THE ITALIAN'S SECRET BABY

MAFIA MASTERS, BOOK 1

RAFFAELLA ROWELL

Mafia Masters series - Book 1

A Dark Mafia Romance

By
Raffaella Rowell

Copyright © Raffaella Rowell and Red Hot Romance (2023)

The right of Raffaella Rowell to be identified as author of this work has been asserted by her in accordance with section 77 and 78 of the Copyright, Designs and Patents Act 1988.

All rights reserved. No part of this publication may be reproduced, stored in a retrieval system, or transmitted in any form or by any means, electronic, mechanical, photocopying, recording, or otherwise, without the prior permission of the publishers.

Any person who commits any unauthorized act in relation to this publication may be liable to criminal prosecution and civil claims for damages.

This is a work of fiction. Names, characters, places, brands, media and incidents are either figments of the author's imagination or are used fictitiously. This book is licensed for your personal enjoyment only.

CHAPTER 1

Rocco

The anticipation was over. The time had come. Soon, Rocco LaTorre would unleash his wrath.

It had taken him months, but he finally tracked the man down, the retribution long overdue.

As autumn led to winter, the frost had spread over the countryside, shimmering in silver tones under the moonlight. The landscape, a little hazy with mist, seemed eerie and ominous. He would have admired its beauty if he had not been thinking of the job. His thoughts absorbed him.

Rocco LaTorre waited patiently with his men. His task was to storm the farmhouse and get the swine. The bitter chill of the evening had numbed his fingers to the bone as he lingered in his car, waiting for the moment to unfold. He rubbed his hands together, puffing a breath to warm them. A distant owl hooted in the darkness. He shivered for a moment, not from the cold but from the dread of impending death that always seized him before a strike. A sign of loathing he'd never lost since his youth.

"My fucking balls are frozen!" Tito grumbled and massaged his crotch to deflect the biting nip. It was a dull and bleak stakeout on a chilly November night.

"Keep your eyes on the house," Rocco urged him with a glare.

"That asshole has a lot to answer to. And bringing us out here in the middle of nowhere on a freezing night like this!"

"Shut it! Pay attention. Call the others. On my signal, we go in. Tell them to stay out of sight. Zeno will lead his group toward the outbuilding and hit them with all he's got." Rocco paused while Tito spoke through the radio to each car to do his bidding.

"Everyone knows what to do?"

"*Sí, signore.*"

"Ready?"

Nico

"Do it now. Pay me before you fall asleep. You know how it is." The naked girl hovered outside the bathroom, shuffling on her feet.

"You don't trust me?"

"I'm just saying."

"Come over here. You'll have your money." Nico Columbano patted the place next to him. He took his wallet from the nightstand and waved a wad of cash. Her eyes widened. She walked over to him and climbed into bed.

"Is that enough for you, sugar?" He slapped the banknotes on her face, none too gently.

"Where did you get all that?" She winced.

"Never you mind. Your business is to please me, so do

it!" His voice struck a jarring note as his mobile phone rang. He swore.

The evening had been fun. They had dined, drank and danced in town, celebrating his success. The previous night, Nico's gang had robbed money, the entire month's takings, from a top nightclub in Naples. They had also stolen boxes of whiskey, brandy, and more, taking all the stock from the storeroom.

The club was owned by the LaTorre clan. Nico's triumph felt more precious because of this. After the robbery, the band of renegades fled and traveled over three hundred miles to Calabria's countryside. They were now hiding in a farmhouse near Reggio Calabria, at the "toe" of the Italian peninsula.

As the ringleaders partied with the ladies for hours, the foot soldiers counted the spoils of the loot in a cramped outbuilding on the farm.

The mob lived by a code of honor. Nico Columbano had done the unthinkable. He violated his oath—binding the principles of the brotherhood—going rogue on his clan.

Betrayal was a sin in the underworld, punished without mercy, and he had dared it! Nico had upset the powerful LaTorre family. From a loyal foot soldier, he had turned on them, betraying the clan and had been obstructing their business with his deadly attacks and robberies for months.

Nico's gang began the long list of assaults by looting a mighty bulk of booze shipped by sea from England. He and his gang had seized the vessel and cargo belonging to Magda LaTorre, a powerful Camorra Boss. In this quest, they left Ulrico DiMarzio—a LaTorre Capo and Magda's nephew, dead. They killed three of his men, too. A massive blow to Magda's clan.

Rocco

Rocco had hunted Nico ever since, and this new attack had only heightened his desire to find him. Besides, Ulrico DiMarzio had been his cousin, they had played together in childhood, and it was time to avenge him and the clan's men.

Thus, Rocco waited to strike at the doors of this dingy farmhouse. The vermin and his minion shacked up with girls on the second floor of the house. He glanced at his watch.

Time to stop Nico's reign of terror, murder and pillaging.

Rocco and his men broke into the farmhouse without a sound. Wearing dark balaclavas, they climbed up the stairs. He directed three men to the room on the left with a flick of his head while he and Tito aimed to hit the one on the right. At his signal, they busted into the bedrooms in unison, slamming the doors wide open as the occupants awakened with a start.

"Don't move," Rocco yelled, holding his Beretta M9 pistol. The customized grip, crafted in bronze and designed for him, was firmly in his hand. A man and a young woman sat up in bed jerkily. With flashlights aimed at them, their eyes were wide in horror. The guy in the bed ignored his warning and reached for his handgun on the nightstand.

Not fast enough.

Rocco shot him first, and two bullets entered the man's skull.

The girl wailed, terrorized, as the man slumped beside her in a pool of blood. Her eyes shut. Rocco clutched the girl's throat with his left hand, raising her chin to him. As she tried to scream, he pointed the pistol at her temple. He had to stop her from screaming. He tightened his grip on her throat, forcing her to look at him. Her eyes flew open, fearful for her life.

"Quiet! I mean no harm to you." His voice rumbled low, rich, with an eerie calmness. "Do you understand?" It was a firm command. Rocco bore into her with a harsh stare through the holes in his balaclava. His green eyes became aflame with fire, spellbinding her, even in the dim light.

Looming over her, his mighty hand clutching her throat while the lifeless body beside her oozed red gore, Rocco knew he cut an entirely scary, menacing, tall figure. Nobody would have dared to disobey him.

She quivered, responding with a vigorous nod, and quietened down.

"I'm releasing my hold on you, but not a sound." He pressed on, his hand clutched her harder. "And don't move. Understood?" He delivered his words with a chilling edge meant to cut through her like a knife. She whimpered and nodded. He released her. She gasped some air into her lungs and brought her hand over her mouth to keep herself from screaming again. Her face was ashen.

It was all done and over in a matter of seconds.

Rocco checked the dead body. He pulled at his victim's hair, thus lifting his head. He peered at him and hissed.

"Fuck, Agostino Grizio!" He frowned. "Nico must have switched rooms. He's next door! Take the girl. Let's go!" Rocco darted out of the room. He heard shots coming from the back of the building, and blasphemies as black as the night blurted out of his mouth. To his dismay, when he entered the other bedroom, Nico had absconded. The woman in the bed was screaming, but no sign of the culprit or his guys.

"Shut her up!"

"Yes, boss!" Tito, who had followed him into the other room with the girl, began tying the two girls up.

Rocco glanced out of the window. He soon realized his

men were at a disadvantage. They were chasing him, but Nico had a head start. Rocco went down the fire escape at the rear and gave chase. Too late. A car picked up the bastard as he reached the road. They shot after him but to no avail. Nico was gone in a flash.

Rocco knew the man was too far ahead to give chase—a blunder. They lost him.

Rocco

"Are you frigging telling me he jumped? What the fuck, Rocco!" Sebastiano exploded. His countenance darkened. He was seething.

"Agostino Grizio is dead. We have three of Nico's men in the crypt, a massive blow to his gang. They are singing like canaries. Zeno led the assault on the outbuilding. They stormed the place, about three hundred yards from the farmhouse. With a few bullets and a brief fight, they stopped the gang about to flee. They captured them and recovered the loot. We did well."

"Except for Nico!"

"The bastards killed the nightclub manager and a bartender working late. They were civilians, just doing a job. We'll take care of their families. They'll be all right," Rocco went on, ignoring his older brother's sarcasm.

"But Nico's still on the loose," Sebastiano pressed on. "I want him caught. Do you hear me?" His tone assured there was no misunderstanding in his orders.

"According to the girl, Nico had plenty of cash—from the robbery, I presume. She said he had a phone call as we entered the farmhouse. Someone tipped him off."

"How's that possible?"

"An informer."

"Seriously?" Magda LaTorre, the clan's boss, until then

silent, asked. "A mole in my organization?" A nerve twitched in her beautiful jaw. The meeting was held in her study in her home in Naples, in Southern Italy, two days after the events in Reggio.

"Yes, Mother! Rolando has been snitching on us. But we made him talk. I was suspicious for some time as Nico was always a step ahead of us," Rocco informed her.

"What do we know, then?" Sebastiano groaned and rubbed his neck.

"The 'Ndrangheta is involved as we suspected. He confirmed that much. But he doesn't know which of the Calabrian clans is paying him. Rolando never met them in person. They leave instructions in a luggage locker at the train station, or through a brief call. Nico's taking orders, too, in the same way. He's not working alone," Rocco replied.

"The backstabbing scumbags are playing with fire. I bet it's Zilli."

"We don't know who's behind this, Mother. Not yet."

"Jesus! I'm arranging a marriage for Sebastiano with Zilli's daughter. Does that mean nothing to them?" Magda fumed.

"One of the Calabrian clans is double-crossing us, sure. But they are covering their tracks well. We don't know who's leading these attacks yet, but we will."

"Yes, Nico and his gang are executing the strikes, but who is paying them off? That's what I want to know. Who is masterminding them?" Magda paused and then insisted, "My money is on Zilli. I bet he's the one giving the orders."

Omero Zilli was the boss of a powerful, skillful clan. She knew the vile man. He could unleash steady, well-planned attacks, and he was too greedy. The other 'Ndrangheta clans were smaller and too busy on their territories to look elsewhere. If her instincts were correct, this man was a danger to her and her clan, and she had to stop him.

Magda didn't want a drawn-out war between them, too risky for her and her sons. Assuming it was Zilli behind it all. She needed proof. Besides, it would attract attention from the law. It would help no one. She had to be smart.

"Any witnesses?" Sebastiano asked.

"We released the two girls in the farmhouse staying with Nico Columbano and Agostino Grizio. The women were not involved. They were call-girls. They'll keep their mouths shut, too scared to breathe a word. They have no idea who we are, anyway."

"What about Nico, then? Where is he? Any news on his whereabouts?" Salvo Renzi, the family's *consigliere*, and Magda's second husband, asked. "We need to find him."

"Rolando confirmed Nico's gone into hiding in England. Whoever is supporting him, they don't want to push their luck."

"And the men you captured?"

"It all matches, they told the same story. The 'Ndrangheta financed and planned the robberies. Again, they can't tell me which clan," Rocco went on. "They received the instructions the same way. My money is on Omero Zilli, too, backing the bastard. The Calabrese is guiding him, hoping his vile little gang can continue to steal from us to weaken our dominance. Omero wants to achieve this through Nico without compromising himself, the double-crossing pig. I'm assuming he sent him away to cool off for a while. We got too close this time."

"Are you sure Nico is in England?" Sebastiano asked.

"Positive. Besides, Nico knows the country well, having been part of Ulrico's cell in the south of England before his gang killed him and turned rogue on us. He speaks the language. I've spoken to Fabio in London, his men are on it."

"You were at a boarding school in England and speak English like a native. Am I right, Rocco?"

"Mother wanted me out of her way."

"To protect you from your father—" A flush crept up Magda's neck.

"So, what of it, Seb?" Rocco asked, ignoring his mother's comment. He hadn't meant to raise old wounds.

"You'll enjoy a trip abroad."

"Oh, fuck! It will be freezing there. I hate cold weather!"

"Go to England, work with Fabio. Find Nico. I want to know who's his link in the 'Ndrangheta." Sebastiano ordered. As the oldest of Magda's children, Sebastiano was the clan's underboss, her heir. His mother relinquished more of the daily business to him.

"It'll give you a chance to see what Selina's up to. Your sister's upsetting me," Magda added, shaking her head in disapproval.

"Why? Surely, Fabio can check on her." Rocco suppressed a grin.

"Your brother Fabio is busy with his family and the English cell. He's got no time. Your sister is up to no good! I know it. Our princess has given Federico some lip, disrespecting him. He's laughed it off for now. Claiming it's her youthful exuberance. Federico is her fiancé, whether she likes it or not," Magda went on.

Rocco chuckled. The irritated glance from his mother silenced him, but he struggled not to laugh. His younger siblings, his brothers Milo and Matteo, and his sister Selina, the youngest of the brood, were troublesome. They often upset Magda with their lively escapades and high spirits.

"Fine." He nodded with a serious face but couldn't hide the amusement in his eyes.

Selina was doing a master degree in London, but gave everyone the runaround. Anyone would think she was in charge. Rocco had long left his sister to her own devices while Sebastiano and Magda struggled to rule over her without success.

As usual, Rocco had no intention of doing anything about his sister. He would protect her with his life, but he tried to stay out of her affairs. The prince of the Sicilian Cosa Nostra, Federico Santillo, Selina's fiancé, was in for a treat if he thought he would dominate his sister. Rocco reckoned it was a challenge the Sicilian had taken on. He smiled, *good luck, Federico.*

"Besides, our company, Stream Net, needs new markets. England is ripe for it. We need to feed our legitimate businesses, too. As the Managing Director, Rocco, you are brilliant at running the staff and operations. It's doing so well, so explore the English market while out there. When the Board term comes up for election, you'll be the ideal candidate to promote to Chief Executive. As CEO, the corporation will be your baby. I'll want you to run it independently," Magda said. "But let's take care of Nico first. Work with Fabio and find him. Uncover who's double-crossing me in the 'Ndrangheta. Don't forget to talk to Selina. Have a safe trip." His mother confirmed the orders.

Magda assumed control of the clan when her first husband, Giordano LaTorre, a drug baron, died.

Giordano had been shot dead in Naples fifteen years ago. His style, power and strength irritated other criminals. Sebastiano, who had been with him then, was wounded in the attack and almost killed. The clan, losing its boss, was in turmoil and in danger, ripe for the taking by other mobsters. Magda realized the police knew who the perpetrators were, but they were not prepared to do anything. She begged them for action but to no avail.

Three weeks later, on a Sunday morning, Magda drove to the church in the town center where the two offending

Camorrists were attending mass and waited for them. After the service, when they came out, she reached into her handbag, pulled out a light revolver, and holding it steady in both hands, she opened fire. Several bullets hit the two men. They crashed to the ground but were not dead. Reloading a gun under those stressful circumstances, in the middle of the street, with eyes on her, and quickly, would have been almost impossible for the most callus mobster—she would have to clear the expended rounds from the chamber of the pistol—but she remained calm and collected under the intense pressure and did it. She discharged a new set of bullets on the culprits, killing them on the spot.

On the way home, she bought herself roses.

She hadn't done the deed to avenge her husband, he didn't deserve her loyalty, but she did it for her beloved son. Thus, a new strong boss of the LaTrorre family had emerged from the ashes, loud and clear. She evaded arrest. Nobody would speak up against her. Soon, she earned the titles of *The Wicked Diva* and *Lady Camorra*.

Magda nursed Sebastiano back to health with loving care, and he grew up to be her underboss. But her husband's death was a blessing for her. It had been an unhappy union. Giordano had been cruel to her and the children, been abusive, and this exasperated her, and left her feeling miserable. His passing had liberated her from the shackles of a dismal relationship and given her freedom.

A few months after his death, she married Salvo Renzi, the clan's *consigliere*. Though remarried, Magda kept the LaTorre name in sync with that of her clan.

When she seized command, she dreamed of turning the business legitimate, lawful and free from crime.

She pulled out of risky Mafia rackets and drugs. She veered the clan into legal projects, backing lawful operations such as real estate, green energy, construction, keeping her casinos and nightclubs clean, too, as both a base of legal operations and means of laundering money from illegal activities such as smuggling, on-line gambling, counterfeited goods and weapons.

She turned what people thought of as a disreputable gangster clan under her first husband into a respected family with her leadership—bringing to the fore her upper-middle-class roots to clean up the family's reputation.

Magda permeated politics, securing control in high places of society, where it counted. She had crooked politicians in her pockets; ministers, undersecretaries, local mayors, district attorneys, and bureaucrats were amongst the leading people she moved with her power. She used it all to her advantage.

Fifteen years down the line, her influence stretched far and wide. She had achieved great wealth in the process, a billionaire many times over.

CHAPTER 2

Evie

Love—with all the trimming—was well overrated. She had suffered the demands of an intense, lengthy engagement, ultimately revealing it was not worth the effort.

Evie Logan was pondering on this with a bruised heart.

The weasel! A grimace marred her face.

She was done with love, too harmful to contemplate again. She felt heartbroken. Her endless musings on this irked her even more.

"Morning," Evie mumbled, halting in the kitchen's doorway.

"There you are! Coffee's in the pot." Selina beamed when her roommate entered, but her smile dimmed, glancing at her friend's sad face. "Oh, dear—cheer up!"

"Cheer up? I had a fidgety night with millions of horrid thoughts running through my head. Not to mention, I have to attend my least favorite class at the university." Evie moaned as she filled her cup with black coffee. "Besides, it's bloody cold and only the end of November." She slumped on a stool at the breakfast bar, somewhat discouraged.

"I'm sorry, darling, but you shouldn't torment yourself with that idiot! Please give it a rest, or you'll make yourself ill. I'm worried about you," Selina countered. "I realize it's only been a couple of months, but I'm glad you found out what a pig he is before you took the big step. Stop brooding about him. Look at new pastures—plenty of fish in the sea. Don't mope around. Live a little." Selina stepped over to her and, placing an arm around her shoulders, gave her a gentle squeeze.

"Three missed calls from him. The dumbass still calls and texts me! I ignore him. I don't answer his phone calls and delete all his messages without reading them, but he is persistent. If he thinks I'll brush this under the carpet and condone what he did to me, he hasn't got a clue. I'm not a complete fool. I shall never forgive him."

"Good on you. Let Jake rot in hell. He is not worthy of you."

"You may be right."

"He isn't, trust me. Forget him. I know it's easy to say but move on. Find a handsome guy and screw his brains out," Selina said. "This always works."

"Experience, have you?" Evie raised a brow.

"No, but—" Her companion reddened.

"Then don't be silly!"

"You know what I mean."

Evelyn Logan, Evie to her friends, sighed. Cocking her head, she was grappling with raw emotions in her heart.

She had broken up the engagement to her fiancé eight weeks ago—*good riddance to him—praise the Lord.* Still, she couldn't help brooding over him. She felt miserable and sorry for herself, having lost a good part of her teenage years and early twenties with a man who was a deceiving bastard.

"We were getting married. Remember?"

"I know, hon, but you must try. Please—"

"Selina! When someone looks as beautiful as you do, it's easy to say. Look at me. How many men like a plump, plain girl, hey? You tell me! They won't be falling over themselves to be with me," she huffed. "Besides, Jake was my first and only boyfriend. I wouldn't know how to talk to a guy now. It's been so long!"

"You silly goose. You are a curvy, sexy girl with a beautiful face and dazzling gray eyes. Soon you'll get a Master Degree in Literature. You are smart and charming and should be proud of yourself. You have a lot to offer to any guy." Her friend went on. "That bastard really chipped at your confidence. Fuck Jake!"

"Perhaps my eyes, my only redeeming feature."

"Oh, God! You are in a shocking mood today. Well, you'll cheer up when you hear this. I've asked my brother about this weekend, and we are going on a big night out on Saturday. Melania, too."

"Your sister-in-law and your brother?"

"Yes."

"Bless them! Fabio and Melania are so in love. Aren't we going to intrude on their parade?"

"Oh, not just Fabio and Melania. My other brother, too." Her roommate beamed as Evie frowned.

"Selina! You've got five brothers! Which one are we talking about now? Not 'Double Trouble'? I love them, but they are a bit crazy. When they came last May, we drank loads. I had an alcohol-induced hangover for two days. It prompted an awful argument with Jake. They'll be too much for me in my current state."

"Hell, yes. They are older than me but can behave rather badly, I must admit."

"Agree!"

"That's why they nicknamed them 'Double Trouble'

when they were children. They were so close in age and temperament—still are, though Milo is a year older than Matteo."

"It figures. Anyway, they'd be too much for me right now. Matteo used to drive Jake furious."

"Jake is not in your life anymore, Evie, is he? So who the frigging cares about him now? You shouldn't! But no. Not Double Trouble. It's Rocco. He'll be in London for a few weeks. Business or something. He promised to take us out to an exclusive club this weekend. All on him, so we are having fun."

"Ooh, Rocco! I suppose he's quite laidback."

"Yes. He's not like Sebastiano, who would wed me off to Federico in no time if I'd let him. But I won't marry him, whatever my mother says."

"I'm sorry. I guess we both have our own crosses to bear!" Evie patted her friend's hand and sighed.

"We need Rocco to cheer us up."

For all her gloom, Evie had perked up somewhat hearing his name.

Rocco LaTorre!

The proverbial tall, dark and handsome fit him like a glove. A glorious man if she ever saw one. She would kill to have those high cheekbones of his, that straight, perfect nose. He had a gorgeous masculine face with harmonious features. His powerful jaw and the fleshy mouth with pearly white teeth were so tempting. *For goodness' sake,* she once dreamt she was kissing him.

He was intoxicating! A forbidden fruit in more ways than one, and the more alluring for it. Rocco's beauty overwhelmed her. He unsettled her with that intense stare and those beguiling green eyes. They seemed to see deep into her soul.

Last year, Jake lost his patience with her and asked her to move out of the apartment, to find somewhere new to live for the same reason. Selina had too many good-looking brothers. It annoyed the hell out of her fiancé, which now, having ignored him, gratified Evie to no end. A mischievous smile hinted at her lip. She would tell her mom about Rocco's visit and ensure it got to Jake.

Yes! Evie thought with a naughty grin. *It'll serve him right!*

Shame Rocco thinks I'm a country bumpkin, she would bet her life on this, even if he always treated her with kindness and courtesy. Of Selina's siblings, he was her favorite by a long mile.

Evie was faultless in her behavior toward Rocco when he visited. She was always ladylike and proper with him. She only looked at him as her roommate's polite brother.

At least on the surface.

How could she do otherwise when she had been engaged to Jake forever. But she had glanced at Rocco with fascination when she thought nobody was watching her.

Evie thought no woman could help it. Rocco was that handsome. Too distracting. Too attractive!

He had something she couldn't pinpoint.

"Did you hear me?" Her companion interrupted her reverie.

"Err... this weekend?"

"Yes!"

"As fun as it sounds. I can't." Evie chickened out. In her current state of mind, she wouldn't put it past herself to do something foolish with this man.

"Why not?"

"I'm not in the mood. I don't want to spoil the party. You go but cut me out." She would ruin the evening with her doom and gloom. Besides, given the girls Rocco went out with, all tall, gorgeous, long-legged models and actresses, she couldn't compete with them.

"Nonsense. Don't be a—" Her friend scowled, but the

doorbell spared her. "Oh, I'll go," Selina said. Evie groaned, not ready to see anybody this early.

She heard the high-pitch voice of Mrs. Jones, their next-door neighbor. The old widow was intent on fattening the girls with cakes and pies she baked like clockwork almost daily.

Evie didn't know Mrs. Jones' age. She had one of those faces she couldn't define. The woman could be anywhere between sixty and eighty. But her heart was in the right place, despite being nosy.

"Hello, Evie, dear!" the old lady chimed as she entered the kitchen, followed by Selina. The woman deposited a large casserole dish oozing a wonderful aroma on the breakfast bar. "Shepherd's pie. I hope this will fill you up. You've lost weight, girl!"

"Mrs. Jones—"

"A little early for lunch, I know. When it cools, please place it in the fridge. You can warm it up in the microwave later. It'll do you good."

"Oh, wow!" Selina's nostrils dilated, inhaling the goodness coming from the pot. "It smells delicious."

"Thank you, Mrs. Jones. You shouldn't have. You are too kind," Evie added, but she was glad that the lady had interrupted the discussion.

She was not going out with them, whatever her friend said.

CHAPTER 3

Evie

They were dancing. Evie could see Selina, Melania and Fabio on the large monitors hanging from the ceiling. They were having a blast. Instead of joining them, she rested in a cozy, expensive, soft leather booth on the upper floor in the VIP lounge. A pristine, elegant, all-white room, a more sedated salon in the exclusive London nightclub in Mayfair.

It wasn't Evie's scene. Too fashionable and stylish to begin with and way too expensive for her purse. It screamed class and wealth.

The LaTorres' beauty and money had allowed her access. She guessed a place like this would not let the likes of her in were it not for them. She wouldn't fit the image even if she had the cash.

Evie knew how men devoured Selina with their eyes. A commonplace occurrence when they went out together—the young woman was so beautiful—and the men in this club were no different. What surprised Evie was the same applied to Selina's brothers. She was astonished at how women in the club ogled Fabio and Rocco shamelessly, outrageously, while they seemed nonplussed. Some would think they didn't even notice.

So frigging normal for them. Evie supposed that's how the other half lived, the gorgeous half of the population.

"I accepted the fact girls stare at my husband a long time ago." Melania had told her once. *"It used to upset me, but now I just ignore it."*

Yes, Evie understood the feeling now. It would annoy her, too, if Rocco were her man.

Fat chance!

She hated how the attractive server beamed a dazzling smile at him without even acknowledging her every time she walked by the booth.

Damn fool!

Evie swirled her gin and tonic in her glass and sighed. Rocco sat beside her. She launched a furtive glance at him. His scent was divine, fresh, citrusy, and so manly. Inebriating! It reminded her of a fresh, luscious spring afternoon under the sun.

Selina had talked her into going out with them and insisted on it until she said "yes". Besides, Rocco looked gorgeous when he came to pick them up. He was more handsome than she remembered, and Evie could not resist gaping at him for a long moment until she snapped out of it.

She had taken great care on her appearance. That evening, one of the few funky dresses she possessed came out of retirement. She wore a short silk sheath, low-cut, silver number, hugging her womanly figure in all the right places, with high matching stilettos which were now killing her feet.

"You look hot, girl!" Selina had said. Evie felt sexy. She applied light makeup, and her friend had done her hair in an elegant chignon.

Now there she was! In this fancy nightclub with him. *What the hell do I talk about now?* She had seen him on and off, occasionally, when he was on a business trip to London and visited his sister and brother. But they had never gone out together. It used to annoy Jake to have this good-looking man around Evie when he called on them, even if she was on the periphery of it. Jake was jealous. He had stopped her from becoming too acquainted with the handsome Italian.

Evie hardly knew him. He intimidated her. She didn't know what to say to him and opted for her second G&T of the evening, hoping the alcohol would help her loosen her tongue. She needed courage.

He seemed relaxed, calm, somewhat aloof, and comfortable.

"What's the matter, Evie? Why aren't you dancing?" he said at last. His deep, rich masculine baritone startled her, breaking the silence.

She glanced his way. She wasn't sure what to say.

"I don't feel like it!" she mumbled, opting for honesty.

Rocco

"You are sulking, sweetheart. Did you have a fight with your fiancé?" Rocco asked with a slight grin, considering all romantic relationships were nonsense.

He was fond of his free and unattached status. He was no believer in love. His mother's first marriage had been a disaster, not an example he wished to emulate. Growing up, he had become quite cynical in matters of the heart.

His mother's second marriage to her *consigliere* was different, but still, in his unorthodox world, such unions were not something Rocco wanted to consider. Marriage was not for him. Besides, where he came from, people didn't have the luxury of falling in love. Couples were matched for business reasons.

"We broke up eight weeks ago." Evie heaved, twirling her empty glass. She ordered another drink from the passing server.

Fuck! I didn't know. What a blunder. His sister said nothing to him about this. *Damn her.*

But why should she? Why would I'd be interested in Evie's world?

"You split up?" he asked, rubbing his chin. It shocked him that the news got him an unexpected reaction.

"Yes." Evie shrugged her shoulders as if it was unimportant.

"Weren't you getting married?"

"We had set the wedding date for New Year's Eve."

"Next month? Oh, Evie." His sultry green moons held her gaze steady.

"My wedding dress was ready and all," she said and fixed her eyes on the drink in her hand instead.

"I'm so sorry."

"Don't be. That's life."

"What brought this on? I hope you don't mind me asking." He wondered what made a good girl like her break up with a long-term partner so close to matrimony. He was curious.

"The cheating bastard did," Evie huffed. Her cheeks pinkened and she smoothed out her dress with her hands.

"Ah!" His eyebrows furrowed, showing a crease on his forehead. Then his expression softened on her.

"Don't look surprised. Selina wasn't. She never liked Jake."

"I don't like him, either," he said, placing his arm around her shoulders and squeezing her to him, wanting to comfort her. Her gray eyes flashed with intensity, then turned misty. She returned a sad grin looking so pretty and vulnerable.

He gave her another squeeze that made him hot under the collar. Blood whooshed to his manhood. *What the hell?* Something came alive in him. An unexpected primitive protective zeal burned in his veins. He wished he could get hold of Jake and punch him in the face for hurting her. The thought troubled him. He was laid back. Nothing bothered him. His reaction to Evie had unsettled him.

As Rocco sat beside her, a new, unrecognizable emotion gripped him. He released her and returned his hand to his whiskey. He circled the rim of his glass with his finger, pensive.

"I've known Jake for all of my life. We are from the same place. My parents have a farm in Lincolnshire, in the Midlands. You know where that is?"

"Yes."

"That's where I grew up. Jake lives nearby in the village. I used to see him around when I was little. We hooked up in high school. We were engaged for five years! Ready to get married, and now, it has all gone up in smoke, puff! Vanished!"

"Don't lose sleep over him. He's not worth it," he said, sounding composed, with no hint of emotion in his voice.

"The bastard had a relationship with someone else. All hush-hush, he was two-timing me," she revealed.

A shot of temper at her ex-fiancé bubbled inside him. Why he should feel this way was beyond him. He peeked at her, wishing he could say sweet words to comfort her, but he was not good at consoling people.

A hostess put a glass in front of her. She took a sip. It surprised him she was pouring her heart out to him. He assumed the alcohol had something to do with it. Then she downed the rest of her G&T and ordered another drink. He frowned. Rocco felt a pang of sorrow for the young woman.

Suddenly, he remembered urging his sister to talk about Evie when he first met her years back, when she came to share the apartment with his sister.

"What's up with this girl?" he had asked then.

Selina replied, *"She has a fiancé, and Jake has been Evie's only boyfriend. So, don't even think about it. She's my friend."*

Rocco had feigned offense at his sister's insinuation, at her warning. But was he considering her then?

He had forgotten all about this. He glanced at Evie and smiled. He assumed the girl had lost her path now without that fucking scumbag after so long.

"What a sleaze!" Rocco cursed, outraged on her behalf. He cast his mind back. Had he met Jake? Possibly. He couldn't say. He could not remember the fellow.

"Apparently, for a year, if you want to know!"

"You're kidding!"

"No. Though a friend swears, it might be longer than that. About eight weeks ago, I returned to the village a day earlier than he expected. I let myself into his apartment, and oh, boy, I got the surprise of my life! I found them in bed." She closed her eyes.

He saw a single, fat tear going down her face, but she swiped it away quickly, trying hard to look composed. Rocco muttered a curse under his breath. He would happily have kicked the man till kingdom come.

"I say good riddance! I know it must hurt. Best to find out now rather than later." He would have broken both of Jake's legs if he had his way. He could think of nothing else. His arm went over her shoulders, squeezing her hard into him. He kissed the top of her head. She darted her eyes at him in confusion, and he released her.

The server placed her G&T on the table, and smiled at him again, ignoring Evie.

"Shall I get you a drink, sir? Can I do anything for you?" the woman asked suggestively, beaming her best smile.

He shook his head without even looking at her. His focus stayed on Evie. She had a massive gulp of booze with a little smirk of victory.

"His loss is some other guy's luck. Plenty of honest men out there," he huffed when the waitress was gone.

"So says the guy, who can't keep women from him. Easy for you to say."

"What do you mean?" He frowned.

"Well, you know…" She blushed.

"No, I don't."

"Is it true girls call you 'Prince Charming'?"

"What?

"Oh, come on, you're being modest. I mean, what about Tanya, the famous model. Isn't she your girlfriend when you come to London? Selina told me. She said you're never short of women wherever you go. These things are difficult for some people. I mean for people like me. It may shock you to know."

"First, I'm no frigging 'Prince Charming'. Trust me. Second, I don't have a girlfriend. Tanya is a friend."

"Friends-with-benefits, aha!" Evie laughed, but he ignored her sarcasm.

"Third, we are not talking about me. And Selina has a big mouth. I must talk to my sister about making me sound like a callous playboy," he added. "I never cheated in a relationship, if that's any consolation." That was somewhat true, but why was he telling her this? It was beyond him. Though he hadn't told her his relationships never lasted long enough to warrant it. They were flings, brief affairs, that was all.

"Umm…" She took a hefty swallow of her drink and ordered one more.

He raised his brows at her drinking bout. She would get herself in trouble if she were not careful.

"Brooding for Jake won't do you any good," he said. She returned a speculative glance at him.

"If you say so." She shrugged her shoulders.

There was a lull in the conversation as the server brought the drink to the table. Rocco had lost count of the number of Evie's gin and tonics, and he didn't like that. She drank a long, satisfying gulp from it.

"When I said brooding was not the answer, neither is alcohol." He took the drink from her hand. She scowled at him.

"Oh, yeah?" She snatched it back and finished the liquor in one long mouthful.

"Evie—"

"There!" She slammed her empty glass on the table with a satisfied smile.

He took a deep breath, not liking her action. He moved closer to her. His side was touching hers, his proximity looming rather tall over her, even sitting. With her eyes on him, she slid back in her seat, placing distance between them. But he grasped her wrist and held her in place tightly.

He lowered his head to hers, his breath fanning her.

"If you were mine, poppet, this little charade would have earned you a good spanking," his velvety, silvery voice whispered in her ear. He raised his big hand, so close to her face, as a warning, invading her personal space. Her eyes grew big.

They gazed at each other for a long moment.

Evie

Blazing at her, his green, sultry eyes flashed with fire. She gawked at him, while a thrill ran down her spine at his words. Silence reigned. For an instant, an electric vibe of desire filled the air between them. She felt it in her bones. Had he?

The thought of him spanking her made Evie's body tingle. She blinked. *Sweet Jesus!* She imagined the scene… in that head-dream, she offered her butt to Rocco, and his firm hand was marking her. No man had ever spanked her, and she wondered what it would feel like. A warmth between her legs filled her with need. The vision of Rocco's large hand connecting with the soft flesh of her backside filled her senses with lust. Her pussy flooded at the power of the image in her head.

Thus, Evie's underlying liking for Rocco, so long latent, hidden and stifled in her subconscious—unbeknownst to her, smoking and smoldering in her heart since she had first met him—ignited her like a wildfire. It burst on her with the force of nature, enveloping her, sucking her in. And she wanted to jump his bones. She craved to make mad love to him, butterflies danced in her stomach. Her hot center pulsated with rampant desire. As if something had shown in her eyes, he gave her the devastating LaTorre smile. She had noticed that wicked, beguiling grin in all the brothers, to some extent. And this one seemed to say, *oh yes, baby, I know, let me take care of you.*

He took her wrist and dragged her out of the seat.

"Come, let's dance." He placed his hand on the small of her back and guided her forward. She was so aware of his hand touching her that heat radiated through her. They pushed through the main downstairs room to the dancing platform and stepped into the crowd of dancers. Placing an arm around her waist, he drew her close to him. Her body responded to his wall of muscles. She wallowed in his arms, sank against the hardness on his chest. The lustful fever in her body raised to a scorching temperature in his proximity.

They danced for a while. Evie's soft core never stopped throbbing as they moved to the music. Her panties were soaked.

"We should go back upstairs." He parted from her.

"Sure." Missing his touch already, she followed him reluctantly. Her friends had also returned to the VIP lounge. Rocco excused himself to pick up a call and went to the hallway.

She ordered another G&T.

"Are you enjoying yourself, Evie?" Selina asked her.

"I am." She smiled and shoulder-bumped her friend.

"Woo-hoo! I knew Rocco would cheer you up." Her companion beamed.

"It's nice seeing you smile again. I've been worried about you." Melania perched on the other side of her and placed her head on her shoulder.

"I'm okay." Evie patted her cheek.

"Worried, my love? Why? What's wrong?" Fabio asked his wife. Rocco's return spared her having to answer.

His eyes narrowed on Evie when he saw she was finishing her umpteen glass of liquor. Selina rose from the booth and winked at her brother. He took advantage and pushed along, sitting beside Evie.

"I told you, no more drinking. You had enough." Rocco's voice was a whisper, but the rebuke was clear.

"You are not the boss of me," Evie snapped. He chuckled as if he considered her retort cute. But the little crease between his eyebrows she liked so much came out at her disobedience, and the frown on his face suggested *you are walking a tightrope!*

"We have to leave," he declared.

"Fine," Melania agreed. "Norina is babysitting Lola. I don't want to tire her with a late night. She's getting old. And my feet are killing me."

"Yes." Fabio nodded in consensus.

"Oh. Not yet," Selina pleaded. "Let's stay a little longer."

"No," Rocco said. "Time to go." He rose. The evening was at an end.

"Spoilsport!"

Evie's last drink was one too many. She swayed on her feet. Before she could crash backward on the seat, Rocco's arm circled her waist and steadied her, drawing her close. His proximity made her giddy. She inhaled, breathing him in.

"Did you just smell me?"

"No!" She blushed like a beetroot.

He snorted.

Fabio held Melania's hand and moved toward the exit. Rocco motioned Selina to follow him while he helped Evie out of the club.

The cars were waiting in the street. Melania and Fabio said their goodbyes and went to their vehicle. Rocco was seeing the girls home, and his driver helped them in. They sat in the backseat of his customized, silver Bentley.

"Wow! A drinks compartment." Evie grinned. "Let's have a glass!" she mumbled merrily, grabbing a bottle of champagne. She waved it around as the car took a corner, hitting Rocco on the head with it by accident.

"Bloody hell."

"Ooh. Sorry…" Evie slurred her words.

His sister snorted. He yanked the bottle from Evie's hands, placing it back. His eyebrows pulled together. He rubbed his head, launching her a censuring look. It was a warning.

The dip between his brows charmed her. Evie giggled

and put a hand over her mouth, covering it, seeking to stifle the sound.

He bent over her.

"You are trying my patience, girl. Watch it," he murmured in his low velvety tone, and her pussy throbbed at the sexy rumble.

CHAPTER 4

Rocco

"Are you okay?" Selina asked her friend as they got to the apartment. She noticed the girl swaying unsteadily.

Evie retorted with something that sounded like, "Hunky-dory!" Her remark was garbled, slurred, almost unintelligible, given with her thumbs up and a vacant grin. Selina chuckled.

Rocco frowned, but he turned to his sister.

"By the way, Mom is upset with you. She thinks you are giving Federico the runaround," he whispered. He had done his duty.

"God, give me strength." Selina rolled her eyes.

"Just saying. Mother's not happy with you."

"And what's new?"

"What are you two whispering about?" Evie glanced at them, still mumbling her speech. The siblings glanced at each other. That conversation was over, and both were glad of it.

"Evie's a little under the weather. I better see her to bed," his sister added with a scoff.

"I'll see to her. You are in no better condition. You both need your sleep," Rocco replied.

"Are you sure?"

"Hey, I'm right here, you know. I can hear you. And I'm fine," Evie sulked, stumbling on her feet.

"Goodnight, then." Selina kissed them both on the cheek and went to her room.

Rocco hardly knew Evie, but despite what she said, she wasn't "fine".

He'd never seen her like this. She was always sweet and well-mannered, her behavior impeccable and exquisite, but she was a handful tonight. Perhaps the fact she had ended a five-year engagement to a guy who behaved like scum to her had something to do with it. Rocco thought she may have every reason to have a drink or two, under the circumstances, in a quirky, outlandish manner. Though it still vexed him.

Evie turned toward a sideboard in the living room. She grabbed hold of a bottle of gin.

"Oh, no, you're not. Time for bed." He glowered, seizing the bottle from her hands, and placing it back.

"I'd rather not. I won't sleep well."

"Tonight, you will, I guarantee. Come on."

"Hey! Let go of me," Evie protested, struggling to disengage herself, but his grip on her upper arm was firm until they entered her bedroom. He removed her coat as she complained, folded it on a chair, and then plopped her down on her bed. She opened her mouth to say something.

"Enough!" he said, with authority in his tone. He loved being masterful, and this girl was out of control.

She gulped, with her eyes wide, but she sat there, quiet as a lamb. Kneeling on one knee in front of her, he held her bare ankles in his large hands and took off her stilettos, one after the other. His touch spread a warmth through her frame as she watched him mesmerized.

∼

Evie

"My feet are killing me," she grumbled to hide her desire. Even in her inebriation, she was so conscious of it. Rocco lifted his head and smiled. His beautiful, devastating beam sent a surge of lust to her private parts, rioting for attention. He rubbed her feet. Her eyelids fluttered. The massage gave her a jolt to the system, and her pussy flooded for the third time that night.

As if her body had a mind of its own, she placed her arms around his neck, and she kissed him on the lips. For a second, he froze. She could tell it surprised him. He stiffened. Then he gripped her wrists to release himself from her hold. Rocco thrust his head back, breaking the kiss instantly. Their eyes locked, and she felt the spark to her core as if lightning had struck her. He felt it, too. She could see it in his stormy eyes. But he shook his head instead as if to say *"No".*

She blushed hotly, not understanding his response, and humiliation flooded her at his rejection. She glanced away. Her cheeks burned in shame, and she could not look at him.

"Evie!" he whispered, his tone letting her know he was aware of her embarrassment at his brush-off. His expression was soft on her. He held her chin in his hand, turning her face to him.

Her name sounded wonderful on his lips, but she was sure it was an apology. So she eyed him stiffly, her cheeks blazing. He gazed at her. Pain and tears showed in her eyes while tenderness flared in his.

"Is it because I'm not pretty enough for you?" she said at last. Her bottom lip quivered.

"Don't be silly."

"Well? Is it because I'm plain and plump? Not one of your supermodels, I know. I guess you don't go for girls like me."

"Evie—you are beautiful."

"Liar!"

Rocco

"Trust me, girl. You are. You look amazing tonight," Rocco added. His sultry eyes focused on her. "I love your body. You have a real woman's body. All those lovely curves. Stunning!" He meant every word he said. He was not lying. Not by a long shot. He liked the silly girl.

A lot!

Not his usual type, true, but there was a first for everything. He found Evie endearing and enchanting, and her body alluring.

"Don't lie to me!"

"I'm not. Stop putting yourself down," he rebuked. "But you are drunk," he chided, raising a brow.

"No, I'm not." Evie pouted. *So adorable,* he thought with a grin.

"Yes, you are. You don't understand what you're asking me." He raked his hand through his hair with an exasperated sigh. As if he was talking to an unruly child.

"You're an ass," she mocked.

He huffed and stood tall, in his full height.

"I prefer my girls sober when I fuck them," he added, staring at her, ignoring her jabs.

Her eyes grew wide, her mouth agape. "Fu—what?"

"When I *'make love'*. I must watch my language with

you." He paused and chortled. "Lovemaking is more your thing."

"Fuck you. Asshole!"

She paused, and he rolled his eyes. This girl was trying his patience.

"I repel you, don't I? Tell the truth," she went on. Her face burned, and anger rose to the fore at his words.

Rocco had never heard her swear before. If anyone else had called him an "*asshole*" or said "*fuck you*" like that, they would have found themselves in the emergency room, or worse, in the morgue. She had crossed the line so many times tonight and didn't even know it. But he found her outburst endearing, so it made him laugh instead.

She frowned and crossed her arms over her chest.

"Don't make fun of me!" she spat.

He sighed in exasperation and flopped beside her on the bed. "Listen to me, Evie, please. I may have done many questionable things in my life, but taking women when they are drunk is not one of them. You would regret it in the morning. You are a decent girl, squeaky clean. The lady in you would hate this on a clear mind."

"Whatever gave you that idea? No. Squeaky clean, indeed!" She turned to him. "You know nothing about me."

"You are."

"No, I'm not. Say what you think. Don't hide behind stupid notions. I'm a big girl. I can take the rejection," she argued. "And it wouldn't be the first time, either!" Her bottom lip trembled.

He thought Jake had gone through her mind then. She was hurt, and Rocco's rejection must have reminded her of her ex-fiancé. Rocco didn't want to hurt her like that bastard had done. She didn't deserve it. Though it was clear, she wouldn't let him see her cry. Her nostrils flared instead, and her chin rose in contempt, even with the quivering lip.

Rocco couldn't help a soft chuckle of admiration at her bravery and shook his head. She mistook his reaction, and this infuriated her more. She scowled at him.

He thought she looked adorable, so flushed with pent-up emotion and temper that he almost forgot himself, wanting to kiss her, but this would only encourage her.

"Okay. Enough of this." Rocco put his hand up to silence her. "I'll tell you what—I'll stay with you tonight. In your bed," he went on calmly. No emotion in his voice. Though if he were honest, the blood roaring to his cock was telling him something different. Maybe he wasn't as calm as he pretended to be during the unorthodox discussion with this girl.

"You will?" She flinched at him, confusion setting in.

"But we'll do nothing tonight. I will only hold you. You want to punish Jake with the same medicine. It seems a good idea to you right now. But it isn't, trust me."

"No, I want you. Not the same," she breathed with burning need. The words slipped out of her mouth before she realized she had given way, out loud, to her infatuation.

Her statement was unexpected and it came with a rawness he didn't realize she harbored. Rocco raised a brow and stayed silent. He regarded her for a long moment.

∼

Evie

Evie gulped, blushing furiously and turned away from him, embarrassed at her admission, rubbing her hands in her lap, anxious.

He rose. Standing before her, he pulled Evie's chin up, his face stony. Was he trying to suppress a hint of a smile on his fleshy, gorgeous lips? She couldn't read him, except his green eyes flashed with a sweltering hunger over her body. His jaw twitched.

Hot blood whooshed through her veins. Her pulse quickened, her control fading at the scorching heat in his gaze searing her cheeks and body.

"I'm honored you want me," he said at last. "I'll sleep in your bed tonight, but nothing will happen between us. Tell me if you feel the same in the morning when you're sober."

"What?"

"You heard me. I'll fuck you if that's what you want," Rocco added in a smooth tone, almost disinterested. Her eyes popped open wide at him.

"I don't need any favors from you."

"Don't be shocked, sweetheart. I'll love nothing better than to fuck your sweet little pussy until it's pink and swollen. But I will defer this conversation to the morning. I'm sure you'll change your mind once you dry out. You are a good girl, and you won't handle it."

"Is that a challenge?" She lifted her chin, defiant, but a red flush crept on her neck.

"Trust me. You won't know what hit you if we do this. If I fuck you, you won't resist me. Now, bed, please. No more arguing," he concluded.

The arrogant sod! She blinked, processing his remarks, somehow, remarkably sober after this conversation. But a fever swamped her entire frame, her panties drenched. A shiver traveled down her spine at the image of him fucking her.

He gave her a wicked grin. He lay her down, covering her with the blanket and tucking her in bed. His tenderness surprised her. She glanced at him in awe, in anticipation.

As he stripped off his clothes with rapid efficiency, Evie lay on her side with her head propped up by her elbow, following his every movement. He was even more glorious in the flesh than she imagined.

Perfect!

A lean and athletic demigod with rippling chest muscles and broad shoulders that tapered to a narrow waist. A cute, firm butt was shown off in the clingy Lycra boxers he left on. *Oh, my!* An outstanding large package bulged out front, showing his hardness. She couldn't stop looking at it. All of this over impressive thighs and long legs. He was so manly, so powerful, so handsome. She almost pinched herself awake, but no. Her naughty dreams came true all at once.

Rocco LaTorre had been the x-rated star of Evie's naughty fantasies once or twice. Only a silly dream. Nothing wrong with having a racy fantasy now and then with a stranger. It was harmless. Besides, at the time, she had a real fiancé. Rage surged in her soul at knowing the years she had squandered with Jake, at the painful memories, but her temper soon vanished as she watched her dream shift into reality.

"Fuck you, Jake," she muttered quietly under her breath. "Look at me now."

"What?" Rocco asked.

"Nothing."

Rocco, the hero of her fantasies, fired an indecent smile at her, full of promise in all his glory and in the flesh. Only, he wasn't a dream. This time, he was real.

∼

Rocco

Rocco climbed into bed beside her. Her back to his chest, he circled his arms around her. True to his words, he held her tight, careful to avoid pressing his hard-on against her ass, even with his boxers still on. Despite his impressive speech, the girl had aroused him. Not her half-hearted drunken advances, but her sweet lips had surprised him. They felt soft, like honey on his. Her innocence and naivety charmed him. She was adorable. A rush of protectiveness for her swept over him, compelling him to want to make everything better for her while he wished to kill the bastard who made her suffer.

She snuggled up to him, wallowing in his warmth.

Within minutes, her even, light breathing told him she was asleep. He chuckled. He had been honest when he said she was beautiful. Her curvy figure was alluring. Touching the silky, creamy skin on her bare legs sent more blood rushing to his dick. Perhaps this was a bad idea. He stayed away from good girls for a reason. They only brought him complications—and he didn't want any in his already complex life. Soon, his rumination ceased, his mind went blank, and he slept.

CHAPTER 5

Evie

The light filtered through her window. Opening her eyes, Evie blinked. It took several seconds for her to focus as she computed the powerful manly arm across her waist. She turned her head. The demigod was wrapped around her frame. Rocco's impressive front package was fully awake, though he slept.

Have we done it? Umm… no, not so lucky.

To her horror, it came back to her. She recalled her shameful, bold advances on him, the kiss, his rejection. Her outspoken truth "*I want you.*"

It appalled her.

Oh, God, I'm a desperate loser. She rubbed a hand over her face in irritation.

She got off the bed quietly so as not to wake him, and sneaked into the bathroom first, then into the kitchen.

She had two glasses of water. Her mind was a little fuzzy after the copious alcohol. She made strong coffee and drank a double espresso in one go. Evie also poured a cup for him and returned to the bedroom.

Placing his cup on the nightstand, she couldn't stop looking at him, admiring his beauty as he slept.

In the light of day, with the alcohol gone, looking at that handsome, powerful man in her bed, her courage left her. She didn't know what to do. She remembered one thing clearly, though. *If you feel the same in the morning, I'll fuck you...* Rocco had said.

It was weird. Despite Evie's shame, she still felt the same. She wanted him with all her might. *Did he mean it? Or was it another ploy to reject me? To let me down gently.*

She studied him for some time. She'll never know now. Evie couldn't return to that conversation with him. She was too embarrassed. Oh, yes, she wished his hands were all over her body. She wanted him to do wicked things to her. For once, she itched to be guided by her lust and desire.

He was right. Deep down, she was a "good girl". Despite her appalling behavior last night, and her shame, she wished she could be a bad girl. Throwing her cares to the wind.

"Are you going to stand there and stare at me all day, or are you coming back to bed?" Rocco muttered in a low rumble without opening his eyes.

She jolted like a spring on a coil, not expecting it.

"Easy, tiger." He chuckled, still with his eyes shut.

It amazed her how he could do this.

"I made you coffee," she mumbled when her heart rate slowed.

"Thank you." He sat up in bed, glanced at her and smiled.

God, the man is handsome! She handed him the cup. He finished his espresso in one big gulp and patted the place next to him. She blushed, hesitated for a moment, grabbed his cup and put it on the nightstand.

Then, she climbed into bed, all flustered. She reckoned it wasn't a big deal sitting next to him since she was still fully clothed from last night, even if he wasn't.

He turned to her. His green, hungry eyes fired up. Her breath hitched.

"Did you sleep well?" she mumbled.

"Like a log."

"Me, too. I thought you would find the bed uncomfortable, as you are so tall and—" Evie blabbered fast, nervous.

"I'm good."

"Really?"

"Yes. Stop fussing."

"Oh."

"Have you changed your mind?" he asked, kissing her forehead.

"What?" *Is he asking what I think he is?*

"You were tipsy last night, have you forgotten our conversation?" He arched a brow. His lips half curled on one side in a wicked smile.

"I don't know what you mean." Her cheeks reddened, feigning ignorance.

"I knew you would," he said. She saw a fleeting flash of disappointment in his eyes. "And that's fine."

It's now or never, girl! Her inner voice urged her. *Come on. Do it! Be daring.*

"No. I did not forget," she admitted, her face burning scarlet. Evie closed her eyes. *What the hell am I saying?*

"I warned you would have regrets if we had done it. That's why I was adamant we shouldn't. You changed your mind. But that's okay, poppet. I was expecting it, anyway."

"No. I haven't changed my mind, if you must know. I'm game if you are. Just sex! No strings attached," Evie muttered all in one breath before she lost her nerve.

What the dickens am I saying?

You are playing with fire, girl. Her inner voice threw a red alert.

Rocco threw his head back and chuckled. He caressed her cheek with his knuckles. She shivered. He regarded her for a moment.

His sultry eyes fixed on her face. He pulled her down with him on the bed. She gasped as she lay beside him on her back. His arm went around her waist, and he tugged her closer. His nose was inches from hers.

"Are you sure?"

"Yes." She blushed uncontrollably.

"Are you ready for me?" His grin spread across his face.

"Ready as I'll ever be. Or is it *you* who's not sure about this now? If so—"

"Oh, poppet, trust me. I want a feel of your pussy and to fuck the daylights out of you." He winked.

She gasped, not expecting his dirty talking. It gave her goosebumps. Liquid heat bubbled between her thighs.

"Rocco!"

"See what you've done to me?" His palms covered her ass, and he pulled her closer to him to let her feel his steely shaft.

A bark of nervous laughter came out of her mouth. She felt out of her depth. The tiny crease between his eyes was visible—the one she adored. She dabbed it lightly with her fingertips, caressing it. He brought her hand to his lips, placing small, delicate kisses on her palm and wrist. Desire struck at her core.

Emboldened by his kisses, her lips brushed his. This time, he didn't pull away.

At first, they barely touched. He feathered her lips, getting to know the tender flesh. His thumb tenderly circled the shape of her mouth, exploring her tempting pout. Then he fisted Evie's hair in a tight knot. Her scalp tingled, and her eyes flew wide open. She sought to move, but he kept her in place. He devoured her pouty, rosy lips. He kissed her long and fiercely, absorbing her in the moment. It was a hungry, all-consuming kiss, probing, intense, intoxicating her with his sweltering passion until she was breathless. No one had kissed her like that, not even Jake.

Rocco released her hair. His hand caressed the length of her hip until it veered under her dress, between her thighs, teasing her folds over her panties, exploring, palming, massaging. She hissed a slow breath. She became wet.

Bold as brass, she pushed him firmly on his back with both hands, giving in to her naughtiness. She was a strong girl, a farmer's daughter. He grinned, delighted at her daring, letting her take the initiative. Evie brushed her lips on his as she fumbled under her dress. She was still wearing the short dress from the club and reached for her black lace panties underneath. Taking them off, she held them up, dangling them in the air in front of him like a trophy.

He chuckled, enjoying this surprising side of her, and kissed her again, cupping her face in both hands. He tasted her mouth at length, deliciously, wallowing in the lingering moment. Affectionate. Amorous. When they parted, he grabbed her panties from her hand.

"I'll keep these, thank you." Rocco rose from the bed and put them in his trouser pocket.

Evie regarded him with a naughty smile, enjoying the gorgeous sight of him. He took off his boxers and his enormous erection popped free. His size and beauty made her gulp. He drew a condom from his wallet and unwrapped it, giving it to her with a grin.

"On my dick," he commanded.

Her brows shot up. He lay beside her on the bed, on his back, his hands beneath his head resting on the pillow, with elbows spread wide, entirely at ease. She stared at him briefly with the rubber in her hand, her mouth agape, but she obliged. She squatted on her haunches and, starting from his pink wet tip, Evie rolled the condom down over his thick shaft. She was slow and deliberate, touching him, feeling his hardness, nibbling at her bottom lip, flushed.

His breathing lowered. His manhood throbbed. And he couldn't resist her, his fingers went to her folds, and he skimmed her length. She sighed, closing her eyes enjoying the rubbing against his hand.

Emboldened by his reaction, she straddled him. She was not wearing any panties, and it felt liberating. He pushed her dress up and gripped her ass to steady her. He placed his dick at her entrance. His massive manhood probed her folds, rubbing, teasing her, taking his time.

"You are so beautiful," he mumbled, lifting her up a notch, pulling her down as he eased in a little. "So tight!"

"Rocco, oh, God!" she moaned, her body tensed.

"Relax!" In an abrupt movement, he inverted their positions. He loved to be in control. He ended up on top of her and entered her folds with a thrust.

Evie bellowed a high-pitched cry. Her gaze grew wide.

Rocco

Rocco saw it in her eyes. Panic! He halted, concerned.

"What's wrong?" he asked, his breathing labored as he withdrew his manhood from her. "Was I too forceful? Did I hurt you?" He peeked down at her red pussy. His eyes almost popped out of their socket at seeing his shaft, smeared with scarlet gunge.

Blood!

He stilled and gawked at her, astonished. Rocco was shocked, speechless. A slight grimace of pain was on her face. He glanced at his cock and back at her in bewilderment.

It couldn't be.

A virgin!

He blinked. An array of emotions swamped him.

What about Jake? He had not touched her! More shock. He didn't know what to make of it.

"R-Rocco..." she said softly, uneasiness in her eyes.

Soon, his hard mask vanished. His expression became soft, with a languid smile. He caressed her pretty face with tenderness, gazing at her, and a notion so primitive raised within him, taking over his senses. He hadn't cared about it before. Never! He made a point of staying away from virgins.

Somehow, this seemed different.

A possessive, proprietorial passion for her burned through his frame, so raw and primeval, from the tip of his head to his curling toes. Blood pounded in his veins. His smile widened, and he couldn't help but grin like a Cheshire cat.

He was her first man!

She smiled back at him, hesitant. Her face softened following the burst of pain as he broke her barrier.

"Are you all right?" he asked, suddenly anxious for her. "If I had known—"

"Don't stop." Her voice was barely a whisper.

"Evie, I—" Doubt began to assail him.

"Please, I want this," she whispered, rocking her hips under him, arching her body toward him. Offering herself to him, showing how much she coveted him.

He mellowed at the precious moment between them, and he couldn't wait to satisfy her desire. His lips captured hers in a fierce entanglement. He kissed Evie repeatedly, with a passionate, overwhelming greed for her.

Rocco eased himself in with eagerness, lifting her hips

and pressing harder. *Bloody Hell! I'm taking her like a schoolboy on his first thirst, and she's still wearing her dress.*

"Am I hurting you?" His erection pulsated inside her as she wriggled beneath him with need. He had to go slow with her, but his control was ebbing away.

"No, don't stop."

A virgin, bloody hell!

The women he went for differed from this girl. They had nothing in common. Yet, at that moment, he wished to be with her more than any woman. He was forsaking all others. And he rammed into her, claiming her, possessing her.

Evie gasped and writhed under him.

"Are you okay?" He struggled to control himself.

"Yes," she said in a breathy puff.

She felt delicate and small under him. He was renowned for his prowess in the bedroom, but this felt strange.

Jesus, I'm messing this up for her, ruining her first time.

Rocco's ardor to have her redoubled. So, he forced himself to slow down. He kissed her ravenously for a long moment, not moving, allowing her to get used to his size, stretching her. Then, he resumed his lovemaking slowly.

"Jesus, you are so tight, Evie."

∽

Evie

Every one of his strokes bewitched her under him. His hands drifted up and down her frame while his vigorous strokes brought her to the edge in no time.

"Oh, sweet lord," Evie mumbled, wriggling. "Oooh—Rocco!" Her heartbeat was pounding, her blood surging in her veins. Her temperature soared deliriously, and she felt every delightful stroke in her pussy until her release erupted, walloping her hard. Her fantasy man had taken her virtue, bringing her to the apex, and she spiraled out of control. He was all she had ever dreamed of, she knew it now, and he didn't disappoint. She was feverish with joy.

She sighed when she came back to earth. But he was relentless. He unzipped her bunched-up dress and tugged it over her head, dropping it in a bundle on the floor. His hands were all over her silky skin. Her flesh tingled with bliss. In a sudden move, he switched positions. She giggled. Evie was straddling him again as he pulled off her bra.

Her beautiful, firm, round, ample breasts popped free, his smile indicating his delight, and his cock sank deep into her. Her bosom bounced with each thrust. And he seemed to love that as well as his smile grew. His eyes roamed over her body, and he took a deep breath as if drinking in the dazzling sight of her.

"You are a vision!" he said. She was inexperienced. In her keenness to please him, she mistreated his cock somewhat. It made him chuckle. So he shifted positions again. He was reverting to being on top of her, to guide her enthusiasm for him.

"Are you fucking me? Or doing athletics?" She chortled irreverently, with a mix of sexiness and humor when she was under him.

"You cheeky minx!" He smacked her thigh and kissed her mouth until her lips were ruby red. "You are adorable!"

His mouth moved to her generous bosom, and he suckled a delectable pink nipple between his lips. He was licking and nipping at the heavenly, aching bud. Then he moved to the other. Her eyes rolled in ecstasy as he sunk in and out, deep inside her, until she reached a second orgasm. He countered with one of his own, blasting his seed inside the condom, reaching the pinnacle.

"Jesus!" He lay on top of her.

He pulled back after a moment and plopped beside her.

They lay motionless, silent, for a minute or two, their breathing still labored. He disposed of the condom. He picked up a few tissues from the bedside table cleaning himself and then her with reverence.

"Are you okay? Did it hurt?" he asked, gazing at her with a tender curiosity.

"A bit at first, when you know…" She shook her head with a sweet smile. "But no. You did well. It was all good—" She giggled, playful, unable to finish her sentence.

"Good?" He chuckled.

"Well, it was great. Does this satisfy you?"

He turned to her with a grin and slapped her ass. His nose almost brushed hers.

"Ouch!" she snorted.

He caressed her face with gentle strokes. He whispered tender endearments in his Italian sing-song. She had no idea what he was saying to her, but if he wished to call her my *micina,* so be it!

"What does it mean?"

"My little kitten."

"I'm too plump to be a kitten." She chortled.

"Nonsense! This nickname suits you well, down to the letter! You are my *micina,* now." He glanced at her with a grin. "And stop saying you are plump, *amore mio.* Those are delicious, sexy curves you got on you. I adore them."

"Umm…" *Did he call me "my love"?* These endearments sat well with her, leaving a satisfied smile on her lips.

"You should have said you were a virgin," he finally prompted her in all seriousness, caressing her dark hair.

"Why? What difference does it make?"

"Was this your retribution to Jake? Umm?" he demanded, raising a brow, doubting her motives.

"No! Of course not," she blurted. "I'm glad I didn't give myself to him. Look, if you must know, there was petting between Jake and me. I had orgasms before, you know."

She blushed as she spoke the words. She would not allow him to think she was a total novice at this.

∽

Rocco

Rocco's body tensed, and he clenched his hands into fists at the images of her with Jake. *If that bastard touches her again, I'll kill him.* The possessive thought burst into his mind unawares. He sighed at his silent outburst.

"You don't say?" he said instead, mocking her lightly to hide his possessive streak.

"Sure. I'm not as innocent as you think." She rammed his shoulder with hers hard.

"Hey!" he scoffed.

She massaged his shoulder with her hand, giving him tiny kisses.

"Jake and I were saving ourselves for our wedding day. Bastard! I was, but clearly, the pig wasn't."

"I'm overjoyed and honored, *micina,* you saved yourself for me." Rocco cupped her face. His mind-blowing kiss meant to erase any notion of Jake from her mind in no time.

CHAPTER 6

Selina

Selina was nursing a terrible hangover that morning. She went to the kitchen for a coffee. It was then she heard them.

Evie's idea of dealing with a hangover was new. They were "doing it" by the sounds of it. Her friend was having a good time. After the heartache with her ex-fiancé, she deserved a bit of joy. Nonetheless, the situation troubled Selina. She would tell her brother off.

Rocco had broken many hearts. Evie did not need more pain and should have been off-limits to him. He knew that. *Damn him!* But her roommate was a big girl. She could make her own decisions.

Blast! The awful hangover throbbing in her head worsened as she reflected on what was happening in the other bedroom. She stayed out of their way and would kill her brother if he hurt her friend.

Rocco

They spent Sunday together, lounging around, chatting and lovemaking. By lunchtime, Rocco was ravenous and wanted to cook.

"You got nothing in your fridge. Seriously? No food?" he asked, astonished.

"We were supposed to get groceries today. I'll call for Chinese takeout. You can cook for me some other time." Evie convinced him instead, kissing his cheek.

The appetizer dumplings she ordered fascinated him. He couldn't get them to taste this good in Naples. They left a portion for Selina in the kitchen.

"This one reminds me of you," he said, sharing a dumpling with Evie. "It's juicy and yummy like that sweet pussy of yours."

"Rocco!" She reddened, not used to dirty talking. He laughed playfully and kissed her soft lips with fervor.

"I love your little dumpling, *micina!* You are so hot. I want to feast on it all day!"

"God, you're a rogue!" she said, though she encouraged him like a love-struck teenager. After lunch, the doorbell rang when they were in the living room. They looked at each other.

"I'll get rid of whoever it is." She kissed his forehead and went to the front door. He laughed. She liked his laugh, a sonorous, low rumble. So masculine! "Well... I like everything about him," Evie muttered under her breath.

Steps advanced toward the room.

"Uh-oh—Hello, dear." The old lady stared at him as she entered the place. Her eyes were big and wide in confusion.

"Hello!" Rocco greeted back, giving her his most dazzling smile.

The woman peered at Evie and raised her brows with a shrewd grin at this handsome man sitting on her young neighbor's couch. He wore dark chinos and a loose, unbuttoned, white shirt displaying well-toned muscles on his chest.

"Sorry, darling. I didn't realize you had company."

A blush crept up Evie's cheeks as she lingered in the doorway, shuffling her feet.

"I'm Rocco LaTorre. Selina's brother," he introduced himself. He stood and stretched out his hand to greet her, seeing his girl flustered. The woman deposited a large, ornate plate with a cake on the small table and then took his hand.

"I'm Mrs. Jones."

"He's in London on business," Evie said as her face burned as she explained his presence.

"Pleased to meet you, Mrs. Jones," he went on, sounding relaxed. Evie looked as if she wished the earth would swallow her up instead.

"I live in the apartment next door. On business, are you? Umm… I see," the lady said with a smug smile. She was old but not a fool.

"Quite!" He smiled, unfazed.

"You can have a slice of my red-velvet cake with your coffee, perfect." The woman's gaze darted from Rocco to the girl, and her grin broadened. Evie was unable to meet her eyes, fidgeting, appearing ashamed.

"It looks delicious, Mrs. Jones. Thank you." He winked at her. *It appears words are failing my bashful girl.* He reckoned Evie was mortified at being caught with him.

My girl? Get a grip. You barely know her. You don't want this complication. His inner voice was quick to remind him.

"It's Evie's favorite," Mrs. Jones went on. "I'll leave you to it then. Good to meet you, Rocco." He was about to follow her. "No. Don't bother. I know the way out." The widow winked at her young neighbor as she left.

Rocco snorted when he heard the front door close and

regained his place on the couch. Evie sighed. She sat beside him, her cheeks still burning. He pushed a lock of hair from her face.

"You look so cute when you blush. How can I resist you?" He grasped the back of her neck with his large hand and pulled her to him. He kissed her ruby lips with passion until she was breathless.

"Sorry about my neighbor, she means well—" she mumbled when the kiss ended.

He released his grasp on her. "No need, poppet. Mrs. Jones seems like a friendly lady."

"She is a dear. So sweet. She checked on me every day when I broke up with Jake. She fed me, cooking casseroles to fatten me up. Claiming I had lost weight, saying he wasn't worth it."

"Well, he isn't. I like her." His tone was mellow, but his face was serious. He would have broken several bones in Jake's body for hurting her.

"I know she's right. She reminds me of my grandmother who passed away two years ago."

"Oh, I'm sorry, Evie. Were you close to her?" He played with a strand of her long dark hair.

"Yes. I first met Jake at school. Granny wasn't sure about him even then. She warned me and didn't mince her words. I suppose with time, she realized I loved him and accepted that we were together. But she warned me not to sell myself short."

"Too right! You shouldn't. You are beautiful, and you have lots going for you, *micina*. Never forget that." He tried to ignore her remark about loving Jake. His thumb brushed her bottom lip in a kind of proprietorial gesture.

"She encouraged me to study. To believe in myself."

"That's sound advice." He lifted her chin, staring into her eyes. Those gray marbles of hers gave him goosebumps. They were so innocent, so pure, and he stole a quick kiss.

"Granny told me I could become anything I wanted. She inspired me. She was lovely, and I miss her."

"Oh, I'm sorry."

"Don't be. She lived a full life."

"Sounds a bit like my granny, a strong woman. I bet they would have liked each other."

"Really?"

"She is as fit as a fiddle at eighty years old."

"Oh, good for her."

"Quite." He chortled.

"Selina never tells me much about her folks."

"My sister doesn't like to talk about our family."

"I gathered that."

"My parents come from, let's just say, 'unorthodox' families."

"Oh?"

"*Nonna* Flora, my grandmother, is a beautiful lady. So loving. She's a star, strong and chipper. She's as sharp as a razor, and you cannot fool her. The woman endured a deep pain in her heart all her life. She despised her husband for giving her two daughters away, my mother first, as the oldest, then my aunt. My aunt was lucky with a good match, but my mother not so much!"

"What do you mean?" Evie covered her mouth in shock.

My micina has led a sheltered life. Bless her! He caressed her hair back, pulling a lock behind her ear.

"The families weren't exactly model citizens, pumpkin. We still aren't," he scoffed. "I come from a long line of unpleasant people!" He paused and gave her a quick kiss, but he went on. "My maternal grandfather, God rest his soul—likely he is in hell. Burning high, I should think—" He chuckled. "Eraldo Montelli wasn't quite an example of endeavors, a well-to-do man from a rich merchant family. But he was overwhelmed by his vices. A gambler, a liar and a cheat. My mother was seventeen then when it happened. Southern Italy, you know. A long time ago." Why was he telling Evie all this? It surprised him at how effortless it was to talk to her. Sure, the story was not a secret. Everyone knew the background of his family. However, he would never speak of it willingly.

"I'm sorry," Evie replied with a tender gaze. She squeezed his hand and he was sure she felt a pang of sadness for him. She would have cuddled him, he was certain, the sweet girl, if they had known each other better.

"Selina never told you?"

"No."

"I suppose it's not something to broadcast. My grandfather gambled and lost all his money. His hefty inheritance soon went up in smoke, and he became riddled with debt. He was about to lose everything, including his home. Creditors came to cash in on their dues. So, my father paid Grandad's debts in return for his beautiful young daughter," Rocco lamented. "Dad came from a long line of criminals instead. As it turned out, he purchased himself a young, educated, beautiful wife with a good family name—an appalling, arranged marriage. Father died years ago—rotting in hell now, no doubt."

"Oh, dear!"

"*Nonna* Flora opposed him, trying to save her daughter, but she was no match for two cunning, strong men. A long story—for another day. Anyway, Granny is my rock. She's the only person who could stand up to my father. At least she tried."

"Oh, Rocco," she said as she embraced him.

This girl wears her heart on her sleeve.

He shrugged his shoulders.

"*Nonna* protected us kids and Mom against my dad. Let's say he wasn't a traditional father or husband. He was brutal. This is the reason I have no intention of marrying or having children, bad blood, you see!"

"Don't be silly."

"True. Over the years, Mother learned how to handle him, but he was awful. Anyway, it was a long while ago. My father died years ago."

"I'm sorry."

"Don't be. I wasn't. I have a stepfather now, he's a good man. Mother remarried after the death of my father. She deserves a little happiness." He glanced up at her, dismissing it all. He stared past her.

A daytime nightmare suddenly flashed across his vision.

∼

The endless welting on the raw and bruised skin was agonizing.

"Please, God, make him stop!" The boy prayed to the heavens silently. He wouldn't dare cry out for his mother in case she came in to help him.

So he took the blows bravely, struggling to blink back the tears. His father hated it when he cried—if he did, it would be worse.

The boy couldn't tell why he was being punished.

"A bastard weakling! That's what you are," his father growled at him.

Whatever that meant. Be brave—the boy willed himself. He felt his ragged breathing soaring against his ears. The fear and the pain crept all over his skin like thousands of spiders suffocating him, his heart thundering in agony.

She rushed to his rescue. To save him from the whipping. At least, she tried. She challenged him, but he was too fierce for her.

"Mommy!" He had to spare her, the boy thought. Small as he was, and full of bruises, he launched himself against the mighty man who simply pushed him to the ground with a swipe of his

hand. His father went on battering her. His punches struck her hard. She fainted. The monster hit the boy one last time with his fist before leaving the room. Imprecating against them.

Nonna Flora showed up to pick up the pieces, to console them. To patch up their wounds.

"One day, Nonna, when I'm big and strong, I'll protect Mom. I'll kill him." The boy's tears of fury and pain, run down his face.

"Shush, darling." She rocked him to sleep in her arms.

∽

Rocco

"Rocco?" Evie touched his arm, bringing him back to her. "You went quite pale. What's the matter? Are you okay?" Her eyes were misty.

He took a deep breath. He could control these daytime nightmares. He hadn't had one for years. What brought this memory on? He wasn't sure. Evie's expression was riddled with anguish for him.

He had said too much!

∽

Evie

"Rocco?" She cupped his face, and he leaned on her.

"I'm fine." He stole a quick kiss.

"Are you sure?"

"My grandmother would have liked yours."

Evie's heart ached for him. She had a flashing glimpse into his life as he opened up. When she started asking questions to know more, he shut down. He changed the subject. He had moved on, but he pulled at her heartstrings. What demons lurked behind his playful facade? Behind the Prince Charming? In his soul? In his family?

She would ask Selina. However, her friend was an

expert at avoiding discussing her family. She hardly ever talked about her background.

Evie worried. A dark aura had descended upon him. A gloominess surrounded his joyful disposition. She sensed it.

She cut the cake. They had a slice with their coffee in companionable silence. His spirit became playful again after the cake. Evie was beginning to think Mrs. Jones' cakes were not only delicious, but indeed miraculous.

Soon, the kisses mounted and made them forget everything, and lovemaking occupied the afternoon.

Rocco

Alas, Monday morning came too soon, and Rocco had a hectic schedule. He liked Evie and felt comfortable with her. But business called for the rest of his time in London.

Besides, he preferred one-night stands, and he had already spent too much time with her.

Out of character for him, still, no denying it, he had enjoyed every minute of the weekend. But something tugged at him. He could not say what it was. An unfamiliar emotion he did not recognize.

It's ridiculous, man! Get a grip on yourself. It was just fucking.

Evie's sweetness, innocence, and eagerness for him, in a body full of sinful, beautiful curves, had raised his pulse with passion, making him feel something new.

He saw a fleeting shadow in her eyes. *Melancholy?* Was she upset because he was leaving? It would please him, though.

"Are you going to be okay?" he asked. He had showered, dressed, and was ready to go.

Usually, he'd kiss his women goodbye with no fuss and

go, but he was reluctant to move. He stood by her side. She was on her haunches on the edge of the bed, still semi-naked from the red-hot amorous night. He wrapped his arms around her neck. She felt warm and silky at his touch, and he wished he could make love to her again. Alas, no time for it.

"Do you mean having spent Sunday in bed with you, and now you are scooting off? Abandoning me?" she said with half a smile in mock insult.

"Uh-huh… something like that."

"I'm a big girl, you know. I can take it."

"You are not used to this," he claimed. His gaze became soft. All the tension left him. He caressed her hair back from her cheeks and kissed her. He was not a fan of sappy goodbyes, but he had to admit his concern for her burned him. *Would she be okay?* She wasn't like his other women.

"Do you think I'll despair and kill myself, Mr. LaTorre?" She raised a brow with a grin.

"No," he scoffed. "But you are not—"

"Don't be so arrogant! I'll survive, I assure you."

"I'm sure you will. I meant that you're not the type for a one-night stand."

"I'm the one who suggested 'just sex, no strings attached'. Remember?"

"Yes. You may have done, but you are not that type of woman."

"You don't know what type of woman I am. And correction! It was not one night. Strictly speaking, it was two nights! And we spent an entire day together eating red velvet cake and Chinese dumplings. There is a new me coming out of this."

"Never change, Evie. I like you as you are—"

"Stop talking, Rocco. Don't you dare pity me!"

"I'm not… I loved every minute with you."

"That's great. And now, you have to go. I get it. So go.

That's the end of it." She brushed her lips on his for a quick kiss and then waved her hands to push him off.

"Evie—"

"Shoo! Go! Have a good time in London."

So, he captured her lips in a lingering, tender, goodbye kiss.

She cried the whole day after he left, missing him already.

∼

Rocco

He threw himself into his work. Rocco worked on his technology company, Stream Net, to open up other opportunities in the English market. A legitimate sector of the business, he was busy for days. Moreover, he and Fabio set everything in motion to have his men pursue Nico Columbano's whereabouts in England and investigate his connections with the 'Ndrangheta. The bugger had to be found. It was paramount.

But that little thing tugging inside him wouldn't quit.

Rocco had no intention of seeing Evie again. But he paid her another visit a week later. He couldn't help it. Her honeypot was too sweet, and he wanted to taste her anew.

"Man! This is a mistake," Rocco muttered as he parked his car outside her apartment block that afternoon. He almost turned back. He saw a shadow as he glanced up at the building to her fourth-floor window.

He went up.

Selina was out, but he hadn't come to see his sister.

Evie's surprise was evident. The smile on her lips, though, and her beaming eyes, told him she was as pleased to see him.

His kisses soon made up for his absence.

So they enjoyed a more forceful, amorous exploit for a

few hours. He meant to return to her two days later, but it wasn't to be.

Sebastiano recalled Rocco home with urgency. So he returned to Italy the next day.

The clan always came first.

~

Evie

Evie blinked back the tears until he went away. She had been the one to say, *just sex, no strings attached,* and she meant it. Still, she couldn't help feeling an emptiness in her heart when he returned home.

It had surprised her to see him again that afternoon. She was not expecting him, but his return had delighted her. She felt wanted and cherished. She hadn't stopped thinking about him since that weekend.

Rocco brought her flowers. She liked roses. To her surprise, he also brought her a present, a dainty Moonstruck Topaz silver bracelet. He called it—*a small thing to remember me by*—as if she needed a sign.

She loved it.

"God, this has been the fuck of the century!" she said to him after one particularly exhilarating lovemaking session that afternoon, wearing nothing but his beautiful bracelet to Rocco's great amusement and manly pride.

Her pussy had been sore for days, a sweet reminder of the things she did with him. At least he had taken her mind off Jake. Evie did not think of her ex-fiancé once. She had moved on.

To Rocco!

CHAPTER 7

Rocco

On his arrival in Naples, Rocco tackled the aftermath of a recent attack, which had ravaged and smashed a LaTorre nightclub to smithereens. A new foe had been troubling them, trying to muscle in on their territory. So, the clan unleashed fierce retribution on two Bratva nightclubs, zapping them to the ground.

Though there were no casualties, the financial losses were considerable for both clans.

Thus, following the assaults, Maximilian Ivanovich Belov, known as Maxim, the head of the Bratva in Southern Italy, asked to meet with Magda. Before the warring got too far, he wished to discuss a truce and a potential partnership.

Fabio's men had also stormed Nico's hideout in England on a tipoff but missed him by a whisker only two days ago. Rocco fumed—an umpteenth blunder. He forced himself to stay calm. It always paid off in the end. They would get him.

Rocco was also moving forward with Stream Net. This legitimate side of the clan's empire drew a massive effort from him.

All these matters had kept Rocco busy. Though, invariably, his mind would return to Evie. It shocked him he was still in contact with her six weeks later. He never gave a second thought to any girl after a brief interlude. God, the lass was a find! Sassy, sweet, fun, and in bed, she was a firecracker. She surprised him with her eagerness, her hunger for him, and under his expert coaching, she was blooming into a sexy siren. Evie was so pretty. He loved it when she blushed. Her innocence beguiled him, her passion dazzled him.

She lived in a different world from him. On the surface, they had nothing in common. But that night in the nightclub, somehow, they had bonded. They had got on so well the entire weekend, and the sex had been amazing.

He texted her a couple of days after returning to Naples, intending it as a friend and was ecstatic when she replied immediately. They had a lot of banter via text following that. They were developing a closeness.

Some of it turned sexy as hell.

Miss me? She messaged him once with a picture. The saucy minx sent him a selfie of her voluptuous breasts in a sexy, lacy, see-through red bra.

Another time, it was an extraordinary picture of her backside in black lace panties to taunt him. *What would you do to me now?* The curvy goddess had asked. He'd taken a cold shower.

He phoned her often. Their chats came easy to them. They had gone on like this for six weeks after his return. But in the last ten days, he noticed a change. It came gradually.

She seemed to have cooled down. Her responses didn't

come back fast enough when Rocco texted her. Hours passed. Sometimes, even days and her replies grew stilted. No humor, no pictures. She was not picking up when he called her, making rather lame excuses.

Women had never broken up with him. He invariably had the dubious task. *There is always a first for everything.* Why he fretted about Evie was beyond him. He had too many responsibilities to squander his time on this sappy nonsense. They had grown close, but now it was all changing.

Was she getting cold feet before they became too attached?

Perhaps, she had discovered what he did for a living exactly. Had his sister told her something? Who he was. Did Evie know about his family? He couldn't get her out of his mind.

It was torture!

Selina had given him a piece of her mind for getting into bed with her best friend. She had reprimanded him when she came home for Christmas, and he couldn't blame her. She urged him not to hurt her. But his sister had got it all wrong.

He had the feeling Evie was about to dump him instead.

Magda

"I don't trust him, Mother. Maxim is too clever. You should refuse the meeting. We have to get him out of our territory. If word gets out that the Bratva is seeking a truce and we are considering it, the other clans will say we've gone soft. They'll come after us," Rocco said.

"I agree. They'll view it as a weakness. It's likely Zilli in the 'Ndrangheta is backstabbing us, sponsoring Nico and his gang to weaken our organization. We will give Zilli a new excuse to bad-mouth us if we meet with the Russian. It's dangerous." Sebastiano shook his head.

"We are losing money. I hate the buggers, but I'd like to resolve this without casualties. We must be smart. I'll stall Maxim for now," Magda replied. They were in the extensive library in her home in Naples.

"There could be a way to stop the Bratva's attacks," Salvo stated as he rubbed his chin, deep in thought.

"How?"

"I hear Maxim is in the market for a bride."

"Go on." Magda raised an elegant brow.

"We offer him one of your nieces. Ulrico's youngest sisters are pretty, good girls. Any of them would make a good wife. Perhaps Greta, or Gala, or Ginevra, you choose. Your sister was blessed with three daughters. I know she still mourns her son Ulrico. Soon, we'll avenge him when we catch Nico Columbano. But the girls are of age now. They could be useful to us."

"I wouldn't use the words 'good girl' when describing Greta," Sebastiano scoffed, and his eyebrows shot up. "She's one of my best spies in high circles. How do you think I get the dirt on corrupt politicians? I can't lose her."

"Ginevra is fickle and spoiled, a real handful. Too young for marriage at only nineteen. Gala is so single-minded when she gets an idea into her head, so stubborn, Maxim'd be at loggerheads with her daily. Yes, Salvo, my nieces are pretty and clever lasses, but I'm not sure they'd make quite the dutiful wife you think." Magda chortled.

"That would be Maxim's problem, not ours," Salvo replied. Magda chuckled again.

"The Italian mob will see an association with the Russian mafia as a threat," Rocco grumbled.

"True, but not if we are smart about it. We can't fight

Nico and the Russian at the same time. We need alliances, and one with the Bratva could prove useful. Yes, not Greta. She's too valuable to us. Perhaps Ginevra or Gala might appeal to him. If he agrees, we'll invent a story. We'll justify it as a 'matter of honor'. Everyone is indulgent when honor is concerned. We could say the girl acted foolish, fell in love with him and ran away. So, we had to marry her off to him. We could explain the marriage that way. Settle on a plausible story with Maxim. He'll comply if it means a partnership with us," Salvo went on.

"Perhaps! But if so, it'll be with the proviso the girl agrees to it. She must want the marriage. I hear Maxim has a way with women. He'll have to woe her. I will not force a wedding on the girls. Selina hates me for betrothing her to Federico, but that couldn't be helped. My sister suffered enough with Ulrico's death. I don't want her to suffer anymore. So if Gala or Ginevra agree, we'll do it. It might work." Magda was mulling it over.

"Surely, you won't offer any of our girls to that scum. I forbid it! We don't need Maxim. I don't like him," Rocco vented, appalled at the idea. His brother rolled his eyes.

"This strategy works, Rocco. Let me think about it. I'll tell him we'll meet him soon. This should stop his attacks. Our resources are running thin, with fighting two sides. We can't go on like this. We need Maxim on our side," Magda pressed on.

"I don't like it, Mother," Rocco countered.

"Neither do I, but it could be a solution." She paused. "Please, Rocco, promise me, you'll find Nico. That's a priority. I promised my sister I won't allow that traitor to get away with killing her son. Nor do I want Nico to continue robbing my nightclubs and killing my men. This has to stop."

"I'm on it."

"We are in danger as long as Columbano lives. And you need to find out who's backing him."

"I'm working with Fabio. His men in London are doing all they can to find him."

"Find out if Zilli is backing him. I want proof. We've got to figure this out."

"We will."

"You know I have political aspirations for Milo and Matteo. These attacks from the Bratva and Nico are pushing my agenda back." She intended to drive the organization toward legitimacy. Political connections were one way to it.

She wanted these attacks stopped.

∽

Rocco

Rocco returned to his office. He tried to work, but his thoughts strayed to her again.

Evie had gone cold on him in the last ten days, and it made him nervous. This was the first time a girl caused him to feel this way. He was confused. He didn't know how he felt about her. These feelings were new to him.

He didn't believe in love or matrimony, nor in having children. With a father like his, he couldn't allow it.

The marriage between his parents had been a disaster. It was an awful example for him, and Rocco would not repeat that mistake. Though Magda's second marriage to Salvo had shown him a different face to marriage, one that could be happy, Rocco remained cynical. His dismal childhood was a testament to how his own father abused his children and wife. He still carried the physical and mental scars of the injuries at his dad's hands.

He had his bad blood. Why would he differ from him?

Would he end up the same bastard as his father was? It was anybody's guess. He couldn't risk it with his genes.

So he decided long ago to stay away from love, marriage and children. Love was a myth to him. It didn't exist anyway.

Still, it hurt him that Evie had cooled off toward him.

CHAPTER 8

Evie

Six weeks had passed since her passionate affair with Rocco in November. At the end of the Christmas holidays with her family, Evie returned to London, agonizing over the situation. She had been delighted to see her parents but hadn't enjoyed the festivities. Oh, no!

Not. One. Bit.

Evie's eyes stung from crying. There were better ways to start a new year.

She had been back in London for a week, but the news still scared her. She swung her legs over the side and got out of bed, crying her eyes out as she brushed her teeth in the bathroom. She scrutinized her image in the mirror. *Sweet Mary! I look awful. How can I face him?*

She fingered the bracelet on her wrist. The one Rocco had given her and wept again. She never took it off. An enormous sigh left her lungs. She missed him so much it hurt.

He was a clever man, but would he understand?

"Evie, are you okay?" A knock at the door jolted her. Selina's voice interrupted her dark musings.

"Fine." She sighed, but another sob escaped her.

"What's wrong?" her friend asked her through the door. "Don't shut me out. You have been so unhappy since your return from the holidays. Did something happen at home? It's freaking me out."

"I'm fine."

"No. Open the door. Come out of there, please." There was a click, and the door opened. "Come, darling," Selina said, gently pulling Evie by the elbow to the living room. She plopped her on the sofa. "Don't move. I'll get some coffee. Then we'll talk." Five minutes later, Selina returned and placed two steaming cups of coffee and two croissants on the small table.

"Thank you," Evie said.

"Are you going to tell me what's wrong? I'm going mad with worry."

"I-I—"

"Has Rocco hurt you?" Selina squeezed her shoulder as an encouragement, her beautiful face full of concern.

I should explain. Selina is my best friend. Eventually, she'd put two and two together. *Besides, I need to tell someone.*

"God, no! He's lovely."

"Then what's wrong? Is not Jake again, that scumbag, is it?"

"Oh, no! Not that bastard."

"Then what?" Selina shrieked. "Please tell me!"

There was no way to sweeten the pill.

"I'm pregnant!" Evie sighed. She put her head in her hands and sobbed.

"What?"

"Pregnant. Having a baby!" Tears streamed down her cheeks.

"Oooh." Selina was stunned. Then, she wrapped her

arm around her friend and patted her back. "Don't cry. Is it Jake's? I mean, the baby's father? You look so miserable."

"Jesus, no! Not that jerk!"

"It's not m-my bro—No!"

"Yes."

"Jesus!"

"Yes. Rocco's baby," Evie whispered. She launched a glance in trepidation at her companion.

"Flipping heck!"

"I never meant for this to happen. I'm so sorry."

"That weekend, in November. I thought, good for her! But I wasn't expecting you to make me an auntie, not so soon. Did you go, ahem—commando?"

"Commando?" Evie scoffed. "Of course not! We used condoms. The bloody suckers! Nobody mentioned they were not one-hundred percent safe! One must've been faulty, a hole or something. I don't know. What a disaster."

"Have you told him?"

"Rocco? Sweet mercy. No!"

"But, darling—"

"I'm not sure how I feel about this myself yet." Evie was tugging at her hair in anguish, torturing the poor strands.

"But why? You're not having an abortion?"

"Good God. No!" Evie huffed. She touched her right temple, massaging it.

Selina smiled and for the first time, visibly relaxed.

Though Evie was scared out of her wits at her new situation, she had started rubbing her tummy tenderly and talking to her baby, often in a childish voice. Yes, she wanted the child! She already loved the little creature growing inside her with a passion. But the idea of parenthood was scarier than she'd imagined, and that of telling the father even more so.

"I'm glad. Then if you're having the baby, you must tell Rocco. He's the father."

"I'm not ready. I need time."

"He deserves to know. Besides, sooner or later, he'd notice. You won't be able to hide your pregnancy for long."

"I haven't figured out what to say to him yet." Evie could not look at her friend.

Selina frowned. "Tell him the truth. Rocco has a heart of gold."

"I need to think this over."

"Evie—"

"Oh, Selina. You must keep my secret, please. You are my best friend. Besides, if I didn't tell you, I would explode."

"Sweetheart—"

"With all due respect, Selina. I'm a farmer's daughter, but I know right from wrong. While your brother belongs to, umm... well, I don't get the ins and outs of your family background, but yours is not your average family, is it?"

"I see. Is that what it is?"

"No, but can you come clean with me now?"

"Jesus!"

"Please…"

"Evie is best if you don't know—"

"Please."

"Okay." Selina hesitated. "Magda LaTorre, my beautiful mother, is a Camorra boss in Italy. She's a powerful woman," she blurted out in one breath before she lost her courage. Her hand was over her chest.

"Mafia?"

"In Naples, we called it Camorra, but yes, we are mafia. Though my mom is a businesswoman above all else these days, she has many legitimate companies to run."

"And Rocco works for her?"

"Yes, but Rocco's a powerful man in his own right. He operates genuine, lawful businesses, too. It's not all doom and gloom, Evie. He's a good person and would never hurt you or your child. He is not a psychopath if you are worried about this."

"I believe you. But if the mafia isn't bad enough, Rocco is also a womanizer. Have you forgotten the stories you told me? He is a master playboy! He is often in the papers with his women. I googled him. I couldn't understand all the captions in Italian, but he is—"

"My brothers are often in the tabloids and magazines in Italy. They are handsome, rich and powerful men, and the ladies love them. Their stories sell newspapers. It would be best if you didn't believe everything you read about them. The papers make things up," Selina huffed.

"He dates actresses and models. I've seen the photos. They have angel faces and bodies like goddesses. While I am…"

"What?"

"Well? Look at me."

"Evie, you are a lovely, beautiful woman, and Rocco likes you a lot. Trust me, I know. Don't overthink it. If you are worried about these things, don't be."

"Oh, God."

"Besides, he worked so hard on his technology business. My mother has approved for him to take it over. Soon, he will make a move full-time. If his life scares you, he'll be free of the more unorthodox business when he takes over Stream Net as CEO. He's quite a wizard at it, you know. In five years, the business is already worth two billion Euros."

"Two billion—you see what I mean. I can't."

"Evie—"

"Please, swear you won't tell him."

"Blast!" Selina rolled her eyes.

"Promise me."

"Okay. I promise. Perhaps, when you have time to think, you'll realize a child needs its dad." Selina would be the first to admit that her own father had been a scumbag. She and her siblings were better off without him. Her father was dead; she was glad they were rid of him. But Rocco was nothing like his father. He had a good heart, and Selina was concerned for him and Evie.

"You know what I said to him that weekend, 'this is just sex, no strings attached,' you understand that?" Evie cleared her throat. She blushed to the roots of her hair.

"You said that? To my brother?" Selina's eyes grew wide and she snorted.

"Yes. Rocco was cool with no commitments. We agreed. He told me he had no intention of marrying or having children. Rocco was categoric about it. He doesn't want any. How can I bring this news to him now?"

"Everyone says they don't want marriage or children, but they always do. Look at Fabio and Melania. When he met Melania, the rest was history."

"Those two are an exception!"

"No, they are not! Rocco will kill me if he finds out I'm keeping this secret. It is a huge thing. My death will be on your head!" her companion lamented, leaping forward to repercussions.

"Don't be so melodramatic." Evie had not regretted making love to Rocco. Oh, no! If she had the chance, she would do it all over again. Sex with Rocco, the demigod, was one thing, but to share a baby with him was a different ball game. She needed time to think. She feared his lifestyle, her pregnancy, and above all, she feared his womanizing.

What would Rocco do with a woman like herself? They had nothing in common. He would find her boring. He would tire of her within six months, and then where would she be? Rocco would turn to other women. He would crush her soul as Jake had done. No, she couldn't tolerate this again.

This time, she was in charge, not Rocco, not Jake. She wouldn't allow another man to hurt her. To break her heart as Jake did.

"He'll kill me for not telling him, and he won't be thrilled with you, either."

"Nonsense. Your brother loves you."

"Let's hope you know what you are doing, Evie. God help us because if he finds out before you tell him, we'll be in deep trouble! I can guarantee. You don't want to experience him when he's not Prince Charming."

As the days passed, Evie got even more scared.

The two billion Euros of his company played on her mind. He was a billionaire. *He'll think I'm a gold digger!* That she had done it on purpose, to trap him. She worked herself up into a frenzy.

She resolved to keep her secret. She had no intention of telling Rocco.

What's more, she devised a lie instead to protect herself and her baby.

CHAPTER 9

Rocco

Rocco was working in his office, until his phone pinged.

I'm going home for the weekend to Lincolnshire. Jake wants to talk to me. Evie's message read on his phone.

Jake? Are you kidding me? The asshole who cheated on you?

I owe it to him to listen.

You owe him nothing. Rocco almost broke the screen on his cell, thumbing the words in a fury.

Bloody hell! How could she be so naïve? He realized it now. She had cooled off with him because of Jake. Rocco convinced himself Evie had slept with him to get back at her fiancé. To get even. It made sense now. He swore profusely!

He speculated on what sappy stories Jake devised to entice her back to him. The frigging bastard!

Please, Rocco. I've known him since I was a child. I was engaged to him for five years. This is something I have to do.

He cheated on you for a year! He had another woman! How can you trust him?

Rocco had no rights over her. Evie wasn't his woman. Even if they had carried on from that weekend, their motto was still *'just sex, no strings attached'.*

Fuck!

The girl got under his skin. Bloody vixen!

Besides, I'm visiting my parents. Evie wrote.

Your parents, yes! But asshole number one, no! I forbid it.

You can't forbid anything, Rocco! We agreed—no strings attached. I wish to see Jake.

Evie, don't!

She stayed silent, no response. Billowing fury rose and spread like fire through his frame.

Rocco texted her again but got nothing from her. He waited. He tried to call her, but she didn't pick up his calls.

He brooded over it for days.

∽

Rocco

A week later, he received another text from Evie.

I'm with Jake again. We have too much history to let things go. I have forgiven him, and we are back together. Please be glad for me. Let's stay friends. Yes?

Rocco was furious. He paced his office like a caged lion. Zeno entered the room to say something.

"Out!" he yelled, ready to pounce on someone, anyone!

Rocco sought to talk her out of it. But she wouldn't hear of it. He couldn't stop the silly girl from ruining her life. He wracked his brain wondering what to do about her until he received word from Evie two weeks later.

Hi, Rocco, some exciting news. I'm going to have Jake's baby. We are thrilled. Marriage is in the cards again, and I'm a little overwhelmed. I hope you can be happy for us.

"No!" he yelled at the top of his lungs. Rocco's world crumbled like a deck of cards as he read her text message three times with wild eyes. On the fourth time, he launched his phone against the wall with an almighty bang. It shattered into smithereens.

∼

Evie

"Oh, Evie. That's dreadful. Why would you say a thing like that to him? It's a pack of lies!" Selina shook her head with a scowl. Her arms crossed over her chest, and disapproval was written all over her face.

"I'm sorry!" Evie's body was filling with the baby growing inside her, almost four months after she had been with Rocco on that weekend of passion. She had panicked.

Earlier in her pregnancy, she convinced herself she had played it well to throw Rocco off the scent and lied to him about the identity of her baby's father. She was thrilled with the story she made up, pretending it was Jake's baby and not his.

Now, she was not so sure.

How can a mobster be the father of my child? What kind of example would he be? She kept repeating to convince herself she had done the right thing. True enough, she believed it, but she used it as a shield to protect herself more than anything.

She was lying to herself.

Yes, Evie feared his mobster life and his family, and she believed Rocco would think her a gold digger. That she wanted to trap him. Though what worried her the most was Rocco's womanizing.

He had the most beautiful women in Italy after him. Even if by some miracle she managed it, she would become tedious to him, dull within months. He would want to move on to new pastures soon enough. Then where would she be? Rocco would crush her spirit like Jake had broken her heart with his deceitfulness. No! She wouldn't allow this. She couldn't permit a man to hurt her again.

Evie could not admit this to herself; this fear petrified her above all others, and there were many.

So, she came up with an elaborate plan to push Rocco away. She lied, informing Rocco that Jake was the baby's father and that they were back together.

All a big fat lie!

It served her purpose. Rocco hadn't contacted her again after that.

Evie's lies had done nothing to lessen her ardor for Rocco though. Every time her mind went to him, and it was often, with his baby growing inside her. She missed him like mad, his kisses, his caresses, his body wrapped around hers, the chats, even his bossy attitude. He was constantly in her thoughts. She dreamt about him, her pussy tingled. One night, she had an orgasm, dreaming about making love to him.

Above all, her lies weighed on her. She had behaved like a vile snake to Rocco and betrayed him with her lies, and the guilt was killing her. She felt remorseful.

"No wonder my brother won't speak to me. It makes sense now. He probably thinks I was complicit in getting you back with Jake."

"But I'm not with Jake!"

"I know, but Rocco doesn't. He thinks the baby is Jake's?"

"Yes."

"Oh, Evie, how could you?"

"What was I supposed to do?" she mumbled, mortified. Her face was a mask of sorrow. She couldn't backtrack now.

"You silly girl."

"Don't look so horrified, Selina. It worked. I have not

heard from Rocco since then. He didn't need much encouragement to go his way."

"But you told him you are having another man's baby, engaged to Jake. What is Rocco supposed to do with that? This is not like you, Evie, to lie like that. You are being unreasonable. My brother wouldn't hurt you."

"I'm sorry. It seemed a good idea at the time," Evie said. "Would he be mad if he knew I lied?"

"Let's not talk about that now." The hair at the back of Selina's neck stood at the thought of Rocco finding out.

"How could he settle for someone like me, anyway? I'm so ordinary."

"Evie, that's nonsense, and you know it. You're many things, but certainly not that! You are working yourself into a frenzy."

"I made matters worse, didn't I?" And she burst out crying with her head in her hands.

"Hey. Don't, sweetheart. It's all the hormones in your body. They are not making you think straight." Selina sat beside her and patted her back.

"I don't know how to get out of this mess." Evie's mascara streaked her cheeks.

"Stay on the sofa. Don't move. I'll make us some coffee, and Mrs. Jones brought in a pie this morning. You'll soon feel better. We'll fix this."

A few minutes later, Selina returned with a tray holding two coffee mugs and two plates with slices of pecan pie.

"You are a lifesaver. Decaffeinated, right?"

"Yes."

"What would I do without you?" And Evie hugged her friend. She cut a bite from the pie and shoved it in her mouth. The goodness of the pie lightened her mood instantly. *God bless Mrs. Jones and her miraculous baking skills!* "*This* is so good!" She sipped at her coffee.

"Heavenly!" Selina agreed, taking a morsel, closing her eyes, enjoying it.

"I have to figure this out. If I tell Rocco the truth, he'll take me for an idiot! A cunning liar." She took another mouthful from her fork.

"Not if you say how you feel. He'll understand. You mentioned you were getting along fine with him, weren't you? Texting and talking over the phone. You told me it was a great weekend when he came in November."

"The best of my life!"

"You see? Rocco made you happy. I know my brother. He never calls girls back. They call him. But he called you!"

Could it be? Evie finished her slice, pensive. With an enormous sigh, she brushed away some crumbs from her belly, caressing her baby bump. *What shall I do, pumpkin?* This question silently went to her child before she glanced at her companion.

The front doorbell rang. Selina huffed but got up to answer it.

CHAPTER 10

Nico

Nico Columbano was living on borrowed time. His enemies had been close to apprehending him twice, but his luck would run out sooner or later. He knew it. Before then, he would strike at LaTorre's core before his demise.

Thus, he was where he needed to be, where he would do just that.

Nico sat in a British Gas cargo van, wearing a uniform as if he were an employee of the company. The previous night, he had stolen the vehicle from a British Gas depot in North London. He changed the license plates on it at the front and back. So, although stolen, the number plates belonged to a legitimate van. It wouldn't raise suspicion. He had also taken the jumpsuit overalls he was wearing from the depot's changing rooms.

He was parked in a leafy side street near Hyde Park, off Bayswater Road. The apartment was on the fourth floor. He had a good view of its windows from the van. He had been there early and assured himself Selina LaTorre was at home. She had answered his mysterious phone call on the land line earlier, thinking it was a wrong number.

For the last month, Nico had watched her. He followed her every move. He studied her routine and learned she shared her apartment with another girl. Sometimes, the girls went out together. When he could, he would listen to their conversation in a coffee shop, where he would sit—well camouflaged—at a nearby table. He realized the other girl, she called her Evie, was pregnant, but he couldn't catch the name of the baby's father. Besides, he was interested in Selina, not her roommate.

It had been easy to follow her. She didn't seem to have a bodyguard, which surprised him.

Everyone knew Selina was Federico Santillo's fiancée. No man would mess with Federico. He was a beast of the underworld, feared and revered by the most eminent Cosa Nostra families, the Sicilian mafia. One day, he was sure, he would be "The Don" of the mob, the "capo di tutti". And he had picked Selina as his woman. The reason, Nico thought, why she went about freely. No one would dare harm her, the retribution too enormous to contemplate.

Though Nico was a dead man walking, and he had no family, it didn't matter to him; and Selina was Magda LaTorre's daughter. The woman who had signed his death warrant.

He glanced at the concierge on the ground floor. His disguise as a British Gas engineer would allow him to go in. People didn't notice this type of serviceman.

He looked at himself in the rearview mirror. He had grown a beard and shaved his hair to a buzz cut. A blue cap on it covered half of his face with its peak. No one would recognize him. Besides, Selina had only seen Nico once, in passing, assuming she had even noticed him when he was part of the clan as a foot soldier. Before the time he had shown his true colors and betrayed them. She wouldn't remember him. With his guise now, she would not realize who he was.

Federico would kill him only for looking at his girl. Nico laughed out loud. It didn't matter what he did now.

The idea of upsetting Federico Santillo and Magda LaTorre, in one go, appealed to him.

He left the vehicle and made his way to the building. He chose a time when the concierge was dealing with a large delivery. The foyer was busy with the consignment, delivery men and a huge sofa. So, Nico strolled through the atrium nonchalantly. He pulled up the fake he'd made of the identity card all energy employees had to show and flashed it at the concierge.

He nodded.

Nico's uniform, cap, phony identification badge, and the large delivery in the lobby allowed him to fool the busy attendant without a problem. Nico took the lift. He pushed the fourth-floor button and went up.

"Good morning, British Gas to check the meter." He flashed his identity card. He had changed the photo on it with one with his new image. Selina peeked at it.

"Oh. Hello. It's in the cupboard. Please follow me." She smiled.

Evie grinned absentmindedly at the fellow in the blue overalls as they went by in the hallway. He touched his peak in salute.

"It's somewhere in here. Sorry about the mess. Can you spot it?" Selina asked him, opening the sloppy, tiny room's door.

"I'll find it." He busied himself, pretending to search for the gas meter.

"I'll be back in a minute," she said. The man didn't look at her. He nodded, and she returned to the living room and her friend.

The first step of his plan went without a hitch. Nico

was in, and Selina had not recognized him. She didn't harbor any suspicions he was not a legitimate British Gas employee. He pretended to look for the meter.

Nico Columbano's heartbeat soared, as it always did when he closed in for a kill. The woman left him and disappeared into the living room. The other girl was there, too—no time for hesitations. He would do it. It suited him that the girls were in the same room. *I'll take them both.*

He adapted hastily to a new execution plan. In any event, he had identified this risk of having to shoot two instead of one. It didn't bother him.

Now. Do it! His inner voice urged him.

A rivulet of sweat ran down his forehead and strayed into his eye. He wiped it with his hand. His gaze flashed along the corridor and with a fast, silent peek into the other rooms, he determined the girls were alone in the apartment.

He unzipped the front of his overalls and pulled the gun from his shoulder holster. He fixed the silencer to his fully loaded Glock 17, ready to fire. His Adam's apple wobbled in his throat in minor agitation. Or was it with the hunger for the kill?

His breath quickened. A rush of adrenaline whooshed through his body. With a sickening shine to his eyes, he made his way toward the women.

∽

Selina

"British Gas is checking the meter," Selina huffed. "Where were we, Evie?"

"I'm sorry, I—"

"That's okay. I understand, but you have to tell Rocco the truth."

"I know."

"Look, I'm sure he will love being a dad. He'll cherish you and the baby."

The intercom buzzer rang loud, making them jump.

"What now?"

"Jesus! It's like Piccadilly Circus today. I'll go." Selina went to it. She said a few words over the intercom and returned to her roommate. Her face burning, eyes wide in horror.

"What is it?"

∽

Nico

A stroke of luck! That is an unexpected piece of news. The ladies' conversation was a revelation to him. Nico had crept toward the living room, handgun in his grip. He paused in the hallway outside.

Rocco's baby! Who would have thought? A devilish smile showed on Nico's lips. *Two birds with one stone. No. Three!* He almost laughed out loud.

He was about to enter, the gun steadfast in his hand, ready to fire, when the intercom buzzer stopped him in his tracks.

Shit!

He darted back to the cupboard, and stuck the pistol back in the holster, hiding it from view. The girls were now in different places in the apartment. A little trickier. *I'll wait until she returns to the room.* He listened to Selina's talking over the intercom. *What?* He swore under his breath. He saw her dash back to the room and heard the girls' high-pitched tones, somewhat in panic. It confirmed what he thought he'd heard.

Fuck, Rocco.

In the first instance, Nico thought of killing him, too. The surprise element was in his favor, but then he realized it might be too risky. The women seemed agitated, and they would scream, making a racket. With three against one, his chances were uncertain. They might even put up a fight. Even if he succeeded, after a commotion, leaving the building undetected was unlikely. Besides, he had spent precious seconds indecisive. Rocco was on his way up, and it would be only a matter of moments before he was at the door.

It was a split-second decision. Nico aborted his plan. For now.

"I'm done, ladies. I'll let myself out," the bogus British Gas man spoke instead. He had to leave that instant. His enemy was coming up.

"I had forgotten all about him." Selina glanced at her friend and poked her head out of the doorway. "Everything okay?"

"Fine." The bogus serviceman nodded.

"Thank you."

He left the apartment quickly, closing the door behind him. Nico rated his options, and he saw the elevator moving up.

Damn.

He needed to get out of that building and fast. He was on the top floor already, and there was no way up. He peered down the stairwell—his only chance to escape.

Shit!

The delivery guys were coming up, blocking the staircase with their large sofa delivery.

Fuck!

He lost precious seconds dithering. His hand went to the gun inside his overall. He knew if he didn't hit first, Rocco was a great shot. Then a door opened behind him. He turned. An old lady carrying a casserole dish came out of another apartment.

"Morning, madam. British Gas, I need to read your meter." He flashed his card at her.

The elevator pinged to a stop. Nico panicked. He was about to face his nemesis. His hand inside his overall grasped his gun tight.

"Come in, young man," the woman said. "I'm Mrs. Jones."

He followed her swiftly into the apartment. As Rocco emerged from the lift, Mrs. Jones closed the door.

Nico missed him by a whisker.

CHAPTER 11

Evie

The doorbell rang.

Rocco was on her doorstep.

"Dear God!" Evie leapt from her seat as if it had caught fire. "Please, Selina, let's stick to my story that I'm happy with Jake, and he is my baby's father—if Rocco asks. I'm not ready to reveal the truth to him just yet. This is so sudden."

"Jesus! Sit down. Okay. Stay calm," Selina urged, quite jumpy herself.

"Oh, sweet Mary."

"If you are not telling him, then pull yourself together or you'll give yourself away."

"Do I look okay?" Evie's voice had taken a nervous tone. She fretted.

"Beautiful!" Selina said with a soft smile. "I better see to him. Breathe!" She patted her friend's arm, reassuring her, and went to the door.

Evie sent a brief prayer to the heavens. She was hyperventilating, but retook her place, striving to stay calm. She smoothed her hair back. Perspiration erupted on her upper lip.

∼

Rocco

"Hi. Why didn't you say you were coming?" Selina kissed Rocco on both cheeks.

"Hey, sis! Long story, business." He came in and followed her to the living room.

He saw Evie on the couch.

She flushed scarlet. His sultry green eyes scrutinized her. His gaze fell on her round silhouette as she rubbed a hand absentmindedly across her belly. She glanced away from him.

Rocco hadn't come to argue with her but to protect her from that asshole of her fiancé Jake, baby or not.

He went to her without a word, and leaning over, he kissed her forehead. Another flush of heat spread across her neck and face. Her reaction gave him a clue. Whatever the girl said, she was still not immune to him. His lips curved at one side. He positioned himself beside her on the couch. She bolted a notch in the opposite direction.

He would have laughed at her response. It took all his self-control not to.

"Hi," Evie squealed, her voice high and pitchy.

She coughed, and Rocco could see she struggled to pull herself together. His presence affected her. That was clear to him.

Good, because the silly chit is affecting me. He thought in astonishment.

"You look well, glowing. Motherhood suits you. Are you okay?" He regarded her steadily, studying her. Her curvy figure was more alluring than ever, even with her baby bump growing. He did not expect her tummy to show like this. It surprised him. He did some mental arithmetic about how far her pregnancy was.

A few weeks since she had told him she was pregnant with Jake's child. *A couple of months at the most, and she's already that big?* But what did he know about these things?

It hurt him, though. *Evie must have gone to bed with Jake that same weekend when she texted me she was going home to talk to her ex-fiancé.* They did more than talk then.

Rocco was disappointed. He thought she had cared for him. It was clear to him.

She went to bed with me only to get back at her ex.

∽

Evie

"I'm okay," she mumbled.

"All well with the baby?"

"Yes!"

"Good for you. Lucky Jake!" Rocco replied, his voice calm, nonchalant. But she noticed he bunched up one hand in a fist.

"Yes, he's happy," Evie added. Lying was horrid, but she couldn't stop herself. In reality, she hadn't seen or spoken to Jake since the breakup. Evie clasped her hands tight on her lap, feeling remorseful at her lies. She glanced at Rocco for an instant but soon lowered her eyes, wringing her bracelet on her arm.

She knew he recognized it. She was still wearing it. A big mistake! It had all happened too quickly she hadn't even thought of it.

"Your eyes look red. Why?"

"Huh?"

"Have you been crying?"

"No." Shocked at her vehement denial, she added, "I've

been working on an essay for class. My eyes are red because I've been on my laptop for hours. How long are you staying?" She couldn't face him. She kept looking somewhere over his shoulder instead while his stare was intent on her. He was not wavering. She peeked at him but soon averted her gaze.

"A few weeks. Business."

"Oh," she said with a tentative smile. "Weeks?" she repeated, blinking fast and taking a calming breath.

He nodded.

"Where are you staying?" Selina asked him, "With Fabio?"

"My house."

"You have a house in London? Since when?"

"There was a house for sale when I was here in November. By chance, a few doors down from Fabio's, on the same street. We talked about it, remember?"

"Oh, yeah."

"I bought it. I thought it best since I'm coming to London regularly. I have had a contractor's team working on it ever since, renovating it. It's almost finished now. Still a few things to do, but mostly cosmetic. I'll stay there while they complete the work."

"I'd love to see it," Selina said.

"Anytime."

∽

Rocco

"Would you like to see it, too, Evie?" Rocco's eyes were steady on the girl, never leaving her.

"Yes." Her face burned.

Evie's so cute when she blushes, prettier than I remember, pregnant and all.

He had the urge to crash his lips on hers. The desire

was so strong; he had to master all his self-control not to leap off the couch, take Evie into his arms, and kiss her senseless. He didn't want to scare her. There was Jake's child between them that complicated matters now.

Jake will not have her. The blasted man doesn't deserve her, baby or not. This girl belongs to me.

"Shall I pick up the two of you for dinner tonight?" Rocco was a patient man. He would bide his time.

"Somewhere nice and trendy, then!" his sister agreed.

"Sorry. I'll pass, a study night," Evie replied instead.

"I assumed that was tomorrow." Selina scowled at her. She knew what her friend was doing.

"No. We changed it to today." Evie cleared her throat and bit her bottom lip. His gaze stayed on her mouth, and her action drove the blood to his cock.

He drew a deep breath, but his eyes darted from Evie to his sister. It was clear his girl lied.

Your girl? Not yet! His inner voice retorted as a wakeup call.

Not yet, no. But she'll be mine.

The first item on Rocco's agenda was to prevent her from marrying Jake. Then, with a bit of luck, and a lot of romancing, she'd become his. But it was clear to him she was trying to avoid him. *That's okay.* He had to give her time.

Her red, crying eyes did not sit well with him, though.

"No worries, some other day," he said. *I should talk to Jake. Frighten the life out of that asshole because if he's making Evie cry again, I'll kill him.*

"I'll leave you to it, then. You'll want to catch up. I need to finish my essay." Evie rose from the couch and stepped toward her bedroom, but not before her companion frowned at her.

She ignored Selina's chastising glare, turned a slight smile on him, and left.

Evie

Evie nearly died of an apoplectic fit before leaving the room when he winked at her in his sexy manner. Heat pulled at her core. God, how would she endure having him around for weeks? How would she manage with all those lies between them?

It mortified her.

She plopped on her bed limply, picked up a pillow, and dragged it over her face. A small scream escaped her lungs. The padding muted the sound. Jesus, he looked better than she remembered. So handsome, while she resembled a whale with clothes that were too tight for her size. She should go shopping tomorrow and buy something fashionable.

She had detected a new intensity in him, directed at her. Once or twice he even looked slightly menacing and dangerous. He had a renewed power about him. He seemed to be on a mission. What that mission was, she had no idea.

Am I imagining this? Blast, he didn't take his eyes off me. Does he suspect something? Is that why he's here?

"Argh!" She made another shriek into the pillow.

She got up and pressed her ear to the door. *What the hell are they talking about? I hope his sister doesn't give me away. No, my secret is safe.* Selina was her best friend. She would not betray her. Her phone pinged. She glanced at it. There was a text message.

Damn!

It was from Jake. *Will he never give up?* He was persistent. It had been six months since she had broken up the engagement with him, and her stupid ex-fiancé was still pursuing her. It made no difference to her. She was done with him. Period!

As if having Rocco's baby and lying to him wasn't bad enough. She had too many problems to give Jake a second thought. She deleted his message without reading it, as she did to all of his messages. She threw the phone on the bedside table and cursed at men in general.

Evie paced the length of the room. She would have to tell Rocco the truth, but how? What would he say?

Rocco will think I'm a rotten liar. An idiot! He'll assume I've done this on purpose, got pregnant to trap him. Besides, he's not likely to leave his bachelor's lifestyle to settle with me just because I'm carrying his child. Forsake all his gorgeous women to stay with a plump, pregnant girl, even if the baby is his. He's going to hate me. A fat tear came down her cheek.

She closed her eyes, inhaling and exhaling, seeking to calm herself. She fell into a frightful sleep.

She awakened in darkness. Evie switched on the lamp on the bedside table and peered at the clock. It was seven pm. She had been asleep for hours. The apartment was deadly quiet. She sighed in relief. *They've gone out.*

∾

Rocco

He didn't return to the apartment for the next three days. On the fourth day, Rocco showed up. Selina had invited him for supper. They swapped pleasantries, but Evie pretended she was busy.

"Sorry to miss dinner, but I have a study evening with a friend. Can't miss it." Her face was burning. He nodded with a hint of a grin. His phone rang.

He left the room, taking the call.

"Evie, you must stay for supper. I'm doing this for you. So you can talk to him. I'm trying to make it easier for you." Selina was none too pleased with her.

"I—"

"Instead, you are avoiding him. You're just putting off the inevitable."

"No. I'm not."

"You are!"

"I'm not ready."

"Then, when?"

"I-I—"

"What are you two whispering about?" he asked. The girls stopped talking the moment he returned to the room.

"Nothing!"

"Girl stuff," his sibling blabbed on instead. Selina scowled at her companion.

"I see."

"Well, I have to go." Evie scurried toward the front door. "Enjoy yourselves!" she shot over her shoulder.

"How long is she going to keep this up? She runs for cover every time she sees me," Rocco countered, as if on cue, looking bemused when Evie fled.

Selina shrugged her shoulders and snorted, a little uneasy.

Evie spent the rest of the evening in a coffee shop with a book to avoid him, and she cursed herself.

CHAPTER 12

Evie

The following week, it was Evie's twenty-third birthday.

She had arranged a dinner party on the Friday night and hired a private area of an Italian restaurant to celebrate. If it wasn't for a slight detail she had overlooked, she would be over the moon.

Fabio, Melania and Rocco were invited to her celebration.

Evie fretted when she realized her mistake. She had not invited Jake to the party. Why would she? The trouble was Rocco believed her child to be Jake's. How would she account for his absence? Rocco thought they were back together. How would she explain Jake missing her birthday party? Her lies would catch up with her. Rocco would ask questions, and hell would break loose.

She hadn't seen or spoken to her ex-fiancé since she broke up the engagement six months ago. Recently, matters had turned for the worse. A friend had revealed a rumor going around the village that Jake had only been interested in her parents' farm. Not in Evie. This had cut her like a knife knowing she had trusted that calculating, conniving, cheating bastard. She was unsure which—Jake's cheating streak or this new greedy revelation of his—infuriated her the most.

Jake was a vile man.

Besides, he had turned into a pest. The scum kept pleading for her mercy. He wished to revive their relationship, pestering her with texts and calls.

The slimy bastard! How dare he?

She didn't pick up his calls or return messages, giving him a consistent message. She wanted nothing to do with Jake.

But with her birthday party hours away, she had a problem.

She was getting ready, vexed to the extreme. Selina was helping her with her hair.

"What are we going to do? What if Rocco grasps something is wrong?" Evie said, agitated. She had been fretting for days.

"If my brothers or Melania ask, tell them Jake will be late. Say he is coming back from a business trip. A commitment that kept him abroad all week. Then, later in the evening, we'll say his flight was cancelled and rescheduled for the morning so he won't make it to the party. You'll pretend to be upset and all that. It should solve our problem. But you wouldn't be in this mess if you'd told Rocco the truth. It's not fair."

"I know, and I'm sorry! But I don't want drama at my party. Let's get through tonight first, shall we?"

"Okay."

"Do you think our plan will work?"

"Unless you have a better idea?"

"No. Melania keeps asking me about Jake. She suspects something. I can feel it."

"Oh, nonsense."

A knock at the bedroom door made them both startle.

"Girls, are you done?" Rocco's voice took them out of their reverie. "It's late. Come on, and I'm hungry."

"Just a minute." Selina glanced at her wristwatch. "Let's go."

∼

Rocco

Rocco whistled when he saw them all dolled up.

"Wow, girls! You look beautiful," he said though his focus was on Evie. She wore a knee-length, deep-toned claret soft dress with a flattering crossover neckline and three-quarters sleeves. The frock fit her to perfection. It draped beautifully over her body. Her makeup was light and dewy. Her lips were the same color as her outfit. She looked stunning.

Rocco didn't know what attracted him to this woman, even when sporting a baby bump… *another man's baby.* She got under his skin. He had the urge to kiss her, his self-control restraining him. He gave up trying to understand why he liked her and went with the flow.

Selina introduced her brothers to their friends when they got to the restaurant. Rocco paid close attention to the men in the group.

"Which one is Jake?" he asked Melania.

"He's not here," she said, looking around her.

"No? Why? Ask her?"

They were about to be seated.

"Where is Jake?" Melania turned the question to Evie. Rocco's ears perked up.

"He's been away on a business trip all week, he's back tonight. His flight was delayed. He'll be coming along later." Evie blushed when she saw Rocco's scrutiny on her.

Evie

Of course, Jake wouldn't be coming at all. *Oh, boy. I'm in for trouble if Rocco becomes suspicious.* A call came on Evie's mobile phone to spare her more lies.

"It's Mother. Excuse me." She moved outside the restaurant to take the call.

"Hi, Mom."

"Evie, dear. I'm sorry Dad and I will miss your celebration tonight. You have fun."

"That's okay, Mom. We'll have the weekend together. I'll be home tomorrow afternoon. We'll celebrate on Sunday."

"Yes, darling, but a word of warning. Jake is on his way to London."

"What?"

"It seems he's familiar with the restaurant."

"Yes, he is. But how did he know?"

"Oh, darling! That's my fault. I met your friend Violet in the village this morning. We were chatting, as you do, and I brought up your dinner celebration. The girl told someone in the pub about it at lunchtime. And this someone blabbered it to Jake, and right now, he's heading to London to catch up with you at the place. He's making the most of this situation by assuming you won't make a scene in public since you barred him from entering the apartment building. When Violet realized what happened, she tried to convince him it was a bad idea. But he was unshakable. Jake is going to be there soon."

"But he can't. He'll spoil everything. I don't want to see him." She could practically feel her face turning pale.

"You must tell him to leave. Be firm with him."

"Oh, God!"

"My apologies, sweetheart! I hope he doesn't ruin your party."

"No worries, Mom. I'll deal with him."

"What's going on?" Selina asked her when she saw her friend all flustered.

"Jake!" Evie whispered and explained the issue. "What do we do now?"

"Oh, hell! What if Melania says something like 'congratulations on the baby' to him? Then what? All your lies will unravel at once."

"Oh, God. He must not come in!"

"Right."

"I'll ask the restaurant manager to watch out for him in return for a generous tip to his staff. He must not allow him in until I can talk to him first. Jake will know then he's not welcome. I'll ask him to leave," Evie whispered, not wanting anyone to hear.

"Good."

"What are you two whispering about?" Rocco asked. "What's going on?"

"Nothing! Take your place at the table. They'll be serving dinner soon. We'll be back in a minute," Selina mumbled. The girls hurried to the front of the restaurant.

The dinner got underway. Everyone was having a great time. The party was intimate but fun, with fifteen people attending, and the meal was finger-licking-good.

The starters came up in silver trays, bringing a riot of colors to the counter with bruschettas and various focaccia loaves of bread. A platter with olives, pickled vegetables, and cured meats didn't last long. To follow, the service brought in three gigantic bowls with fresh pasta dishes for all to share.

Rocco sat opposite Evie. He watched her, studying her interaction with the other guests. She was like a rare pearl, and everybody loved her. Her friends looked at her as if she were the best creature in the world.

His soul swelled for her. It was then he resented Jake's existence with all his might. He had never envied anyone in his entire life, but he hated the man. Rocco wished her baby was his.

"Hand me your plate. I'll serve you. What would you like first?" Rocco said, overcoming his thoughts when he saw her trying to figure out what to have. The aroma was making her mouth water.

"Selina ordered the food, so I'm not sure what all these are."

He removed the tongs from the first bowl.

"These are pumpkin and spinach ravioli." He had tasted them all. He placed a portion on her plate. Then he got to the second dish. "These are cannelloni with zucchini, ricotta and chilli."

"Yes, I know. I like the ravioli. I'll try the cannelloni."

"What about spaghetti puttanesca?"

"Yes, but that's too much, Rocco." She stared at the amount piled up on her plate with wide eyes.

"You are eating for two. You have a baby to nourish." He arched his brows. She scoffed.

"Have you tried them?"

"Do you need to ask?" He cocked his head.

She put a hand over her mouth and giggled.

God, she's so cute.

"Rocco is the best cook in the family, aside from Dora, my mother's housekeeper. Her food is to die for. He learned from the master when he was young. My other brothers are hopeless in the kitchen." Selina chuckled.

"Hey? I do a wonderful carbonara." Fabio frowned at his sister.

"True. Though I intend to teach him something else. It's all we get when he's cooking," Melania teased her husband.

"But it's good, huh?"

"Oh, yes, delicious, darling!"

So, the dinner went on in good humor.

∼

Rocco

Half an hour later, the manager said something in Evie's ear. Her eyes grew wide. She glanced at Selina in panic, and with a slight motion of her head and tight lips, she indicated to follow her. They rose and moved out of the room.

Rocco followed their movements through the large archway separating the rooms, as they reached the front of the restaurant.

He saw Evie talking to someone in the foyer, but a pillar obscured the other person. He could see Evie and the arms of a man in a suit. His sister stood a little back from them in plain view.

What was going on? These girls were always whispering when he was around. They were concealing something, and he didn't like that. *Were they in trouble about something? Who's this guy talking to Evie? Is he Jake? If so, why is he not coming in, then?*

He didn't know what to think.

∼

Evie

"What the hell are you doing here?" Evie glared at him. Her lips pursed. Her ex-fiancé had turned up at her party uninvited. What gave him the right?

"Happy birthday, sweetheart." Jake offered her a small box with a bow.

"I want nothing from you. Please, leave. Right now. You

are not welcome here." She dismissed him, waving his gift away.

"We need to talk."

"We have nothing to say."

"Evie—"

"Jake, you had a wasted journey."

"Darling, why are you not answering my calls… you know how sorry I am. Let me explain. Please."

"Explain? That woman in your bed explained everything. And don't 'darling' me," she said, jutting out her chin in defiance. "Leave and don't come back. We are finished! Get it through your thick skull. Get out of my life."

"Sweetheart—" Jake's fingers reached for her arm, trying to touch her. But she swatted his hand away.

"Leave me alone. Go away."

His nostrils flared, but she was determined. He would not intimidate her.

"Why did you do that? To taunt me?" He glared at her baby bump. "Who's the father?" Jake tapped it lightly with his hand, his eyes in slits on her.

Evie gasped in dismay, not expecting this. Jake had delivered a slight slap on her bump. Though it didn't hurt, it was outrageous. She instinctively caressed her tummy and covered it with her arms to protect her baby, glancing at him, horrified. Then she darted her eyes to Selina. Her lips trembled, and she looked back at him.

The insolent smirk on Jake's face released a surge of fury in her blood. A white-hot rage flared inside Evie. How dare he do that to her child? So she kicked his shin harshly. He hopped in pain.

"Don't you touch my baby again."

"You are a slut!" He grasped her upper arm in fury.

"You are a bastard, and I'm so glad I got rid of you!" She shook him off with another kick.

Patrons in the restaurant started to whisper, all their eyes on them in the foyer.

Selina turned to glance at her brother in the other room for an instant, then back to her friend.

Rocco still couldn't see what was happening at the front of the restaurant or hear what they were saying, the pillar obstructing his view.

Though his sister needed no words, her face revealed a plea.

∽

Rocco

"Let her be," Selina warned Jake as she reached them in two strides. The situation was getting out of hand. She put her body between them and pushed him off with both hands. "Go. Do it now, or you'll be sorry."

Jake shoved Selina aside with his hand and seized Evie's wrist. She yelped.

"You stupid girl!" he swore, shaking her. His chest puffed up. "Look at the state of you."

"Leave her alone!" Selina punched him in the ribs.

"You bloody tramp!" Jake breathed out. The punch, though strong, had not moved him. He slapped Selina hard.

"Jake!" Evie cried out, horrified. He went for his ex-fiancée again. The brawl escalating, was turning ugly. The manager was about to intervene.

In a split second, Rocco grabbed Jake by the collar amid the kerfuffle and dragged him out of the place and onto the street, virtually lifting his feet off the floor.

He tossed him against the wall outside hard.

The girls went after them.

Rocco flung two jabs at the man's face in a fast one-two combo boxing technique, landing powerful punches.

"Fuck!" Jake's head snapped back and he winced in pain. Blood gushed down his nose. The metallic taste flooded his mouth. His lip was cut.

"Stop. Let Jake go," Selina yelled at her brother seeing the red gore, while Evie seemed dumbstruck. But it wasn't over. Rocco struck one more blow to Jake's stomach, making him double up in agony.

Evie could not speak, staring at them as if paralyzed.

"Don't touch these girls again, understood?" Rocco's pulled him up by the hair, and his other hand clasped the man's throat. His thumb and forefinger dug in. "Am I clear? Answer me."

"Y-yes."

"Now, apologize to them. Your apology to Evie's long overdue."

"Fuck Evie!"

Rocco saw red. Billowing fury swelled in his veins, eyes bulging as if he were a bear with a sore tooth. He would have severely hurt the fucker, but he restrained himself in front of the women watching in alarm. He was sure his *micina* had never witnessed a real fight before, other than in a movie.

As it was, he limited himself to punching Jake in the abdomen with all his might. The fellow was about to crumble. But he squeezed his palm on his neck in sufficient force, pinning him in place, choking him.

"Jesus. Rocco, no! Jake's not worth the trouble." At last, Evie found her voice, but he ignored her.

"Don't talk to Evie again. Don't come near her again, or I'll crush every bone in your skull. Apologize, now." Rocco jabbed him.

"S-sorry!" Jake moaned in misery.

"No, no! As if you mean it," Rocco said, nailing another blow, striking his ribs. "With genuine remorse, this time!"

"I'm s-so s-sorry, Evie."

"Good!"

"Please, Rocco…" Selina tried to pull her sibling off the guy.

"What the fuck are you doing? Do you want to get arrested?" Having reached them outside after hearing the commotion, Fabio struggled to tear his brother off the bastard.

"You heard the ladies. Leave. Do it now or you'll wind up in a bag." Rocco released the man, shoving him off. "Go! Before I change my mind and I kill you." His eyes blazed fire at him.

The moment he was free, Jake legged it without a look back.

"Are you okay?" Rocco scanned her from head to toe to reassure himself she wasn't injured.

"I'm fine." Evie nodded, shaken but unharmed.

He did the same with his sister. The girls were unhurt, and he hissed a sigh of relief. He turned to Fabio with a quick, meaningful flicker of the head. He needed a word with his *micina,* alone.

"Come on, let's go inside. Let Evie take a breather for a moment. Rocco will look after her," his brother prompted, catching his plea. Selina patted her friend's arm with a heartening smile but followed Fabio inside.

"So sorry you had to see this, poppet." Rocco raised her chin to him when they were alone. "But when he touched you…" His words faltered.

Evie felt relieved he hadn't seen Jake tap his hand against her baby bump maliciously. She surmised, her Italian demigod would have murdered the man for sure if he'd known.

"That's okay. Thank you, but I had it all under control."

"Oh, yeah?" He raised his brows with an amused grin. She blushed. He removed a lock of hair from her face pulling it behind her ear, caressing the line of her neck with his fingertips. His thumb went to her upper lip, circling the contours of the soft flesh. Hot blood swooshed through his veins.

"Rocco!" Evie's spine tingled in anticipation, but in sudden panic, she stepped back against the wall with her heart thundering in her ears.

He advanced and placed his hands on either side of her, trapping her in, breathing in her sweet scent. Their eyes locked, and desire filled the air between them. It sizzled and flashed around them like a storm unleashing its bolts faster and faster, whipping them up into a frenzy of passion. His gaze went to her plump, sugary lips, and like a beacon of light guiding a ship to port, they called out to him, enticing him.

He kissed her.

"Rocco." Evie sighed in his mouth. Her eyelashes fluttered. Her pulse quickened. His lips were on hers, pressing the silky flesh for access. Evie allowed him in, and he probed her generous, sensual mouth with his tongue. Her hot honeyed pot tasted so good, he grunted in her mouth. She was so kissable. He relished it. One arm circled her waist, and her tummy bumped into him first as he drew her to him.

She giggled when he drew back and glanced at the round tummy on her. He echoed her laughter, but it didn't stop him from kissing her again. The kiss was powerful and possessive this time, masterfully claiming her until she was breathless.

CHAPTER 13

Evie

"Rocco, we are in the street," she breathed out, panting, placing her palms on his chest.

"Who cares?" He raised her wrists to his lips.

A sharp intake of breath filled her lungs. "Ooh..." she said.

"I don't know what happened between you and Jake, but you can't have him treating you like this. I want you to end it." Though his words were a whisper, there was no mistaking his tender command. He kissed her over and over.

I should tell him now. Do it, woman. Evie willed herself. *Tell him you aren't with Jake.*

But her courage failed her. She was enjoying his kisses. So she let the moment pass.

"I don't want to talk about him." *Not now, anyway.*

"Evie! He's scum."

"Okay, I'll leave him. I promise," she blurted, prepared to say this, no harm in it, which pleased him.

He kissed her again, gratified, unleashing more passion. Technically, she was still lying.

Be truthful, woman! She admonished herself, compelling herself, but the brush of Rocco's lips on hers was so divine she would ruin it all with the truth. She didn't want this moment to end. He would hate her once he discovered her secret, her lies. She felt it in her bones. Her heart ached at the mess she was in and the one she would create for him once the truth was out.

"We must go inside, my guests, my party…" she mumbled.

"Sure, in a minute." He smiled, caressing her cheek. He pulled out a small, red-velvet box from his jacket pocket and gave it to her.

"What's this?"

"Your birthday present, *micina*. You didn't think I'd forgotten?"

"Ooh—"

"Open it."

She complied eagerly.

"Oh, my God." She lay a hand on her chest over a quickening heartbeat. "They are beautiful." She fixed her gray eyes, big in wonderment, on the most extraordinary earrings.

"Glad you like them."

"Are they…"

"Real?"

"Are they?"

"The pearls or the gold setting?"

"Silly."

"They are Baroque pearls, poppet, from the South Seas." He winked at her. "I'll put them on you." He reached for the package in her hands.

Her skin tingled. She sucked in Rocco's inebriating manly scent, turning giddy. Her clit pulsed.

"Stop smelling me."

"No, I'm not."

"Don't move or we'll be here all night. I'm trying to put these buggers on you." He fiddled for a minute with the trinkets, placing the jewels on her. "There!" His head drew backward to admire them. "They look lovely on you."

"Do they?" Evie's fingertips caressed the raindrop-shaped pearls on her ears. "Thank you, but it's too much. They must have cost a fortune."

"Nonsense. These are perfect for you. Let's slip back inside before your guests think you're rude," he said. "Ah, and I'll stay with you tonight. I'm not taking any chances in case that idiot is still in town," he added in all seriousness. "Someone has to protect you."

And her heart melted for him.

∞

Evie

After the party, he drove the girls home.

"Are you okay, Evie?" Selina put her arm on her shoulders. They were in the living room, in the apartment.

"Aha."

"I'll look after her. I'm going nowhere tonight," Rocco said.

Selina's eyes grew large, and she did a double take between her brother and Evie. She grinned, pleased with herself and winked at them. Evie blushed. Selina wished them goodnight and retired to her bedroom.

They sat on the sofa.

He drew Evie to him, noses an inch from each other. He knotted his fist in her hair and pulled her back. Her scalp tingled, and it traveled straight to her pussy.

"You look beautiful! I love those earrings on you." He kissed her, devouring her. His other hand caressed her round bump, and the baby kicked. He removed his hand abruptly as if it had burned him.

She snorted.

"Bloody hell! He kicked!"

"He?"

"Well, he or she…" He grinned.

She took his palm and placed it back on her belly.

"Don't be afraid, it's fine. Touch it." A glow of pleasure lit up her face as he caressed her round bump until it rewarded him with another kick.

"Wow! That's amazing," he said in awe and brushed his lips on her tummy. "That bastard doesn't deserve this."

Evie felt awful. Rocco was still under the impression the child was Jake's.

You moron, tell him now! Her inner voice urged her. But she was too anxious Rocco would get upset with her. Too afraid the dream would end. She craved him. If she told him now, it would open a can of worms.

So, she cupped his cheeks instead and yanked him to her for a kiss. His palm slithered up her thigh under her dress. She gasped, and her soft center ached with need. He reached for her panties and moved the gusset aside. He fingered the length of her moist folds.

She inhaled a sharp breath.

"Good girl, you are so wet for me."

She sighed when his finger plunged into her core. Then another. A slow, deep hiss came out through her lungs. His breath meshed with hers, and she called out his name. He strengthened the pressure and depth.

He finger-fucked her.

"Sweet Lord. Oh, my…"

"That's it. Let yourself go." He increased the intensity of the strokes in and out, watching her.

"Ooh. Rocco—" And before she finished her sentence, her orgasm burst on his fingers, gushing her juices on him.

Her moans grew louder, but his mouth on hers muffled the sound.

It had been some time. Heaven, she had missed him and his expert touch.

As her climax subsided, he scooped her into his arms and dashed to her bedroom. She giggled. He placed her on the bed and undressed her. When he took her bra off, her beautiful breasts sprung free. "These are fuller than I remember."

"Pregnancy does that," she said.

He gorged on her pert nipples while she gave tiny moans of ecstasy. Her tight buds were tender and becoming sensitive with her pregnancy, but she allowed him to do it. The mix of pain and pleasure heightened her senses.

He stood and stripped off his clothes in a flash. She watched him, mesmerized. How could she keep such a handsome man? No woman would truly ever own him.

Her gray moons went large when his fiery manhood jutted out, long, iron-solid, ready to battle. She wanted him inside her and reached for him, touching his shaft, and he growled a primitive sound. Her delicate hand around him made his blood rush to his cock. It throbbed in her palm.

"In your mouth," he said with a hint of command, and her eyes sparkled. She obeyed him.

Her alluring lips circled his moist tip, and he grunted his appreciation while her soft hand curled around his hard length. He inched into her mouth, bit by bit. He fisted her hair, pulling her back and dictating the pace. Her skin and scalp tingled, her bosom was engorged, and her center ached with need. He held her in place and moved at a rhythm. Every thrust a little deeper.

"Sweet girl! Letting me fuck your irresistible, generous mouth." He groaned in satisfaction.

She welcomed him in greedily, not expecting she would

love this so much. He sank in until her ruby lips were too much for him. His orgasm exploded. His seed filled her, warm and salty. She swallowed every little drop, and her pulse surged. He withdrew from her.

Incredible how she affected him, somehow his manhood was still rather hard.

He pulled her up, kissing her long and hard, tasting himself on her. He seemed to enjoy savoring her. Rocco lay tiny kisses over her face, neck, and shoulders, making her quiver. He turned on her swollen breast and sucked on her pink-tipped nipples to his heart content. Her pussy pulsed, demanding fulfilment. He eased her to the edge of the bed. He took off her panties.

"Open your legs," he said. Evie obeyed. He pushed her knees down and watched her lying there, open and ready for him. His heartbeat spiked. "You are glorious."

"Liar."

"You are! Never forget that." He slid inside her, bit by bit, stretching her. She received him with a gasp of joy, but he paused.

"Is this okay, Evie? It won't harm the baby, will it?"

"No, it's fine." A small smile curled the side of her mouth. "Don't stop."

"Are you sure?"

"Positive," she mumbled with a snort, and he called for no further invitation. He buried himself in her and then moved in long, deep strokes. She arched her back, her hips matching his moves, clenching his cock within her walls. He grunted his hunger for her and covered her mouth in a possessive, fiery kiss that made her dizzy with love.

Oh, God, I worship him.

She had missed him all these months, but she wouldn't hazard a guess at what would happen when she told him he was the father of her baby. This was stuck in her mind, but not for long. His relentless thrusts soon rendered any thought inconsequential. Her pussy was tight and wet as he slammed into her. She wriggled in ecstasy under him, calling his name in tiny bursts of breath. Their desire became frenzied, their bodies meshing into one until her world twirled around her.

A powerful orgasm rocked her body. Every cell in her frame was wired to the climax. Elation took hold of her. She was on the brink of passing out.

His turn came. He erupted inside her in a wild, mighty release that shot through his body. He withdrew and collapsed beside her in a spent heap. He kissed her shoulder with closed eyes, whispering sweet words in Italian.

He called her *amore mio*.

"I know what that means."

"Do you?"

"It means—my love."

"Good, *micina!*"

"I haven't forgotten this one, either."

"Have you been learning?" He propped up his face on his elbow.

"Maybe."

"Umm… it'd give me great pleasure if you learned my language."

"I'd like to."

"I'll teach you." And he began with the parts of the body as he touched and pleasured her.

That night, vigorous lovemaking swept over them until slumber caught up with them.

∽

Evie

The next day, he wouldn't allow her to go to the station to take the train to Lincolnshire and travel to North

Kesteven alone. Not when Jake may be lurking in the village. So he drove her all the way home. When they reached the farm, Evie's parents would not let him leave. They insisted he should stay the night.

"Please, Rocco, call us Callum and Bridget. Okay?" Her dad showed him around the farm, and they soon hit it off.

"So, what's going on with this handsome fellow? Hey?" Bridget asked her while Rocco was out. So Evie told her how he had chased Jake off at the party.

"He was masterful and scary, Mom. But it was lovely to think he was defending me and the baby."

"I guess it's his child, too."

"Mom!"

"I'm not a fool. When he came to London last winter, you couldn't stop talking about him. Then, you got pregnant and didn't want to talk about the father. I know you too well, Evelyn! So tell me the truth. Is he the one? No more nonsense."

When her mother called her by her full name, she knew she was in trouble. Besides, she wanted to. So, she explained everything.

"Oh, Mom. What do I do now? He'll be upset if he discovers the secret unmasking my lies."

"No, he won't. Rocco'll be delighted. He is a good man."

"Mother, he's not quite… he is…"

"I know what he is, darling. Your dad and I are well aware."

"You do?"

"He's very fond of you. He seems smitten with you."

"Give over!"

"It's true."

"You don't mind, he is what he is?"

"We thought Jake was a good man. But what do we know? He lied, he cheated on you, wanted our farm. I rather have Rocco a hundred times than that spineless, greedy pig of your ex-fiancé who treated you like dirt. But the sooner you tell your Italian man the truth, the better. Or it will end in tears."

"I promise."

They had dinner, and later they went up to bed. Her mother assigned Rocco a separate bedroom for proprietary sake, which Evie found rather hilarious given the circumstances. Though it didn't put him off. He sneaked into Evie's that night to make love to her. He had his hand on her mouth twice to block her from screaming her orgasms out to the household.

The following day, he was out on the fields at the crack of dawn. It was still dark. He worked with her father for hours, milking the cows, feeding the piglets and more.

They had a full English breakfast when it was light. Rocco understood why a simple croissant and an espresso wouldn't do after this hard physical work.

"Are you ready for more?" Callum rubbed his hands after breakfast. "You are a pro at this."

"Daddy, you'll tire him out. He's not used to this."

"Sure, let's go." Rocco winked at her.

"You realize you don't have to do this."

"Darling, I want to." He rose from his seat, and they set off to the fields. Evie was so proud of him, her heart burst with joy.

They celebrated her birthday again with a glorious lunch. Rocco thought he could eat nothing after the huge breakfast. Though he was hungry after all the hard manual work, it was exhilarating.

All the food was produced and grown on the farm. It was an earthy, delicious luncheon, starting with bite-size canapés. The bread, puff pastry and butter were all homemade and served on a beautiful platter. A juicy, tender leg of lamb with roast potatoes and spinach followed. It made his mouth water. An enormous red-velvet cake with twenty-three candles ended the celebration.

Evie blinked back the tears. She was on cloud nine. If the truth didn't hang between them, it would have been one of the best weekends of her life.

After the meal, Rocco needed to go. He was bound out west with Fabio for a week. He did not mention it was to follow Nico's whereabouts. Rocco summoned Zeno, his lieutenant, to pick up Evie and drive her back to London. It astonished her he would do this for her.

"This isn't necessary. I can take the train," she insisted, but he wouldn't hear of it.

"Ready, Miss Logan?" Zeno urged when he got there.

"Take good care of her."

CHAPTER 14

Rocco

"Uncle Rocco, are you staying in London forever?" Lola, Fabio and Melania's seven-year-old daughter, stuck her hands together as if in prayer, wishing he was.

Rocco was having dinner at his brother's home that Friday. The girls were there, too. He and Fabio had returned that morning from a week spent out west. Rocco had not seen Evie since her birthday weekend, but they talked on the phone every evening.

"For a little while, *stellina.*" He rumpled his niece's hair and kissed the top of her head, placing his arm around her shoulders and squeezed her to him.

"Can you take me to school tomorrow?"

"No school on Saturdays."

"Umm… what about Monday?"

"Sure."

"Yeah!"

"Lola, please, behave," Melania said. "Eat your pie."

"She's fine. Let her be," Rocco said.

"Uncle Rocco is driving me to school in his car, Daddy."

"Really?"

"I might walk you there, *stellina*, not necessarily drive you."

"But I like your car. We go fast."

"You speed with my daughter in your car?" Fabio scowled at him.

"No, I don't," Rocco scoffed, caressing Lola's cheek. "Compared to you, Fabio, everyone drives fast."

"There are cameras and speed limits in this city, you know."

"Right!"

"Can I have a bite of your pie, Uncle Rocco?" Lola had finished hers already, wanting another piece of dessert.

"Sure, go ahead. Help yourself."

The child picked an enormous lump of pie from his plate, but instead of making it to her plate, it fell from her fork over the pristine tablecloth and on her. There was apple pie everywhere.

"Wait, I'll come over," Melania said, ready to clear up the mess.

"No need. I'll see to it." Rocco plucked all the crumbles from the dinner table and his niece's dress. He brushed off the few remaining crumbs with his napkin.

"Oh, I'm all sticky now," Lola grumbled after helping him pick a few pieces of pie from her lap and shoving them into her mouth.

"Let's wash our hands, then. Excuse us." Rocco walked his niece out of the room.

"All clean!" Lola stuck her palms up to show them when they returned soon after.

Rocco helped Lola back into her seat at the dinner table. Then he took his place beside her.

His gaze settled on Evie, and he smiled at her.

My woman looks lovely this evening. His eyes lit up. *Yours?*

Umm... are you sure she's not Jake's? His inner voice teased him. Rocco rolled his eyes.

Evie had assured him she would break up with Jake after her birthday party. But had she? She wouldn't talk about him when Rocco had raised the subject over the phone a couple of times in the past week, and he refused to turn into a jealous boyfriend. So he didn't press the matter with her. In Rocco's mind, he and Evie were an item again. What sort of item, he wasn't quite sure—the baby issue hung over them.

Rocco was sitting between his niece and his brother on the opposite side of her. With Lola wanting his full attention, he didn't have the chance to direct much conversation to Evie yet. Still, he studied her every move. He was blatant. He felt possessive about her. He watched her all evening.

As they locked eyes, she blushed, averting hers.

"Can I feel the baby in your tummy?" Lola's tiny face was full of affection.

"Sure!" Evie said, "Come over here."

Lola leapt from her chair, but Fabio intercepted her before she went any farther.

"Not now, darling. Don't bother Evie. You've asked her five times already," Fabio chided. "Come on, children, time to go upstairs. It's late."

"No." Archie, Melania's five-year-old nephew, staying with them for a few days, replied with a pout. He crossed his little arms over his chest. "I want to watch cartoons."

"No, sweetheart, it's bedtime," Melania prompted, ruffling her nephew's hair and kissing him. "You, too, Lola. Say goodnight."

"I want to feel the baby first. Can I, Mom?" Lola pleaded. "Please?"

"What did I say?" Fabio glared, chastising her.

"But, Daddy—"

"I don't mind. Really. Let her." Evie beckoned the kid with her finger.

"Fine, two minutes, then upstairs, both of you. It's past your bedtime."

Lola dashed to Evie who smiled at the child's eagerness. She rose to step away from the table. The child placed a hand on her abdomen reverently, then her ear on Evie's tummy with a giggle. She listened with a focused expression.

"The baby kicked," Lola boomed in a high-pitched voice.

"A huge kick." Evie's face glowed, caressing her bump. She turned to Rocco, who was watching them captivated. She gave him her sweetest smile.

The scene gave Rocco a warm, fuzzy feeling. His hair prickled on his neck. For a moment, he wished the baby was his. He mastered his control to avoid saying something stupid.

Ridiculous! His inner voice said, *that's some other man's kid you are after, man.* He ignored the devil messing inside his head. Rocco wished he could put his hands on Evie's hips and kiss her round, full belly, inch by inch.

She glanced his way, almost as if in a calling. His sultry, green moons looked tenderly at her. Her gaze locked on him. She blushed.

Every cell in his body wanted to dart to her and crash his mouth on Evie's.

Make her yours, man. Yours and yours alone. Be done with it. Don't you see how she looks at you? She needs you as much as you want her.

Evie was not like his previous women. She had lived a sheltered life. He had to go easy on her. That evening, glancing at her flushed, pretty face, her round, womanly hips, and her cute baby bump, it finally dawned on him. He wanted Evie with all his might, body and soul, baby and all, and for good, even if the child was not his.

She's mine. My woman!

∼

Melania

"Come, Archie, say nighty-night," Melania said to her nephew. Her sister's child was a darling, but sometimes Archie could be stubborn. "Lola, you too," she went on, but the youngsters had no intention of moving. "Chop, chop."

"No!" the boy bellowed. "I want to watch cartoons."

Rocco grinned. At least it got him out of his reverie.

"What if I read to you? Guess what I have in my handbag?" Selina ruffled the boy's hair.

"What?"

"A new book!"

"A story?"

"Yes!" She rummaged in her handbag and picked up a storybook about a cat and a dog going on an adventure with beautiful drawings. She showed them the cover. Lola's eyes sparkled at the fun book cover.

"Goody!" hooted the little girl. "But can Evie come, too?"

"Sure."

"Okay," Archie pouted, in a grudge, still in two minds.

"Let's go. Did you say goodnight?" Melania prompted her nephew.

"Mom, I felt the baby's kick. Honest!" Lola told her with big, wondrous eyes. "A big kick."

"How lucky, sweetheart."

"Is it because the baby likes me?"

"Yes, he does. Now, off to bed."

"He?" Evie's brows shot up, and they laughed.

The kids said goodnight. They spread a considerable

number of kisses all around. Evie reached for Lola's hand while Melania took Archie's. Selina followed them at the rear.

The ladies and the children went upstairs.

∽

Rocco

They left the brothers alone in the dining room.

"God knows I love these kids, but peace at last." Fabio rose from his seat and went to the sideboard. He picked up two crystal tumblers. Fabio was Magda's second son, a year older than Rocco, and commanded the LaTorres' cells in England, managing their local business interests.

"They are great kids!" Rocco nodded with a soft smile. "And Melania is a wonderful mother and an amazing wife to you."

"True." His brother laughed, that little happy laugh he knew well. "Brandy or whiskey?"

"Whiskey, neat."

Fabio poured the amber liquid and brought the glasses to the table. They savored their drinks in a quiet peacefulness.

"Smooth. Damn good scotch, man!" Rocco said at last, taking another sip.

"Glenmorangie Elegance, single Highland malt, twenty-one years old."

"Fancy!"

"*Salute!*" His brother raised his tumbler with pride.

"*Salute!*" They clinked glasses in a toast.

They sipped the liquor for a while.

"What's this thing between you and Evie, then?" Fabio took a swig of whiskey and peeked at his younger brother over the tumbler's rim, breaking the silence.

"What thing?"

"Come, Rocco. I'm no fool," Fabio said, with a quirk of his brows. "You haven't taken your eyes off her all night. And she looks at you when she thinks no one is watching her."

"Nonsense."

"Is it?"

"You punched her fiancé almost to a pulp last week."

"I think she's left him."

"You think?"

"Umm…"

"I hear you spent the weekend with her after her birthday party."

"What if I have? Fuck! For all I know, she might still be engaged to that scum. She won't talk about Jake when I ask her. And I'm not turning into a frigging jealous idiot! Don't forget, she's having his baby."

"I see."

"She's not like my other women. She's different."

"Different?" Fabio scoffed. "How?"

"Uh-huh…"

"Be honest, man!"

"Hell, I suck at relationships. They never last. You know that. I'll ruin this, too. Likely, the silly girl will end up marrying the dickhead who cheated on her."

"But that's just it."

"What is?"

"Melania says there is something fishy about it."

"What do you mean? About what?" Rocco straightened up in his chair. He raked a hand over his dark hair and stared at his brother.

"You may not realize this, but Melania worked as an a— before she married me. Ahem… years ago, that's how we met, she—"

"She worked for the English security service, MI5?"

"You know that?"

"Of course, I fucking do. The entire family has always known, bro! Mother overlooked this because Melania loves you, and you adore her. Besides, she didn't pass any important information to MI5 when investigating you."

"You knew about MI5?"

"Geez, Fabio. You've been in England too long and forgotten how we operate. We know everything! The reason we kept quiet was that you were happy, not to mention determined to have her. Mom took a gamble on Melania, and it paid off. Now you have a wife besotted with you and a lovely child."

"MI5 is over for her."

"Yes, fine. All in the past. But what about Evie?" He tapped his fingers on the table, his patience wearing off. His sixth sense began sniffing trouble.

"Melania thinks something is off. She doesn't quite know what, but she is certain Selina knows."

"Off? Spit it out, man." Rocco was exasperated. Fabio was talking in riddles.

"Evie and Selina are lying. Melania can tell, her training—"

"Lying?" Rocco was getting irritated. "What about?" It was taking so long for his brother to get to the point.

"About the baby and Jake."

"What do you mean?" Rocco's attention grew exponentially. He sat ramrod straight in his chair and turned toward him. Something clicked in his mind, too.

"Wait a minute! Sometimes, I hear Selina and Evie whispering. They stop when I enter the room. When I ask them what they were talking about, they deflect the question." Rocco scratched his forehead, pondering.

"That's what Melania said. They do the same with her. She thinks they are hiding something. Something big. Otherwise, they would have told her."

"I put it down to girl talk. Is it something to do with Jake?"

"I don't know. But listen to this. Archie is here to give Melania's sister a break."

"I don't follow you."

"Melania's sister is expecting her second child, four months into it, to be precise. That's what sparked Melania's doubt. Besides Melania remembers when she was expecting Lola, too."

"I still don't follow you."

"It's the size of her sister's tummy that raised my wife's alert. It's around the same size as your girl. Though Evie claims she's been carrying the child for only two months. Melania doesn't believe her! She is too big for that. Either that or your girl is having twins."

"Where the hell are you going with this?"

"Rocco, for fuck's sake. Are you thick or something? Think! Weren't you in London in November? If Evie is four months pregnant and not two, ring any bells? Four months! Didn't you spend a weekend with her then?"

Rocco felt the color drain from his face. He froze on the spot with his drink in mid-air. He blinked, processing what Fabio had just said.

Then, it hit him.

"Bloody hell! You are not suggesting—" He placed the glass on the table.

"I'm saying it!" Fabio boasted.

Rocco squeezed his eyes shut, taking a deep breath in.

"Mine?" His voice was barely audible in wonderment.

"Melania swears the baby is yours," his brother said.

Then Rocco drowned his whiskey in one gulp.

"I'll be damned!" He rose and paced the length of the room. He looked at his sibling. "The baby is mine?" Rocco plopped back in his chair and closed his eyes, shaking his head again.

"Melania thinks so."

"Does she?"

"My wife can still piece two and two together, you know. The investigator in her won't lose the habit of a lifetime."

"No! Melania's wrong." Rocco stood up abruptly. He took the bottle of whiskey from the sideboard and refilled his drink.

"Wrong?"

"We used condoms," Rocco argued, his head clearing, his coherent thoughts coming back to him. He refilled his brother's glass, too.

"The suckers fail sometimes, you know. It can happen."

"No. It can't be."

"I tell you, it makes sense."

"No."

"Why not?"

"Why would Evie tell me the baby is Jake's child, then? She wouldn't lie to me." He rubbed his jaw, disbelief setting in.

"Think of it? Not difficult. She's a farmer's daughter, squeaky clean. I bet her folks have never had even a traffic ticket! While we—our family—you—"

"She knows who we are? I talked a bit about the family, but I don't think—" he huffed, plopping in a chair beside Fabio.

"Wouldn't you research her? If you had to? I suppose Evie researched you!"

"And she didn't like what she found."

"I guess not. And I don't blame her, either," Fabio scoffed.

Rocco launched a scowl at his brother. "No. She wouldn't lie to me! There must be another explanation. Perhaps Evie's having twins, and the babies are Jake's."

"I doubt it. That's just the point. Melania tells me that

before Evie had that fling with you in November, she always talked about him. Jake this and Jake that. She would never shut up about him. Now she doesn't talk about him, and she's supposed to have his baby? No. Even when Melania asks her, Evie limits herself to saying he's fine. My wife asked her how she went back to Jake, what he said for her to forgive him for his past indiscretion—"

"Indiscretion? He had an affair with another woman while engaged to her. For a fucking year! Hardly an indiscretion, was it?"

"All right! But Jake has not been to London since this supposed reconciliation. He's been absent, other than at her birthday last week when you chased him off the premises. Isn't that strange? When Melania asked Selina what had happened at the party, she was as mysterious as Evie. Their behavior is odd. See why my wife thinks they are lying?"

"You think so?"

"I do, man! There is a chance that baby is yours."

"A chance is not good enough. I must be certain. If she's lying, only one way to find out."

"Ask her."

"No. No point in asking Evie or Selina, from what you say. If they lied so far, they'd continue to lie. I need confirmation with my own eyes from another source. One that cannot lie."

"And who's that?"

"Her medical records."

"What?"

"You heard! I must verify the pregnancy and delivery dates. Her medical file will have that information. It cannot lie."

"I suppose so... and you'll do that?"

"No, not me. You!"

"Me?"

"Yes, Fabio, you!"

"No! Out of the question. If I get caught…"

"Please."

"Dozens of Stream Net employees can do this for you. They are masters at this. Why me? My skills are average at best."

"You are good, and you know it. My technology firm is legitimate. My teams at Stream Net are 'ethical hackers'. They do it with the permission of the companies we work with. They hack them to identify potential weaknesses in their software systems, so that any bugs can be fixed and secured. They don't do illegal stuff. I'm trying to keep things clean. I prefer not to compromise the position of my company. Besides, if you do it, it'll stay between us. No one will know."

"No."

"Fabio! You told me I may soon be a father, and you won't help?"

"Fuck! The risk is greater for me, our web is not wide enough in England. Ask someone in Italy to do it for you."

"I want to keep this between us."

"No!"

"Do you want me to live in doubt for the rest of my life? Or jeopardize an entire legitimate company? The law is scrutinizing me. They are waiting for me to put a foot wrong," Rocco said.

"I won't do it. Why don't you ask Selina?"

"If she kept the secret this far, she won't tell me. I need to see Evie's medical records."

"Ask Zeno to do it. He can work this out. Didn't he spend some time with Stream Net as an intern to learn this sort of thing?"

"Yes. But I want this to remain private in case we are mistaken. You have to do it, man."

"Jesus!"

"Please?"

"I'll think it over."

"Fabio!"

"Okay. Let me figure it out, and—"

"No, Fabio. We must do this tonight. I'll drive the girls home, and then we'll do it."

"Fuck. You owe me," Fabio huffed, rubbing his neck.

∾

Rocco

The women returned to the room.

"Drinks, please!" Selina said. "Fabio, can you make us margarita cocktails? We have earned them, reading to the children for an hour and getting them ready for bed."

"They were exhausted. They are fast asleep, the sweet darlings," Melania added.

As Rocco turned, he glanced at Evie. His gaze went from her face to her baby bump and back again. She smiled at him.

His body stiffened. His nostrils flared, and fury at her deception ignited him. He glared at her. She looked so innocent, so sweet.

If Fabio is correct, she lied to me for months.

She denied me my child.

Hold your horses, man. You don't know if it's true yet. His inner voice warned him. *She wouldn't lie to me, would she? No. Melania's wrong!*

One thing finally clicked, though. He wanted that baby to be his.

But if she lied to me, she'll get the shock of her life. She's mine now! No pussyfooting around her anymore.

His eyes were on her in tiny slits, his stare cold and harsh. She gulped and shifted her feet as if unsure and worried at the sudden hostility in his demeanor.

"No. It's late, Selina, and you had enough alcohol for one night. I'll give you both a lift home," Rocco growled at his sister, but his eyes stayed on Evie.

"Hey, wait a minute! Don't be such a grump. It's only ten thirty. The evening is not over. Fabio, why can't we have a drink?"

"Of course, we can. Rocco, help me out with it." Fabio took his brother's elbow, pulling him toward the sideboard. "Melania, take the ladies to the drawing room. We'll bring the drinks in soon."

"Thank you. You are a darling. A non-alcoholic one for Evie." Selina kissed Fabio's cheek and stuck her tongue out —bold as brass—at Rocco. He scowled at her, but she ignored him. The girls left the dining area.

"Fucking margaritas?" Rocco barked once they were alone.

"Calm down, man. Don't ruin the evening," Fabio said, ignoring his brother's temper as he prepared the refreshments.

"Are you insane? How could I sit with her when I know?"

"We know nothing for certain. We got theories and suppositions. But we have no confirmation. So, until then, you'll relax and act civilized."

Ten minutes later, the girls were humming "ahh," enjoying their drinks.

"Can I taste yours?" Selina turned to Evie.

"Sure. I want a drop of yours, too." They exchanged glasses, but before Evie could bring Selina's to her lips, Rocco bolted from his seat like a spiked stallion and snatched the glass from her hand.

"Don't you fucking dare," he whispered into Evie's ear. She blanched. He gave it back to Selina and took the non-alcoholic drink back from his sister. "This is yours!" He glared at Evie. She reached for her glass with a trembling hand, open-mouthed, as if not knowing what to make of his bossy, brutish attitude—not appreciating his impudent behavior.

"What's wrong with you? She was going to have just a sip, you moron." His sister rolled her eyes.

"Come on. Finish up. Let's go," he grumbled, and he moved toward the door and said goodbye to Melania. Fabio rolled his eyes.

The party was at an end.

∽

Evie

Rocco drove the girls home. Selina sat in the backseat, and Evie in the front seat. She glanced at him furtively a few times but got no reaction. He looked straight ahead on the road, silent and brooding.

What's wrong with him? What brought this change after dinner? Evie was astonished.

One moment he beamed charm and charisma. Next, he turned demonic. Since Evie's return from taking the children to bed, he barely looked at her, and when he did, it was with cold, menacing eyes. She hated that expression, not like him—her "Prince Charming".

When they arrived at the destination, Rocco dropped them outside the building, said his goodbyes cold as ice, waited until they were inside, and left.

It didn't add up. He hadn't even kissed her.

"What's the matter with Dr. Jekyll and Mr. Hyde? What gave him the hump?" Evie asked her friend as they took the lift to the apartment.

"Hell, don't ask me." Selina unlocked the front door. They went inside.

"One moment he is so sweet with me, can't take his eyes off me, the next he's all moody and bossy. Threatening me with God knows what if I take a sip of your drink? He baffled me."

"Welcome to the family, Evie! Men behave like this in my world. They don't give explanations. So you better get used to it."

"Well, I won't! What's his problem?"

"Perhaps he got a call when we were with the children. Something about work upset him? No idea."

"That's no reason to pick on me."

"Oh, ignore him, Evie. He'll be fine in the morning, but it would be best if you told him about the baby. He's been in London for weeks. You had plenty of opportunities. It'll be worse the more time goes by. What if he finds out?" Selina huffed, launching a grimace at her.

"You don't think he-he…"

"No. You would have known if he had, trust me! But you must tell him, no more waiting."

"I promise, we will tomorrow!"

"We? Are you out of your mind? Oh no! *You* do it." Selina shook her head vehemently.

"No, I mean, you can be my moral support."

"Fine. I am. That's for sure."

∽

Evie

Evie couldn't sleep. Her thoughts were in turmoil.

Rocco hadn't taken his eyes off her at dinner, and when she met his gaze, it was like a bolt from the skies, straight to her core. The electricity in the air between them was strong. He felt it, too, she was sure, and it soaked her panties. She had enjoyed the evening at Melania's despite Rocco's questionable behavior toward the end of it.

She was still under his spell.

They had become amorous again since her birthday.

She was over the moon about it. Evie was so attracted to him every cell in her body screamed for him. It disappointed her when he left without telling her the reason, no excuse, without even kissing her. She had hoped he would stay the night.

Does he suspect something? No! It can't be. He would have said. I'm just paranoid.

She wished she had never lied to him. She craved to confess to him the baby was his and was proud of it. Evie knew her stupid fears had overwhelmed her, and she went about it all wrong. Now she languished in this mess.

Rocco didn't deserve her lies.

She observed how wonderful he had been with Lola and Archie. Making them squeal with laughter as he twirled them around. He was lovely with them, answering the many questions they fired at him. So wholly at ease. He would be an excellent father to her child. Thus, she resolved to tell him the truth.

No more lies! She would tell him everything in the morning. She promised herself she would.

On that note, her heart lightened, and she soon fell asleep.

CHAPTER 15

Rocco

Rocco drove off at high speed through the streets of London, back to his brother's home in Kensington, a stone's throw from Hyde Park. Fabio was already in his study when he arrived, perusing through his laptop.

"The things I do for you, Rocco. Melania is mad at me. She knows what we're about to do."

"Why did you tell her?"

"She's my wife! Her 'conjectures' and I quote—'were for my benefit only, not to be broadcasted'. She's so pissed at me that she went to bed," Fabio huffed.

"Broadcast? This is my child we are talking about."

"She says it's a betrayal—to her and Evie. Can't you talk to Evie instead? Ask her. This is upsetting Melania. She's adamant these are only suspicions and could be total nonsense."

"If true, Evie had four months to tell me, but no. Not a peep out of her. What makes you think she'll do it now?

Even if I ask her. I need an independent validation to be certain."

"You should give her a chance to come clean."

"No. I've been here for weeks. She had plenty of opportunities. I must know tonight, for sure."

"We could be wrong."

"Only one way to find out."

"You owe me."

"If you say so. Now, get to work."

"These things take time."

"Get on with it, then."

"Don't be an ass." Fabio went to work on his laptop. "Let's see, Copeland. Let me conduct a quick search on him. Assuming Evie saw her local doctor," Fabio mumbled as he got busy with the job at hand.

"Yes. Dr. Copeland. That's him. The same doctor as Selina's, when in London."

"We'll soon find out."

They were silent while the clicking and clacking of Fabio's fingers on the laptop keyboard boomed in the room as he began to work.

"How long are you gonna be?" Rocco heaved out of his chair ten minutes later, pacing the room.

"How long is a piece of string? Why don't you get us a drink?"

"Okay," he said on tenterhooks. He went to the sideboard and filled two tumblers with whiskey. He placed one beside Fabio's laptop, who glanced up and smiled. "Are you in yet?"

"No! Relax."

"Hurry!"

"Rocco, if you keep fucking nagging me, I'll send you home to wait. Sit down and enjoy your drink." Fabio pointed at an armchair by his desk.

Rocco flopped in it, allowing him to do the job. Later

on, impatience surged again. He got up and stared at the screen over his sibling's shoulder.

"Stop bothering me. It won't make me work any faster. Sit, and stay calm."

"Fuck! How the hell am I supposed to stay calm?" He reverted to the armchair and played with his phone, trying to distract himself. Two hours had passed since Fabio had worked on hacking the doctor's filing system. He was losing faith.

"If you can't do it. I'll have to call Zeno or someone at Stream Net to do it."

"Backstabbing asshole!"

"Hell. I don't want to."

"Then, don't. Be patient."

"Blast! She's maybe carrying my child. I got to—"

"Gotcha!"

"You are in?" Rocco leapt to his feet and was by Fabio's side instantly.

"Yes, my man. I'm in!"

"So?"

"Patience, I'm not on her records yet. So, Evie Logan."

"Evelyn Logan. Evie is the short version."

"Okay. Evelyn." Fabio typed. "Here we go."

"Jesus!"

"Uh? She used to suffer from mild panic attacks?"

"I could have told you that… a mild form of anxiety when she was a teenager. That asshole Jake and the breakup of her engagement brought it back briefly."

"Oh, poor lamb. She's fine now, by the sounds of it."

"I know, Fabio. Let's get to the fucking point!"

"That is what I'm doing."

"Crack on, then."

"Bingo!"

"About time."

"Let's see what her file says." Fabio went through Evie's

medical records until he found what he wanted. "She's a Primigravida."

"A what?"

"A woman who's pregnant for the first time."

"Well, that's a relief. And I knew that."

"Sure."

"Moron!"

"Got it. Evie's LMP."

"What's that?

"A woman's Last Menstrual Period. That's how they count how far gone the pregnancy is and when the gestational period starts. I remember it from Melania's pregnancy."

"And?"

"There's no date."

"What do you mean?"

"Wait. The age of the fetus was based on the actual date of conception rather than on her last period. Your girl seemed fairly sure of herself. When exactly were you in London? When you and Evie…"

Rocco checked his schedule quickly.

"Let's see. I arrived in London on Friday, the twenty-six of November. We went to the nightclub the next day, on Saturday. Then I fucked Evie the next morning, on Sunday the twenty-eight."

"You have that in your diary?"

"Not that, only… bloody hell. Get on with it."

"Girls like Evie are not for the like of us, bro! That was badly done by you!"

"Oh, please, don't. Evie was quite keen if you must know."

"And you obliged."

"More than once. But that's none of your business. Look, Evie's so sweet and sexy, beautiful! God, who could resist her."

"Indeed!" Fabio chuckled. "And that's how all babies come about."

"Get to the point."

"That's what's on her record, the twenty-eighth of November! Bingo. Dates match."

"Jesus!"

"Her due date is the fourth of September! Forty weeks from your first fuck to the day! Congratulations, bro, it's yours."

"Bloody hell!" Rocco sank into the armchair, flabbergasted. A shock, even if he somehow was expecting it, willing it. He sat there dumbfounded for ages and heard furious typing and the printer go, but his mind was blank.

"Done! I got out of the system. Covered my tracks, I suspect no one will ever know we broke into this one record in a busy clinic. Here, I printed the page. Just the one that interests you."

"Thanks!" Rocco glanced up at him, but his eyes were stormy.

"We need a drink." Fabio took the empty glass from his hand and went to the sideboard. He refilled the tumblers. "Cheers, Rocco!"

"Shit! *Salute!*"

"*Salute e figli maschi!* You'll be a great papa."

"To health and sons?" Rocco scoffed at the old Neapolitan saying. They clinked glasses. "Before you get too carried away, I must figure out if the lying chit is still with Jake. If Evie thinks she can give my child to that scumbag, she's a frigging fool."

"I doubt it. Evie may have only told you so you were not suspicious."

"She lied to me for months!" He bolted from the armchair as if an electric current had shot through him. He paced frantically. This time, anger saturated his soul and raised his blood. He was incandescent. His brother watched him with a benevolent expression.

"How could she do this to me? I'll wring her bloody neck!" Rocco spat at last, his green gaze full of fire.

"Hey, hey! Relax. Don't be stupid. Talk to her."

"Oh, you bet! I'll teach her not to lie to me again."

"Rocco, calm down. You are upset but think of the baby. Don't do anything rash. Think this through."

"I have! Thank you, bro." He gulped the rest of his whiskey, squeezed his brother's shoulder, and left.

Rocco's first impulse was to go to the girls' apartment immediately. Then he looked at the time, 3 a.m., thought better of it and turned back. The cool night air became a welcome respite for his angry mood.

It'll keep 'till the morning.

He didn't sleep a wink all night.

CHAPTER 16

Selina

The alarm clock buzzed at the crack of dawn. She wanted to beat London's peak-time traffic jam. Selina showered, dressed, and was now making breakfast. She had an early class to attend. She prepared two slices of toast with creamy avocado and berries for Evie. Her roommate would be up soon.

The doorbell rang, startling her. Selina glanced at her wristwatch. Six-thirty a.m. barely gone.

"Rocco!" she said, surprised when she opened the door. "What are you doing here at this hour?"

He moved past her without a word and went straight to the kitchen. She followed him in with a frown. The smell of coffee from the Italian mocha at work was strong. It had just bubbled up, the intense aroma spreading across the apartment. Rocco turned the gas off and poured two cups. He gave one to his sister and sat on a stool at the breakfast bar, brooding over his espresso.

Selina knew him well. He had not spoken for five minutes while she had her morning meal.

"What's wrong? You weren't yourself after dinner last night. Is it Mother? Sebastiano? Double Trouble?"

"Everyone is fine. That's not why I'm here."

"Thank God, I thought—"

"Tell me, when is Evie's child due?"

"What?"

"Evie's baby."

"Uh?"

"You heard me."

"I don't—"

"Answer my question!" Rocco drew a sheet of paper from the inside of his jacket, placed it on the counter, and pushed it forward toward her.

"What's this?" Selina lifted the paper; her breath hitched when she realized what it was. "Where did you get t-this?" Her voice cracked with apprehension.

Heck!

"You and your friend lied to me!" He snatched it back from her hand, folded it with care, and placed it in his pocket.

"I—"

"I can imagine why Evie would, but you are my sister. Damn it, Selina! I had a right to know!"

"I'm sorry, Rocco. Look, she's my friend. She was distraught at the news when she found out. It's a big thing, you know."

"I know it's a fucking big thing.

"Please, don't be mad!"

"Mad? No."

"No?"

"No, I'm not mad." He paused. "I want blood! You two are in deep trouble." He bolted from his seat and made her jump. She gasped and put a hand on her heart.

144

"Rocco, Evie's emotional these days. All those hormones... I tried, but—"

"Is she back with Jake?"

"Jake?"

"Yes. Jake! Is she back with him?"

"No." Selina shook her head, closed her eyes, and she sighed.

"Is he under the impression the baby is his?"

"No. Rocco—"

"If Evie thinks she is going to give my child to that scumbag—"

"No. Of course, not."

"All lies then."

"Look—"

"Yes or no?"

"Yes," she whispered, disconsolate.

Rocco despised liars. A catastrophe was about to occur, and Selina sensed it. He would not forgive and forget. Not this, not so easy.

"Pack your bags," he said in a commanding manner.

"What?"

"You are moving in with me—no more freedom. Mother is correct. You are out of control."

"Don't be ridiculous."

"That's my child you lied about."

"I swear, I pleaded with Evie to tell you. It was her choice, not mine to make. I couldn't ignore her wishes. She's my friend. I couldn't betray her confidence."

"But you could betray me. Your own brother. The family! If Fabio and I hadn't supported you against Mother's scheming, you would be married to Federico by now. And this is the thanks I get! So, unless you prefer me to tell your fiancé he should speed up the wedding plans, get moving."

"You wouldn't dare!"

"Try me." He peered at his watch. "We leave in forty-five minutes. You'll stay with me where I can keep an eye on you. Wake up your roommate. She must pack her things, too. My men will escort you both to my home."

"Evie?" A look of horror crossed Selina's face.

"The very same!" The glare he pinned on her lacked warmth. His smile, tense as a wire, did not fool her. She knew all the signs. Inside the calm exterior, he was furious.

"Are you insane?"

"Nope!"

"Look, I'll come with you if you insist… but Evie? She may not want to."

"Not want to what?" Evie stood in the doorway wearing a matching silk blue camisole and shorts. She rubbed an eye with her hand, still sleepy, and a big yawn escaped her.

∽

Rocco

Rocco scanned her from head to toe. His cock stirred, despite himself, and a nerve twitched in his jaw, indicating the conflict of sentiments warring within him.

"Oh, sweet Jesus!" Selina gulped.

"Speaking of the devil!" Rocco uttered in a voice that had a rough edge to it. He launched a broad, dangerous smile at Evie. His eyes blazed with a primal urge. He wanted to hurl the girl over his shoulder and take off with her. The thought had his pulse racing. His self-control won by a whisker.

"Rocco!" chimed Evie when she computed they had company. She cast a languid, innocent beam at him. "What are you doing here so early?" No doubt she was glad to see him.

"Please. Be reasonable," Selina beseeched him.

"I'm reasonable." He paused, a full grin to his sister, his

tone calm, but the dangerous glint in his eyes was a warning. His patience was at an end. "Off you go, sis. Get ready."

"Rocco—"

"You'll be wed before the week is over, Selina, if you are not careful. So, run along."

"What's the matter?" Evie felt the tension. She darted her gaze from him to his sister.

"I'm sorry!" Selina whimpered to her friend, blinking back her tears as she ran away from the room.

∽

Evie

"Why is she crying? What's happened?" Evie asked.

Rocco waved a hand dismissively.

"Sit! Have your breakfast." He handed over the plate with the two slices of toast with creamy avocado and berries. He poured a cup of coffee for her, checking first the brand was decaffeinated. She watched him do these things, not knowing what to think.

He sounded calm but not his usual self, she could tell. He had that expression she didn't much care for. The one she saw last night for the first time. Rocco hadn't said hello to her, not even kissed her. His behavior was still odd. His cold, deadly tone had made sister cry.

Why? It was not like him. Not the "Prince Charming" she knew.

"Thank you. What's wrong with Selina?" she asked, with an uneasy note in her voice.

He seemed composed but somewhat dangerous. His green, sultry eyes, usually full of life, were dark and stormy. There was a menacing aura about him.

"Come, *micina*, eat up." He watched her in silence for a long moment, leaning on the breakfast bar with his arms folded over his chest, a fake grin plastered on his lips.

Evie gulped. She took that somewhat baffling grin as a bad omen. She could almost see her undoing. Her ruin was upon her. But she kept silent.

Dear God!

She launched a fitful of tiny smiles his way as she ate her breakfast anxiously under his scrutiny, slowly, to buy herself some time, not knowing what was up precisely, but deep down she knew her time was up. She finished her morning meal, not daring to speak.

Rocco took the sheet of paper from his pocket.

"Read," he prompted, sliding it on the counter toward her.

"What's this?" She sipped her espresso and picked up the paper. Her eyes went wide, and it didn't take her long to understand. She whooped and sputtered on her coffee, choking. He patted her back several times. He opened the fridge swiftly, filled a glass with orange juice, and gave it to her.

"Drink!" he said, in a tone reminiscent of a military order. Evie coughed some more and clutched the glass, clinging tightly to it and sipping, peering at him over the rim. She took her time sipping the liquid to delay the conversation she wished not to have. Her face became paler with every passing second.

"How did you get this?" she asked at last, her voice weak and croaky. She cleared her throat to give herself confidence—the paper shaking in her hands.

"That's not important." He yanked the paper from her hands and tucked it back in his pocket. "Why didn't you tell me?" He leaned back on the counter, crossed his arms over his chest, and watched her intently, waiting.

"I-I was going to."

"When? When my kid came of age?"

"Today. I was going to tell you today. Ask Selina. It's the truth, Rocco, please forgive me. I'm so sorry. I—"

He put his palm out to shut her up.

"You are carrying my child! Have the guts to say it, then." It wasn't a question. Nonetheless, he craved to hear it from her.

"Yes, I'm—" she breathed.

"You're what? Say it!"

"I'm having your child," she admitted, flushing bright red. Her voice was barely audible. She couldn't look into his eyes.

God, help her! Is that a tiny hint of a smile I see on his face? But it was fleeting. He soon put his stony mask on again.

"Are you back with Jake?" He knew the answer, but he ached to hear it from her.

"I'm sorry. I-I—"

"Yes or no? Are you with him?"

"No."

"That was a lie, too, then."

"I didn't mean to lie. Please accept my apologies. I was confused and—"

"Why?"

"Why what?"

"Don't fucking play games with me." He gripped the side of the counter, and his knuckles turned white at the strong hold.

"I-I—" She tried, but nothing came out. "I-I—" Words failed her.

"Jesus. Give me strength!" he yelled, incensed. He took a deep breath. "If you finished breakfast, run along and pack. We'll talk later." His voice was calm again but firm. She couldn't miss the implied order in it.

"Pack? What for?" Her spine straightened, and she blinked.

"You and Selina are coming with me, moving into my home."

"Your house? Why?"

"So, I can look after you and my child. Keep you out of mischief."

"Rocco, darling. I'm sorry, truly. You are upset and—"

"Upset? I'm not repeating it, Evie. Get your things. Now. And don't you fucking 'darling' me. Move. I have some calls to make. When I'm done, we'll go."

He left the room. Her mouth was agape.

∽

Rocco

Rocco moved to the living room to make a few calls. When he finished, he proceeded to her bedroom. He pushed the door handle and went straight in.

"Hey!" Evie scolded him. "You can't come in like this."

He caught her in her underwear, about to get dressed after her shower. His eyes grew wide. He couldn't help a good peep at her body. Her smooth, glorious skin, long legs, and feminine curves were alluring. Her beautiful full bosom was delightful, and her waist was still tiny. The round tummy's bump was sticking out, turning her into a hot mama siren. *God,* he wanted her more than ever.

His cock stirred.

Goodness me! She's carrying my child. His heart swelled at the thought. He had to master all his self-control to stop himself from caressing her, from kissing her fleshy, pouty lips.

Sweet heaven! He wished to fuck the daylights out of her until her pussy became red and swollen. As he came closer, she covered herself with her robe and stepped back.

Evie was glowing. Her pregnancy made her look prettier, sassier. Rocco fancied her with all his might, despite her back-stabbing betrayal.

"I've been in your bed before, you know. That's how you got knocked up in the first place."

"Even so. Do you mind?"

"May I remind you I've already seen you naked?"

"Darling, look—"

"I told you to pack."

"Rocco, please, forgive me. I beg you. If I could take back the lies, I would, but I can't. I hurt you, and I'm so very sorry," she pleaded.

"Get dressed, and pack. You are coming with me."

"I apologize for what I did, unreservedly, but I'm staying right here. Please be reasonable—"

"We'll leave soon, Evie."

"I'm not moving."

"Your last warning. Hurry!" His velvety, silvery voice was soft, but there was a coldness to it. He crossed the threshold out of her room as if she hadn't spoken at all. His arrogance annoyed her and she slammed the door shut behind him.

He froze for a second and turned.

"Ten minutes, *micina*. I'd hurry if I were you unless you want my men going through your drawers," he called out through the door.

∼

Rocco

"Are you ready?" Rocco asked.

"You're a dickhead!" Selina huffed.

"I wouldn't push it if I were you. You are so close to the line."

"Please!"

"Ready?"

"Rocco—"

"Yes or no?"

"Yes," Selina said. "That's all I could pack."

"Fine."

"How long am I going for?"

"Until the baby's birth."

"What?"

"Don't worry; my men can pick up the rest of your things later."

"That's not what I'm worried about. What have you done to Evie?"

"Done? Don't be ridiculous."

"Where is she?"

"I'm waiting for her to pack her stuff."

"Look. I'm used to these crazy things, but Evie isn't. She's not from our world. She won't move in with you, not like this. Not when you are forcing her."

"She will."

"You won't harm her? Will you?"

"Don't be absurd!"

"Rocco—"

"Let's go." He took her wheelie suitcase out of the room.

"*Buongiorno,* signorina." A young man stood in the hall.

"Zeno! You're still in London?"

"Sebastiano assigned me to Rocco for a while, *signorina.*"

"I see."

"Take her home, Zeno," Rocco said, rushing them. "Then come back here. I've got an inkling her friend won't be so complaint."

"*Sì, signore.*" Zeno took the wheelie suitcase. Selina scoffed but followed him.

"You'll go easy on Evie, won't you?" She glanced at her brother over her shoulder.

"Go!"

∽

Evie

Evie had dressed but had yet to follow his instructions.

She had begged Rocco's forgiveness. But she wasn't leaving her apartment. *Certainly not as if I'm being punished.* No matter how much she still wanted him. Besides, the reasons she had kept her secret were still valid. Her concerns had been genuine, but this was getting out of hand. *For crying out loud!* They hadn't even talked about the situation properly, as it should be, and he was ordering her about it.

That won't do.

She figured Rocco may have broken into her doctor's records to find out the truth. *Hell!* That was against the law. And he acted unconcerned about it?

Two possibilities flared in her mind, her fears taking the better of her.

He's not pleased with the baby! I knew it. She convinced herself. *He thinks I want to trick him into marriage and that my lies are an elaborate plan for entrapment. That's why he got to my doctor's records rather than asking me.* She sighed and cursed herself for lying to him. *But I'm not moving in with him! Not like this, with bad vibes between us. Without a proper conversation! That's not how it works. And certainly not because he's ordering it.*

So, she casually sat at her desk instead. She was due to Zoom in with her fellow students when he returned to her room.

"Are you ready?" Rocco asked with a burning stare from the doorway, his green eyes dark and deadly in disapproval.

His commanding tone displeased her. She straightened up in her chair. Her head tilted, her chin high in rebellion, and she returned to what she was doing.

God, this is not going well. Why didn't I tell him when I had the chance? I'm an idiot.

"Why are you not packing?" he asked when she ignored him, his nostrils flaring.

"Rocco, knock before entering. This is my room, you know. And stop giving me orders. I'm not one of your men," she retorted over her shoulders, annoyed at his arrogance. She huffed. Then she turned fully to him with pleading eyes. "Look, I'm very sorry I hurt you. I really am. If you wish to talk about our situation like an a-adult, come back when you've calmed down. You are upset now and not making any sense. Don't get me wrong, you have every right to be. I know I was an idiot, but this is not the way. Please, c-calm down. W-we can talk later." She struggled to keep her voice composed, though she couldn't avoid slight tremors in it. But he had irritated her with his dictatorial manner.

She wouldn't allow him to intimidate her. Even in her anxiousness, she noted his stylish blue Saville Row suit fitting him perfectly. For a moment, she had flutters at her core. He looked divine. Tall, darkly handsome, in more ways than one, with stormy eyes, and all lean muscle, as if he were a menacing James Bond prepped for a kill. His fiery green eyes were closer to a steely gray that day, blazing daggers at her. He was now scratching his jaw out of annoyance.

Boy, he is stunning, even when he's furious. It did something to her insides. Evie inhaled deeply. *Damn!*

Rocco launched her a feral glare, closing the distance in two long strides. Before she knew it, he was upon her.

"Right, *micina*, your time is up!" He pulled her up and tugged her toward the door.

Evie screamed, not expecting this. *Sweet Mary, mother of Jesus!*

"You are behaving like-like—" She stumbled, but he placed his arm around her waist, steadying her. His touch upon her skin sent a pang of desire through her. She flushed in anger at her own lustful yearning. His palm circled her arm and he shuffled her out of the room. "Get your hands off me!" she yelled, seeking to hide her dichotomy of irritation and desire for him. God, those pregnancy hormones were causing havoc. *Why am I thinking of sex when he's behaving like a caveman?* She struggled to liberate herself from his clutch. But he clung on to her. He brought her to the living area.

"Sit!"

"Heck! I'm not your flipping dog," she blurted.

He grinned despite himself. None too gently, he caught her wrist and yanked her down until she sat on the sofa.

"How dare you? Who do you think you are? I said I'm sorry. How many times do I have to apologize?" Her lips were in a thin line.

"Let me make this clear to you, princess." He stood and leaned over her, his proximity overbearing, his fierce, handsome face a whisker away from hers.

Horrified, she sank further into the settee to pull away from him.

"You have lied to me for months. That's unforgivable. This is our child, and you won't keep me on the fringes of it. Understood? You deserve a good spanking, poppet, for what you've done, but I'll take a rain check because right now, I'm too damn annoyed for it," he said, pointing at her ass.

She was about to reply. She opened her mouth, but Rocco stuck his hand up to stop her. Evie closed it abruptly. Then she realized he had referred to the baby as "our child". It softened her heart. Tears came into her eyes, and she blinked them away, putting on a brave face, and proving strong. She would not cry.

"Rocco, please. I'm so sorry—" she said softly, willing to make things better.

"I intend to stay close to my flesh and blood, whether

you like it or not. Don't make things difficult for me, sunshine. Or when the kid is born, I'll take him away from you. You'll never see him or her again. So I suggest you cooperate."

She sucked in some air, stunned, horrified. With her palms on his chest, she pushed him, forcing him to backtrack a step, not predicting her reaction. She rose from the couch defiantly and stared straight at him, her fists curled at her sides. She was furious, too, now.

"Don't even say that as a joke. It's not funny."

"Do you see me laughing?"

"You wouldn't dare! We have laws in this country. And, for the record, I'm not going anywhere with you."

"Oh, but you are coming with me. Now sit," Rocco said, getting so close to her, invading her personal space. She flopped backward on the couch to escape his proximity.

"You are an ape, Rocco LaTorre. A Neanderthal!" she mumbled.

Rocco scoffed, containing a grin and sat beside her. He grabbed his laptop from the small table. He had paused a Zoom call with somebody earlier.

"I suggest you pay attention, Evie."

"What's this?"

"Graham, are you still there?" He resumed the Zoom call.

"Here, boss." The man replied as they looked over at the screen. He was standing in a vast space.

Evie's brows narrowed.

"Show me what you have," Rocco added. Another call participant popped up on the split screen of his laptop. The second man seemed to be in a cockpit, wearing headphones, airborne. Then, on another section of the screen, there was an aerial view, and the small plane moved into view.

"It is a light agricultural aircraft. Graham, tell Evie what that plane does."

"I know what it does! I'm a farmer's daughter. We hire similar planes as an aerial application for crop dusting or fertilizers. What's this about, Rocco? I don't understand."

"Oh, you will, *micina,* soon. Go ahead, guys."

"Where are you now? Phil, do you read—over? Please tell us your flight position," Graham called out.

"I copy. I'm flying over North Kesteven in Lincolnshire."

"What the heck?" Evie yelped.

"Where exactly?" Rocco urged.

"What the hell is going on?" She darted her gaze from Rocco to the screen in front of her with a scowl.

"Passing over Logan Field Farm just about now. Can you see it?" A clear view of the farmhouse, the outbuildings, and the surrounding fields was now on the monitor.

"Good God. That's my parents' farm," she uttered. Her eyes were fixed on the screen. Then, she glared at Rocco beside her, astonished.

"Your plane does not have fertilizer, Phil, or dusting today, does it?" Rocco claimed nonchalantly.

"No."

"What do you have?"

"Toxic waste." The pilot replied.

Evie gasped in shock.

"Thank you, Graham and Phil. Please standby, and wait for further instructions. We'll speak later in a few minutes," Rocco said, disconnecting the call and closing his laptop.

"What the hell?" Evie stood up, a fiery expression on her face.

"Sit!" He reached for her wrist and pulled her back to her seat.

"You are an asshole!" She spat, yanking her wrist out of his hand.

His eyebrows knitted, but he showed her the LaTorre Hollywood smile instead. The one she liked so much, though right now he wasn't her favorite person in the world by a long shot.

"Call your parents. Here! Use my phone. Ask them if they can see the plane."

"No, I won't. It will only worry them. What are you doing with that thing over my farm? What's the meaning of this?"

"You have a choice, *micina!* You are coming with me, right now, or toxic waste will fill your land." It was Rocco's turn to lie to her, there was no toxic waste anywhere in that plane, but she wasn't to know. He was bluffing.

She gulped, astonished. "That's preposterous. You are a monster!" She lashed at him with her hands as tears filled her eyes.

He stood and pulled her up with him. She lashed out at him again but he grabbed her wrists and dragged them behind her back. He drew her to him. Her body crashed into his as she yelled.

"I want to spank you so bad, *micina,* until your ass is blistering red all over. You don't get it, do you? You think because you said sorry, everything is fine?" He paused, inhaling in irritation. "But not now. I need a clear head when I spank you good and proper. Because right now, I'm so furious at you." That much was true! His voice kept his silvery tone, but his menacing words were unmissable.

"Let me g-go. You b-bastard." Evie struggled to pull herself free without success.

He pulled her closer to him, their noses almost touching. Tears flowed down her cheeks, the mascara running. The tension of the last few months exploded in her. Fear was building in her guts, too.

He could not mean these menaces, wanting to take her child away from her. No! He threatened to pour toxic waste over the farm, for goodness' sake. *Was he out of his mind?* Rocco had met her parents and worked on the estate with her dad. *How can he say such a thing? I was correct all along about not telling him about the baby.* His behavior was appalling.

His "Prince Charming" side was only an act. *I bet this is the real him—a nasty man.* So, why was his proximity still affecting her? It exasperated and baffled her when she realized she would gladly let him fuck her, even after all his hideous threats.

I have no shame! I drop all sense of perspective when this man is near me. His closeness did something to her insides. Her brain had lost all thinking power even when she despised him. His manly scent, a mixture of cologne and body heat, was inebriating, dizzying her.

She felt faint with mingled feelings about him.

"What will it be, *micina*? I don't want any trouble from you. Do I tell Phil to go ahead?"

"No!" She jerked her head back.

"Then, you'll comply? Are you coming with me?"

"Yes," she whispered as a sob left her lungs.

Who's this monster?

CHAPTER 17

Evie

Zeno drove her to Rocco's home in Kensington while his boss had gone to a business meeting.

"He won't hurt you." The young fellow sought to reassure her. She stayed silent, ignoring him. "Come, Miss Logan. We're home," Zeno said on arrival at the enormous townhouse.

She glanced at him bewildered. "For the record, this is not my home!"

They walked up the steps from the underground garage to a grand foyer. Evie followed him through a hallway, then up the magnificent staircase.

"You'll stay here," he said when they entered a bedroom on the second floor.

Shocked, when he left, she realized he had placed her under lock and key. Evie released a wail of anger. She was aghast. It was all too absurd. She tugged at the door handle, attempting to open it by force, but it proved useless.

Had she misjudged Rocco all along? Got him all wrong? *The man I love is a callous monster.*

Wait a minute!

Love?

No. I can't possibly love Rocco. Not now, when he's treating me like this. No! Is this the real him? A flipping beast?

"Let me out, you assholes. Do you hear me?" Evie called out at the top of her lungs. Her fists thumped on the door with all her might, making a racket. Not one inclined to swear, that morning Evie uttered black curses.

"Tell that fucking bastard I'm going to kill him for what he's doing to me. Open this bloody door right now." Distinctly unladylike, she screamed colorful expletives, reflecting her rage with little discernment. Evie kept on yelling until her voice became hoarse. Exhausted by her prolonged rantings and ravings, her body slid down in a heap against the wall, and she cried her eyes out. Nobody showed up to free her.

She was Rocco's prisoner, his captive.

I'm in the heart of London, for heaven's sake! How can this be happening to me? There were laws against this. *But that devil believes he is above the law.*

The pig!

A tap took her out of her raging thoughts. The click on the lock announced someone was coming in.

Rocco? She jumped to her feet. It disappointed her when Zeno came in with a tray. He placed it on the table. Another fellow outside locked the door behind him.

"I brought you a juice, *signorina,* made with fresh red oranges from Italy. The cookies are delicious, homemade," he said with a satisfied smile.

"You don't say!" The sarcasm in her tone was apparent as she wiped away a lingering tear. She forced a grin. A closer inspection would have unveiled the rigid set of the jaw and the thin lips on her face, a precursor of the incandescent fury whooshing through her veins about to explode."Let me out. Do you hear me?" she said through gritted teeth. Her voice was weak from too much yelling, and her fingernails dug into her palms as she clenched her fists.

"I'm sorry, Miss Logan. I can't. Please drink your juice and have some cookies. It'll do you good."

Evie marched to the table in stomping strides. She took a cookie and snapped it in two in irritation. Then tossed it back on the table. She grabbed the tumbler and smelled the liquid.

"Umm… lovely!" She pronounced it after a small taste with a mischievous grin. Next, in a sudden move, she threw the drink, cookies, tray and all at the wall.

Shattered glass scattered everywhere. Juice splattered all over. The plate of cookies cracked and smashed.

Zeno lifted his brows, but he said nothing. She caught a fleeting disappointment in his eyes. Perhaps it blended with sorrow, but his impenetrable mask returned. He tapped on the door. It opened, and he spoke to somebody outside in Italian.

Within minutes, three maids came in. One girl picked up the glass and plate shards from the floor. A maid washed the surfaces and walls while another cleaned the sticky juice from the flooring.

They crept about working silently while Zeno watched Evie instead. He unsettled her, and she blushed.

Evie felt foolish now for having done this. She created more work for these girls. They were not to blame for her situation. They cleared the mess in no time, leaving no trace of her outburst.

They all left without a word, and the door-lock clicked in place.

Evie broke down. A white-hot rage permeated every pore in her body, inflaming her blood.

I'll tear Rocco from limb to limb when I catch him, the cruel swine! He was administering his savage revenge on her. If she would have told him the truth, perhaps… too late for regrets. But this was too much. He was unreasonable, and all his threats were unacceptable. So, she seethed for a long time.

When she calmed down, she realized, with regret, there was no point in yelling. Nor exhausting herself or throwing a tantrum. Too tired and stressed to think straight, bursting for a wee, Evie glanced around her. There were a few doors she hadn't bothered with. She opened one, and bingo!

The ensuite was three times the size of that in her apartment. There was a massive, freestanding white bath and a walk-in shower. The marble floor was light gray with matching fancy tiles halfway up the wall, the rest painted white. A large washbasin with an ornate, antique brass mirror hanging above it was a focal point.

She spotted a dainty armchair in red hues in a corner. It turned into a recliner at a press of a button. *Who has a recliner in the bathroom?*

It seemed Rocco frigging LaTorre did! She cursed him.

She saw fluffy towels neatly folded on a rack. Two soft robes hung on brass hooks. The outburst and the yelling had exhausted her. It had drenched her in sweat.

She opted for a bath, hoping it would soothe her. Besides, she couldn't do anything else. She undressed as she perused through several bath salts on a brass shelf. She chose a vanilla and rose blend. God knew she needed a much-deserved relaxation. It even had actual bits of rose petals in it. So, she poured a good amount into the bathwater. It smelt divine. She inhaled and felt a pinch better already.

"Damn him!" she said aloud as she lowered herself into the hot tub. "Oh, this is heaven!" She closed her eyes as she nestled into the water like a mother duck, allowing the scent and the warmth to engulf her senses. Her mind went blank as she soaked for a while.

She flicked her eyes open. She was sure she had fallen asleep.

The water had become cold. Evie got out of the bath and clasped a large towel from the rack. It was soft and fluffy. She dried herself off and wrapped the white bathrobe around her body. She went back to the bedroom to dress. She would have liked a change of clothes, but she had none, all her things were still in her apartment. The barbarian had commanded her to his home with nothing but the clothes on her back. So, she dressed in what she had on earlier.

Now calmer and more settled, she inspected her surroundings.

It was an enormous bedroom. Light and airy, elegantly furnished with expensive rugs and antique pieces. The wall behind the bed was upholstered in silk cerise stripes. The splendid king-size bed was in cherry wood. A cerise Victorian *recamier* brought an energetic, vibrant presence at the foot of the bed. She could easily imagine herself reading while reclining on the French chaise. The crystal raindrop chandelier in the middle of the room seemed regal to her, but not pompous amongst the overall style and size of the place. The white polished wood of the antique dressing stand and matching bedside tables with intricate ornate details were beautiful. They matched a table and chairs in a corner, too.

Massive windows on one wall overlooked the magnificent gardens as she peered out.

She opened the wardrobe and, to her dismay, she saw several maternity clothes. All in her size, meant to fit and flatter her, cut in designer tailored shapes and fashionable colors. Some dresses seemed daring for a pregnant woman, alluring. *The monkey beast!* Others were made for comfort. She noticed sexy lingerie in a drawer and more.

Does the bastard think he'll buy my consent with these? I don't want them, even if I'm dying for a change of clothes.

She was irritated by the clothes. At the same time, they had absorbed her attention, so she missed a part of the room. She entered a cozy alcove through an archway, where a comfy two-seater loveseat, facing a beautiful stone fireplace, matched the Victorian *recamier.* There were bookshelves on both sides and a T.V.

It was a glorious suite, but she could only think of it as a gilded cage.

∾

Rocco

Rocco had no intention whatsoever of throwing toxic waste over Evie's farm. It wasn't his style, he revered the land, but she did not know this. It was all an elaborate ruse on his part to push her to move in with him with no fuss.

His family owned the agricultural aircraft in question, a business they had gained in England. Phil's plane contained fertilizer that day, nothing else. But Evie didn't know that, either.

The trick had served his purpose. She believed in his threats and submitted to his will. He had achieved his aim. She was in his home and under his protection.

The young woman was now bound to him, whether she liked it or not, the silly lass had his baby in her womb.

For the first time, though, he felt uneasy at being so rough.

He'd never given a second thought before when he behaved in such a bullish manner when the occasion required it in his unorthodox line of business. The difference? This time, he had been heavy-handed with Evie. This made him uncomfortable—a sentiment he was not used to, which infuriated him all the more. In his view, she deserved it for feeding him absurd lies and for denying him his child for months.

She'll yield to me.

Rocco ordered her bedroom door locked at all times. He stationed a guard in the hallway for good measure. She could not escape.

Her bedroom windows were shut, opened only under Zeno's supervision. The glass wouldn't break, anyway if she tried. The windows were made of polycarbonate panels, and although they looked and functioned like ordinary windows, the material composing them was unbreakable. Even if she was lucky, there was no easy way for a pregnant girl to flee from a second-floor bedroom window.

High walls enclosed the property, anyway. A security guard patrolled the gardens at all times. There were surveillance cameras, too, and perimeter sensors—all the latest technology to keep them safe.

This was a rule in all the family's homes, and there were many. Rocco's was no exception.

The LaTorre family built their homes like fortresses to fence off intruders. On this occasion, it was to keep Evie in.

In his world, his enemies may regard her as a bargaining chip. With Nico still at large and with the Bratva causing mayhem in their territories, he was not taking any chances. He wished to ensure her obedience to protect her and his child, keeping them safe from external threats.

The only way out was if Rocco released her. *No chance!* He wouldn't, wanting Evie's submission instead. Besides, he still liked the blasted chit, lies and all.

The girl has a strong character behind that vulnerable facade and she's stubborn. He doubted she would submit willingly, but he would have a damn good try. Besides, he liked a challenge.

Evie hadn't experienced this brutal behavior before, the shock at his menaces in her lovely gray eyes had been remarkable. He perceived her fear. And though he didn't want her to fear him, a tiny part of him was pleased she did. She deserved her punishment for lying to him. He would teach her a lesson.

He was fully aware this would ruin their romantic affection, but it was a small price to pay to protect her, to keep her safe in his uncertain world.

It satisfied him that she was in his home and locked up. A clear message as to whom was in charge after her shenanigans.

Evie had only known the easy-going fellow in him that could woo any woman. Everyone admired the calm, lovable Rocco. The Prince Charming! As his nickname vouched. The one who made her laugh. The thrilling handsome man who raised her blood—aroused her. The one who whispered sweet Italian words to her. The witty fellow. Women didn't resist that captivating side of him, and Evie had not been immune to him, either.

Though this morning, she had experienced what it was to be on the wrong side of a LaTorre. She had unmasked Rocco's brutal force with her lies, and his dangerous power, exposing the ruthless part of him. The one Rocco set aside for the violence sometimes called for in his unorthodox line of business, even if he had no intention of carrying out any of his threats against her.

He realized this new status quo would be tricky for them—a contentious path in their new relationship, which could end in only two ways.

He had no idea how she felt about him after today—if he had to hazard a guess, not good!

He assumed she would be confused. The important matter was that she was in his home, under his protection, which satisfied him.

Since she left her apartment with Zeno, Rocco hadn't seen her. He was back in the house now and was working at his desk in the study. There was a knock at his door.

"Enter." He lifted his eyes from his laptop's screen. Zeno brought in a tray with an espresso and a croissant. It was mid-morning. He placed it on the counter for him.

"Everything okay, Zeno?"

"*Sí,* Rocco."

"Are the girls in their rooms? Locked up as instructed?"

"*Sí.* Tito returned about half an hour ago with the rest of their things. He delivered Selina's first."

"What about Evie's stuff?"

The young man furrowed his brows. Rocco knew that look, his way of announcing trouble.

"Miss Logan yelled for ages, for over an hour, calling us colorful names."

"Did she?" Rocco scoffed.

"She caused an uproar. The maids were looking at me like I was the devil."

"Right!"

"It was bloody awful."

"What did Evie call us?"

"Assholes."

"That's it?"

"No. She called you a 'fucking bastard'. She promised to kill you." Zeno snorted.

"I see." Rocco chuckled.

"She's quiet now."

"Tell Tito to deliver her things, except her phone and laptop. My girl needs to learn some manners."

"She won't be happy! I better help him with it."

"Why?" He glanced at him. "It doesn't take two big men to bring a suitcase to Evie's room."

Zeno furrowed his brows again.

"When I brought her a snack earlier from the kitchen, she hurled it at the wall, shattering glass, plates, the lot."

"She threw a tantrum?"

"Your woman's not from our world, Rocco. Her—"

"She'll get used to it. How's Selina?"

"No trouble. But she's worried about Miss Logan. She wants to talk to you."

"Maybe later. When you deliver Evie's things, ask Lara to bring her lunch. She's having my baby, you know. Tell the cook to make balanced meals for her. On second thoughts, healthy meals for everyone," he said. Zeno's brows shot up. "No more junk food! The boys will adhere to it."

"Fine. Congratulations on the baby."

"Thank you." Satisfied, Rocco smiled.

Evie's misbehavior did not surprise him. It was proof that there was a strong girl behind her vulnerable facade, but there was no way back for her. She'd have to manage the new status quo. She was his woman now.

Mine and mine alone!

The intensity of his possessiveness toward her amazed Rocco. He'd had countless women in his bed before her, much more beautiful than Evie. Yet he dismissed them all without a second thought. He walked away from them all because of her. It astonished him. He couldn't help liking her. A lot!

He had not seen Evie or his sister since the morning. *Let them stew for a while longer.*

He assumed Selina wanted to plead their case, keeping a low profile, given the threats he had launched at her about having her married.

He had no intention of calling Federico about his sister,

either. The threat was enough punishment for her. Besides, when Evie calmed down and settled in, she would need a friend to reassure her and support her, and Selina was that friend.

∼

Evie

Evie heard a knock. Soon after, the lock clicked, alerting her that someone was about to come in.

Rocco?

It disheartened her when Zeno entered with her suitcase. A housemaid accompanied him with a tray.

"Hello, Miss Logan," the maid said. "My name is Lara. This is your lunch. I'll leave it on the table."

"We got your things," Zeno added, slipping the case on the ottoman. "Lara will unpack them. The clothes in the wardrobe are for you with Mr. LaTorre's compliments."

"Tell him to stick them up his ass!" she quarreled with hostility.

Zeno's eyes grew wide.

"Do I unpack now or after lunch?" Lara asked her, trying her utmost to repress a laugh.

"Unpack? What for? You had no right, Zeno, to take my stuff from the apartment. I want to go home." Her tone was high-pitched. Though she required a change of clothes.

"I'm sorry, *signorina*," Zeno said and left the room.

She glanced at Lara and sighed. Evie started unpacking.

"Please, miss, let me help you."

"Fine." Evie selected a few things from her case. "I'm going to the bathroom to change." She changed into clean underwear and a dress and returned to the room.

"You should eat your lunch, miss. It will go cold."

"I'm not hungry." She engaged herself in helping the maid to unpack. It was a brief respite from the turmoil raging in her mind and soul. *Can I run away? Umm...* Evie thoughts were still in confusion, but she couldn't allow him to treat her like this.

"Mr. LaTorre bought some lovely clothes for you."

"I don't want them, I said. Get rid of them."

"I can't remove them, miss. Sorry."

"Lara, I'm looking for my laptop and my phone. Did they leave them behind in the apartment?"

"Uh? No."

"Where are they, then?"

"Umm-uh?"

"Lara?"

"Yes?"

"Who's taken them?"

"Zeno, under Mr. LaTorre's orders."

"Aargh!" She plopped herself on the bed and wept. The maid fretted.

"Please, miss, d-don't cry," the girl stammered, shuffling on her feet. She gave her an awkward pat on the arm, which made Evie feel foolish at the complete lack of restraint on her emotions.

She straightened up and sighed, drying her eyes.

The maid smiled when she finished unpacking Evie's things, ill at ease as she knocked on the door. When it opened from the outside, she left quietly, giving her one last anxious glance over her shoulder. Then the door was shut and locked behind her.

CHAPTER 18

Evie

Evie removed the silver domes covering the plates. The waft of a rich, succulent meal rose in the air, permeating the place with the aroma of the chicken stew and roasted vegetables.

It was mouthwatering.

She stared at the inviting meal and would have demolished her lunch, but Rocco had isolated her. Evie had become his captive. She missed her best friend. He had taken away her laptop and phone. She felt sick in her stomach, unable to reach the outside world stuck in that room. Her mom would be worried sick for a start.

Yes, I lied to him, but Rocco had been too heavy-handed with her. What was he trying to prove? She glanced at the tray and sighed. Evie had the baby to consider, but she couldn't eat a morsel. *If I take a bite, I'll puke.* So she left her meal untouched and paced the room in anxiousness instead.

"Wait until I get my hands on Rocco!" she growled under her breath.

Or would you rather he had his hands on you? Her inner voice came back, mocking her.

She gasped at her thought. After his appalling behavior, how could she even think about this? True! That morning, Rocco looked so tall and handsome in his perfect suit. It fit him like a glove. *How can such a monster be so attractive and push all my buttons?* A thunderbolt struck at her core at the memory of his hands on her body the night of her birthday.

Horrified, she denied herself dwelling on this memory. Shame turned her cheeks hot-red. She was annoyed with herself for thinking of him in those terms, with desire bubbling all over her. Evie couldn't deny the attraction was still there, notwithstanding the turn of events. The sparkle was so intense she was unable to extinguish it.

She cursed for being such a weak floozy.

A click on the lock startled her out of her warring thoughts. She spun to it. *No knock. I bet it's him. Arrogant bastard!*

"Rocco!" she hissed as he stepped into the room. "Still bloody rude, I see. I'm not surprised. You are a frigging pig!"

He raised his eyebrows with a pinched expression.

"Watch your mouth!" His tone was harsh, with displeasure on the face of it, but a slight grin appeared on his lips despite himself.

This enraged her more.

"You have no manners. You are an asshole. How dare you do this to me?" Evie blurted out with vehemence, glaring at him.

"Is that so?" He whirled toward the exit, nonplussed.

Is he leaving? She watched him while he locked the door from the inside with his key. It ignited her fury even more.

"Give me the fucking key. I want to go home," Evie said, full of bravado. Her jaw jutted mulishly. Her voice had regained a certain calmness, despite her foul language. Her hand reached out to him, facing upward, waiting for him to place the bedroom key in her palm, tapping her foot with impatience. She strived to control herself, but her eyes were narrow, shooting daggers at him with an insolent expression.

"No," Rocco said—with a cheeky grin—willing her to dare him as if playing with her.

Evie became incandescent. As if her blood were hot lava, it gushed through her veins, spewing dangerous energy—and her temper blew like a volcano. Her face turned red. She propelled herself at him to snatch the key from his hand. He moved out of her way. She missed her step, clutching at thin air while he pocketed the key in his trousers. He reached out to steady her with his other hand and circled her waist. She cursed at him and he tugged her to him.

"This is your home now, *micina*. And no more swearing," he warned, kissing her forehead as he held her in his arms.

His proximity, his embrace and the kiss raised her pulse. It did things to her soul, despite her resentment. As if an electric current of desire streamed between them, it confused her. She breathed in his scent, a blend of fresh aftershave and masculinity that sent her salacious hormones into overdrive. She couldn't deny he smelt divine!

Focus, you stupid cow, don't let your pussy overrule your brain, Evie willed herself. His arm pulled her tighter to him. A surge of lust spread through her frame. He was dizzying her. As if her body had a mind of her own, entirely disassociating from her brain.

She trembled and lifted her head to peek at him. Their

eyes locked, and a new wave of warmth hit her. As if a flash of lightning had struck her womanly parts, making her quiver, her clit throbbed.

He must have seen something in her expression. An amused smile lit up his face.

She was losing the battle, failing in her intent to tear him from limb to limb as she had promised herself. He bent over her, his face a whisker from hers. She was sure he was about to kiss her, and her lips parted of their own volition. *I'm a total wimp.*

He had treated her abominably, and she was about to welcome his kiss. Her body reveled in his embrace.

No! She recovered her resolve. Still trembling, she pushed him away with all her might. He was too strong and didn't budge. Evie struggled with him and kicked his shin. He swore, limped with pain for an instant, but released her.

"Open that door this minute, you rotten Neanderthal. Give me the key!" Evie screamed at him. He massaged his lower leg.

"Jesus, Evie, you have a good boot on you. If we have a boy, I hope he can kick like you—at a ball, not at people." His tone was soothing and velvety, light in mockery, but his eyes had a fire in them, cloudy, not pleased with her.

She registered his words *if we have a boy—we?* His remark confused her. Her mind framed the cozy picture of a small boy kicking a ball—their little boy—and it made her eyes soften on him. She even displayed a hint of a smile.

"But enough of this. I'll punish you if you hit me again or throw another insult at me, understood?" His statement was firm and clear, delivered with the same calmness, though a little eerie in how he uttered it.

Her soft spot for him didn't last long. She quivered in outrage as she computed what he had just said. Her chest tightened, constricting her. Her white-hot rage returned with force. She was glowing with it; it was so intense that her nostrils flared at his words. Her gaze, ablaze, flashed at him, wanting his blood.

"Punish me?" she yelled, but hesitated seeing a scowl on his face, but went on. "How dare you? Aargh! I want to leave. Now!"

"You know the answer to that," Rocco said. A sigh escaped his lungs as if to say, *God, give me patience!* But he did not intimidate her.

She inhaled. *Calm down, Evie,* she thought to herself. *This argument is getting you nowhere. Try to reason with him.*

"Look, Rocco…" She changed tactics, struggling for a sweet note in her voice. "You are upset with me because I lied to you. I get that, and I'm very sorry I did. Honest! But you proved your point now. Please, let me go."

"No!"

"This is insane. You can't keep me locked up like this."

"But I can, and I am."

"Please, Rocco…"

"No. This is how it is until I can trust you. Or do I have to remind you Phil is ready to fly over your farm on my orders?"

Her mouth was agape for a moment.

"You frigging swine!" Her rage, just now barely controllable, flared up again. Blood rushed to her brain. She saw red. Evie launched herself at him like a wild cat. Her blow struck him square in the face with all her might.

"Bloody hell!" His head snapped back with the hit, not expecting it. She was about to punch him again when he caught her fist. She tried to fight back to no avail. Rocco grabbed her other hand, too. He held both her dainty wrists behind her back in his massive hand.

"Let me go, you cocky damn fuck!"

"Jesus, what a mouth. I thought Selina said you don't

swear." He paused, stunned that his sweet girl had such foul language in her arsenal. It amused him, though, but he would not encourage her.

"Only to you. Fuck. You." She accentuated the last two words with deliberate intent.

"Right! That's it," he said, exasperated. "I warned you to stop this. You are quite stubborn, poppet. Your language is appalling. I've had enough of your terrible behavior. May I remind you I'm the injured party here? *You* lied to *me*."

"Let me go!" she screamed, but he dragged her to the bed. He sat and hauled her over his lap, facedown, with her butt in the air.

"You'll stay right here. With me." He accommodated her tummy bump between his legs so as not to hurt her or make it uncomfortable for the baby, adjusting her position over his knees.

"What the hell are you doing, you infernal devil?"

He lifted a brow at her insult, and his palm flattened her buttocks without warning.

"Aah!"

"You told me fibs for months." Smack! "You punched and kicked me." Smack! "Not to mention your appalling language and tantrums today. This is long overdue." He highlighted her every misdeed with a firm hand branding her backside.

"Aw, aw. Stop," Evie yelled. He crumpled her dress to her waist and tugged her panties over her thighs. These floated downward to her ankles.

"Oh, I like it pink!" He oohed over her bare, flushed backside. A smirk lifted on his lips. "Quiet, now." The palm of his hand resonated with the soft flesh of her buttocks as two smacks came down in quick succession.

"Aargh!"

"Stop being a brat. You are not leaving. So, get used to it." He massaged her scorching backside for a moment.

"And No. More. Lies!" He punctuated each word with a smack.

"Please," she pleaded and wiggled on his lap.

"This be a lesson to you," he said with another cracking blow. He rubbed her scarlet bottom for a few seconds to lessen the sting.

She couldn't help a moan at the welcomed massage after the blistering heat scorching her flesh, but he soon resumed.

Smack, smack, smack! The spanking, though flaming her bottom, was not too harsh. He was clearly controlling his strength.

"Bastard!" she wailed amongst two other not-too-kind expletives.

"*Micina!*" Rocco spanked her with two well-timed, eye-watering, powerful smacks that sent her body limp.

Tears gathered in her eyes. A sob broke out of her mouth, but pain and desire suddenly mingled. Her clit felt the exquisite pleasure of each smack landing on her buttocks, her body rioting between pain and longing. Her pussy drenched with need.

"Please. Let me go."

"You are not going anywhere. So quit asking." A searing whack thundered down. Her posterior was on fire, glowing red.

She felt humiliated and angry with herself. How could she think of this mind-blowing lust for him when he did this outrageous thing to her? Her wet channel was in a happy land, no denying it, contracting in anticipation with each smack. She couldn't believe the spanking had aroused her. She had never been spanked before, and somehow, despite the heat on her flesh, she wanted him, even in her fit of temper. Pain, pleasure and desire burst through her body, overwhelming her.

"From now on, Evie, you'll stay with me. Where I can keep an eye on you and protect you."

"I don't need protecting," she muttered as he massaged her backside.

He would have laughed, but it would only encourage her.

"You must cooperate, *micina*. Is that clear?" Another blistering whack. "Answer me!"

"Okay!" Evie grumbled, nodding her head in consent. "Now, stop, please." Her body was limp and exhausted. She tried to be brave, but it was useless. Her backside was sizzling.

∽

Rocco

His manhood throbbed at the gratifying sight of his handiwork on her behind as she sniffed and took one more spank. Her flesh had turned crimson, and it gave him great satisfaction.

"Please, Rocco, stop!"

"Will you behave? So we can have a meaningful conversation about our situation?" he asked, pausing and rubbing her skin.

"Yes." She nodded eagerly, almost managing to suppress a moan at his massage of her scarlet backside, glowing like a beacon of light, but he still heard it.

"Good! And for the love of God, don't push me like this again. Understood? Promise me."

She nodded.

Evie had taken the spanking bravely, and he was proud of her. He reckoned he drummed his point long enough, but his possessiveness of her intensified.

"I promise." She sniffed away lingering tears.

As he massaged her derrière, her legs parted—he wasn't sure whether she realized it or not.

Was it an invitation? He couldn't help his kink, and he touched her. His fingers skimmed the length of her wet folds.

"What a-are y-you doing?" she stuttered, surprised.

Rocco loved it when he soaked his women with his spankings. He had spanked his previous girlfriends for mutual fun as a quirky, sexy game to heighten their lovemaking rather than a punishment. Evie's lies had made him furious, though. So he used it to drum his point across as an over-the-knee discipline session. He could not reward her now with sex! It would defeat the purpose.

He had enjoyed spanking her, and by the looks of it, so had she, despite whatever she said to the contrary. He had embraced the challenge of mastering her wholeheartedly.

Her submission, however brief, was thrilling.

Still, he should not indulge her with sex. Seeing her like this, submissive after all her morning tantrums and defiance, still desiring him, caused his cock to throb. His substantial shaft ached for her. He wanted her as much as she did.

But he stuck to his plan.

Rocco pulled her up into a sitting position on his lap, trying to resist her. To his surprise, she leaned her head on his chest, sniffing her tears, exhausted and limp. He embraced her, and she responded by circling his waist with her arms.

"That's okay, *micina*. I'm here for you now. You can count on me," Rocco said, caressing her hair, pulling some strands out of her face and behind her ear, and kissing her forehead.

"I'm sorry," she whispered. "I never meant to lie to you. To hurt you."

"I know. No more lies, okay?"

"I promise."

"But why did you lie, though?"

"I was scared," she blurted with a sob.

"Of me? Of what I do?"

"A bit of both," she said, as he dried a streaking tear on her cheek. "At first, I was frightened of what you do. Who you are."

"I would never harm you. You know that, don't you? I want to look after you and our baby. It's a big thing. The child will need my protection, and so do you."

"I-I—"

"There are rules now that you have entered my world."

"If you say so."

"You fear what's ahead of you?"

"Yes, but this isn't what alarms me the most."

"My family scares you?" He massaged her back in a circular motion, encouraging her to talk.

"A bit! Yes. But that's not it, either."

"I'm sorry if all this frightens you, but we are no longer the family we were under my father—the terror of the high seas that was all illegal activities and violence—granted, we are not quite out of the woods yet, but we are more gentrified these days." He paused and laughed, caressing her. "My mother has reacquainted us with that side of her upbringing. Her connections give us a more legitimate face. My family will never hurt you."

"I know. Selina said your family makes more money from your legal businesses now, as opposed to that of the clan. All steps toward your mother's legitimacy goals." She peeked at him and realized she should shut up. So, she bit her bottom lip.

His brows arched with a frown. Evie knew more than she let on. His sister should be careful about the things she blurted out, even to her best friend.

"Did she now?"

"But your family is not what scares me the most."

"Then what kept you from telling me the truth?"

"Uh…"

"Well?"

"I-I—"

"Tell me."

"Well, look at me," Evie mumbled, flapping a hand over her body.

"What about you?"

"You have all those fine, beautiful women. How long before you tire of me? You'd leave me for one of them. And where would I be then? I'll have a broken heart. That's what Jake did, and I couldn't allow it again. So I lied."

"You silly girl! I'm not Jake, you know. You've got to trust me. Besides, you are sexy and sassy, beautiful. That's what you are." He captured her hand in his, brought it to his lips and kissed it gingerly. Then lay it on his erect cock. "Look what you do to me. This is all you, *micina!* I want to fuck you senseless."

"Ooh." Evie's eyes grew wide. Their eyes met.

From her soaked pussy and hard nipples, he knew the pain and pleasure of his punishment still tingled her womanly parts, and now sitting on his lap, with him caressing her face and her hand on his hard cock, she licked her bottom lip.

He caught the motion of her little tongue over the silky flesh, and he couldn't resist her. Rocco captured her mouth fiercely, forgetting his intention of no reward after the spanking. She responded in kind.

He was ravenous on her, possessive. His hands caressed her inner thighs, and her arms went around his collar. She pulled him closer to her. He fondled her drenched folds, and she gasped. He mumbled sweet, incomprehensible things to her in Italian. She groaned, obviously enjoying it as he sank a finger inside her. Then two.

"Oh, God!" she panted, her breath mixing with his.

"Jesus, Evie, you are so fucking wet!"

She moaned in ecstasy at his thrusts. He adored her little sounds of passion as he made love to her. It was music to his ears. He increased the depth and the pace.

He finger-fucked her.

Her breathing became ragged, unabashed in her desire, and wantonly charmed in his embrace. She was on the verge, her body tensed with his thrusts, and then her orgasm exploded.

"Rocco," she mumbled his name in his mouth. Her frame shuddered with ripples of pleasure flooding over her. He relished it when she climaxed in his embrace. He lifted her in his arms when her orgasm subsided and laid her on the bed.

She was still dazed.

He unbuttoned his shirt and discarded it at his feet. As Evie lay there on her back, watching him undress, she closed her legs, likely feeling exposed. He parted them, giving her a small smack on her thigh. Her cheeks flushed, reddening to the roots of her hair. Her sudden coyness made him smile, given what he had just done to her.

Do not move from this position. I want to admire your beautiful pussy. I've missed it," Rocco said with a wink and a croaky voice as he took off his clothes, piling them on the floor. His boxers joined the heap, too.

~

Evie

Her eyes grew wide as his massive hard-on was set free. She marveled at his beautiful body, tight and muscular in all the right places. Her breathing turned shallow with anticipation. She removed her dress. She kicked off her panties, now lying around one of her ankles. Her bra ended on the floor, too.

"You are gorgeous! Never forget that," he said. Rocco gazed at her with a heated, passionate look. He leaned on her, giving her tummy tiny kisses all over. She rejoiced.

"Hello, baby, this is your dad!" he said to her tummy. She giggled, as her eyes went misty. His lips traveled south and savored her wet folds. She hissed a little cry as his velvety tongue slipped in to make love to her. He gorged on her pussy.

"You taste like honey, *amore.*" His face buried deep between her legs as he worked his magic on her. Her hands nestled in his soft hair. He licked and sucked as she moaned her way to another orgasm. A wave of bliss rushed through her until she was satiated with love. Her climax hadn't subsided yet when his stiff shaft sank into her. She sighed. His strokes became steady, in and out of her, according no truce. Her bosom heaved up and down, and he captured a nipple with his mouth.

"Ouch!" she shifted under his lips.

"What is it?" He drew his head back to look at her, concerned.

"My nipples are sensitive in this last week, the pregnancy. It's okay, but—" Evie sighed, his enormous cock still filling her pussy.

He displayed his best LaTorre smile. It fired her insides to mush. Rocco nuzzled her.

"It's okay, *micina.* My suckling will ease the soreness in your nipples. Aside, I frigging love your breasts, it will encourage the baby to latch onto your nipples more easily after birth." He winked at her. "Trust me!" Thus, his mouth returned to her pink buds. With this in mind, he grazed her ample bosom for a while, suckling and teasing the aching buds. After a time, amazed, her discomfort eased, and pleasure replaced it instead.

"How did you know that?" she asked. She was astonished at her pert nipples feeling much better than they had. Under Rocco's expert touch, her lust was pulling her quivering core into a frenzy. She was needy and smoldering with heat.

He lifted his head.

"What?"

"About my nipples."

"It was in the pregnancy book." And Rocco latched onto one again. But she grabbed his cheeks in her hands, pausing his actions so he would look at her.

"You read about pregnancy?"

"Surprised? Evie, I do read! I couldn't sleep after I knew about the baby last night, I finished the book," he said.

Tears formed at the corner of her eyes. It made her delirious with joy he had taken the trouble to read about it, and she pulled him down to her, giving him a ravenous kiss.

He resumed his licking and nibbling on her pink-tipped beads to his heart's content. He increased the pace of his strokes at her core. Her lush, creamy boobs swelled and throbbed. Her channel drenched, and soon all thought became inconsequential. She was on the verge again, quivering, pulsating.

"God, Evie." He plunged in and out of her. Her climax ripped through her body in a current of acute fever, wild, as she mumbled his name repeatedly. He followed suit and jetted his seed inside her. After the almighty sex blast, Rocco withdrew from her. He rolled over and lay beside her in silence, not wanting to crush her. He propped his cheek with his hand and caressed her tummy with the other.

"Are you okay?" he asked, placing a peck on her belly button. It tickled her, her eyes misty.

He brushed her lips with a soft, lingering kiss. Then, he

leapt to his feet out of bed, and picked up a few tissues from the nightstand and cleaned himself, then her. He went to the bathroom. She heard the shower running.

When he returned, wearing only a towel around his hips, beauty personified, he moved to the table and lifted the silver domes covering the dishes. He sighed with a frown.

"Evie, you haven't eaten a thing all day. Take a shower. I would have asked you to join me in there, but I'd fuck you again, and you need a rest." He winked at her. Her cheeks burned, and her coyness seemed to amuse him after the vigorous lovemaking. "You must eat. I'll ask the cook to send over hot food. This is cold."

"No, it doesn't bother me."

"This meal is best warm. So, come on, lazy bones." He pulled her up from the bed. He typed his orders on his cellphone, in the house app. "Go, hurry." He slapped her backside, encouraging her toward the bathroom. She yelped, then giggled and skipped to it. He followed her in and unhooked a bathrobe and put it on.

"Would you prefer a bath? Shall I run one for you?"

"No, a shower is fine." And she went for it. When done, she returned to the room wearing the other bathrobe.

There was a knock on the door. He searched for his trousers. They lay in a heap on the floor.

He had the key to her bedroom in them. Evie tensed as it reminded her she was still his captive. Rocco unlocked the door, and Lara came in with a new platter. He picked up the old one while the maid transferred hers to the table.

"Miss Logan's supper, sir," the maid said.

"Thank you, Lara. Please, take this back to the kitchen." He gave her the tray with the cold meal. When the girl left, he closed the door behind her and locked it anew. Next, he pocketed his key, placing his slacks on the *recamier* at the foot of the bed.

All of Evie's good humor faded quickly watching this action. A pang of sorrow pierced her heart. *I'm still his prisoner. He doesn't trust me, even after we made love.*

Rocco didn't pick up her sudden mood change, busily lifting the silver domes from the plates.

"Come, eat. You must be starving." He beckoned her with his finger. She sat at the table.

Though the realization of being his captive had hit her hard, she tried not to show it. Besides, she was hungry now.

"Why did you lock me in again?" she asked, side-glancing at him after wolfing down most of her food.

"Evie! Please don't spoil it now." His impatience was visible.

"Spoil it? You have a nerve." She rattled the fork on the plate.

"Hey, I won't quarrel with you again. And you won't win, Evie. You have to earn the key."

"What? That's ridiculous. You have no right to do this. You don't need to lock me up." She blinked rapidly, tears pooling in her eyes.

"Come on, *micina,* finish up your food. We had a nice afternoon, didn't we? I don't wish to argue with you. You look tired," he said. "I think the sex and the tantrums of this morning have drained you. You need to rest. I'll stay with you until you are asleep." He ignored her statements and caressed her face. She flinched away from him. Rocco drew her to him and kissed her forehead.

She let him do it even though she was tense. She wondered what he meant about "earning the key". *He doesn't trust me!* It figured. She couldn't blame him after all the lies she had concocted.

Though his capriciousness at shutting her in was driving her mad, in particular, now they were amorous again, she chose not to push the point. Evie was exhausted and had no strength left to assert herself. Her battle could wait.

"I wonder what your grandmother would say about your pregnancy." He wished to lighten the mood. He was struggling to make some concessions. "Would she approve of you having a kid? Out of wedlock, I mean?"

She snapped her head up to him, somewhat appeased. *He remembered what I said about grandma after all these months?*

"She loved children. She didn't want me to be an only child. But it didn't happen again for my mom."

"Siblings can annoy the hell out of you. This from someone who has five of them!"

"No. I don't believe you." She laughed that girly laugh he liked so much. "But Granny would have been happy with my baby if I was."

"And are you?"

"Yes, very much."

"What about your parents? They seemed okay last weekend. Though I had no idea it was mine then."

"They are fine. They are very supportive."

"Do they know I'm the father?"

"Mother knows it's yours. Well, she pulled it out of me. She lectured me about lying to you. But Father doesn't know yet. I'm sure Mother will tell him soon though."

"Are you ashamed of me? Is that why you didn't tell him? Because of what I do?"

"No!"

"Remember, *micina*. We said no lies." His brows knitted with a crease on his forehead.

She sighed.

"I don't want to worry Father, that's all. But he likes you."

"I like them, too."

"Really?"

"Of course. Come on, finish up."

"No, I can't eat another bite. This was delicious, but I'm too full."

"Do you want to watch T.V. or read before the nap?"

"No, I'll brush my teeth and go straight to bed. I'm tired."

"Good."

She moved to the ensuite but turned to him before entering.

"Rocco?"

"Yes?" He was picking at some of her leftovers.

"Are you happy about the baby? About being a father?" She became coy, shuffling on her feet, gripping one side of her robe in her fist. His head snapped up, and he gave her that beaming smile which always raised her pulse.

"Sweetheart! You and our child are the most important people in my life." He closed the space between them and kissed her forehead. "You believe me, don't you?"

She studied him for a long moment. At last, she nodded.

"You don't think I did this on purpose, do you?" she whispered.

"On purpose?"

"Yes, as in wanting to get pregnant."

"What? No."

"To trap you."

"Don't be silly. Go." He snorted. She moved to the bathroom but returned to the doorway.

"Rocco?"

"Yes, darling?" he said with tenderness in his tone.

"Don't you wish the mother of your child was one of your model girlfriends? I mean, rather than me? A beautiful one…"

"Jesus, Evie! You are in a silly mood. For the record, you are my only girlfriend. And look at you. You are gorgeous.

And if you don't hurry, I'll fuck you so hard. I'll show you how stunning you are. So scoot!"

She giggled and skipped to the bath. When she returned to her room, he was in bed.

"Come," he beckoned. "Curl up to me. I'll stay with you for a bit."

She lay down beside him. He covered her with the coverlet, her back to his chest, and his hand stretched gingerly over her belly, caressing her. The baby rewarded him with a kick, to his great shock and delight.

"Bloody hell, he does kick like you." And he kissed her cheek, stroking her tummy. She laughed and curled up to him with pride.

"What if it is a girl?"

"Oh, that would be lovely, too, sweetheart. If she's anything like Lola, she'll wrap me around her little finger in no time."

She soon drifted to sleep, getting comfortable and cozy in his arms.

CHAPTER 19

Evie

Evie opened her eyes in the darkened room. She squinted.

Rocco's home. She knew he'd planned to stick around until she had fallen asleep, but he must have changed his mind as he was nestling up to her, joining her in the land of dreams.

Her backside was still tender and tingling, and her pussy was sore. The recollection of Rocco's spanking and the afternoon's lovemaking soon flooded back. A lazy, soft smile spread across her lips.

Moreover, the cat was out of the bag. Rocco had assured her he was over the moon about the baby. After months of agonizing, this was a joy to her. She stretched her limbs with a yawn. Rocco's warm breath tickled her nape, and she curled into his body. His muscled arm draped around her tummy. She sighed, contented, wallowing in his glow for a while.

That niggling thought in her mind reappeared, though. *He still has me locked up in this bedroom*—her only vexation.

She rolled her eyes and peeped over her shoulder. His breathing was slow and steady. The chiseled lines of his manly face looked handsome and restful.

He must have been exhausted.

She didn't want to disturb his peaceful sleep, but she needed to pee. She wriggled out of bed quietly, stark naked. When she glanced at him, the sheets scrunched down his hips, baring his sexy, sculpted torso, and just about covered his cock. By the size of him, it seemed the man was still hard. She snorted. *Quiet, you fool,* and sticking a hand over her mouth, she hurried to the bathroom. When she returned to the bedroom, she flipped through a pile of garments scattered about. She gathered her clothes from the floor and caught sight of his trousers on the beautiful *recamier.* Her eyes widened, and she remembered.

The key to the bedroom was in his pocket, and with it, her freedom!

Evie froze. A thousand thoughts flashed through her mind. *Should I do it? He wouldn't like it.* She bit her bottom lip in agony, pensive for a moment.

Then, she took action.

Evie seized Rocco's trousers and scoured his pockets until she found it. Her heart pounded in her chest. She dressed at the speed of light and picked up her handbag. Her movements were furtive.

Quiet as a mouse, she dived for the door and unlocked it with the key she had just stolen from his pants. The click in the bolt boomed loud in the quiet place. Holding her breath, she turned to glimpse at him. Her thundering heartbeat buzzed in her ears.

He stirred but did not wake up. He must have been tired. Rocco had told Evie the baby's news had kept him awake all night. The notion softened her soul.

She should stay.

No!

As much as I adore him, the man has me captive. Her inner voice groaned. *And it's brutal.* She paused, reflecting. *Perhaps, I should talk to him instead. Oh, God.* Doubts assailed her. Guilt engulfed her. They had got on so well this afternoon. Would she ruin everything by leaving? Evie chewed at her bottom lip and almost went back to him.

He made his point to her.

Too bad, it won't do! He couldn't treat her like one of his lowlifes—her turn to make a point.

Get out. Now.

She stepped out of the room and bolted the door behind her. Her naughty side was getting the better of her. She giggled and put the key in her purse. *See if he likes his own medicine.*

Evie scanned the hallway, but nobody was about. Rocco must have dismissed the bodyguard outside since he showed up in her bedroom. She tried to find her bearings and wished she had paid more attention to the layout of this enormous house. She had no clue where she was going, but the household was quiet. It was late.

She peeked over the banister. She was two floors up, so she turned toward the staircase. She wondered at a landscape mural forming a canopy over the domed stairwell.

Hurry, girl! No time to admire these things.

Evie crept down two flights of stairs, looking for a way out. She hastened along the paneled hallway on the ground floor. She almost dithered, wanting to open doors to other rooms. *Hurry, you fool!* She came up to the large foyer.

The entryway!

～

Rocco

The first click on the bolt didn't wake him when Evie

opened the bedroom door. The second one—locking it back behind her—did.

Rocco found her space empty when he stretched his arm next to him.

"Evie?" he called out. When he had no reply, he leapt out of bed. He plucked his slacks from the sofa and peeked in the bathroom and into the adjacent alcove swiftly—no sign of her. There was no key in his pocket, either. He cursed.

He opened the house security app on his phone in haste. He pressed the emergency button, and the locks came into play. His home had the latest, most advanced security system and locking mechanisms money could buy. He sealed his home shut to the outside world.

Had he done it in time? Or was she gone?

He alerted Zeno and the surveillance team on the grounds with a text. He blurted another blasphemy. Rocco hadn't tested the door handle yet, but he needn't be Einstein to guess what Evie had done. When he did, his immediate reaction was a laugh bubbling up despite himself.

Lo-and-behold, the door didn't budge.

She had locked him in.

∼

Evie

Evie heard loud clicks but made a beeline for the entrance door. She attacked the handle several times, but she found the door locked. No sign of the household keys. She opened the drawers of the hall furniture, but there were no keys.

She tried the other door, the one she remembered went down to the garage when she first arrived, but it was shut, too.

She panicked.

She went to the windows. Try as she might, she couldn't open them.

Think, woman, think. The back door! She made her way toward the rear of the house.

~

Rocco

He dressed quickly and waited for Zeno. As the realization hit him, he had to force himself to calm down. He needed a clear head when he dealt with her.

The damn flirt!

Rocco would never live it down.

Evie had played him like a schoolboy, using sex to run away. The oldest trick in the book. A slip of a girl had the upper hand on him. If his brothers knew, they would tease him to the end of time. He cursed. His manly pride was dented. He chuckled at her daring, though. Despite himself, he had to take his hat off to her, *the bloody minx!* He would have to swear Zeno to secrecy.

But her deception soon cut him like a knife. This woman wasn't his sweet girl, the one in his heart. This one was a lying, backstabbing, stubborn brat who stopped at nothing to get her way, he convinced himself. Her intentions were clear now, it all made sense.

She won't get away with this.

Zeno unlocked the bedroom door.

"Don't say a word!" Rocco warned him, watching the young man struggling to contain an amused smile.

"I didn't say a thing."

"You don't have to."

"No!" Zeno snorted. Rocco rolled his eyes.

"Where the fuck is she?" he barked instead.

"The monitors picked her up downstairs."

Rocco released a sigh of relief. She was still in the house.

~

Evie

Evie had to find an exit. She crossed over to the rear of the mansion. Locating the back door, she forced the knob. No luck! It was locked, too! *What the hell is going on?* She grew baffled when she undertook the windows. She couldn't unfasten them. Then it hit her.

The frigging brute has some automatic locking mechanism!

It didn't put her off. She would find a way out. Evie spotted the kitchen, and the staff stared at her when she entered.

Lara was sitting at the wooden table, having a night cup of tea with the cook. They stopped abruptly and rose. They nodded.

"Miss Logan," Lara said. "Anything I can do for you?"

"No. That's okay."

"I'm Mrs. Caruso, miss, the cook. Do you need something to eat?" asked the middle-aged, gray-haired, round woman in charge of the kitchen.

"No. Thank you. Can you open the back door in the hallway, Mrs. Caruso? Let me out?"

"No. I'm sorry. I can't."

"What about the kitchen door?" Evie decided to take her chances through the garden.

"No. Everything is shut, miss. No one can go in or out of the house."

"You don't have any keys?"

"No. Sorry."

Evie ran to a window and tried to open it.

"You can't, miss. The system barred all exits, doors and windows."

Bloody hell! Her cheeks turned pale. Evie was trapped. *No way out!* Her eyes darted to a heavy, large stainless steel frying pan with a long handle lying on the counter. She seized it and, dashing to the door to the garden, she hammered the knob with it with all her might. The staff was shocked. Their eyes wide, watching her horrified, but no one said a word as they held their breath.

She was denting the door knob with the loud clinking and clanking, hammering it. But it held. On her fourth attempt, she lifted the pan higher, pushing it far back behind her head—she needed a solid momentum to strike the handle harder—but it stuck in mid-air instead. Evie tried to pull it forward with all her strength but couldn't bring it down. She turned her head over her shoulders, and to her horror discovered Rocco gripping it with a devilish grin.

She yelped.

He snatched the pan out of her hands and tossed it on the counter. He grabbed her wrist.

"Zeno, lead everybody out of the kitchen, please. Now! Close the door and wait outside." Rocco grunted his order; no one argued. They obeyed. When they left, Evie grappled with him to free herself, but his hand held on to her.

"Rocco, please!"

"You haven't won yourself any points with this charade, *micina*. And you've broken this fucking door handle." His gaze was dark and stormy, pointing at it.

"Listen to me." She reached for his forearm, seeking to appease him. To her alarm, he jerked backward as if she had burned him.

"What's the meaning of this, Evie? I thought we reached an understanding." He paused with a scowl. She hung back, avoiding eye contact. "But no! Instead, you manipulated me to break out of the house. It almost worked," he went on. His tone was sharp and cynical. The girl had rattled all his feathers.

"No." She put on a brave face. "I didn't."

"Be honest. You had no intention of ever sharing the baby with me. That's why you lied for so long. And this afternoon, you used sex to get your way out." His expression was calm anew, but his tone had an edge of steel.

"No, that's not true." She grew weary at his accusations. "I explained to you why I lied about the baby. But this situation is your doing! You locked me in as if I were one of your hoodlums. You pushed me to this! By keeping me a prisoner, even after we made love. So, don't you take the high ground with me! And I didn't have a plan this afternoon. It just happened. It was unpremeditated if that's what you mean." She defended herself with vehemence from his recriminations.

"Was it?"

"Please, let me go. You must realize it now. We are too different. It's over, whatever this thing between us was. It's not good for us. You don't trust me. It won't work," Evie said. "Don't worry. After the birth, you can visit the child any time you want."

With a stony mask, he hauled her to him. She yelped. His thunderous green eyes went dark and flashed at her. His control was ebbing at her words. He was scary, and she gulped.

"Obviously, you learned nothing this afternoon. Lean on the table, high on your forearms. Feet on the floor, ass in the air!" His patience was at an end.

"What?" Her jaw lifted in rebellion, and she tried to turn away from him. He held her tight.

"You heard me. Do it and don't struggle, or you'll hurt yourself. Move." He growled the last word, and her breath hitched. "Take your punishment in silence, or my staff will hear you," he went on in a chilly tone that left Evie no doubt. He meant business.

"Please, Rocco…"

"The more you argue with me, Evie, the worse for you."

After more protestations, she complied. She took the position. Rocco readjusted the spread of her legs with his feet. He grabbed a thick cushion from a chair and placed it on the counter under her belly, even if her tummy was well away from the counters, just in case, so she would not hurt herself or the baby.

"Don't move, understood?" He swatted her ass with his large hand, and she squealed, swaying. "Stay still." Rocco scrunched her dress to her waistline and tugged her panties down to her knees. These slithered to her ankles, thus exposing her delicious backside to him. Then he saw something on the kitchen counter.

He grabbed a long, thin, smooth wooden paddle from it, contemplating it for a moment.

The first swat with it, though not harsh, left a pink glow on her soft skin. Evie cried out a curse. She wasn't expecting it to hurt so much, but he did it again.

"What's that?"

"It is a paddle, *micina,* because you have been a very naughty girl." He connected two more swats with her posterior. She tried to be brave, but a simpering hiss came out of her mouth. Her already pinkish complexion flushed scarlet. She wiggled her bottom.

"Stop. Please…"

Her bottom was tender following the afternoon spanking, but if she thought his firm hand had left her skin glowing red and hot, the paddle was in a different league. She had tears in her eyes straight away. Her face grimaced.

"The hell with visiting rights, Evie. If you don't wish to stay with me, that's fine. You can leave after the birth. But the baby stays with me. I won't repeat myself, and you'll remain with me until then. Understood? This is not negotiable!" He cracked two consecutive swats harder, and she uttered a yelp, nodding vigorously.

She was miserable, ashamed, and fired up at his accusations and menaces. All sentiments mingled. She didn't know whether to call for mercy or to murder him outright. She opted for silence instead, not to aggravate her case.

"You lied to me for months, and now you deceived me with your scheming sex plan to run away."

"No. There was no plan," she cried out. "It was on impulse. I felt hurt when you locked me in again after we made love. How could you?" She went on, sniveling her displeasure. Though as much as he irritated her, she didn't want him to think she cajoled him into sex for her purposes. He caressed her face with his hand and pulled a lock of hair behind her ear.

"Didn't you?" He trashed the crease between her buttocks and thighs, one on each side.

"No, aw, aw. Please, believe me. Stop." She sobbed.

"We'll see about that."

"You're a brute!" she said through gritted teeth, flinching in agony. Her backside was on fire with heat and pain.

"I won't let you go, Evie. So don't try this again. And if you run, I'll find you, and I'll bring you back. No more tricks. Do you understand?" He delivered a set of hard whacks on her backside.

"Yes," she whimpered. Her tears flowed as she went limp on the table. Her tinted bottom stinging and scorching. He tossed the paddle on the table and massaged her backside. Rocco parted her legs. He couldn't help to inspect her sex and touch her. He grinned, satisfied with himself.

"What a-are are you doing?" she simpered.

"You are still wet for me, *micina*. Be honest?" He paused.

"No matter what you say, you still want me. We are not done yet. Certainly not where the baby is concerned."

"Please…" Evie pleaded.

~

Rocco

He would've wanted nothing better than to assert dominance by fucking her hard, but he refrained from it. It would only confuse her. So Rocco massaged her buttocks, releasing the blistering heat. This time, he would not humor her with sex and wanted his punishment to resonate with her—no more lies or tricks! He would not dilute his massage with sex.

He pulled her up from the table.

Rocco raised her panties instead and lowered her dress to make her presentable again. He sat her on the bench. She winced, her backside too raw to sit in comfort. She seemed exhausted, still whimpering, with tears streaking her face.

"Are you all right?" He studied her, checking he had not overdone it. He lifted her chin, and with a tissue, he dried her tears with gentleness.

"What do you think?" She sniffed, massaging her backside. He glanced at her with tenderness and would have kissed her hard if she hadn't made him so mad.

He called out to Zeno instead. The young man came in.

"Take Miss Logan to her bedroom. Ask the staff to return to the kitchen. Tell security to deactivate the lockdown."

"After you, miss." Zeno pulled her up gently from the seat, but she stopped.

"Rocco, please hear me out."

"Evie, don't force it. Go." His mask didn't waver. She was out of the room, dejected.

He was incandescent. His temper was ruling his head, but he wasn't one for big outbursts. So Rocco inhaled deeply, closed his eyes and counted to ten in his mind to let his grim humor out. At least for now.

"Mrs. Caruso, can you bake a cake in the morning?" Rocco asked when his staff returned to the kitchen. *Well, Evie's upset.* Even in his anger, he was still concerned about her.

"Yes, of course."

"Can you bake a red-velvet cake? It's Miss Logan's favorite," he said, feeling somewhat uncomfortable with punishing her and making her cry. So he knew the cake would please her.

Why do I indulge this girl? What's wrong with me? She didn't deserve a reward for her behavior.

Evie and Rocco craved each other. At least their bodies did. To distraction! Rocco was conscious of that. *It's a little point in our favor. But why is everything else so complicated with her?* He rolled his eyes. He was uncertain of what it was between them. A relationship? Certainly not a normal one. *Fuck!*

"Sure." the woman smiled. "Miss Logan is so pretty. The baby's so precious."

"Yeah."

"She's young, and a baby is a big commitment. You have to give her time and be patient. I'll make her a lovely cake," the cook concluded with a smile. He arched his brows but made no reply.

Perhaps Mrs. Caruso was right. He'd have to be tolerant, calm, and allow her space.

∾

Evie

When Zeno locked the door, Evie wept, unsure if she

cried for herself or her man. Rocco had accused her of never intending to share the baby with him and that she had used sex to escape him, convinced she betrayed him all over again!

How can he believe that? Yes, she had lied to him, but this? No!

Why did she fret about what he thought of her when she was still his captive and treating her abominably? It made no sense to her.

He now despises me.

Evie felt lonely, unhappy and vulnerable. Without Selina to talk over her distress, and with no phone or laptop to call her mother, she sobbed herself to sleep.

∼

Rocco

Rocco wouldn't admit to it, but Evie's deception hurt. He had planned to stay with her that night but regretted even indulging her in the afternoon. The minx had bewitched him.

Forget her. You wasted enough time with this girl.

They were not meant to be together, despite the baby. They were doomed. Besides, someone in his line of business had no right to a proper relationship with a woman, anyway. The odds stuck against him, regardless of how difficult the chit was.

Was she still in love with Jake? The reason she didn't want him?

A surge of red, furious jealousy coursed through him. It flashed through his veins like a monster eating him up. *I should have killed that bastard when I had the chance.* He wasn't comfortable with these jealous emotions. Nothing made sense to him anymore. Rocco punched the wall hard. His knuckles bled.

He would have to keep Evie safe until the birth. *But stay away from her,* he cursed. He would let her go after that if she wanted to. He resolved.

A LaTorre through birth, his child wouldn't be safe with Evie, needing the clan's protection—*the baby stays with me.*

CHAPTER 20

Evie

Evie hadn't seen Rocco in three days. Since her notorious attempted escape, he'd stayed away. Lara showed up daily, carrying her meal trays. A futile exercise. Evie's stomach was in knots, and she couldn't eat a morsel.

The first day, she'd picked at her food. Even a slice of red-velvet cake wouldn't go down well, intense nausea had settled in her stomach. She became sick, vomiting, and couldn't keep anything down. So, she stopped eating, achieving only small sips of water or juice.

It was now 1:00 p.m. on the fourth day. Lara came in with Zeno.

"Hello, Miss Logan," the maid said chirpily. "Are you still in bed?" She squinted in the darkened room.

"Why are the drapes closed?" Zeno reached out to open them. The sun filtered in, and he unlocked the windows for fresh air.

"I opened them this morning, but Miss Logan wanted them closed." Lara deposited the tray with lunch on the table and frowned. "Oh, no, miss. Why won't you eat? You had no breakfast. You can't go on like this." Lara glanced in her direction with a sorrowful expression. Then she turned to Zeno and glowered at him in disapproval.

"Hey, not my fault." His tone was conspiratorial, and he raised a hand in defense. The young man moved toward the bed. He sat beside Evie, who had buried her head under the blanket against the light. He took the covers down to peek at her. She blinked rapidly at the glaring light from the windows, but her eyes were red, her face blotchy. He presumed from crying. Her hair looked messy. She was very pale.

"You must eat something. It's not good for the baby. I know you are, how do you say? Sorry, miss, my English—"

"Under the weather? Sick?" Lara helped him in an undertone, still disapproving.

"I can't keep any food down. I vomit if I eat," Evie said, and covered her face with the blanket again.

Zeno groaned and went to the table. He motioned to the maid to pick up the untouched breakfast.

"Try, Miss Logan, even if it's a little food," he insisted.

"Please take it away. The smell makes me sick," Evie mumbled, her voice feeble, popping her face up from under the covers.

"I'll leave your lunch. You may be hungry later," Lara said. Evie hadn't even bothered to get up from bed. It was a bad sign. The maid was concerned about her.

"I'll leave the windows open. The fresh air will do you good," Zeno said, and they left.

When they closed the door, Evie sighed with relief, glad they had gone. She wanted to be alone. What was the point of getting up if that monster had trapped her in his gilded cage? She was anguished. Disconsolate.

Mother must be out of her wits with worry. She had yet to speak to her for four days. *What's he doing to me?*

She wept.

~

Rocco

Rocco was in his study when Selina burst into the room.

"What are you going to do about Evie?" she blurted out. He had allowed his sister to roam around the house as she pleased. But he wouldn't let her see her friend.

"I didn't hear you knock!"

"Rocco, I'm worried about her. I want to see her. She is isolated up there, please. I hear she's unwell."

"Nonsense. It's probably one of her tricks."

"Rubbish!"

"Mind your own business. You are still in trouble. So don't push it."

"Evie is my friend, so she's my business."

There was a tap on the door.

"Enter," he huffed. Zeno paused in the doorway.

"What is it?" Rocco asked, and seeing him furrow his brows, he sighed. "Come in, spit it out."

"Is Miss Logan, Rocco." Zeno guessed Selina was pressing her brother about the same issue, noticing the tension in the air. So, he pushed on. "She hasn't eaten for three days, and I bet she won't touch food today, either." The young man liked Evie and couldn't bear seeing her so unhappy.

"See? Lara said the same thing." Selina scowled at him. "This can't go on. She's expecting a child, in case it hasn't sunk into your thick skull yet! She's sick because of you. She may lose the baby. Is that what you want?"

"Why is she not eating? A whim? More tricks, manipulation?"

"What? Don't be ridiculous. Evie hasn't got a manipulative bone in her body."

"She cannot keep her food down. She's ill, vomiting, and I'm concerned," Zeno spoke with a steady voice.

"I told you she was sick!" Selina said, impatiently.

"Sick?" Rocco stood up abruptly. "Why didn't you say?"

"I tried to tell you yesterday, but you wouldn't hear of it as soon as I mentioned her name," Zeno challenged.

"Call Evie's doctor. Dr. Copeland, is it?" Rocco's eyes flashed in warning.

"Yes, he's our local doctor in London. Can I go to her now, please?" Selina pleaded. "She's not well."

"Fine. Zeno, after you call the doctor, take my sister to her friend. Fifteen minutes only. I don't want to tire her if she's sick. Tell me when Copeland gets here."

"Sí, signore."

"Thank you." His sister smiled gratefully.

When they left, Rocco sat back in his chair and pinched the top of his nose. *Is she sick because of me?*

He had stayed away from her, feeling too raw. Rocco believed she had manipulated him, played him like a schoolboy. Even if his sister denied that possibility, he felt betrayed by her attempted escape. Betrayed twice over! But perhaps he had overplayed the situation in his mind. As a result, his child would suffer the consequences.

His sister was right. Underneath it all, he believed Evie to be a sweet girl. He had pushed her too far. Besides, who wouldn't be scared of him and his family? He couldn't blame her for lying to him, for trying to protect her child from toxic people like him and his mob.

The baby's my child, too! He couldn't ignore that point.

Evie

"Evie?" *a* voice said.

The girl uncovered her face from under the blanket, where she was hiding from the newcomer. Recognizing her friend's voice, she raised her head. "Selina?"

Her friend dashed to her, and Evie sat upright in the bed. They hugged and cried.

"Oh, dear. You look awful." Selina said when they had settled after the reunion.

"Thanks a bunch!"

"You know what I mean. You've got to eat."

"I can't keep my food down. Besides, what's the point? I have no hope."

"You have a baby coming, remember? Look, my brother was shocked at finding out the truth. He's stubborn as hell and upset, but it'll pass. You'll see."

"Will it?"

"He's dealing with this in the only way he knows how. Sorry, darling, I'm not excusing him, but he cares for you. I'm sure he does. Give him time."

"Well, that's a funny way of showing it."

"Dr. Copeland is coming to see you."

"I don't need a doctor. I'm fine."

"No, you are not!"

"I-I—"

"What?"

"Rocco hates me. He's treating me as if I were his worst enemy, not the mother of his child. He said I manipulated him into sex to escape. But I didn't. It just happened. Besides, he's the one who doesn't trust me. He locked me up in here even after we made love. How do you think I felt after that?"

"I know, darling. It'll be all right."

"He said I never intended to share the baby with him. How could he accuse me of this?"

"Ignore him. He'll get over it."

"Will he?"

"Come on. I'll run you a bath. Your hair looks like a wasp's nest."

"I haven't combed it in three days." Evie snorted. She felt a little better already, for the simple reason Selina was there.

"It figures."

∽

Rocco

"Dr. Copeland," Zeno announced.

"Thank you for coming, Doctor." Rocco shook hands, greeting him. "I'll show you the way."

They climbed up the stairs.

"Rocco!" Evie had finished her bath and sat with Selina in the alcove.

"Dr. Copeland is here," he said.

"I'll be back later." His sister kissed her friend, greeted the physician and went out.

"So sorry, you had a wasted journey, Doctor. I'm fine," Evie said instead.

"I'll be the judge of that, Miss Logan. Mr. LaTorre, can you please leave us?"

"Leave?"

"I think it's best." The doctor said while Evie lowered her eyes. "I'll stop by your office when I'm done."

"I'm not sure—"

"We'll be okay."

"Fine." He relented but looked at her over his shoulder one last time before he left.

∽

Rocco

"What's wrong with her?" Rocco asked, sitting at his desk. The doctor was facing him after he'd seen to Evie.

"Her health is my priority. Miss Logan is stressed. She has been crying. She won't say what's bothering her, but her anxiety is back. It's making her feel ill to the extent she has nausea and can't eat. And what little she eats, she vomits. All due to anxiety, it has nothing to do with her pregnancy. She wasn't nauseous at all in her first trimester."

"Well, I wouldn't know about that, would I?" he said like a petulant child. "I knew nothing about her pregnancy then."

The doctor sighed.

"She's exhausted, Mr. LaTorre, which is not surprising given she has not eaten for four days. She sounds worried about her baby's future. Do you have anything to tell me?"

"No!"

"I see. These are early symptoms and can relent if circumstances change. They can also deteriorate fast. The fetus will get distressed if the expectant mother is distressed. So, if it is in your power, you better fix this and pronto. Do you hear me?"

"Is the child all right?"

"The baby is fine, for now. I haven't given her any medication except rest. She scoffed when I suggested this. She said that's up to you."

"Me?"

"Yes. I don't know what Evie means or what's going on. She didn't elaborate, but I'm sure you know. She requires a peaceful environment and needs to relax. Allow her to do so, and her anxiety will ease. Then her stomach will heal. She'll be able to keep her food down. Call me if she hasn't improved in a couple of days."

"Of course."

"Good day, Mr. LaTorre."

CHAPTER 21

Evie

"Selina!" Evie bolted from the couch when her friend entered the room the following morning.

"Sit down. Look what I brought you."

"What is it?"

"Open it." Selina offered her a box and plopped beside her. Evie was excited as she unraveled the package.

"My phone and my laptop!" she squealed. Tears formed at the corners of her eyes.

"Hey, no crying. Just enjoy them."

"He approved of this?"

"Yes."

"Am I allowed to call Mother?"

"Of course, anyone you like. But beware, ahem… you cannot say certain things."

"Is he monitoring my calls?"

"Not as such, but particular words may trigger a recording of it."

"I see." She nodded, conscious of what her friend was telling her.

"You can do your college courses online for now. I'm doing mine, too. But Rocco said, next week, Tito will drive us to lessons."

"You are the best!" She embraced her friend. "Can I Zoom with my study group? Will I be able to do my exams as I was preparing to do?"

"Yes. Everything as it was."

"Oh. What a relief!"

"Do you fancy a walk in the garden? Fresh air will do you good. You've been cooped up in here long enough."

"Can I?" Evie asked, her gaze wide with wonder and misty at all the changes. She blinked back the tears and forced herself to smile instead.

"On the home grounds, for now. Next week, he'll give us more freedom. One step at a time. I asked Lara to bring our meal to the dining room, so we'll have lunch together."

"Oh, Selina. How lovely! I thought I would spend the rest of my days like this. Die in here, alone."

"Shush, you silly goose! Let's go for a walk."

"Can I talk to my mother first? She'll be so worried."

"Yes, of course. I told your mom you had the flu with a sore throat, and lost your voice, that you were resting in bed, to explain your complete silence."

"Oh, what would I do without you? Thank you."

"I'll leave you to it."

She had finished the call with her mom when Selina returned. Evie looked forward to her stroll. She could now appreciate the wonderful mural of a landscaped garden over the domed stairwell, immersing it in a lofty canopy of greenery and blooms. With its fretwork railing balustrade, the graceful curve of the staircase completed the superb feature.

"It's a mural of our gardens on the Island."

"Island?"

"My family spends the autumns and winters in Naples, the warmer months on Capri, an island in the Bay of Naples. Rocco loves it there. He asked an artist to portray a Mediterranean garden to remind him of home."

"Our apartment must look so small to you if you're used to grand homes like this."

"Our apartment is gorgeous and bijoux. Who knows, Rocco might let us return to it. I love it there."

"So do I."

"Come." The two girls went on their way.

They reached the first floor. Selina showed her around the house first. They went through a sequence of rooms. Evie could see how Rocco had devised the ideal combination of old-world charm and modern glamour in this large London townhouse. Lacquered walls, oversized artwork, and statement lighting made the living spaces charming.

They went down to the ground floor.

"Behind this door is my brother's study. It's out of bounds unless he summons you."

"What's he hiding?"

"Evie!"

"Sorry. Gotcha."

"Come. Let's go for a stroll. Let me show you the gardens."

The hallmark of his gardens was order, as expressed by symmetry and an ultra-manicured look. Evergreen shrubs meticulously sheared into short hedges lined the walkways.

They strolled along a stone pathway.

The gardens are in tune with Rocco's temper, Evie concluded. She was in awe.

They interpreted his nature as a man in perfect harmony. The greenery was austere in some places. In contrast, it displayed color and playfulness in others with its brightly tinted blooms. It fit him.

The scent of lavender spread in the air, giving the gardens a unique fragrance. With its use of hardscape, formal lines, and what she imagined must be extensive maintenance, it was a home garden full of Italian flair, ornamental, and matching the gorgeous man himself in all its beauty and splendor.

They stayed out until it was time for lunch.

"A kitten!" Evie called out to her friend. "Whose is it?" Evie picked up the tiny creature on the path, a fluffy black-and-white ball of softness.

"We don't know. We have given him food and lodgings, poor lamb. I bet he's only a few months old. But it is not Rocco's. The kitten comes and goes as he pleases. Sometimes, he's absent for days, and then he reappears. Quite a tomboy."

"Aww. You're a lovely little thing, aren't you?" Evie stroked the cat. He seemed to have taken an immediate liking to her. She held him in the crook of her arm, running her fingers over his fur, and the silly creature enjoyed the attention, purring happily in her arms. When they were about to go back in the house, she stopped on the threshold and placed the kitten on the pavement outside, but he followed them inside and up to the first floor into the dining room. They laughed when they realized he had kept up with them. Selina brought food and milk to a corner for him.

"If Rocco catches you are feeding him in here, it'll be trouble. He does not mind him in the kitchen, but he won't allow him to roam around the house," Zeno warned them when he peeked into the room.

"Well, he's with us now. So there!" Selina grumbled.

"Don't say I didn't warn you," he said, but the kitten brushed himself against Zeno's ankles, purring. "Oh, no.

You won't win me over, little fellow. You should be thanking the ladies, not me." But giving a tender smile, Zeno couldn't help petting him several times.

⁓

Evie

No wonder the morning's events—Selina's company restored, the chat with her mother, a blind devotion from a kitten, and the relaxing stroll in the gardens—felt liberating. So, when they sat down for lunch, Evie was ravenous. She wolfed down half a plate of tagliatelle with a light ragú sauce and a small green salad. The most she had eaten in days.

Her stomach had settled as if by magic. Unsure if it was because she was reclaiming her life back or feeling somewhat free again, but whatever the circumstances, it suited her. Though one thing still troubled her.

"Why is your brother avoiding me?" Evie asked.

"What?"

"I have not seen him for five days if I disregard the minute he came in with the doctor yesterday."

"Who knows, darling. Though the phone, the laptop, our walk, our newfound freedom is thanks to him." Selina munched on a mouthful of tagliatelle.

"Yes, I gathered that. But why is Rocco ignoring me? Does he still think I betrayed him?"

"Give him time."

"He hates me."

"Don't be ridiculous—"

"He does!" Evie sighed. "Jesus! Rocco and I make one step forward and three backward. It will never work between us. We are too different."

"Nonsense. Rocco likes you a lot!"

"Is he really pleased about the baby?"

"Of course he is! Why do you think he got so upset about you not telling him about it?" Her companion frowned. They ate in silence for a while.

"The big scars he has on his chest and hip, amongst other smaller ones, how did he get them? Fighting some mobster?" Evie asked. Her companion's head snapped up.

"You could say so," Selina scoffed, unsure what to say, and studied her for a moment.

"What do you mean?"

"Yes, he has a few scars from fights and scrapes in his line of business. But the big ones, the ones on the chest and the hip were inflicted at my father's hands. He did that to him."

"Your father?"

"Yes! Father's dead now, thank goodness."

"Selina!"

"No, Evie, it's true. My father was a wicked man. A monster!"

"You are exaggerating."

"No. I'm not. Father was abusive to Mother and to us. He had no love for his children, except perhaps for me. Even his love for me was a bit off. My brother Sebastiano was Dad's heir to the family's business. Well, he's Mother's heir now since she now commands it all with Salvo, her second husband. Fabio was the spare. So, Father taught them the ropes to our, ahem, let's call it 'unorthodox' way of life, the respect for the clan, and all that shit! Though the evil bastard was rough and autocratic with them, he didn't hurt them much, only when necessary, so they wouldn't forget a point he made. But for some reason, he despised Rocco. Milo and Matteo came much later when Mom became more cunning, had more power, and could protect them. So they didn't suffer much.

"But Mother was very young when my three older brothers were children, had no experience with the likes of my father, and had little power. So, Rocco suffered all the consequences of Daddy's lack of talents other than those for violence. Only a young boy when my father punched and stabbed him in the hip in one of his horrible moods, inflicting a gash on his chest, too. Rocco was ten years old. Sebastiano tried to defend him, but he was hurt, too. Mother got a broken arm for trying to help them. After the attack, Rocco spent two months in the hospital. Everyone thought he was going to die. He doesn't remember the attack at all to this day. The doctors call it 'selective amnesia'. He remembers all the other incidents at Father's hands, but that one—mercifully, no."

"Jesus!" Evie was horrified.

"Sebastiano and Fabio were older, but they were children, too, and no match for a fierce, grown-up man; they couldn't protect Rocco. Mother tried to protect him but she got as many beatings as he did. So Dad abused him with punches and whips. Until one day, Rocco finally snapped and fought him back, almost killing him. He was thirteen years old. After that, my father never touched him again."

"Oh, Selina. It's horrible. I'm so sorry."

"Mother sent Rocco to boarding school in England then, for his safety, and he stayed for college, too."

"That's why he speaks English so well?"

"Yes. When Rocco returned to Italy, he was quite the grown-up gentleman, so proper, so elegant, charming, but underneath that facade, he had become a tough guy. Shortly after his return, he embraced the world of the clan. Father was dead by then." Selina paused. "I learned all these horrible truths over the years, I was too young then."

"Sweet mercy."

"It's a miracle Rocco survived Father's attack. But despite all, my brother is a good guy and clever."

"He tried to tell me once, I think, but I had no idea the extent of it."

"Not something to broadcast, is it?"

"God, no!"

"Welcome to our very dysfunctional family and our crazy world! I say this now so you can understand Rocco better. But don't fear him. He is nothing like my dad. Rocco can have a temper if pushed and wants people's loyalties, but he has a good heart. My father was born without that organ. That's the big difference between them. When Father died and Mother turned into the clan's boss, things eased for us children. Hell, for everyone. We could breathe again. He's out of our hair for good now, thank goodness. Salvo, my stepfather is a fine man, he loves Mother."

"Oh, Selina…"

"Sometimes, I wonder how Mother survived all those years with Father. Not to mention the attacks from the other clans when she got to power. I'm glad she has Salvo. God, what a life. Though I may disagree with the life she leads, I take my hat off to her. She saved her children from that monster, survived, and came out on top."

"Dear me!"

"All water under the bridge."

"Poor Rocco!"

"Please don't tell him you know."

"No—I won't."

"But enough of this gloomy shit. Let's talk about something more cheerful. What about a great slice of red-velvet cake produced by Mrs. Jones' magical hands?"

"Mrs. Jones?"

"She's coming this afternoon for tea and bringing the cake. What do you say to that?"

"I say yes, bring her on! I miss her."

"So do I."

Rocco

"How's Evie doing?" Rocco asked when Zeno entered his study and placed his espresso on the table after lunch.

"She seems a lot happier. All she needed was a little freedom, see? I'm glad you allowed it. She'll be herself in no time." The young man glanced at him with a determined smile as if to say, *I told you so.*

"Good. What's she been up to?"

"She's been with Selina. The kitten follows Evie everywhere like a shadow."

"Yes. I saw them in the garden earlier. She seems fond of the little bugger," Rocco said. "But has she eaten today?"

"*Sí*. More importantly, she kept her food down."

"Excellent!"

"She's looking forward to seeing Mrs. Jones later, but—she's worried about you."

"Me?" Rocco snapped his head up.

"Evie hasn't seen you for days, and she's hurt you are avoiding her."

"I think you're enjoying listening to the ladies' conversations a bit too much, aren't you?"

"You told me to do that!"

"I know."

"Rocco, you accused her of being manipulative. She's upset. If you want my opinion—"

"Then, I'll ask for it."

"Sure," he said and shut his mouth. Zeno knew when to stop.

"Okay, fine. Let's hear it." Rocco rolled his eyes.

"She thinks you hate her!"

"Unbelievable."

"And she knows everything about your father, and what he did to you."

"What?"

"Selina told her."

"Fuck! My sister's got a big mouth."

"Oh, there is Evie." Zeno moved to the double doors to the garden, watching her. Rocco swiveled in his chair.

"Where?"

"The cat's on her lap, under the pergola. Look. She's called the kitten Oreo. Can you fucking believe that? Cute, ha?" Zeno laughed.

"Oreo?" Rocco snorted. "You can go, Zeno, thank you. Tell me when Mrs. Jones arrives. Watch them when she's here, just in case."

"Sure."

Rocco gulped his espresso in one go. He rose and moved to the floor-to-ceiling window to look out for her. Evie was sitting under the pergola with a book. By the size of it, he supposed it was one of her college textbooks. The kitten was basking in her lap as she stroked him.

"The little bugger is having all the fun," he muttered. A pang of longing flooded him.

He studied her for a long moment. Her profile was exquisite. The beautiful lines of her long neck made him want to taste the hollow of it with his tongue, feel her pulse raise under his expert hands.

As he observed her, she bit her bottom lip. That movement sent a rush of blood to his cock.

Bloody hell! He had missed her. He hadn't even realized it until then. Perhaps he should have dinner with her tonight. Try to woe her over again after his less than gentlemanly behavior toward her.

Lara reached her. He didn't hear what she said, but a text pinged on his phone. It was Zeno telling him Mrs. Jones had arrived.

He saw Evie's face light up and she followed the maid into the house, the kitten in tow. He laughed, seeing the cat follow her like a shadow. He was pensive for an instant, then made up his mind.

∽

Rocco

"You want to do surveillance?" Zeno asked, lifting his brows, surprised at seeing him in the security room as he sat beside him.

"Yes," Rocco said. "Where is my sister?"

"Babysitting appointment with Lola, a last-minute thing."

"Who said she could go?"

"I decided it was for the best. Otherwise, Selina would have bothered you for the rest of the afternoon until she got her way."

"True! Send her to me later. I don't want to give her any special privileges yet. My sister kept this secret from me for over four months. I'm not forgiving her so easily. Besides, I must tell her to watch her mouth, blabbering all the family secrets. Is Evie with Mrs. Jones?"

"Yes, in the blue dayroom." Zeno showed him the monitors on the closed-circuit television.

"I like the old woman. Nosy, but she's good to the girls." Rocco had the most advanced state-of-the-art in CCTVs. So, they settled to watch the screens and listen to the exchange between the two women as Evie greeted Mrs. Jones.

∽

Evie

"Evie, darling. I missed you." The elderly lady hugged her with delight.

"Please sit down, Mrs. Jones."

"Where is Selina?"

"She's out; went to see Melania, her sister-in-law. She's babysitting Lola for the afternoon. Sad to miss you, though. She'll be back later."

"Miss Logan, shall I bring in tea or coffee?" The housemaid asked as they made themselves comfortable on the dark blue velvet Chesterfield sofa.

"Mrs. Jones?"

"Tea would be lovely, thank you. Wait! I made your favorite, a red-velvet cake." The woman placed a box on the coffee table and unwrapped it.

"Oh, yummy!"

"I'll take it and place it on a stand. I'll bring in some plates," Lara suggested.

"Yes, perfect. Thank you."

The maid took the cake and left. The cat, who had followed Evie in the dayroom, suddenly jumped onto the old lady's lap.

"Oh, dear, and who's this?"

"We don't know who owns him. I've called him Oreo. Isn't he adorable?"

"You are a cute little fellow, aren't you?" Mrs. Jones rubbed him on the nose, talking gibberish to the kitten.

"He's so sweet," Evie said with a tender smile. The woman regarded her thoughtfully, tilting her head as she stroked the cat on her lap. "What?"

"You lost weight, sweetheart, pregnant and all. You look pale. Are you well?"

"I'm fine. Tired, that's all."

"Are you sure?"

"Yes."

"Perhaps I should have brought you a casserole instead. Do they feed you in this house?"

"Yes, of course!"

"Umm…"

"Please, don't fuss."

"If you say so." Mrs. Jones shrugged her shoulders and glanced around her. "God, this house is fantastic."

"It belongs to Selina's brother."

"What's his name?"

"Rocco."

"Ah, yes. And?"

"And what?"

"I may be old, but not a fool, dear. Is Rocco your boyfriend?"

"No!"

Meanwhile, unbeknownst to the ladies, in the security room, hearing her words, Rocco scowled at the monitor. Zeno snorted, but with one glance from his boss, he shut his mouth.

"No? You are telling me a fib, young lady," Mrs. Jones said in the dayroom. "And the baby? You didn't fool me for an instant with that silly story about Jake."

"But… I—"

"Come, Evie. Your child is Rocco's, isn't it?"

"Did Selina tell you?"

"No, she didn't. But since I haven't seen Jake with you in over six months, unlikely, don't you think?" The old woman asked with a triumphant smile, nodding, seeing her young friend blush crimson.

The maid came back with a trolly, interrupting them.

"Thank you, Lara." Evie sighed with relief. They stayed silent while the maid placed the items on the coffee table, poured the tea, cut a wedge of the luxurious red-velvet cake for each of them, and left.

Oreo raised his tiny head on Mrs. Jones' lap; he was sniffing the goodies on the small plate in front of him. He sought to reach the table with the delicious dessert.

"You want a bit, hey? Sure," the old lady said absent-mindedly to him as she stroked his fluffy fur and started feeding the cat bits of cake with her fingers. The kitten devoured the pieces.

"He likes it but isn't chocolate bad for animals?" Evie asked.

"A little bit won't hurt. And everyone likes my cakes." The lady sipped her tea. The cat suddenly shivered, gave a high-pitched howl, and jumped from her lap to the floor. He hid beyond the settee. "What's up with him? Had enough cake, Oreo?" Mrs. Jones said to the tiny creature. Then, turning back to her companion, she went on. "Oh, darling, such a nice afternoon. So glad to see you."

"Me, too. And I can't wait to taste your cake. It looks delicious." Evie put down her teacup and picked up the plate with the slice of cake.

Mrs. Jones picked up her slice, too. They hadn't tasted it yet. Evie was raising her fork toward her mouth when, halfway there, the door blasted open with a bang.

"Stop! Don't eat it," Rocco yelled, bursting in like a bolt from the skies. Zeno and Tito rushed in after him with a few guards.

Evie trembled and dropped her fork at the fright as she leapt off her seat in shock, not expecting it. Mrs. Jones bolted off the couch, too, and screamed. It all happened too fast.

For a moment, there was a great commotion in the room, pandemonium all around, and a lot of yelling. Rocco snatched the plate from Evie's hands and gave it to his man. He seized Mrs. Jones' too. His men grabbed everything from the small table and took it all away in a split second.

"What the hell? What's going on?" Evie blurted out when she had a moment to recover.

He moved her with him behind the sofa.

"Oh, my love," Rocco said to her, his tone permeated with softness. His stormy gaze, clouded with grief, he turned to the cat behind the couch. They all followed his line of sight and stared at the sweet animal.

A few seconds was all it took.

The pussycat was coughing and spitting in distress, then howled, vomited, and had several severe muscle spasms. Then, Oreo ululated a horrific, high-pitched, mournful wail and convulsed.

To Evie's horror, the kitten then went limp.

"Oreo," she cried out, bending over, trying to pick him up.

"Don't touch him." Rocco grasped her, halting her movements. "Take her to her bedroom. Stay with her."

"*Cazzo!*" Zeno cursed. He drew her by the elbow, his eyes misty, staring at the prostrated kitten.

While he moved her toward the exit, Evie kept calling "Oreo, Oreo" over her shoulder. But there was no movement from her furry friend. "Please, Oreo... no." Not understanding what had just transpired, she was taken away in torment.

The kitten lay on the floor, inert.

Rocco lifted the cat's limp body with tender care. He cursed. His ear bent to Oreo's mouth. His fingers were on the kitten's teensy chest, stroking him, working on him, trying to revive the poor creature. He persevered for a minute or two, he even attempted to make the kitten vomit, but Oreo was not breathing.

After a while, Rocco shook his head and conceded, "Oreo is dead." Blasphemies as black as the night bellowed from his lips.

"Take her away," he yelled thunderously. Mrs. Jones, who was still standing there, paralyzed by shock with all the goings on, was seized by a guard.

CHAPTER 22

Rocco

"What happened?" Selina cried out the following morning when she returned to the house. Fabio had asked her to stop overnight after the incident, but she was too worried about her friends to stay away for long.

"Jesus. Don't burst into my office like this!" Rocco grunted. He was sitting at his desk.

"Well?" she barked.

"Mrs. Jones' cake, if I hadn't—"

"You are not serious."

"I am!"

"Where is Evie? Is she all right?"

"She's fine, resting upstairs, but she's shaken."

"Thank God. But it can't be Mrs. Jones. You're mistaken."

"Enough!" he yelled and stood up, tired of all the antics. His chair rattled with force. His nostrils flared. Zeno was with him, and his eyes widened.

What if I hadn't been watching the monitors? Rocco bristled. He had witnessed Oreo jump up from Mrs. Jones' lap after she fed him her cake concoction. The kitten gasped and puffed behind the sofa, his little body convulsing.

Rocco knew the signs. He had seen them before. The cat's reaction to the cake hit him like a shot. Poisoning was not an unusual occurrence in his line of business. If his curiosity hadn't pushed him to listen in on Evie's conversation and watch her on the monitors, his girl and child would have died. His gut twisted.

"You don't believe that, do you? Mrs. Jones? It makes no sense," his sister insisted as he paced along, struggling to control his fury.

"I paid good money to a vet to rush in a necropsy. Poison killed Oreo, and I'm not talking about chocolate though it's toxic to cats. There is no doubt about it. We analyzed the cake. It contained strychnine. It was meant to kill. You'll pardon me if I'm not in the mood."

"No way."

"Here." He handed her some papers. She took them. It was the necropsy report, and she read it.

"It's ludicrous. Where is the old lady?"

"Downstairs!"

"Not in the frigging basement! Sweet Jesus. She must be terrified."

"She's denying everything."

"Of course, she is. Because it wasn't her," Selina exclaimed. Zeno lifted his brows, and Rocco pinched the bridge of his nose with a sigh, but she wasn't finished. "Why would she do such a thing? She's been my neighbor for over three years. Why now?"

"I don't know. But the old goat will talk."

"It's preposterous! Let me speak to her."

"No!"

"But—"

"She's hysterical, anyway."

"And this surprises you? You have a sweet old lady locked up in your basement, treating her like a criminal. She's not one of your mobsters."

"Enough, I said."

"I can talk to her. I can make her relax without your heavy-handed tactics. I'll have something out of her. She's innocent. I bet my life on it. Poison, indeed. I don't believe it."

"She's of no use right now—"

"Well, if she's with your men, no wonder. Please, Rocco, let's try my way."

"Fine." He relented. "We got nothing to lose—Zeno, bring Mrs. Jones up here."

"Ask Lara to serve some tea. I'll pop up to see Evie for a moment."

"I locked her in for her safety. Tell her it's only temporary until we find out what's happening."

Evie

"Selina!" Evie jumped to her feet. "Little Oreo is dead."

"Are you okay?"

Evie nodded as tears streamed down her face. She hadn't stopped sobbing for the little creature. They stayed silent for a while, hugging and comforting each other.

"Zeno said Mrs. Jones poisoned the cake. Why would she do that? She was about to eat it with me. I don't understand," Evie said at last.

"I know. I'm going to speak to her now."

"I'll come with you."

"No. Rocco won't like it."

"I have a right to know."

"Please, Evie. He's just barely allowing me to talk to her."

"They haven't harmed her, have they?"

"No. But the poor woman must be so scared. Let me do this. I promise I'll tell you everything."

"Okay."

Her companion moved toward the door, but before she reached it, Evie called out to her, "Selina?"

"Yes?"

"I was about to put a piece of cake in my mouth. If Rocco hadn't walked in, the baby-I—"

"Shush, you are both fine." Selina went back to hug her. "We'll get to the bottom of this."

∽

Rocco

"Oh, sweetheart!" Mrs. Jones ran into Selina's arms. "They say I poisoned the cat."

"Come, sit down." Selina helped her to an armchair. The old lady plopped down on it. She sniffed in her handkerchief.

"They are accusing me of wanting to poison you and Evie. That's ridiculous." Mrs. Jones burst out crying. They were in Rocco's study. He and Zeno were there, keeping a low profile.

"Have a cup of tea. Come on, have a sip. It's nice and sweet. It'll calm you down," Selina sweet-talked her.

"Thank you, dear!" Mrs. Jones sniffed, shaking her head in misery. Her companion gave her a clean hanky to dry her tears. "You don't believe I would do such a thing, do you?"

"Of course not. But please, now think back. It's crucial. Did anyone touch the cake after you made it?"

"No. Not until I came here yesterday afternoon. The maid took it away to place it onto the stand."

"We talked to Lara, searched her and her room, and the

other kitchen personnel. We interrogated them all. We thoroughly vet our staff. There is no evidence of poison anywhere in the house or on my people. I trust them all. I'm satisfied they had nothing to do with it," Rocco replied. His tone was ice, his eyes cold and stormy.

"And you think I did it?" the woman squealed.

"Evie was about to eat it. My child and my girl would have died," he boomed, making everyone jump.

"There was strychnine in your cake," Zeno added his tone cold, staring at her.

"Strychnine? Oh, my—but it can't be!" Mrs. Jones gulped and stood, jutting her chin out in defiance. "I love these girls. They are like family to me."

"Calm yourself. No one is accusing you." Selina enticed her back into the armchair. She glanced at her brother and pressed her forefinger to her nose as if to say, *be quiet!*

"He's accusing me." The old lady pointed at Rocco, and a sob escaped her.

He tapped a fist against the table and huffed at the impasse.

"Mrs. Jones, please. Think," Selina prompted her. "Did anybody touch the cake other than yourself? Before you brought it in here. Or while you were making it?"

"No! I just told you."

"Did you have guests in the house?"

"No! I don't have visitors; my friends are in retirement homes. I call on them. I'm the only one still holding out—but after this... you aged me a decade." She glanced at Rocco with a hand over her forehead.

"Are you certain?"

"Yes. Maybe the flour or the eggs were bad or something. How should I know?" Mrs. Jones picked up the teacup, but her hands were shaking, and she placed it back on the table, unable to control herself.

"We analyzed the contents of your pantry. We found

nothing there. The only poison was in your cake. It means someone took great care to put venom in it when, or after, you made it," Rocco growled at her.

"But it can't be." Mrs. Jones burst out in tears.

Selina narrowed her eyes on him, scowling, and patted the woman's back with tenderness until she calmed down.

"Are you sure?" Selina resumed.

"I said no! No-umm-uh—"

"What?"

"Well, no, unless you count the British Gas man."

"Who?" Rocco and Zeno straightened up, intrigued.

"That nice young fellow!"

"Which fellow?"

"The guy from British Gas." Mrs. Jones paused. "He saw me making a cake the first time he showed up to read the meter."

"A man was in your kitchen?" Rocco came closer to her.

"Yes. Remember? He had just been in your apartment, too." Mrs. Jones glanced at Selina. "I told him the cake was for the ladies next door. Then, he mentioned my gas meter was too old and needed replacing. So, I made two cakes when he returned to change the gas reader; one for the girls and one for me. Well, for him. The young fellow and I had a nice cup of tea and a slice of the second cake in the kitchen. He had two huge wedges—no poison in it, you see. I'm still alive, am I not? He was fine, too, when he left. You're mistaken in accusing me, Rocco. There must be another explanation. I had forgotten about him with all this upset."

"He knew you made cakes for Selina and Evie?"

"I suppose I must have told him."

"Wait! True. We had a visit from British Gas, too. Some weeks back," Selina recalled, frowning. "On the same day, you arrived from Italy, if I'm not mistaken. Yes, it was that day."

"Well, he came back! The cakes had just come out of the oven. It was the day before yesterday. I was cooling them down on the rack when the gas man arrived."

"Can you remember his name? Did he have a badge?"

"But I was with him the whole time. He couldn't have done anything without me seeing it."

"His name, Mrs. Jones?"

"I-I—"

∼

Rocco

The following morning, Selina paced the breakfast room, restless. The atmosphere was tense. She stopped by the large window to glance at the sky but soon resumed her anxious pacing.

"You'll wear the rug off, dear. Come," Mrs. Jones said, patting the vacant seat on the couch beside her. Evie sat on the left of the old lady, her face giving form to her worry by the fixed lines of her mouth. They held hands after the stressful events of the previous two days.

A bodyguard was in the room by the wall, while another was stuck outside in the hall. Rocco was not taking any chances. The girls' security turned paramount. The door opened.

"Rocco!" Evie leapt from the sofa. "What's going on?"

"At least Mrs. Jones is no longer the suspect in this fiasco," Selina huffed. They had urged the old lady to stay the night for her safety.

"That's correct. Mrs. Jones, I hope you realize your interrogation was necessary to—" he began, but she cut him short.

"No matter, Rocco. Forget it. You did what you had to do. But why would a British Gas worker wish to poison my cake?"

"We still have a lot to investigate, but my men worked through the night and made some progress. We've established enough poison was in that cake to kill a horse," he added. They gasped. "It appears the man was a bogus British Gas employee. A sham! The I.D. card was fake, so he was masquerading as one. We confirmed this with the company. He only inspected your apartment and Selina's that first time. On the second visit, he targeted only you, Mrs. Jones. It was premeditated."

The nightmarish circumstances about the poisoned cake were coming to light.

"Was he the same guy in both apartments?" Evie asked.

"Yes, the same. We checked the cameras in the building. When he was in Selina's apartment, he must have postponed whatever he had planned to do then. My arrival put him off. A blessing I showed up when I did. I dread to think what might—"

"Twice, now," Evie whispered, then clearing her voice with a tiny cough, she said, "I mean, you were in the right place at the right time for us."

"Three times, poppet, if you count Jake at the restaurant." He winked at her. "But I'm not keeping tabs."

"Rocco has become your guardian angel, dear!" Mrs. Jones concluded.

He laughed, and Evie's cheeks pinkened.

"My brother has been called many things, many of them unrepeatable. But never an angel," Selina scoffed.

Rocco's brows lifted, but he ignored her sarcasm.

"The man was disguised, but we'll get to him," he continued instead.

"Who is he? Why is he doing this?" the old lady asked innocently.

"We'll find him, don't you worry." Rocco had recognized the man. It was Nico Columbano. The fellow had moved up another gear from robbing their nightclubs and murdering his men. The bastard now wanted to take a swipe at the very heart of his family. Rocco didn't mention this to the girls. This was the clan's problem. The less he said to them, the better. No reason to frighten them more than they already were.

"But how did he put the poison in my cake. I was there with him the entire time."

"We may never know exactly. I could hypothesize the man had a syringe with the poison with him. He would have needed only a few seconds to inject the cake while you were somehow distracted or turned the other way. Who knows."

"How dreadful. And to think I was there, it gives me the shivers."

"But why?" Evie insisted.

"What's important is you are all safe now. But you must be careful and vigilant. I've doubled security in the house. Fabio has done the same in his. Follow our instructions. Do what we say."

"We will." Selina understood soon enough this might be something related to the clan. She drew a deep breath but opted for silence—no need to upset her friend in her condition.

"Please stay together as much as you can."

"Why should anyone want to kill us?" Evie asked.

Rocco went to her and caressed her face with his knuckles, his eyes soft on her, at her innocence. His world was far too removed from hers. He had to admit it. She couldn't imagine any such thing. Bless her! He tucked a loose strand of her hair behind her ear.

She leaned into his touch.

He hadn't spoken to her for the last week. Only fleeting seconds here and there. He missed her. Now in the gloomy atmosphere, he craved to wrap his arms around her. To comfort her, to hold her, to protect her.

"This was not meant for you, *amore*," he said. He glanced at his sister, who rolled her eyes and could guess he was lying for Evie's sake. Rocco was sure Selina and Evie were both Nico's targets, but he chose not to burden her with this, not wanting to alarm her. "This bogus gas employee poisoned the cake. I'm certain. Whatever his plan, we nipped it in the bud. You are safe now. We'll find him. I promise."

CHAPTER 23

Evie

Greenery was sprigging out of the earth with the power of nature. New leaves unfurled as plant life resumed its cycle. The early spring blossoms with their colorful shades lifted the spirit. The tepid winter sunshine yielded to a more vigorous incandescent star as the new season eased in. The days were becoming longer, lighter and warmer, though the nights were still chilly.

However, Evie's mind drifted to Oreo with a heavy heart. To his soft, cuddly fur and tender purrs when she stroked him. To his cruel death! That man meant this death for her and her friend. Even if Rocco tried to shield her from it, she knew. She wasn't a fool.

Who could have done such a thing? She missed the lovable kitten so much but chose to disengage from these gloomy thoughts.

Evie had a bath after supper. The pleasant glow and plenty of scented salts in the water revived her. She felt calmer, but keeping her anxiousness and sadness at bay was difficult. She opened a large towel, dried herself off, and then wrapped herself in the bathrobe. It was fluffy and enveloped her in coziness. As if enormous arms were flooding her with bliss. She sighed.

That night, the crispy nip in the air slipped into her bones despite the warming robe. A slight shiver subdued her. Perhaps it was because of the weariness of her situation or what happened to poor Oreo.

"I'm fine, Lara. There is no need," she said as the maid entered the room with an armful of logs. "Please, don't fuss."

"You had a shock, Miss Logan. Besides, these are Mr. LaTorre's orders."

"And, of course, we cannot disobey him, right?" Evie said with a mischievous smile, and they both smuggled out a sonorous, naughty giggle. Lara piled the logs in the hearth, kindling it until she got the fire going.

"Goodnight, Miss Logan."

"Thank you, Lara, goodnight." The maid left her.

Evie sat on the couch in the alcove facing the fireplace. The wooden logs flickered and smoldered, blazing heat from the hearth. The crackling and popping sounds of the timber burning seemed to comfort her, and it felt homely. A log fell from the central bunch. She knelt by the grate and poked it to shove the drifting wood back into the flaming fire. She returned to the loveseat and picked up her book.

As an hour passed, she became warm and stretched on the settee in the cosseted room.

Though her heart was still heavy with sorrow for Oreo, Evie released part of the stress that had plagued her, feeling more human again and a little pampered.

She had yearned for Rocco, now more than ever. He had turned into the elusive man. He had spent no time with her for days, brief moments here and there when they were all together. *Was he still upset with her?* She drew in a sharp air intake and hissed a long, slow breath out.

"That's a big, wondrous sigh!" The velvety, manly voice came from behind her.

"Rocco!" she squealed, rising abruptly. He moved around the settee to stand a few steps from her. It took all her self-control to stop herself from rushing into his arms.

"Are you okay, *micina?*"

"Yes."

"I'm so sorry about Oreo, Evie," he said. His voice had a gentleness to it, and it caressed her ears. His eyes mellowed on her.

"I know you are." She felt slightly awkward with him since her attempted escape. But he grinned.

Sweet mercy, he looked like a dish in his fitted light-blue cotton turtle neck and dark gray chinos. With no socks, the black loafers on his feet made him look so continental, demure, *and damn hot.*

She had always liked him from the first day she met him. Of Selina's handsome brothers, Rocco had been the one to tickle her fancy. Even engaged to Jake, as she was then, Evie had admired Rocco's gracefulness and attractiveness. His charm and wit had stirred her soul. She had even spotted his menacing, sultry greened-eye stare once or twice, showing so darkly, making her shiver.

Maybe it was the eyes.

Oh, the fantasies she had about him... *nothing wrong with fantasies,* she told herself. Every healthy woman had one, and Rocco was hers. It wasn't until she broke up with Jake, she transformed her dreamy fantasy into reality. It still filled her with shame at how she begged him to make love to her that night in November.

Rocco had saved her life, she owed him her life. These were the confusing thoughts, rioting in her mind, as she appreciated his beauty now.

"You are glowing! Your cheeks are red," he said, his voice soft.

"The fire…" she mumbled, but she peered at her bare feet. She shuffled, self-conscious. Her nakedness underneath the cozy bathrobe felt a little naughty, and when he scanned her from head to toe with hungry eyes, a thrill ran down her spine. She secured the knots on the belt of her robe tighter with an awkward smile and wrapped her arms around herself.

"You should be in bed, resting. You had a shock, a stressful time. I'll see you to bed," Rocco said, his gaze fixed on hers. An amused, sexy half grin graced his lips, and heat spread between her thighs. She flushed.

"I'll read for a while—" Evie mumbled, but a call came in on his phone. He flipped through his cell, massaged his temple and muttered an imprecation in Italian.

"I need to take this. Give me ten minutes. I'll sleep in here tonight."

"What?" Her eyes grew big and round. "With me?"

"On the couch. For protection." He pointed at the alcove.

"I see."

His phone kept ringing. He sighed and took the call. He winked at her before moving outside to the hallway.

Oh, sweet Jesus.

The warmth at the apex of her legs grew. Her heart was thundering in her chest. A rollercoaster of emotions, delight, desire, longing and excitement mingled and conflicted within her. Her inner voice told her *calm down, don't get too excited.* She glanced at the settee and at his big retreating frame as he left the room.

It was clear he had not forgiven her for trying to escape, despite the concerns about the poisoning. He regarded it as a betrayal, not to mention her lies about the baby. His week's absence and the evidence he wished to bed on the sofa were all a testament to it.

She picked up her book while waiting for him, but try as she might, she couldn't focus on a single line.

∽

Evie

Evie's thoughts absorbed her, so she didn't hear Rocco return to the room.

"I told you to go to bed," he said, his eyes narrowed on her.

"No. You said you were coming back to see me to bed. I was waiting for you."

"Are you going to argue with me?"

"No, I'm just—"

"Good." He took the book from her hands and placed it on the small table. He gently pulled her up by the elbow and marched her out of the cozy room into the main bedroom. He let go of her arm. He reached for the collar of her robe, ready to take it off. But she slapped his hands away and bolted backward as if he had burned her.

"What's the matter?"

"Nothing!" She shrugged her shoulders, and she averted his gaze.

"Are you cold?"

"No."

"Take off your robe, and get into bed." He eyed her up and down. A hint of an amused smile passed over his lips.

She blushed.

"Maybe later."

"We have a big day tomorrow. You must rest tonight."

"Why? What's happening?"

"Do as I say. Off with the robe and go to bed."

"No!" She closed it much tighter over her body. Her

cheeks flushed scarlet. She had omitted to tell him she was nude underneath. Her nakedness would suggest she was inviting him. As if she had done it on purpose to tempt him, so she wanted to maintain her pride. But something must have shown on her face as a grin curved on his lips. She realized he was playing with her.

Arrogant man! He knows I'm naked underneath.

"What's the matter, Evie? Why won't you take off the robe?"

"I'm not sleepy yet. I'll read for a bit if you don't mind."

"Oh, but I do mind!"

"What?"

"I bet you are wearing nothing underneath."

"Rocco!"

"I've seen you naked before, Evie. Don't be coy with me."

"Yes, but we are in the friends' zone now. We share a baby, but—"

"Friends? What the hell gave you that idea, woman?" he barked in irritation.

She flinched. "You are right. Perhaps we cannot even be friends and—"

"I beg your pardon?"

"Well, you haven't talked to me in days other than when necessary. Tonight, you sleep on the couch. What am I to think?"

"May I remind you, *micina,* when I caught you that day trying to run away from me, you said that you and I were over! Adamant that it was the end for us, remember?"

"Well, I-I was upset. And we argue a lot."

"And you lie!"

"Ah! You haven't forgiven me then."

"I want to make love to you, Evie. God knows, I do!" he said. His eyes were full of promise, gazing at her. And the image of his cock plunging into her pussy drenched her.

"But you ignored me for days. You wouldn't be here if someone hadn't tried to poison me."

"Do you still wish to leave my home? Get away from me?"

"I can't now. Selina and I may be in danger with that guy still lurking around."

"If there was no danger, would you go?"

"I owe you my life, Rocco—"

"Never mind that," he pressed on wanting an answer. "Would you?"

"And I thank you. My baby and I would be dead if it weren't for you."

"It's our baby, *micina.* But that's not what I asked you. I guess, you'll be glad to go when this is over. Admit it."

"Me?" She frowned, confused, rubbing her tummy relentlessly. *Oh, no, not at all!* She blushed furiously, thinking it was the other way around, but she would not give herself away by saying it. She shuffled on her feet like a kid instead, not liking the way this conversation was going.

∼

Rocco

With his other women, Rocco had alternated between sex, passion, and long periods of silence in the midst. He never missed them during those long absent periods. Hence, it was easy for him to disengage from them when it came to parting. He offered not much of himself other than sex. But with Evie, it felt different. This wasn't only about the child, no, or just sex.

First, Rocco had yearned for the girl with surprising intensity, making his resolution not to see Evie during that week much more challenging than he thought possible—

which had greatly exasperated him. It had taken all his willpower to avoid her for that long.

Second, the absolute joy of being with her again now overwhelmed him, more than he was willing to concede. Even the frivolous matter about her robe amused and thrilled him. *Her coyness is adorable.*

Still, he wanted an answer.

"Do you want to go? Tell me!" His tone demanded a reply, and she shrugged her shoulders. Her eyes bounced from him to anywhere in the room, to avoid his penetrating gaze before she gave herself away.

"You said you want me here until the birth, but you know I wouldn't leave my child!"

"We are going in circles, Evie. That's not what I asked. Let's leave the baby aside for a moment. I'm talking about us. Do you want to leave—me? Yes or no?"

"Would you let me go?"

"Christ, answer me!"

"No!" she whispered, blushing furiously.

"No, what?"

"No, I don't want to go," she mumbled averting his gaze.

"Good. You see. That wasn't so hard, was it?" Rocco uttered, caressing her cheek, his gaze soft on her. "Take off your robe, poppet."

"I'd rather not—"

"Now, Evie!"

"I-I—" she started, but he grabbed the lapels of her robe and yanked it open, sending it off her shoulders and down her arms.

She yelped as she stood there, stark naked before him, shielding herself from view with her arm and her hand as the garment pooled at her ankles.

Rocco took a long look reveling in her delicious body. His nostrils flared. His eyes darkened. He turned her around and fisted her hair. She gasped.

"You are so beautiful, *micina,*" he whispered in her ear.

"Rocco…"

"Forearms on the quilt, and spread your legs, feet apart." He startled her as he dragged her by the elbow toward the bed. "Butt in the air. You know the posture." His tone was imperious as he helped her into the position. He placed a pillow under her tummy for comfort. "And hold your head up."

"Please…" She knew what was coming.

"You need to learn some obedience, *amore.* Or we will argue forever." And he spanked her twice briskly. She wailed and wiggled her bottom. "Don't move!" He steadied her, grabbing her hips.

"Rocco, please." She clenched her buttocks, to prepare herself for the next round. He followed with a pair of smacks on each buttock. Her flesh stung, bringing tears to her eyes.

"Tell me again. This time straight! No going in circles. So, you are staying with me, then."

"Yes," she whimpered, and she meant it, despite her blazing backside.

"No more running away?" An almighty wallop flattened her pillowy backside.

"No. I promise. Please…" she pleaded.

"No more arguing? No tricks or lies?" he asked as he smacked her again, making her wriggle.

"No."

"At last, we agree." He stared at her heavenly, cherry-red bottom with his handiwork stamped all over it, and he delighted in it. Rocco fondled her flesh, massaging it, and a low hiss left her lungs, somewhere between a moan and a mumble that sounded much like "wow" to him.

He smiled and slapped her ass with a light hand, playfully now, alternating it with tender strokes on her skin. Then his fingers teased her wet opening, and she moaned.

Evie

Her pussy was drenched and throbbed.

"You like my spankings, Evie?"

"Rocco, I-I—"

"Remember, no lies!"

"I do," she sniffled. Her face flushed at the admission, and he grinned delighted.

"I can see that. You are dripping wet. Do you want me to stop touching you?" he said, still teasing her folds.

"No, don't stop!" she moaned.

A crisp laugh left his mouth, but his fingers slid inside her, her hips rolling through each thrust.

"Do you like it when I do this?" he asked close to her ear, with a long thrust inside her.

"Yes," she breathed. The heat raising in her body searing every nerve-ending as he pumped her. She wriggled her delectable bottom. Her blood surged in her veins. Her heart pounded in her chest as her climax exploded, shuddering her frame.

"Do not move," he commanded when her orgasm subsided.

Rocco undressed. His steely manhood was free at last to have his fun.

She glanced at him over her shoulder, still in the same position with her backside in the air. Her breathing was labored.

He leaned over her and he filled her, inch by slow-agonizing inch, as his cock entered her from behind, stretching her pussy to accommodate his enormous erection. He wrapped his arms around her body to fondle her breasts. He pinched her nipples.

Rocco whispered in her ear. She wasn't sure what he said in Italian, but from his tone, she knew the words were amorous. She'd bet they were even romantic if she could understand them. She quivered but egged him on brazenly as he thrust into her.

"Faster!"

"This little pussy is so greedy for me."

"Please…" she begged, and he pounded into her. Her eyes rolled back in ecstasy. He fisted her hair and tugged it backward. Her back arched.

"Who do you belong to, Evie?"

"Darling…"

"Tell me!" Rocco pulled her locks harder while his cock worked his magic inside her.

"To you. I belong to you," she said in quick puffs of breath.

"That's right, *micina.* Mine!"

"Rocco…" Her butt was aching, but the pounding of flesh against flesh after the spanking only increased the lustful hotness in her body, heightening her senses. Her throbbing pussy clenched around him. He lay claim to her body with the strength and the vigor of a man possessing his woman, powerfully, until she screamed his name through her second climax. He soon followed, and his seed blasted inside her. They slumped limply on the bed, side by side.

"Fuck, Evie. I missed you," he said through ragged breath.

"Me, too." Her chest was heaving, and a soft, happy giggle escaped her. She nuzzled his neck. His mouth captured hers. The kiss lingered on and on, and it was the sweetest smooch.

"You naughty girl," he said when they parted from the kiss, caressing her cheek tenderly. He leapt to his feet out of bed. He took some tissues from the bedside table and cleaned himself and her.

"You like it when I'm naughty!" she replied, and he

lifted his brows.

"I knew you were naked under the robe. I saw your PJs on the armchair."

"That's cheating," she uttered solemnly. He snorted and brushed his lips on hers.

"Come. It's a little chilly tonight. We need to keep the baby warm." He tucked her into bed as if she were a child, caressing her face. "God, you are so beautiful. Go to sleep now. I'll join you after a shower."

I'll be damned if I've figured out why a demigod like him is interested in somebody like me. Someone with no grace, no beauty, plump, and with child, even if the baby is his. She dismissed the thought and willed herself to stay in the moment.

"Are you staying on the couch?"

"What do you think?"

She giggled and blew him a kiss.

He didn't stay on the couch that night. Oh, no! When he returned to bed, Evie was still waiting for him, and the earlier lovemaking prelude became a full-blown, powerful symphony of devotion, desire, and ardor throughout the night. Each orchestrated movement of the sweet music between them built to a grand finale—turning their passion into a crescendo of pure emotion—and by the time sleep conquered them, they were intoxicated with love.

∽

Rocco

They joined Selina and Mrs. Jones in the breakfast room the next day. Just before they entered the room, Evie paused, and reached for Rocco's hand.

It startled him. He looked at his big hand folded between Evie's much smaller, softer ones and gazed at her. She offered him an adoring grin. Her beautiful, innocent smile was the loveliest, sunniest thing he'd ever seen, and in his dark world, this sweet light had become a real commodity. It filled him with lightheartedness, soothing him.

What was it about this girl that triggered these sudden emotions? He couldn't say. He kissed her cheek. This cozy, affectionate, and solicitous concern from a woman didn't often happen to him.

Oh, yes! He attracted plenty of attention in a sexy, overt way from women, but this was an intimate gesture, a heartwarming token from Evie, an innermost moment for them. A thrilling joy rushed through him at this very simple, tender and blissful act.

Lifting his hand, still wrapped in hers, he cupped her delicate cheeks in both hands, inhaling her natural flowery scent. Never dropping his gaze, he needed—no, he craved —to say something.

"Evie, I-I—" Overwrought by sentiment, words failed him.

Not sure what he wanted to say, she snuggled closer to him instead. Lifting onto her toes, her lips brushed his almost reverently. Her heavenly tongue slipped into his mouth.

He drew back, still holding her cheeks, and smiled from ear to ear. His mouth captured hers, and her delicious, warm little tongue resumed its sexy tango, insistent and glorious, curling, diving, swirling, plundering him. He allowed her to continue, enjoying the moment and wallowing in her kiss, chirping at him and silently expressing her passion for him. Soon he responded in kind. He returned the kiss with the same fervor, with mighty power, allowing it to do the talking, to reveal how he felt about her. They kissed with ardor. The world around them vanished. Their worries faded into nothingness. Only they existed in the universe, lingering in the pleasure, settling in the swell of the romantic moment engulfing them.

They had kissed many times before, but this one seemed extraordinary. Expressive! Perhaps, it was because the previous night, they had felt their lovemaking so strongly, so profoundly, and in touch with their souls. So, the kiss swept them into an otherworldly magic occasion. As if they'd kissed for the first time, wishing to tell the other a story. When they parted, their eyes met, languorous and shiny, flowing in a current of love. It set off a new stage in their liaison. And they were never the same again.

"Good God—" he puffed.

"Umm..." Evie giggled knowingly, in a similar awe. Her sound was girlish and limpid. Like the chiming of a church bell on a Sunday, it massaged his heart and soul as if it were a soft hand.

"Come," Rocco muttered with a sigh. "Let's go in, or I'll take you upstairs again." He clasped her wrist and pulled her forward, opening the door and guiding her over the threshold.

At last, they came into the room.

"Good morning!" they purred as they took their seats.

"I bet it is. You are glowing, Evie," Selina snorted.

Lara served their breakfast plates with a cappuccino for Evie—decaffeinated, as Rocco insisted—and espresso for him.

"You mind your own business if you want to finish your breakfast," Rocco exclaimed while Evie rolled her eyes at her friend's remark.

"Any progress?" Mrs. Jones asked him with an amused grin.

"What?" He frowned, not getting it, and then realized what she was referring to. "Do you mean with the British Gas man?"

"Yes."

"No, not quite."

"He has been busy with his sweetheart," Selina remarked in a sing-song, still taunting them.

"You are more annoying than usual this morning," he lectured her. Before there was a retort from his sister, a call broke in on his cell. He looked at the caller. "Excuse me. I've got to take this."

"Selina, please stop pestering us!" Evie grumbled when he left the room.

"Oh, 'us' is it?" her friend scoffed. "So you kissed and made up, then?"

"Stop!"

"Sorry, I can't help teasing you, but I'm glad you did. This is how it should be. For heaven's sake, you are having a baby together. Time to grow up," Selina responded with a snort.

"You lovebirds look so cute today. It's a joy to see." Mrs. Jones stood up and picked up a jug from the sideboard. "More coffee, anyone?" She served Selina another cup and helped herself.

Rocco came back in, his cheerful face replaced by a frosty mask.

"What's wrong?" Evie asked.

"Ladies, please finish your breakfast quickly. You need to pack. We are flying home this afternoon."

"You mean to Italy?" Selina's jaw slacked in surprise.

"Yes. We'll go to the summer house on the Island. You'll be fine there." Rocco meant well-protected there. He hadn't said they were stretching themselves thin guarding Fabio's house and his in London. His brother's family was reputed to be in danger, too, as well as the rest of the family in Italy. They would be safer all together in one home.

"What's happening? I thought you had state-of-the-art security here," Selina asked, pale.

"I do!"

"Why then? Is this a crisis?"

"No. Just a precaution, please hurry, girls."

"Why don't you answer my question—" Selina insisted, but he shrugged his shoulders.

"You mean me, too?" Evie asked.

"I do, poppet," Rocco scoffed. "You don't think I'm leaving you here."

"But I cannot go to Italy just like that. What about school?" Evie's apprehension raised at this sudden problem. The danger became more evident, too, her anxiety escalating in her heart.

"You'll do your classes online for the rest of the year. When the time comes, if you cannot return to London to hold your exams, I'll run a team over from the college for you and Selina to take them there. It'll all be valid. Nothing speaks louder than a huge donation to a university's fund. Or the potential to build a new wing. They become creative, then—Zoom in to your study group and lessons. So don't trouble yourself. We'll make it work. I promise."

"But what about Mum and Dad?"

"We have a car in half an hour to take us there. So you can say goodbye. They can stay over with us whenever they choose."

"But the farm—"

"I'll bring in someone to look after the farm while they call on you in Italy. Besides, it won't be forever." He omitted to mention it was the only way to keep her safe.

"What about Mrs. Jones? She'll come, too?" Selina glanced at the old lady.

"Oh, don't fret about me. I was going to stay with my nephew. I've been promising to visit him for ages. Now, I am. He lives in Northamptonshire. I'll be fine there. After all, it's not me that man wants, is it?" The woman stared at Rocco, but he ignored her remark.

"There is no hurry, Mrs. Jones. Settle here until you want to go. I'll leave a skeleton staff, anyway. When you are ready, one of my guards will drive you. He'll stick around until we know you are okay."

"Thank you. You are too kind."

"Girls please, get a move on."

"It means I'll be living with… ahem—" Evie said, all flustered.

Rocco snorted. "With me, poppet, yes!" He winked.

CHAPTER 24

Evie

Evie had never seen a private jet close up, let alone traveled in one.

Her surroundings mesmerized her as she flew to Naples in style that afternoon. She peered at the clouds from the window seat. The luxurious honey-colored leather chair was so soft she sank in its glorious squashiness, still wallowing in it after an hour into the flight.

A brand new life awaited her in Italy.

Yet, Rocco's unorthodox line of business, sometimes his arbitrary behavior, his notorious family, and the danger she and her baby faced worried her. It added to her uneasiness. But she was learning to accept it all. At heart—and she wouldn't admit to this—it thrilled her too, for the simple reason she was with Rocco!

At first, she had denied him fatherhood with her lies. This morning, he implied they were in a relationship.

Go, figure!

An entanglement for sure—doubts still assailed her—

but whatever it was, she shared it with the man of her dreams. In truth, despite the difficulties they experienced, her heart had finally and utterly capitulated to him.

Evie worshipped Rocco and fell for him with all her heart, body and soul. She speculated perhaps she had always loved him, even when engaged to Jake. Who knew! She had been in a nightmarish situation where she had lied to Rocco for months. Now, she would meet his entire family in his home country. And it thrilled her.

Her world had shifted, tumbled topsy-turvy, though she didn't mind it one bit as long as she was with him.

The only downturn was the melancholy of leaving her parents behind. That morning, saying goodbye to them had grieved her. Her parents were worried about her, but they liked her new man, despite what he was. He charmed them. So, when the brief visit ended, Rocco had hooked her folks completely. They were eating out of his hand—more than on his first visit.

On this occasion, to her great embarrassment, when her parents introduced him to a neighbor, they called him "our son-in-law". Her mother had appraised her father about the baby, too.

"Rocco, put a ring on her finger. Don't you feel it's time? Before the baby comes," her father said to him out loud with a pat on his shoulder.

"Dad!" Evie chastised him. It mortified her. Rocco laughed it off instead, with a short deep rumble that did something to her insides.

"Do you think she'll have me?" he asked in his nonchalant, silvery tone with an amused grin, glancing at her as she blushed scarlet.

"Oh, she will. Mind my words," Bridget countered before Evie could object.

"Mum!" She scoffed. "Will you stop this?" To her great

relief, they left soon after, avoiding any more awkward moments.

Rocco's mother wouldn't behave like this. She imagined the woman would be too worldly for such remarks. Assuming Evie wouldn't embarrass herself with the lady, *which I'm more than capable of doing.*

Her mind was in overdrive with these thoughts as they flew to Naples.

Evie was sitting beside Rocco on the plane. He had his laptop open on the mahogany table, talking to Fabio opposite him with Melania. They were in a cluster of four seats facing each other. Selina was across the aisle, coloring a book with Lola. Zeno, Tito and a handful of their men were in a section at the rear of the plane.

"We'll have fun in Capri. It's a beautiful island. The family is great," Melania said out of the blue, seeing a concerned expression on Evie's face.

"Don't lie to her, Mel." Fabio chuckled. "It takes a while to get used to my family."

"Oh, don't worry, they don't bite."

"Not much!" Fabio scoffed

"Leave her alone. She's worried as it is," Rocco grumbled.

"No, I'm not." Evie shook her head.

"You are not worried?"

"No." The truth, she was, but she didn't want to sound silly.

"Good." He put his arm around her shoulders and pulled her to him for a kiss. "You'll be fine, *amore*."

"Come on, lover-boy. We need to talk." Fabio rolled his eyes and rose from his seat. Rocco followed. They moved further back on the aircraft—it was time for business.

"Would you read to me, please?" Lola asked, passing her a storybook as she plopped herself beside Evie.

"Sure, sweetheart."

After a while, Lola fell asleep. Evie covered her with a blanket and moved to the row of seats behind to give Lola space to stretch her legs.

Rocco

"The bastard attacked one of our warehouses in Devon two days ago, stealing the cargo and wounding a guard. He left a message on the wall. *'Next, your girls, young blood'* worries me. I'm sure it's him." Evie heard what Fabio said, and she gasped. She was closer to where the brothers sat in a private alcove on the plane. She lounged low on the seat, pretending to sleep and staying out of sight, while listening to the conversation.

"What's your view? Who do you think he means?" Rocco asked. He couldn't hide the concern in his voice.

"Selina? Lola and Melania? Your guess is as good as mine."

"Fuck, perhaps all our girls, including Evie. Who knows. He wants to play dirty. The girls won't be safe until we deal with him."

Evie drew in a sharp breath. She placed a hand over her mouth to stifle the sound. She realized why they were going to Italy. It wasn't just the poisoning. A man stole from them, wounding people and leaving a warning. She shivered.

Your daddy and I will protect you! She thought, caressing her baby bump, but she stayed on the brothers' conversation, not wishing to miss anything.

"Is it worth talking to Federico about Selina? As her fiancé, he'll want to know," Rocco added.

"It depends on what Sebastiano thinks. But given their friendship, he'll probably tell him. Federico may demand to marry her sooner," Fabio replied.

"His name alone is protection for her. It will discourage anybody wanting to lay a finger on her."

"That murdering son of a bitch doesn't play by the rules, Rocco."

"Perhaps you are right."

"It won't work with that bastard. Remember, his gang kidnapped Mel? Our name didn't protect her then. The pig knows he is a dead man and is bent on causing as much damage as possible. But you should marry Evie, to send a signal to the community. Besides, she is having your child. What the hell are you waiting for?"

"Not now, Fabio! I'll have enough of that when we get home."

"She's a lovely girl. I thought you liked her."

"I do! Very much so. More than you imagine."

Evie whimpered. She placed a hand over her mouth, hoping they had not heard her, but her heart did a summersault.

"You don't say," Fabio scoffed.

"The girls will be safe at home." Rocco switched back to the burning issues, refusing to be drawn into a conversation about Evie.

"Fine!" Fabio snorted, knowing he wouldn't get anything else from him on this.

"Will that scum be aware we left England?" Rocco added. "I want him to know we've gone to Italy."

"I asked my cell in London to blabber about it on purpose. If he follows us, he'll have to expose himself, and it will be easier to capture him in Italy."

"I won't let him harm the girls."

Evie was astonished. A chill ran down her spine, hearing them talk like this. Did they know the culprit? Then, the brothers switched from English to rapid Italian, and she lost the rest of the conversation.

God, I'm over my head with this family. But it was too late. Her heart belonged to Rocco.

Thus, she fell into a frightful sleep for a while. Rocco woke her up.

They were preparing for landing.

They went through the arrival passport formalities on the plane. Several Bentley sedans picked them up at the airport terminal in Naples.

Evie and Rocco were alone in one car. Selina had gone with Fabio and his family. Other cars collected Zeno, Tito, and the other men Evie recognized from the house in London.

A call came in on Rocco's phone. He took it with an apologetic smile. He spoke too rapidly and Evie was unable to understand a word of the Italian uttered.

The cavalcade of cars motored along the elegant promenade in Via Caracciolo, heading toward Mergellina, the second port in the city.

"We'll sail straight to the island. We won't have time to stay at my house in Naples tonight. I'll show you the sights some other time," he said when he finished his call.

Evie nodded, wondering whether their safety was the real reason.

CHAPTER 25

Evie

The port buzzed with people and clamor. They proceeded to the private mooring marina to a grand yacht.

"This is it," said Lola with pride. "When I grow up, Zeno will teach me to steer it. I'll be the skipper, all by myself."

"Is that so, *stellina?*" Rocco ruffled her hair.

"True, he promised. Didn't you, Zeno?"

"Sure," the man answered.

"When?"

"Sweetheart, we need to get going," Fabio prompted her, lifting her into his arms. They all climbed on board.

Evie's eyes grew huge at the sight of the splendid vessel. She had moved from Rocco's luxurious townhouse in London, flew in a regal jet to Italy—bypassing, according to Melania, a majestic villa in Naples overlooking the Gulf—and now, this large pleasure yacht was taking them to the renowned island of Capri. Nobody in the village in North Kesteven, would believe her.

Zeno busied himself with the navigation charts, while

Tito and a handful of men, traveling with them, were helping with the preparations. She wondered if they were there to safeguard them.

They eventually set sail in the Tyrrhenian Sea. The Gulf of Naples glittered in the sunshine like a colorful scenic postcard as they glided away. Rocco must have seen Evie's look of awe. He winked at her from across the deck. *God, he is handsome!* A tingling between her legs reminded her of the vigorous night of passion. Her female parts were still sore. A warmth spread through her at the recollection.

Mercy! Rocco had made her body sizzle. His lovemaking had been intoxicating. He had marked her in a few spots and her pussy was red and swollen. She'd seen a faint imprint—in the rough shape of his large hand—on her buttocks in the mirror that morning.

Our best night yet.

She sighed.

"Come." Lola showed her around the imposing and luxurious boat.

Selina and Melania had prepared refreshments in the galley below deck. She helped them carry out the beverages to the upper bridge. A cool breeze picked up as they cruised along.

Evie brought a tray to one end of the bridge, housing a study.

Rocco and Fabio stopped talking when she entered, the brothers having retired to it soon after boarding. She placed the tray on the large desk. She had an inkling of what they might be discussing. She glanced around her. The ambience was rather dark and severe in contrast with the light and relaxed atmosphere on deck.

The decor was stately in black stained high-gloss wood and gold-leaf panels on two walls, while highlighted with red lacquer on another. The wide desk in ebony had gilt detailing and an oxblood-red leather top, with matching high-back chairs in red leather—where they now sat in comfort. It had a floor-to-ceiling window on one side with a balcony, giving it an expansive view over the waters.

"You have a balcony out to sea?"

"Evie, we left orders not to be disturbed," Rocco spoke with a frown.

"I know, but I thought you may like a drink," she said, ignoring the mild rebuke. "How come I haven't seen this before? The balcony, I mean, from the outside."

"You didn't because it wasn't there. It's retractable. I can deploy it out using a button, with a single click," he explained with an indulgent expression, like talking to a child.

"A fold-out terrace?"

"Yes." He sighed patiently.

"Show me." Her eyes wide like those of a kid with a new toy.

"Evie—"

"Please!"

"Right," he huffed. Sometimes, she could be cute and so annoying altogether like at this moment. But he complied and, pressing the button, the balcony retracted. Then, it went out to sea again. "Happy now?"

"I'll be damned!" She stared at it, rooted to the spot, her mouth agape.

"Evie?"

"Yes?" she asked absentmindedly, still in awe, looking at it.

"Thank you," he said drily, with half a grin. "You can go now."

"Oh, sure. Sorry." She moved toward the exit, glanced over her shoulder at the retractable balcony, and scoffed, shaking her head. Then she directed a glimpse at him before leaving. She could tell he wasn't best pleased with the interruption, but he winked at her, somewhat amused.

The rest of the party settled on deck.

Zeno was at the controls in the cockpit at the helm, steering the vessel.

They sailed on the Tyrrhenian Sea, a branch of the Mediterranean, off the coast of Western Italy. Their destination was the island of Capri, in the Gulf of Naples just off the Sorrento Peninsula in Southern Italy.

As they sailed along, the island emerged from the waters. Selina pointed it out to her. Evie had read in magazines about the picturesque island with exotic scenery and its dramatic coastline peppered with beautiful villas, the glitziest and most glamorous of the islands in the Gulf. As she contemplated it now, it was a striking vision.

"There you are. We thought we'd lost you," Melania teased as the brothers joined them on deck.

"Beautiful, isn't she?" Rocco said, referring to Capri, seeing Evie staring at the place. "It is said that Charles Dickens once noted: *'There is no place in the world with such delightful possibilities as this little island'.* So true."

"I'll say!"

"Did you enjoy the crossing?"

"I loved it."

"There! Our house. The one in the far corner." He pointed to it as it came into view.

"The white one? I thought you said it was a summer house, but that's a grand villa."

"I suppose so."

She saw a magnificent mansion perched atop the cliff in Punta Carena nestled between luscious greenery and unobstructed views of the sea. It was Palladian in its dimensions, soaring above the waters.

"I hope you like it," he added.

At the junction of the two Gulfs, the villa's location opened up to stunning panoramic views that stretched from the Faraglioni and Marina Piccola on one side to the

Gulf of Naples on the other. The remote spot and the extensive grounds evoked a sense of tranquility, wealth and affluence. The pristine white house was built on four floors, with one going below ground where the carved square windows were visible in the rock. Its seclusion gave the owners of the large estate the privacy they desired.

"You bet," she chirped.

The family transferred to a speedboat for the last leg of the journey, whisking them away.

"Zeno will moor the yacht at the wharf in Marina Piccola, just south of the island. The motorboat will take us home," Rocco said.

The speedboat moored at the LaTorre dock in the secluded, private cove below the house.

The sun looked like a ball of fire, low in the skyline with a blend of reds, yellows and oranges, skirting the water on the horizon as the day began to fade. They disembarked and walked the length of the wooden jetty and up via steep stone steps toward the villa.

"It's unnecessary, Rocco. I'll be fine," she said with a sweet smile at his insistence.

"No, Evie. These steps are treacherous at the best of times. I'm not taking any risks." Rocco wouldn't hear otherwise. So she relented. He carried her up in his arms as if she weighed nothing. As they climbed, Mediterranean-style terraces and gardens opened up at various levels. A large pool nestled in, too. The scent of the sea filled the air. It mingled with that of citrus trees, vibrantly colored bougainvillea and sweet jasmine. Her senses perked up.

"We should go shopping. The island has wonderful stores," Selina proposed with a bright smile.

"You do realize why we are here." Rocco frowned. "Let me be clear about this. I wish to be informed of where you are at all times. *Capito?* No going off without our permission." He directed this instruction to the girls, but his eyes were fixed on Evie. They all nodded. Fabio agreed with his brother, warning Melania in the same manner. Selina rolled her eyes and feigned a military salute.

It didn't surprise Evie. Rocco had become more protective of her after Oreo's poisoning. No wonder, given what she had heard on the plane.

He was turning proprietorial about her, possessive, and none too subtle.

And somehow, it pleased her.

CHAPTER 26

Evie

The group sat around a massive oak table on the large terrace, basking in the scented dusk.

Members of the staff came out with refreshments to welcome them.

"This is Miss Logan," Rocco introduced her to an older woman. "Dora is our housekeeper. She's been with us for an eternity and is like family to us, similar to a dear aunt." He kissed the rotund, white-haired, still full of beans, woman's cheek.

"You make me sound like a relic from a museum."

"You'll look after my girlfriend while she is here, right?" he whispered in Dora's ear, who, shocked at his admission, raised her eyebrows when her gaze landed on Evie's pregnant belly. Her mouth was agape.

"This is Romina, *signorina*." Dora snapped out of shock and introduced the housemaid beside her.

"Lovely! Hello."

"Anything you need, Miss Logan, ask Romina or me,"

the housekeeper added. The pretty maid, who seemed not a day past eighteen, returned a warm grin.

"Thank you."

"Evie! I didn't know you were coming. Welcome to our home," Matteo, Rocco's youngest brother, said with a kiss on her forehead as he joined the group.

"Oh, here I am, at last." She shrugged with a blush.

"Stellina!" Milo, another sibling, boomed to Lola. He was a year older than Matteo, but they were much younger than the three LaTorre older brothers. Milo and Matteo made a formidable duo since childhood being so close in age, earning the nickname "Double Trouble" for their many escapades through their teenage years. Milo seized his niece and threw her up, catching her like a ball on her descent. Lola bellowed a high-pitched shriek of glee.

"Wait a minute! Are you pregnant?" Matteo stared at Evie's bump as she stood to greet the newcomer. "Wow, wonderful—look at you!"

Oh, sweet mercy! She gulped. It dawned on her, Rocco might not have said a word to his family in Italy about the baby yet. Milo stopped bouncing Lola abruptly and deposited her back on her feet.

"More, Uncle Milo!" his niece cried out, but he didn't hear her. He gaped at Evie instead, scanning her up and down. His lively hazel gaze took in her plump tummy.

"It seems so!" Evie mumbled, caressing her baby bump with a nervous laugh.

"Congratulations. Did you get married to your fiancé? What's his name? I forgot." Matteo reached out to touch her tummy.

"No, she didn't marry him!" Rocco intervened with gritted teeth, smacking away his brother's hand from her belly. "And she never will. The baby is mine. Okay! Let's cut the story short." He fixed his younger brothers with a dark glare, daring them for a reaction.

His brothers' mouths gaped as quizzical, incredulous stares darted from Evie to Rocco. Matteo tried to say something, but no sound came out. Everyone stopped talking. There was a long pause, all eyes on them.

"Fuck. Congratulations!" Milo snorted, breaking the silence.

"Daddy, Uncle Milo said a bad word." Lola put her hand over her mouth, and a giggle slipped out.

"Watch it!" Fabio scowled. Melania rolled her eyes.

"*Minchia!*" Matteo then roared with laughter, following suit, guffawing.

"Daddy, Uncle Matteo also said a bad word!" Lola shrieked with glee.

Fabio's arms went wide at his sibling's 'no shit' expletive. "Please, guys, stop!" He was sure his daughter would grow up fully bilingual in all the foul, dirty profanities the Italian and English vocabularies had to offer.

"What the heck is so funny?" Rocco scowled at his younger brothers. He was not amused.

"Does Mother know?" Matteo asked when his laughter finally subsided.

"Not yet!"

"Tsk, tsk!"

Now, this troubled Evie.

"*Signor* Rocco, your mother would like to see you straight away. She's in her office," Romina, the maid, told him.

"I guess news travels fast, bro!" Milo chuckled.

Evie's heartbeat raced.

"I'll catch you later," Rocco said and kissed her cheek. This action produced more laughter from "Double Trouble".

"When the hell did this happen? And why didn't we know?" Milo chided with a snort. "Sorry, Evie. We are not making fun of you. We are delighted for you. Hell, for both of you. It's just we are not used to seeing Rocco with a girlfriend. A pregnant one at that!"

"Daddy, Uncle Milo said *hell*!" Lola chirped in, giggling, and Fabio rolled his eyes.

"He never brings women home, you know. It must be serious," Matteo explained to Evie. He seemed thoroughly amused by the situation. "He looks all fatherly already."

"I dare say it's serious. Evie's expecting his child," Selina cried out. "Rocco, tell these two—*coglioni* to stop bothering my friend."

"Mommy, what does *coglioni* mean?" Lola asked.

"Selina!" Fabio barked, closing his eyes. Melania huffed, shaking her head.

"Oops, sorry." Selina gave them an apologetic smile for calling her brothers assholes. "Nothing. *Stellina,* forget it."

"Romina, can you please show Evie to her room?" Rocco tried to control his temper at his unruly siblings.

"Come this way, Miss Logan."

He turned to his sister. Selina understood his plea. She nodded with a wink and trotted after Evie as he went to call on his mother. He could still hear, as he walked away, Milo and Matteo making fun of his impending fatherhood.

He sighed, resigned to the banter.

∼

Evie

"Oh, *signorina* Selina, I'm so glad you're here." The maid spoke, leading them up the long, gently curving staircase to the second floor to the guest quarters. "I need ideas on a dress for my cousin's wedding."

"Of course, Romina, anytime."

"You look so well. And with Miss Logan having Master Rocco's baby…" The housemaid said, overexcited. "Not that I eavesdropped. I couldn't help hearing, err—the news."

"No worries," Selina added with a laugh. Everybody liked the sweet, young maid. She was a breath of fresh air.

"Sorry, Miss Logan, I didn't mean to be impertinent," Romina went on, looking a little awkward.

"That's fine. Don't worry."

"Knowing 'Double Trouble,' it's going to be carnage for Rocco and Evie about this. Milo and Matteo will amuse themselves for ages," Selina scoffed.

"Here we are, miss. Your suite clean and ready. I saw to it, myself," Romina pointed out with a smile. "It's the prettiest in the house. "

"True!" Selina led her into the rooms.

"Tito will bring up your luggage when they return from Marina Piccola."

"Wonderful, Romina. Thank you," Evie thanked the maid and entered. "Oh, my-my, I never!"

∽

Rocco

"What the hell is going on?" Magda LaTorre demanded the moment her son came into her study. She remained behind her large mahogany desk as the epitome of authority. Her brows drew together with her glare fixed on him.

"Gee! And hello to you, too, Mother!" Rocco scoffed, undaunted.

Raising her chin with a jerky movement, Magda asked him to take the chair opposite her. "Hey, buddy!" he went on, fist-bumping his older brother. His demeanor was calm. His older brother, Sebastiano, sitting beside him, seemed rather amused by it all.

Salvo, the clan's *consigliere,* and their stepfather, standing next to Magda, frowned, perplexed. Magda's expression was thunderous. Rocco was weary of it. Usually, the precursor to a fit of temper from Lady Camorra.

"Nico poisoned a cake destined for Selina, but I stopped it in time," Rocco said in his suave, silvery voice, nonchalant.

"We are well aware of that! The reason the girls are here is to protect them. To bring that pig back to Italy, where we can catch him. Once we do, he'll pay for it, don't you worry. And we'll talk about this later. But that's not what I asked, and you know it."

"What?" Rocco faked ignorance, and an innocent grin danced on his lips.

"Guess what she means, bro!" Sebastiano snorted, struggling to suppress a snigger.

"Don't you dare laugh!" she yelled at Sebastiano, and her eyes became tiny slits when she fixed them back on Rocco.

"Huh?" he persisted, the fake smile still plastered on his lips. She would have to draw him out. He was not offering.

"That girl, the pregnant farmer!"

"Mother!" Rocco bolted from his chair. This time she had rattled him. The smile was off his face. "Don't you dare any of your shenanigans with her! She's a sweet girl."

"Sit down, you moron." Sebastiano chuckled, but he ignored him.

"Is it true, Rocco?" Salvo asked. "Is the young woman having your baby?"

"What if she is!" He drew himself to his full height, hands on his hips, his posture straight and stiff. His gaze challenged them, defiant.

Magda sighed and rolled her eyes. Her shoulders sagged.

"Why did you keep this a secret?" Sebastiano wasn't laughing anymore; his eyes were intent on his younger brother. "Well, the mighty playboy has capitulated to a slip of a girl and is about to become a father. Who would have thought?" he went on amused, but as the underboss, he had to display the clan's displeasure—not at the news per se, but at the secrecy of it. The family couldn't grant the luxury of privacy in such matters. Rocco should have told them. He knew the rules. The fact that his mother had been sending him pictures of potential wife matches with other families should have given him a clue about the significance, but he knew Rocco was stubborn.

"Is it true? Is she carrying your child?" Magda went on.

"None of your business."

"Rocco! I'm losing my patience with you. I'd expected something like this from Milo or Matteo, but you? At thirty-one? Unbelievable."

"Mother, accidents do happen," he said, and his brother almost convulsed with laughter. He ignored him and went on stoically. "But Evie and I are happy with the news. She's having my baby, and that's all there is to it."

"When is the wedding?" Magda faced the facts head-on. Rocco had brought home a girl who was not part of their world. An outsider. Without even giving them a hint. No discussion! It wouldn't do! He was out of line. But in her own way, Magda was an honorable woman. The least her son could do in the circumstances was to wed the chit. She wouldn't allow her grandchild to be born out of wedlock.

"I doubt she wants to marry me."

"What? Have you proposed to her?"

"Uh? Err... no. I mean, she's sweet, loving and—"

"Okay. I've heard enough. Blasted man! We'll come back to this later," Magda hissed. "What should we do about the potential brides I picked out for you?"

"Your problem, Mother! You were wrong to offer me as a husband. You know how I feel about this. That's not changed."

"But you are marrying Evie now, surely?" Sebastiano said, brushing aside his remark.

"It's for Evie and me to consider... it doesn't concern any of you. We're in no rush."

"If you haven't even asked her, how would you know how she feels?"

"We are done here. Do you want to meet her or not, then?" Rocco asked. His mother and Salvo had never met Evie. His gaze was stern on them, expecting them to refuse.

"Of course." His mom sighed. "She's carrying my second grandchild, and I'll be damned if I'll miss this because you were secretive about it."

"Fine!"

"Be prompt for dinner! We'll meet her then."

Rocco had only known he was the father of Evie's baby for about ten days. So there was no time to tell anyone. But he hadn't said this to his mother, or she would blame Evie for the secrecy. He could not change the past, but he would manage this in his own way.

∽

Magda

"What do you think, then?" Magda asked Salvo when Rocco left the room.

"My opinion? Let them get on with it. He seems to care for the girl, or he wouldn't challenge you. Write to all those who expressed an interest and politely decline their offer of matrimony as Rocco made his choice. Tell the truth, it won't be a secret for long."

"Nico might know this if he was in Selina's apartment. If so, Evie is in danger, too. We'll keep an eye on her. She'll be attracting everyone's attention now," Sebastiano added.

"He must marry her. Our name will protect her," she insisted.

"Magda, don't meddle!" Salvo warned her. He was the only person who could somewhat control Lady Camorra.

"What?" she growled, but even Salvo had his limits.

"Besides, Nico's not playing by the rules, name or no name."

∽

Evie

"How did it go with your mother? Did you tell her?" Evie asked as Rocco entered the suite.

"Were you taking a nap?" Rocco ignored her questions.

"No." She sat up in bed. "I was lying down to admire the frescos on the ceiling. God, they are amazing. This suite is stunning." She pointed to the ceiling and behind the bed, her eyes sparkling with delight.

Evie had loved Rocco's London townhouse. But this magnificent, white-colored villa on this marvelous island topped everything. The inside of the place had revealed itself as equally wonderful as the location. The high ceilings, the two curving marble staircases leading to the grand wings of the house, the beautiful murals and frescos, the spacious rooms with views from picture-framed windows flooding the place with light, the expensive rugs, the ornate chandeliers, the long hallways, the valuable paintings mixed with colorful local artwork were impressive. And the splendid gardens and terraces overlooking Punta Carena and the sea all contributed to making the place heavenly.

"This suite is quite private on this side of the house. The family quarters are in the west wing. We'll be well away from prying eyes here. I guess we have raised too much attention already. They'll get used to the idea that we are together, and we are having a baby… eventually! Besides, this suite is my favorite. What do you think?"

The grand suite had two bedrooms, with the main one having a romantic-like vibe. There was also a day room with all the comforts. Stunning frescoes were a feature throughout the place.

"Oh, I love it. The frescoes are a work of art."

"Glad you like it! That sensual goddess depicted up there reminds me of you."

"No, I'm too ordinary for that."

"Stop saying that. You are beautiful, *micina*." He moved a lock of her hair from her cheek and placed it behind her ear, kissing the top of her head. Her cheeks burned, but she liked the compliment.

"That one is you." She pointed up at a figure on the ceiling.

"Who that? No."

"Yes."

"No. That one is Ares, the God of War. Ares is throwing lightning bolts down on the Titans from the heavens. We are in the realm of Greek mythology on these murals."

"It reminds me of you, anyway." An amused smile played on her lips. "Same as when you were thundering your smacks on my ass!" She paused and giggled. "You had that same expression when spanking me the day I tried to escape from your townhouse in London."

He raised a brow at her impertinence.

"You deserved that spanking, poppet. You were very naughty that evening."

"Only because I took the key from under your nose. I wounded your manly pride."

"Watch your mouth! Or I'll spank you right now."

"Is that a promise?" She launched a sultry glance at him.

His eyes widened at her sexiness.

"Vixen!" He kissed the hollow of her neck.

"So, what did your mother say? About me and the baby. Oh, do tell." She dampened his spirits.

"We talked business."

"Please. Come on, out with it."

"Fine!" So he told her, roughly, the gist of it.

"You didn't say I lied to you over the baby's paternity? That you had no idea the baby was yours for months?"

"No!"

"To protect me?"

"I suppose."

"Aw, you are a sweet man!" She kissed him on the cheek. "I was worried about this. But it's not fair to you. I'll tell them the truth. That you didn't know."

"Don't you dare! I want them to get to know you first. See how lovely you are. By the time they find out the truth, then it won't matter. And I'm not a sweet man."

"If you say so."

"Dinner is in half an hour, with official introductions and all." His hand was already up on her thigh, though.

She smacked his hand away. "Not now. We have no time."

"Why not?"

"Rocco! You don't want me all flustered and reeking of sex when I meet your mother."

"Get ready, then—before I change my mind," he said.

She strolled to the bathroom but paused in the doorway.

"What?" he asked when he saw her still standing there.

"I heard a snippet of your conversation with Fabio on the plane. That man you were talking about wants to kill us, right? And he won't stop until he does."

"Did your mother ever tell you not to eavesdrop? Don't do that, Evie. I don't like it." He scowled. "And no one is going to kill you."

"I couldn't help that, but if we are in danger, we should call the police."

"No, Evie!" He snorted. *Bless the girl! She still doesn't get it.* "My family doesn't involve the police. We sort our own problems. We'll fix this—"

"Rocco—"

"You and my baby are safe here. No one will hurt you."

"But—"

"You'll be fine." He walked over to her and caressed her cheek.

"What if you don't catch him?"

"We will, darling. I promise you."

CHAPTER 27

Evie

"Do you like our home?"

"Oh, it's wonderful, Selina. My suite is fit for a queen. Look at this beauty." Evie waved her hand at the enchanting bay under the starry night.

"You'll enjoy it here."

"But aren't you worried about the man who's after us?"

"You shouldn't worry. We are safe here." Melania squeezed her shoulder, giving her a reassuring smile.

"It's Nico, Mel. He's the problem!" Selina huffed with a frown.

"Nico?" Melania's brows shot up, then she muted her speech to a whisper. "The fucker who kidnapped me?"

"The same."

"Kidnap? What? When? Evie asked, her face blanched, glancing at them in horror.

"Hush, lower your voice."

They were having pre-dinner drinks on the terrace,

and the three girls now hushed their tones so the rest of the family would not hear their conversation.

"Yes, he did," Melania whispered. "Nico Columbano abducted me last year. He wanted to extort the clan's money after turning rogue against them and killing Fabio's cousin Ulrico."

"But he messed with the wrong girl!" Selina said. "Melania worked with MI5 before she married Fabio, you know, and they trained her well. So she fought back and escaped."

"What? No!" Evie squealed.

"Shush! Oh, yes. I was an investigator with MI5. That's how I met Fabio. I interviewed him on an inquiry I was working on. He was a suspect in the case, but it wasn't him —on that occasion," Melania said with a breezy laugh. "I never expected, in a million years, we would fall in love. And indeed, thanks to my training with the agency, I escaped Nico. That scumbag would have killed me, I'm sure."

"Unbelievable."

"I was lucky!"

The thought of an abduction alarmed Evie, hearing her friend's account. She realized her life with Rocco might not be as smooth as she anticipated. The clan had a set of rules, nonconformist, callous and dangerous. Sometimes, they were openly hostile and brutal.

Rules that she didn't understand. Her friend's tale only corroborated her suspicions. She wondered if she would be up to the task if need be. Fire a gun point blank at a man as Melania had to do? No. Evie doubted she could. She would have died if she were in Melania's shoes.

As a farmer's daughter, Evie had experience with firearms. But she used a shotgun only for her clay-shooting competitions. A clay disk was her flying target, not a living, breathing person.

Oh, dear God! A shiver came down her spine.

"Nico won't get away with it this time. My brothers have every man on it," Selina added.

"The bastard is working with one of the families in the 'Ndrangheta—that's another word for Mafia in Calabria," Selina said for Evie's benefit. "They are certain someone is sponsoring him. Sebastiano thinks it's Zilli. That's why Nico has been able to get away with it. Someone is giving him resources and money to carry out these attacks on us."

"Isn't Zilli's daughter scheduled to meet Sebastiano soon? I gather she is to become his wife. Is that not the case?" Melania asked, surprised.

"Sure. There is an agreement between our two clans. Sebastiano is supposed to marry her. I doubt they'll marry if all this is true, though."

"I see."

"My brothers say Zilli is behind everything."

"How do you know all this? Rocco tells me nothing," Evie grumbled.

"Sebastiano discussed this with you?" Melania asked her. "Not even Fabio tells me anything."

"Good God! No," Selina scoffed. "My brothers won't debate these matters with me. But don't worry! I have my ways of finding out these things. If you want to know something, come to mama!" Selina tapped her nose with her finger in conspiracy with a satisfied grin. "But keep this to yourself, ladies. Don't tell anyone, or I'll be in trouble."

"You mean you have mastered the art of listening at doors without being caught." Melania laughed.

"The only way."

The library was the place where her brothers liked to discuss matters amongst themselves. Fabio had related all that had transpired in London to Sebastiano and his suspicions. So Selina had eavesdropped; their conversation was an eye-opener. The same one she had just related to her companions.

∽

Evie

"Sorry, ladies, do you mind if I steal her for a while?" Rocco asked, not missing the fact that the girls had stopped talking when he was near them.

"Has Mother summoned her?" Selina chimed.

"Come, let's go." He ignored his sister and put a hand behind Evie's back, moving her gently toward another group of people on the terrace. She glanced at him, but he gave her a reassuring wink.

"Evie, you have met my older brother, haven't you?"

"Sure. Hello." She smiled. Sebastiano hadn't lost his menacing look. Taller than all the brothers, with broad, powerful shoulders, his prominent physique made him scary. He was built like a mountain, and fair-haired like his sister. Evie had only seen him twice in London, and when he came to visit Selina, Evie stayed away. He terrified her. Blessed with the same harmonious family features, his more angular jaw gave him a rugged look. Sebastiano's overall hallmark seemed harsher because he smiled very little. The same rich deep-blue eyes, reminiscent of Selina's, were now staring at Evie intently. His gaze was burning her.

She gulped. He grasped her upper arms with his large hands, kissing her on both cheeks.

"Welcome to the family, Evie," Sebastiano said with a hint of a smile. Though this brief, boyish beam turned him into a remarkably handsome fellow, it lasted three mere seconds.

"Thank you," she mumbled.

"This is Nonna Flora—my grandmother," Rocco said,

leading her to a mid-height woman with stylish coiffured silvery hair. She was an impressive figure, even at her venerable age, so elegant and every bit as dignified as a queen. Evie realized the origin of the recognizable intense, bedazzling blue gaze.

"Oh, it is such a joy—"

"You are so lovely, my dear. I'll be a great-grandmother again. How wonderful! Rocco, you didn't tell me your girl was so pretty." After shaking a finger at him, the lady kissed Evie.

"This is *Signor* Renzi. My stepfather." He introduced her next to the clan's *consigliere*.

"Nice to meet you, sir." Evie felt encouraged, seeing a broad smile on the man's lips. She thought he had a pleasing face. Perhaps nearing his sixties, she calculated, he was still entirely handsome and somehow looked familiar. Strange. Evie had never set eyes on this fellow until today, but he reminded her of someone. Not a clue who. *Nonsense, you idiot,* she told herself.

"Please, call me Salvo. The pleasure is all mine," he said, holding her hand and kissing her knuckles lightly, steadying his gaze on her with his lovely green moons —*and a gentleman, too, the old charmer.* She had an on-the-spot liking for him.

"And last but not least, this is my mother, Magda."

"My p-pleasure, Mrs. Renzi."

"People call me by my first husband's name, Mrs. LaTorre. You may call me Magda," the woman said. Magda had kept the name, even if she was married to Salvo now, as befitting to the clan's boss.

"I've heard s-so much a-about you," Evie stammered anxiously. She was speculating what his mom would make of her. Magda clutched her hand firmly. She radiated charisma with a strong presence. It was no wonder her brood turned out to be so confident. It must be in the genes. Rocco got a sizeable share of them. Indeed, his mother looked commanding and beautiful, like a dazzling film star. Some would claim she had all the hallmarks of a reigning monarch.

Evie understood why all the LaTorre's offspring were attractive. Magda was a stunning creature, considering she was in her fifties. Beautiful. The same bright, sharp blue eyes as Nonna Flora. As those inherited by Sebastiano, Matteo and Selina, while she had deduced, Fabio and Milo's lively hazel moons came from the father's side, according to a photo she had once seen of the man.

And Rocco's? Odd! His eyes—a brilliant shade of green—were unlike all the rest.

"Don't trust any of it, Evie! They all invent stories about me," Magda said, inspecting her from head to toe. "How far gone are you?"

"The pregnancy?" A blush heated her face. "Just under five months."

"I see. Make sure my son puts a ring on your finger, preferably before the baby is born."

"Mother!"

"That's an order, Rocco."

"Please, not now!"

"I won't change my mind," his mom stated.

Rocco rolled his eyes.

"Gather everyone for dinner. Let's all sit down. I'm starving," Magda commanded, moving toward the big table on the terrace.

Evie was glad the introductions were over and moved on with them.

The table was laid out for a big feast, with fresh sweet-scented flowers along the counter, silver cutlery, and a white gold-rimmed porcelain china dinner service. Soon, they all gathered around and took their seats.

A magnificent banquet followed.

They served the starter, and a basket with *fritto misto* arrived, the day's catch from the bay below. The mixed seafood included morsels of deliciousness, such as calamari, squid, shrimp and prawns coated with a lightly fried, crispy, flaky golden batter. The aroma was incredible. It made Evie's mouth water.

"None for you, *micina.*" Rocco poured her a lemonade while everyone else washed down the seafood with chilled, sparkling white wine.

"A sip from yours?"

"No!"

"Spoilsport! Can I smell it, then?"

"Sure," he said. He offered his glass, and she sniffed the citrus tones, but then she drew a tiny sip despite his warning.

"Delicious." She smacked her lips together, savoring it. He seized the goblet from her hand with a scowl.

"Don't push it, *amore,* or I'll have to punish you," he said. She glanced at him, and her heart thundered in her ribcage. She didn't know if it was in anticipation or dread.

"Really?" She giggled, as they served risotto next with white truffles.

"Be a good girl." He leaned into her ear. "Or I'll make you suck my cock on your knees tonight!" he whispered with a wicked grin.

Her eyes went wide, and she almost choked on a mouthful. He patted her back and gave her the glass of lemonade. She drank it to calm herself, then giggled. As she turned, she realized Magda's scrutiny was on them. Evie blushed.

"Behave. Your mother is looking at us."

"Who cares?" He nibbled on her earlobe. She tried to pull away discretely.

"Rocco, stop! Sebastiano is watching us, too."

"Evie, to live with my family, you must learn to ignore them when necessary."

Romina, the maid, interrupted them, serving a silver platter with succulent meats, venison, thick beef steak slices, and lamb.

"More food?"

"You're in Italy, darling. Food is a way of life."

"I don't think I can swallow another bite."

"Come on, poppet. You need to eat for two."

The red wine to go with the meats was flowing then.

"Please, I'd like a sip."

"No, *micina!*"

"You are not the boss of me, you know."

"You wanna bet?" he said, though he relented and allowed her to have a tiny swig.

"Silly man!" she scoffed. When he looked down his nose at her, she giggled, kissing his cheek. And notwithstanding the dangers lurking around them, Evie felt ecstatic. She couldn't believe she was having a child with this handsome man, and he wanted her. Somehow, everything else paled in comparison.

They spent the entire evening on the long, unhurried dinner. Evie talked and laughed, enjoying herself with him and his family. At the end, Sebastiano stood up and clunked his knife on his glass to attract everybody's attention. When they went quiet, he spoke.

"I want to welcome Evie to our family. Congratulations to you and Rocco. We can't wait to meet your baby, too."

"Hear, hear!" everyone cheered.

"The baby will be my cousin, you know," Lola shouted, clapping her hands. Everybody chuckled.

"Thank you." Evie's eyes glittered. Had his family accepted her? She had already accepted them, warts and all.

～

Evie

Rocco and Evie strolled on the rocky beach for a while. She didn't miss two bodyguards in tow, a few yards behind them, as they promenaded along the beach—a sign of the times. They sat at the edge of the jetty in silent contemplation over the expanse of water. The small private cove below the house, a narrow inlet within Punta Carena, was lovely, and with a silvery moon beaming, it felt intimate, amorous. She cherished the tender lull with him in the moonlight.

They were exhausted when they finally returned to the suite. It had been a long day.

"My feet are hurting and swollen." Evie flopped on the bed and lay on her back. She kicked off her tennis shoes. He sat beside her and swung her legs over on his lap. He rubbed her feet with an indulgent, tender smile. At first, she giggled. She was ticklish as he massaged them. Then she relaxed in his capable hands, allowing him to work his magic on her tootsies.

"Oh, this feels so good. You have a talent, Mr. LaTorre!"

"You'll find I have a multitude of talents, and I can prove it." He winked at her, caressing her baby bump. She snorted.

"I can see why they call you Prince Charming!" She turned on her side as he moved to the chaise lounge at the foot of the bed. She propped her head up with her hand as she watched him take his boots and socks off.

"Who told you that?"

"I have my sources. Soon, I'll learn everything there is about you."

"Is that so?"

"Sure." She observed him for a while as he took his shirt off. Then her eyes darkened as she gazed at him.

"What?"

"Is it true that Zilli's clan is sponsoring Nico to hurt your family? They are behind all the troubles. The reason we have bodyguards everywhere."

"Dio Santo!" Rocco's head snapped up to her. "Who the hell told you that?" He stood, straightened up to his full height and narrowed his eyes on her.

"Oh, I-I overheard it on the p-plane from you," she mumbled, sitting up on the bed, realizing her mistake. She couldn't blame his sister for it when it was supposed to be a secret.

"You didn't hear that from me. I didn't mention Zilli or Nico by name on the plane." He glared at her.

"You must have done."

"No, Evie."

"Where else would I hear it from, then?"

"Where indeed. That's what I want to know."

"I told you."

"You are lying."

"No, I'm not."

"I thought we said no more lies between us. You are doing it again."

"No, I swear." She was. She stood up and went to him, trying to touch his cheek, but he pushed her hand away.

"Where?" He advanced on her, and she stepped back, seeing his face darken. His sultry gaze turned cold and stormy.

"I-I—"

"Who told you?" His voice was soft, but she detected the warning edge on it. He took two more strides toward her. She stepped back further.

"Rocco..."

"I'm not in the mood for games." He moved up closer to her. His expression was severe, towering over her. She retreated until she hit the wall. There was nowhere to run.

He planted his hands on the surface, on either side of her, trapping her in.

"Have you been eavesdropping?" His tone was a whisper. She barely caught his words.

"No!"

"Umm?"

"I said no."

"If you weren't snooping, who was it, then? Who told you? I won't ask you again."

"I must have picked it up from you on the plane." She maintained, though she couldn't disguise her trepidation about lying to him anew.

"Turn around."

"But—"

"Turn, I said. Stretch your arms and lay your palms flat on the wall. Spread your legs."

"What?"

"You heard me, do it!"

"Darling, please…"

"Don't make me do it for you," Rocco added calmly.

Evie gulped, seeing the determination stamped on his face. The clenching jaw and the slight crease between his brows she loved so much were unmistakable. Her heart slammed into her chest. A mixture of dread and excitement gained a hold on her. She obeyed. Evie stretched herself into position as he demanded.

"I-I—"

"Don't move from this position. Do you understand?" Rocco spread her feet on the floor.

She nodded, her head bobbing in jerky movements when she got the first smack on her rear. She yelped, not expecting it so harsh, but one more came down before she regained her breath.

"Tell me!"

"Please…" she pleaded as his hand released two more

whacks over her dress. He gripped her upper arm and hauled her with him.

"On your knees, on the bed." He instructed coolly. She tried to blink her tears away, her bottom heating up already.

"Please…"

"Don't argue with me," he said peremptorily. He lifted her dress over her head and threw it onto the floor. Her bra went the same way. "Now!"

Evie complied and was on all fours on the bed. Her backside was sticking out. He pulled her panties down to expose her already pink tush. The sight of her naked beauty delighted him. A smirk hit his lips while a rush of blood flooded his manhood.

He placed a pillow under her belly to protect the baby, even though her tummy was hanging loose without touching the bed.

She clenched her buttocks and closed her eyes tightly, knowing what came next. Without preamble, his mighty hand bounced with a blistering hardness on her pillowy buttocks. The searing heat ignited her frame.

"Aw, aw!" She turned to glance at him over her shoulder to see he was intently focused on administering her punishment. She hadn't seen a more determined expression, a more handsome face, or sensual masculinity in her entire life. It drove her giddy with lust, despite another hard spank. "Ouch!" she yelled. Or perhaps, because of it.

Rocco was splendid. Every angle of his exquisite face whispered poetry to her. She had never seen a better specimen of manliness. It wasn't just his good-looks. It was how he made her feel about herself as if she were the most beautiful woman on the planet to him. Although pushy and often exhibiting unconventional behavior, she had no doubt he deeply cared for her and her baby.

Rocco protected her.

She saw the intensity in his eyes and realized she worshipped him—even now, as he spanked her and set her bottom on fire, she adored him. Evie loved the bossy man with all her heart.

Thus, her pert backside leapt higher, dangling closer to him, offering it to him for the taking. And despite Rocco's hand smacking her with blistering heat, she reveled in it.

Her reaction scandalized her. Though she wouldn't enjoy this from any other man. Oh, no. Rocco LaTorre—was the only one she craved it from.

Her frame simmered with lust as the liquid heat swelling within her raised her pulse. The soft walls at her apex clenched with anticipation. Her pussy let out a dribble, running on her thigh.

Goodness me!

She blinked away the tears. Uncertain if they were because of the harsh spanking or perhaps, she was ashamed that this had soaked her, aroused her.

He paused, but when he resumed, she yelped. Her behind was glowing as he branded her with his firm hand.

"Are you going to tell me? Or shall we do this all night?" he uttered landing another hard smack.

"Ooh, I eavesdropped outside the library. Sorry," Evie finally said. She wouldn't blame Selina.

"See, not so hard, was it? Don't eavesdrop again. I forbid it." He stopped spanking her and massaged her buttocks instead. His hands rubbing the scorching skin made the warmth between her legs sizzle, and she moaned. She wanted him inside her.

"Rocco…" Her voice was soft and breathy. Inviting him. She had never felt such lust for a man.

∽

Rocco

It made his erection throb.

"Umm… I don't know why I punish you if all it does is turn you on." He unzipped his trousers and lowered them with his boxers, taking them off. His manhood sprung hard and erect like a spear. He touched her dampened folds.

"You are soaked, *micina.*" More blood thundered to his shaft as he rubbed her nub.

"Sweet Jesus!" she blurted in a panting burst. She inhaled deeply. He played with her slit, teasing her, provoking her. Her needy whispers called out his name.

"Do you want me? Umm?"

"Yes."

"Yes, what?" He gave her a playful spank.

"Yes, I want you."

"I beg your pardon?" Smack!

"I want you, Sir?"

"That's right, poppet! Say it." A light spank squashed her reddened buttocks.

"I want you, Sir."

"Good! That's my girl!" He put his cock at her entrance and inched into her. "I doubt you'll last long."

"No, Sir, I won't," she agreed and pushed her bottom back against him. He fisted her hair, kissing her neck.

"Rocco…" His name on her lips was intoxicating. He plunged in, stretching her. She hissed, breathing out small quick puffs. His claiming thrusts were meant to send shock waves of pain and delight through her as he smacked her tenderized backside with the force of his pounding hips. Her pussy clenched around him, dripping wet, squeezing his cock. He would not last long, either.

He grasped her breast, pinching her tight nipples.

"Oh, dear God." She panted.

"Come for me, *micina!*" He enticed her, hammering into her. Their bodies tensed and then whirled higher and higher in a vortex of pleasure as they reached the pinnacle until their bodies limp, exhausted, were sated.

He withdrew from her and crashed on the bed, pulling her down. They lay side-by-side.

"Jesus, Evie! What the hell you do to me!" he said, brushing away her hair from her neck and placing tender kisses on her. She smiled, satisfied. She rolled over and buried her head on his chest as he caressed her cheek. They stayed in companionable silence, kissing and caressing each other until they fell asleep.

CHAPTER 28

Evie

They'd been on the island for several days. Evie got to know the family a little more, enjoying her time with them. She discovered all the enchanting nooks and crannies of the beautiful villa with its magnificent grounds. She learned more about his brothers, the people in the household, the names of the staff, and the guards. Much to her surprise, even Magda and Sebastiano looked less intimidating.

Her life had turned out differently than she had envisioned a year ago. Her best laid-out plans about her future were gone out of the window. Nor did she care!

Did she choose this? No. She hadn't bargained on it six months ago, but now that it happened; she welcomed it. She embraced it.

The most significant transformation had occurred within her, in her heart! Each day she lost one more bit of her heart to Rocco. Evie adored him. She even delighted in his bossiness—most of the time.

It was a beguiling feeling. A thrilling giddiness of pure joy hit her as if she were intoxicated with love. She wished she could shout about her passion for him to the four winds so everyone could partake in her bliss. His family knew it, and he did, too. Remarkably, she had soon fit in with him and his life.

Sometimes he would work in their bedroom, at the table, to keep her company while she rested and she would look at him at her leisure enjoying watching him work. Her affections for him had become more powerful than just the physical attraction, greater than the extraordinary pleasure and sinful lovemaking he bestowed on her, more than the allure of his godlike beauty. His thoughtfulness in the small things made her complete. As if he was the missing piece of the jigsaw to her life.

His eyes lit up when he saw her. He drove her to believe in herself again, that she was beautiful, and gave her confidence. She had butterflies in her stomach every time he touched her.

Like a love-struck teenager, she had taken up doodling hearts with his name in her notebook as she studied for her exams.

Evie didn't wish to be foolish, though. She tried to keep a cool head. But what did he make of her? In his heart… she wasn't sure. They were about to become parents, and he wanted the child, but he kept a tight lid on his feelings. She knew he liked and cared for her deeply, but was there more?

Sometimes, she had a glimpse of them when he uttered all those beautiful words in Italian to her on the spur of the moment, but she couldn't make head or tail of them, and he wouldn't translate them for her.

To her detriment, there were times when she thought *I'm only part of the parcel,* by default, as the mother of his child.

Yet, she knew her nature and she belonged to him, utterly and forever.

Rocco

The LaTorre brothers gathered in Magda's study. They were sitting around the conference table.

"Is it Nico Columbano?" she asked.

"Yes. My informant in the border police picked up his passport. He was traveling under his mother's maiden name," Rocco said. "We anticipated that. I just received a photocopy of the passport with the picture. It's him."

"I see."

"He used a private jet to fly to Naples. Arrived three days ago."

"Whose jet?"

"I don't know, but you can hazard a guess when you hear this. We had a breakthrough. Zeno uncovered emails between Omero Zilli and Nico. He hacked into the old man's computer."

"That young man is an asset to us. So, what has he uncovered?" Sebastiano asked.

"Zilli is guilty as hell! He's helping Nico against us, like we thought, supporting him with money and men. It's all in the emails between them. It's all in code, of course. The language is innocuous, but Zeno got it. Omero's a traitor. You should warn Santillo," Rocco confirmed.

"*Minchia!* Federico will be furious. We trusted Zilli, that slimy-toad," Sebastiano blurted.

"We must be vigilant. If Nico is in Naples, we need to increase security on the girls," Magda said.

"The old man plans to destroy the LaTorres' empire. He financed Nico on the attacks, including the one in which he killed Ulrico and his men," Rocco went on. As they debated what to do next, a call on the hotline interrupted the meeting. Sebastiano rolled his eyes and hissed. It could only mean bad news.

"Yes?" Salvo answered the call. He listened intently for a while. He blanched. Then he put the phone down without a word.

"What is it?" Sebastiano asked.

"Multiple strikes. They battered us! If this is Zilli's work again, he's going for the jugular. Two nightclubs and the Diamond Development site in Naples."

"Rocco, find out who did this. It must be Nico under the old man's orders. Find him. I want him alive. I want Nico to talk on Zilli," Magda ordered.

"There are casualties, too."

"Zilli's gone too far." She banged her fist on her desk.

"Everybody will take it as a sign of weakness if we don't retaliate. A fair game for the taking," Salvo claimed. "He's waged a war on us. We respond. We cannot dither. Or we'll write our death sentence."

"I want a plan to deal with Zilli. Salvo, Sebastiano, work on it. But first, we got to return to Naples to assess the damage. The Diamond Real Estate Development is too important for us," Magda called out. "Get the choppers to the island, Rocco. Let's leave within the hour. We'll discuss the plan when we return. Then, we make our move on that old bastard. Our response must be firm and deadly."

"What about the girls?" Rocco rubbed the back of his neck. He was concerned for Evie.

"They'll stay on the island."

"No. I don't like it," Rocco objected.

"They won't be on their own. Fabio, you'll remain here with plenty of guards."

"Yes, of course. Double Trouble can help for once. I'll make sure," Fabio replied.

"Mother, I'd rather stay," Rocco insisted.

"We have an army of men at the villa. They patrol the grounds at all times. The perimeter's walls are secured with sensors, cameras, and monitored surveillance. They are safe. As a precaution, the girls should stay in the house until this is over."

"But—"

"They won't try anything here. Women and children are off-limit, you know that. They wouldn't dare."

"Nico tried to poison them in London, Mother! Abducted Melania. His gang killed Ulrico. He's not playing by the rules."

"Enough, let's move. We have no choice. We are wasting time."

⁓

Evie

"Can't your mother handle this? Whatever this is. Sebastiano and Salvo are going with her. Why do they need you, too?" Evie pleaded half an hour later as he said his goodbye to her.

"Darling, we have gone through this."

"What happened?"

"Don't ask, poppet."

"I must tell you everything, not lie to you, but you won't share a thing with me? How's that fair?"

"Enough!" Rocco huffed and closed his eyes.

"You are impossible."

"Evie, please…"

"How long will you be away? Can you at least tell me that?"

"Just a few days, sweetheart. I'll call you from Naples." He came over to kiss her, but she turned from him. He sighed.

"You bossy boots!" she muttered under her breath. It

seemed she had a new nickname for him. Somehow, he liked it. Half a grin broke at the corner of his mouth.

"Don't be upset, poppet. I'll be back soon, I promise." He took her hand and kissed the inside of her wrist. Her eyes softened on him.

"Is this dangerous?"

"Fabio and Double Trouble will stay here. I'll leave Zeno as your bodyguard. We have security around the clock. You'll be safe."

"You know that's not what I asked. Are *you* going to be safe?"

"Of course I'm." He dismissed her worries.

"Liar!"

"I have to go, *micina*." He cupped her face, and his lips lingered on hers.

"Don't call me that! It won't work," she mumbled in his mouth, but she responded to his kiss. In reality, she loved it when he called her "little kitten," but a few tears rolled down her cheeks.

"Evie… no crying. It's only a few days." He caressed her arms up and down.

"I'll see you off."

"No, you settle in with Lola. She'll stay with you these next few nights to keep you company."

"The sweet child is so excited about it."

"I'll call you later." He kissed her forehead and cheek, and he was gone.

Evie went to the window. The helicopters were ready to leave.

She watched them rise into the utter darkness of the night sky and disappear on the horizon as more tears ran down her face.

CHAPTER 29

Romina

The girl usually returned home once a week on her day off. She had stayed overnight and was now enjoying breakfast in the kitchen with her mother before returning to work.

A loud knock made her jump.

"Are you expecting someone, Mama?"

"No."

"It's so early." She peered at her watch. "Not even seven yet. I'll see to it."

"You'll be late for work," her mom warned her as the hammering on the door grew slightly louder. "Don't dwell on the doorstep if it is Mrs. Nardini; she likes to gossip. She's too nosy. She must've seen you come home yesterday morning."

"Don't worry, Mama." The girl dashed to the front door. From her mother's modest house in the suburb of Matermania, in the mountain above Capri town, she had a twenty-minute minibus ride to Punta Carena, on the other side of the island, to get to work.

She glanced through the keyhole but didn't recognize the man.

"Delivery!" the guy said through the door. "You need to sign for it."

"Are you waiting for a package, Mama?" she called out.

"Umm… no, I don't think so. Why?"

"There's something for you."

"See what it is, then."

"Okay." She unbolted the front door but attached the small security chain out of habit.

"Can I help you?" The girl spoke through the crack when she opened it. The fellow outside smiled. She relaxed when he raised a thin parcel and winked. She took it through the gap.

"Sign there," he said. The parcel, pen and paper to sign burdened the girl's hands. She got distracted inspecting the package, taking her eyes off him, and the man took action.

He shouldered the wooden door with all his might. The thin chain snapped, and the door slammed open with brute force. It hit her hard. She shrieked in pain as it flung her backward, and she lost her balance. She landed on her backside with the battered parcel and paper beside her.

"What the hell was that?" her mother yelled. Two men entered the house, locking the exit behind them.

The girl was still on the floor, stunned, unable to react, when one of the men pointed a gun at her. She gasped. The other moved swiftly onward, bypassing her in haste. The assailant pulled her up, steadying her back on her feet. Fisting her hair, he pushed her toward the kitchen. The other fellow already had a hand over her mother's mouth. Her eyes were enormous in panic.

"W-what's this?" the girl stammered in fear.

"Be quiet, do not yell. Understood?" The man in charge said, pointing the handgun harshly at her temple. His companion lost no time, he gagged her mom, tying her hands and feet to a chair.

"There is little m-money in the house. Take what you want. I won't scream, p-please do not hurt us."

"We don't need your money!"

"What do you w-want, then?" The girl covered her body with her arms. The guy laughed, an awful screeching sound to her ears.

"No! Not that." He tightened the hold on her hair, hurting her.

"Please…"

"You work for LaTorre? At the villa?" he whispered in her ear.

"Y-Yes," she mumbled as these men's intentions hit her.

"What's your name?"

"R-Romina Bonetti. I'm a-a maid."

"You're going to do as I say, Romina. Or you won't see your mother again."

Romina

"What happened to you?" Dora admonished her, glancing at the clock in the kitchen. Romina was very late. It was almost ten.

"Oh, pardon me, Miss Dora. I had no idea it would take this long." The maid wrung her hands anxiously. "My mother was taken ill this morning. I had to call the doctor and wait until he arrived. I couldn't leave her alone after this, I had to wait for my cousin afterward. My apologies, I'm so sorry."

"Is she all right?" the housekeeper asked.

"It's her asthma, you see. I'll make up the hours this evening after dinner."

"That's not necessary, Romina, if your mom—"

"She's feeling better after the medication. My cousin is with her. So I can stay as usual."

"Well, if you're sure."

"Yes, I'm sure."

"Then go about your duties," Dora said.

The young woman nodded and scurried off. But she didn't attend to her work, not quite. Nobody was in the pantry, and Romina got her chance and stole a key from a hook. She hid it in the pocket of her apron. The maid hoped nobody would miss it. Next, as directed, she had to disable the security camera over the private cove below the house. It was more tricky. She waited for the guard in the surveillance room to leave for lunch at one o'clock while she distracted his replacement.

"Is there a new person on patrol, Adriano? Romina asked. As he was about to take his position in the room, she intercepted him in the hallway.

"No, why?"

"I saw a man in the garden at the front of the house."

"A stranger?"

"Yes."

"It can't be. No new staff."

"I'm sure I saw someone, but if you—"

"Okay. Let me check." Adriano went outside to the front of the house to talk to the patrol on duty. He walked on with them to investigate.

Romina entered the security room and disabled the perimeter sensors. These were housed in a cabinet inspected twice daily, at 7:00 a.m. and 11:00 p.m. So, she had hours before the next inspections.

Then, she dashed to the back of the villa. She slipped down the stone steps in a flash. If she got caught, it was the end of her. She gulped. She had previously hidden a ladder for the purpose.

Romina inspected the camera that surveilled the cove below the house. Her heartbeat skyrocketed. She searched for the battery power source. She quickly found the wire and ripped it off from the unit, making it look like an accident, as if a fallen rock from the cliff had dislodged it. She used a laser to disable the optics, too. Her hands were shaking like a leaf. She thought she would die of a heart attack.

They had instructed her with precision, and if she didn't deliver, her mother's life was on the line.

She became drenched in sweat by the time she ditched the ladder and dashed back to the villa.

"Tsk-tsk, Romina. The patrol guards are the only ones out front." He declared when she popped her head into the security room.

"Oh, I'm so sorry, Adriano. I would've sworn…"

"You had a tough morning with your mom not being well, Romina. Besides, Giovanni shaved his beard. So you may have thought he was someone else," he said.

A stroke of luck with Giovanni!

"My apologies. I recognize him, now," she added, looking at the man outside through the security monitor. "He looks so different, though, without his beard. Sorry."

"No problem," Adriano said. As she left the room, she heard him speak on the phone to send someone to look at the cove's camera. It would take Adriano, at best, an hour to rewire the camera, but he wouldn't retrieve the optics any time soon, not today. That would keep that camera out of order for the entire day. And with the perimeter's sensors deactivated, this would give her the space and time she needed.

Later on, at the assigned hour, Romina dashed down the stone steps to the cove. They'd told her to wait by the waterfront on the rocky beach. She glanced along the jetty, but there was nobody there. She fretted. Her chest was heaving, and her palms were sweaty. Dora would miss her if she were too long.

What if Adriano looked into the sensors cabinet before time? *No, he won't.* Or if he fixed the camera and caught her? *No, the optics would need replacement. Calm down!*

She would lose her job over this, perhaps much more.

Romina felt guilty and tormented as she waited on the private beach, not knowing what to expect. There was a sudden movement in the water. A ferocious, high-pitched shriek escaped her lungs. Three frogmen wearing face veils made of camouflage netting mesh over a full-body wet suit, fins, mask and snorkel—similar to those used by military Frogman Corps—rose from the sea.

"Shut up, woman," one man scolded her as he pulled off his net veil, mask and breathing apparatus. They plucked hermetically sealed plastic packages from inside the wet suits. Then, they took off all the gear. They were wearing shorts and vests underneath. They opened the boxes picking up their guns, explosive grenades, knives and other paraphernalia.

If Romina had feared the scary sight of the men before her—not something she wanted to come across on a dark night—her eyes widened in terror at the power of their weapons.

"Do you have the key?" he asked her.

"Yes."

"Give it to me."

She did. The one she had stolen from the pantry—the ignition key to the speedboat.

He gave Romina more precise instructions, giving her the items she needed.

"Do you understand what to do next?"

"Yes," she whimpered, not liking it.

"Go. And do not fail me." He paused. "Remember, your mother's life is in your hands."

Romina

The three patrol guards on the grounds outside would have their dinner after midnight when their shift ended. While, as usual, the other men inside the villa and staff would dine at nine sharp.

Her cue to strike.

Romina agonized.

She had a sheen of sweat on her forehead and upper lip. She wiped it with the back of her hand. Her feet heated, blazing in her shoes as if the leather was strangling them on flaming coals. Her hands were moist and slippery.

She felt she was already in hell!

"*Dio Santo!* You are all fingers and thumbs this evening. Jumpy like a cat. What's the matter with you, girl?" Dora reprimanded her when she dropped another plate as she set the table.

"I'm sorry, miss." The maid swept through the broken shards in haste.

She only needed a few minutes. Would she be able to do it? Romina prayed to God for some miracle. For a sign!

"Do you remember the exact number of pills to dispense in the coffee?" The man had asked her earlier, emphasizing his instructions with no mercy.

"Yes. These are sleeping pills, I know, but what are these?" Romina asked in trepidation, afraid of the answer.

"Antidepressants, custom-made for us." One of the gang sniggered, "A deadly concoction, and combined—"

"Shut up, you fool," his boss yelled at him, then turning to her, he said. "Listen, girl, just do as I tell you, or you won't see your mother again. And don't forget the alcohol, grappa or brandy."

"Yes," she mumbled, swallowing hard.

Romina guessed the antidepressants must have a higher

dose content if custom-made—*a deadly concoction,* the man had called it, and combined with sleeping pills and alcohol... no, no one would escape death.

At first, she'd said, "No!" He hit her and roughed her up, but still, she refused. She even convinced herself she would tell the family everything upon returning to the house. *I'm done with it!*

Then, the guy coerced her into it with an excruciating, distressing call to her mom. A reminder of what was at stake. This call had her in tears after hearing her mother being tortured. She was too upset. A sobering experience. A clear signal of what would happen if she didn't obey them.

Romina was a pretty, innocent young woman. She liked chatting, but weakness and stupidity had no part in her character. She knew these men meant to kill. If she obeyed them, she realized, the LaTorre family, the clan's men and guards, would die with the high-dosage depressant pills, anyway. Let alone tampering with them with a combination of sleeping pills and alcohol into the mix as the man had ordered her to add. Her mother took sleeping pills sometimes, and Romina was constantly worrying about her, fully aware of the risks of mixing them with depressants or alcohol.

He—the love of her life—would die, too.

Oh, sweet Jesus!

The bastards had taken her mobile phone and given Romina a burner cell instead, enabling her only to receive calls so they could communicate instructions to her. Romina was horrified. She would become a killer if she did what they asked.

These men were coercing her into murder, and the realization took a toll on her. She was a sweet girl in a dreadful situation, worrying about her mother. Tears streamed down her cheeks, but she wiped them away.

Not the time to fall apart, she told herself. *Think! Think!*

She made up her mind.

Romina moved to the staffroom and served the supper dishes to the clan's guards and staff. After the meal, she prepared the coffee for them in the pantry as usual. Except, tonight, she put the barbiturates drugs in the coffee. The guards and staff drank it as they talked and joked amongst themselves, unsuspecting. She brought Adriano coffee with the barbiturates in the security room, too.

Next, she went to the family's dining room. She served the same coffee with the pills.

Milo, Matteo, Fabio, Selina and Melania had it, too, unawares.

She realized Evie and Lola were not at dinner. She would have to deal with them later.

~

Romina

Romina had not followed the instructions, though. No, she didn't. Not quite to the letter. On the contrary! She only used sleeping pills to send people to sleep, nothing more. When the push came to shove, she omitted to combine the deadly depressants and the alcohol. So she took a colossal risk, a gamble, but wouldn't do it. She could not murder anyone, no matter the consequences. Her mother's morals would not want her to do it, either.

As time passed, one by one, guards, staff and family fell into a deep sleep with the strong barbiturates.

They had also ordered her to slit the men's throats if they survived the drugs. They'd given her a flick knife. They showed her how to use it.

It sickened her.

It was against her nature.

Nonetheless, Romina counted two immediate problems.

Lola and Evie had stayed in their suite. Dora brought a tray up to them with supper. And no coffee! What would happen if they left the rooms? Evie would know something was wrong. Not to mention, the guards of the security patrol outside were all wide awake. She had forgotten all about them. But they would stay out, patrolling the grounds, until midnight when their shift ended and were replaced by a new one.

Romina fretted, but she couldn't worry about them now.

She worried about the three bad guys on the beach. *The murderous bastards!* What if they entered the villa with their guns to check she had done what they asked? Would they realize the guards, the staff and the family were not dead but just asleep? She pondered for an instant. Of course, they would. It was evident, even to her, they were still breathing, all very much alive.

It would fool no one. She cursed herself.

But what else can I do? I'm not a killer! She vexed.

I should have told the family everything, she thought abruptly, *let them deal with this.* She rolled her eyes. *You stupid girl!*

Too late for recriminations and what-ifs now… Romina would have to live with her decisions, her mistakes, the consequences, and soldier on. She wanted to save her mother, but she was sure about one thing. Those ghastly men giving the orders were not playing games. They were murderers. Romina needed to keep them out of the house, or they would discover her treachery.

What if they checked on her? No one could help her now.

If they came in, they would surely kill everybody, including her, for disobeying their order. Her mother would die, too, for sure. Perhaps she should tell the three guards patrolling outside, but then there would be a shootout, and what if they lost? Those dreadful men would come inside and kill everyone, anyway.

She couldn't risk the man she loved. And her mother.

It was all too futile! She cried her eyes out. Her head hurt.

She prayed to God for a miracle.

Her phone rang, and she yelped at the sound. Her nerves tingled with fear. The man's voice made her shudder as he spoke.

"Did you drug them?"

"Yes."

"How many men?"

"Ten."

"The domestic staff and family?"

"Yes, three staff and five family members, all drugged except for the pregnant woman and the child. The housekeeper is with them now, but Dora had dinner—and coffee with the concoction of drugs. She won't be a problem. But Evie and Lola are eating supper in their rooms. I can't get to them now."

Dear God! Was she out of her mind? She was a blabbering fool when she was nervous and afraid. She couldn't help it. Too late. The words had come out of her mouth, she had given out too much information, and she couldn't take them back. She was her worst enemy.

Why tell those bastards about Evie and Lola? She had an inkling she had just made a huge mistake.

"Damn! We might have to see to them."

I've fucked up! Romina shivered uncontrollably and cursed herself.

"No!" she said. The word came out more forceful than she intended. She willed herself to calm down. "You can't come in now. The guards are still patrolling outside. I was not able to get to them yet. It will be dangerous for you to enter the house now. They have shotguns. You'll have to wait. I usually take a drink to them around eleven." The last sentence was a lie, she never brought anything to the patrol men, but at least it would keep the ghastly men on the beach out for a while.

"How many of them?"

"Six!" Romina said. She had to try. No clue where her idea came from then. "They increased the number on patrol."

The bastards would think themselves outnumbered by three. In reality, only three men were patrolling the grounds. They were even.

"Did you use the knife?"

"No need. The pills are working. Most of them are dying," she lied. The man at the end of the phone was silent. Romina's breathing labored with dread.

"I don't believe you. Listen, girl, if you lie to me, we'll kill you and your mother. Understood?"

"I-I—"

"Silence. The pills you administered, did you use the dose I told you to? Exactly like I said?"

"Yes." She struggled to sound assured and firm.

"Are you certain?"

"Yes."

"If you are messing with me, I'll kill you, but first, you'll watch me taking pleasure in torturing your mother before I kill her."

She whimpered with a sob.

"Am I clear?" he yelled.

"Look, these people are nothing to me. Why should I sacrifice my mother for them? I'm only eighteen. Do you think I want to die for them? No way!" She spat with conviction this time. She was bluffing, but she had to play her cards right. There was silence at the other end. "I tell you. I checked," Romina went on, assuring him with vehemence. It could make the difference between life and death. "I put the number of pills you told me in their coffee, and the alcohol. They will soon be all dead. They are foaming at the mouth. I saw them; it was disgusting."

Is it the right thing to say? No clue.

If the man didn't trust her, they would come into the house to finish the job. To kill them all. And it would be easy for them. She would have no chance against them.

Perspiration drenched her. *I've messed up! I should have come clean with the family about this. They would have known what to do. As it is, I'm in deep trouble risking everybody's life.*

Romina sunk deeper into despair. She needed to ponder her next move. She wouldn't keep the scumbags out for long. She had a feeling the man had not believed her. If he came in, then what? A shootout with the patrol guards outside? What if the guards lost? They would all be dead, including her love.

It was hopeless.

Time was running out for her. But she could not bring herself to kill anyone.

So, in a fit of temper, she had gone to the bathroom and threw the rest of the drugs, sleeping pills, and depressants all down the toilet before she did something stupid with them.

She had worked in the villa for two years. These people were her friends. Some of them she'd known for a long time, knew their families. She would murder no one.

The family paid well. Romina liked them, they were good to her, good employers. She got on with everybody. She loved the house but would not admit her deepest secret. The colossal crush she had on him. Precisely, she thought herself in love with Matteo.

She pined after him. She felt so foolish aspiring to someone like him, so handsome, witty, clever, and rich. He made her laugh. Sometimes she laughed like an idiot at anything he said.

The likelihood, the man thinks of me as a silly, ignorant peasant. He would laugh if he knew I love him, she thought with a tormented sigh.

Notwithstanding the circumstance, she'd be damned if she would allow anyone to kill Matteo. No matter what! Deep down, she realized she had risked her mother and herself to save him. Unconsciously, Matteo had been the catalyst for her actions. She would do anything to save him. But she was out of her depth now.

Way. Out.

Soon, these people would come into the house to find everyone still alive. What then?

"Is it true? Are they dying? Remember, if they don't die, your mother will. And so will you," the man went on.

"I swear, I'm telling the truth." Her fingers crossed behind her back.

"Fine. Do this next." The guy explained what he wanted her to do now. "But first, the patrol must drink something with the drugs, too. No one must stay alive. Understood?"

Shit! I've dumped all the pills down the frigging toilet. God, help me.

"You know what to do."

CHAPTER 30

Evie

"Everything okay, Miss Logan?"

"Zeno! You'll give yourself indigestion. You were only gone a few minutes."

"I went to the staffroom because you insisted. I should've taken my dinner on a tray outside."

"I got a new book, Zeno," Lola squealed.

"Great, *stellina*."

"Dora's gone to the staffroom now, but she stayed with us. So don't worry," Evie said reassuringly.

"Yes, I passed her in the hallway, but Dora is not a guard."

"We are fine."

"Rocco wouldn't like it if he knew I left you. He gave me strict orders."

"For ten minutes? Did you even finish your dinner? You must have gobbled it up."

"I eat quickly. It's a habit. Can I check the rooms now?"

"Go ahead."

"All good!" he said when he ended his security inspection.

"Done?"

"Yes, miss."

"We'll turn in soon."

"Oh, no!" Lola protested. "We haven't finished reading yet."

"I'll leave you to it. I'll be outside if you need me."

"Thank you, Zeno. Goodnight."

The young man closed the door behind him. He had taken his night cup upstairs. *It might be cold by now.* Sitting in the hallway, outside Evie's suite, Zeno gulped his coffee down when he was back in his chair. He hoped it would keep him alert for the long shift.

Little did he know…

∽

Evie

"It's half past nine, darling. Ten more minutes, that's all. Your mom won't like it if she knows I let you stay up so late."

"I won't tell her." Lola giggled with a hand over her mouth, looking a scant naughty. Evie ruffled her hair with an indulgent smile. She began reading again.

"Bedtime, you little rascal," she said when the time was up. She closed the book and placed it on the bedside table.

"Ooh, no…"

She tucked the child into bed. She left the lamp on the nightstand on, giving a faint glow to the place.

"Will you be in the other bedroom, Evie?"

"Yes, sweetheart, right next to yours. If you need anything, call me. I'll leave the door ajar, okay?"

"I like it here. Can I sleep here every night?"

"Sure, while your Uncle Rocco is away."

"No, I mean, always."

"We'll talk about this in the morning." Evie laughed.

"All right."

"Goodnight, sweetheart." She kissed the girl's forehead and went to her bedroom.

An hour later, Evie had watched an episode of her favorite show on her laptop when her mobile phone rang. To her delight, it was Rocco.

∽

Romina

Romina didn't want to do this, but the guys on the beach would uncover her lies if she didn't.

Her guts twisted in knots.

She had not foreseen she'd have to make a choice and wanted to scream. But there was a slight chance that if she followed their orders this time she might get away with it —a remote possibility, and a risky strategy, perhaps her last card.

She pinned her hopes on that tiny chance—slim indeed —that those men would trust her and not enter the house after she did what they asked.

Romina realized she was about to play God and sacrifice two people, but in the process, she was about to save twenty more in the house, including her beloved Matteo and her dear mother. Undoubtedly, the math was in her favor.

Would God forgive me?

Was it the best option?

Think, think! She told herself over and over. *I can't win. Somebody will get hurt, whatever I do! Either this or everybody is dead.*

She wept as she ran out of options.

I'll burn in hell!

Romina set in motion. She disabled the rest of the cameras in the security room as directed. With Adriano out of action with sleeping pills, it was easy.

She ensured the guard by the stairs was out cold, too. He lay at the bottom of the staircase. She dragged the large man around. She was only a slender girl, but she put all her strength into pulling him by the arms to a secluded corner under the staircase. Difficult, but she managed. She had to stop twice as he twitched and stirred, but the drugs were too potent, he didn't wake up.

She went up to Evie's suite. It was gone 11:00 p.m. by then.

Romina found Zeno slumped in his chair in the hallway. The potent sedatives in his coffee had taken effect. She moved him to an empty bedroom beside Evie's suite. He was a much lighter man, athletic, and easier to move. He stirred but remained asleep.

Aside from the three guards patrolling outside, Evie and Lola, the girl had drugged everyone else to the hilt with sleeping pills. When the guards' shift ended at midnight, a new patrol would be expected to take over. They would soon investigate when nobody showed up to replace them and would discover her treachery.

She had to act fast before they caught her.

The maid couldn't give the patrol guards a drink with barbiturates like the bastards on the shore instructed her to do. The guards had their own flasks with drinks. It would have seemed odd for her to bring something to them, out of character. Besides, she had thrown all the tablets down the toilet.

Sweet Jesus! There was nothing she could do except comply with this.

She prayed for some miracle. Alas, there was none.

I'll be an accomplice in Evie and the child's abductions!

Romina sobbed. She dried her tears and slipped into

the silent suite as quiet as a mouse. It was enveloped in darkness. Her breathing lowered. Her heart was pounding. She thought her thunderous heartbeat would wake up the girls. She hesitated. Her eyes adjusted to the blackness with the dim light coming from one of the bedrooms. She made her way to the child's room. She stopped at the foot of her bed and watched Lola, asleep like an angel in her warm, comfortable bed.

Romina almost turned back. A sob escaped her. She used her hand to squash the sound. She lifted Lola into her arms, still asleep. The child moaned and stirred but didn't wake.

Romina covered her with a blanket. *Poor sausage!* Tears streamed down her face. She liked the sweet kid, and she didn't deserve this. With her heart breaking, she beat a hasty retreat out of the room and down the stairs before she changed her mind.

She waited for the patrol guards to be on the opposite side of the grounds. She made a break for it down the stone steps leading to the waterfront.

The men were waiting for her in the speedboat, docked at the quay. The key was ready in the ignition. The one Romina had stolen earlier in the day.

She was unwilling to let the child go as the men tried to take her. But then the kid woke up during the scuffle. In the unfamiliar situation, in the pitch black, Lola cried, calling for her mother. So, Romina released her to the bastards, every cry a deep wound to her heart.

She ran back to the house in agony. *My path to hell is secured!* She had one more job to complete. This one would be tricky. She had to be convincing.

Could she do it?

The only thought still propelling her to do it was, *I'm saving twenty people's lives in exchange for the abduction of two people.* She sobbed.

Will God forgive me? More tears streamed down her cheeks as she reached the suite door again. She dried them, took a deep breath, and went in.

She turned on the lights.

"Miss Logan!" Romina called out, going to the bed and shaking her. Evie stirred, opening her eyes. She lifted her head from the pillow.

"Romina?" she mumbled, not quite awake yet. "What is it? Is it Lola?"

"No, miss. It's Master Rocco. He's waiting for you."

"Rocco?"

"Yes. We have little time. He must return to Naples, but he'll take you with him."

"Naples?"

"Yes, now."

She looked at the clock, 11:30 p.m. Evie rubbed her cheek and blinked.

"Get dressed. We need to go. Please, hurry. Or Master Rocco will be cross." Romina pulled the covers off her.

"What about Lola? She's in the other bedroom."

"*Signor* Fabio took her to her own room."

∽

Evie

Evie stared at the younger girl. "He did?"

"Sure."

"He was here?"

"Yes."

"How come I heard nothing?"

"I don't know."

"But he would have told me."

"Lola was asleep. He asked me to tell you. Please, Miss Logan. Get dressed."

"I'll call Rocco."

"No!" the maid squealed. It was then Evie remembered something Selina had said, "We don't trust anybody!"

"Why not?"

"He's down in the cove, miss. No reception."

"But—"

"We must hurry!"

"Hold on!" Evie said, "I talked to Rocco just before eleven o'clock. He couldn't have returned home from Naples in forty minutes. No chance. Besides, he would have told me." Evie glanced at her with suspicion. Her sleepy brain working again, fast.

"He wanted to surprise you."

"Umm..." Evie leapt out of bed, frowning. Something wasn't right.

"Please, get dressed."

"No!"

"You must."

"What's going on, Romina?"

"Now, move!" The girl pulled out the flick knife and pointed it at her round belly.

"Romina! What on earth—" Evie stepped backward, her arms going around her tummy, protecting her baby.

"If you don't, everybody will die, including us," the maid said in agony. "Get moving. I've taken the girl."

"Lola?"

"Yes."

"Oh, God."

"I'm sorry, they have my mother. I have to do it, or she'll die. They'll kill us all if I don't. They'll come into the house and—"

"Are you insane?"

"Please."

"Where is Lola?"

"In the speedboat."

"My goodness!" Evie shot into action. She grabbed her

gym shoes, her loose-fitting pants and her t-shirt from the armchair and put them on swiftly.

"Poor child, I'm so sorry. I had no choice," Romina said in tears. "Lola is alone with them. She'll be terrified. The men have her."

"What men?"

"I have no idea who they are, miss. But they are bad men, evil. They'll kill my mother if I don't take you to them. They tortured her. Worse, they'll come into the house and murder everybody."

"Good Lord!" Evie gasped. "Wait. Where is Zeno? He's supposed to be outside. He'll know what to do."

"No, he cannot help."

"Why not?"

"He's sleeping."

"Sleeping? I'll wake him up."

"He won't!"

"What?"

"He can't."

"I'll call Fabio then."

"No. You don't understand. I drugged everybody with sleeping pills."

"I'll call Rocco."

"No! Don't. He wouldn't make it in time. It'd be too late. Come with me. Please." Romina poked Evie's upper arm with the knife, cutting her, and her eyes flew wide open with the shot of pain. The maid screamed at the sight of blood, horrified at her actions. "Oh, miss, I didn't mean to do it. I'm sorry, sorry!" Romina wailed.

"You crazy girl. Quit this nonsense this minute! We need to get Lola back." Though it was only a superficial slash, Evie's upper arm hurt and bled.

"No, we can't."

"Yes, we will. How many are there with her?"

"Three men."

"Everyone in the house was drugged?"

"No. The guards patrolling are outside."

"Thank God. Where is Zeno?"

"Next door."

"Okay." Evie pushed past her and rushed out of the room.

"Miss Logan, wait!" After seeing the gash and the blood on Evie, Romina evidently didn't have the heart to harm her again, apologizing repeatedly as she just followed Evie out.

"Come on. Hurry," Evie yelled at her over her shoulder.

"Where are you going, miss? Stop!" the maid cried out, but Evie ignored her. "They'll murder my mother, all of us. And you won't stop them from taking Lola."

"No, they won't take her." Evie turned and grabbed Romina by her upper arms, shaking her. A shot of pain ran through her own injured arm as she did so. "Listen to me. Not if you do as I tell you. And give me that bloody blade!" Evie lifted the flick knife from the maid's trembling hands, closed it, and pocketed it in her slacks with a sigh of relief.

"They'll kill us all. We are doomed."

Evie watched as Romina suddenly began to cry. She supposed the last few hours had taken a heavy toll on the poor maid. Her sobbing became uncontrollable, wretched as if her spirit was crushed.

"We'll help your mom. But first, we need to get Lola back. Do you hear me?"

"Oh, God. We'll die," Romina wailed, closed her eyes and sunk to her knees on the floor. Her skin flushed, and she pounded a fist into her chest, hard, several times, penitent, muttering incomprehensible words in Italian under her breath.

"Pull yourself together. You are not helping," Evie blurted, but the maid continued to bawl, blathering like a crazed woman. "Romina, please!" she went on, but she had no response. So, Evie slapped her, and the maid's eyes flew wide open. "Look at me, Romina." She pulled her chin up. "We can do this. Do you hear me? I know we can. But you got to help me." The girl stopped crying as if she had awakened from a feverish nightmare, from a trance. "There is coffee on my desk from this morning. Bring a cup to me… no wait! It's decaffeinated and won't help. Run downstairs and make a cup, make it strong!"

"I-I—"

"Do you understand?"

"Yes." Romina nodded, still shaking, swiping her tears away.

"Then go. Hurry. I'll see to Zeno." Evie rushed into the next room as the maid hurried off to do her bidding. Evie saw the man on the floor.

"Zeno. Wake up." She shook him hard, but he was out cold. Evie ran to the bathroom and filled a glass with water. She threw it at his face. He opened his eyes, but they were unfocused. He closed them again.

"Please, Zeno!" she yelled and slapped his cheeks. He blinked. Evie continued to try to rouse him until Romina finally came in with the coffee. Evie reached for it and then hesitated. "You didn't put any drugs in this?"

"Oh, no, I threw them all down the toilet."

"Good," Evie said, taking the cup and attempting to get Zeno to take it. "Help us; Lola is in danger! Get up, Zeno! Oh, sweet Jesus," Evie blurted, pushing the cup at Romina. "Stay with him, Romina. Sit him up and make him drink the coffee. Wake him up. I'm going to talk to the guards outside."

"You'll have bloodshed on your hands, miss, if you tell the patrol. The men on the beach have guns. There will be a shoot-out. People will die. And if those bad men win, they'll kill us all."

"If we don't, Lola disappears, and we lose her. For God's

sake! She's seven years old, she must be terrified. Do as I say. Wake Zeno up." Evie rushed down the stairs, and from the corner of her eyes, she saw two feet sticking out from under the stairs. She reached them, and a guard was lying there, unconscious, sleeping off the potent drugs. After taking his gun and torch, she pocketed the items in her slacks and searched for the patrolmen outside.

A massive hand grabbed her by the shoulder in the garden. She shrieked.

"You shouldn't be out here this late, *signorina*." Giovanni, the patrol leader was cautious. "What's the matter?"

She explained everything.

"Get back to the house, Miss Logan. We'll deal with this."

"No, wait. I'll come with you."

"No."

"The hell I'm not. You don't understand!"

"We do, miss."

"They have Lola. They'll kill her if you go guns blazing. We pretend I'm going with them instead. That I don't know anything."

"No!"

"Please, listen. If the abductors see me, they'll think all is well. If they see you, or if you fire your shotguns, we'll place Lola in danger. Who's telling Magda her granddaughter is dead, you? We cannot risk her. I'll approach them on my own. You'll hide somewhere behind me, ready. Once I have the child, I pray you and your men are good shots because you'll have to take the bastards out without hurting us. Can you do that?" she said in a rush.

The man scrutinized her for a long moment, then glanced at his two comrades. They nodded.

"We are ex-soldiers, Miss Logan. We were marksman,

we can. Rocco will kill us if we survive for endangering you, but I think we have a chance at rescuing the child."

They understood her plan.

"Good. I'll go ahead. Stay out of sight." Evie was hurrying down the stone steps to the cove below, and when the lights went out at midnight, she only had the torch illuminating her way. The three guards followed her at a distance, in the dark, so as not to be seen.

She stumbled twice in her haste. Her adrenaline was too high to care. She kept her hands on the side rock wall to steady herself.

Damn! The torch suddenly failed when she reached the last few steps. Evie found herself in the pitch dark. She shook it but nothing; the torch wouldn't work. So she moved forward to the narrow inlet with difficulty in the shadows. She struggled to get to the small wooden structure, battered by the elements, that served the family as a small jetty. It ran along into the sea for about fifty yards. She walked across, toward the speedboat, while her eyes adjusted somewhat to the darkness.

∼

The Enemy

"Shut up, or you'll be sorry." The man grabbed the whimpering child by the shoulders, shaking her with force. "Lie down under the bench and don't move, silence. Understood?"

Lola nodded, frightened, cold, and confused to find herself outside in the dark, in the speedboat, with strangers who were mean to her. She struggled to contain her sobbing, but she obeyed, sensing the danger.

"If that fucking snitch of Rolando hadn't disappeared, everything would have been easier for us. The dickhead! I bet he had cold feet, or worse, he got caught. As it is, we had to use that stupid maid as our inside 'man,' but I don't trust the fucking girl. Romina is lying. We need to wind up this job ourselves," the man added.

"Yes, boss."

"Tell Tadeo to handle the mother before he leaves. I don't want any witnesses. When we enter the villa, let's ensure they are all dead. The maid should have given the patrol a drink with the drugs. But we'll deploy grenades to blow our way into the house. If anyone is still alive, the explosives will do the trick. We leave no survivors when we're done."

"Got it."

"But where is that frigging girl? Why is she taking so long? We need to hurry. We must take the pregnant woman. Having her and the child to bargain with is crucial. After the hit on this island, the LaTorres in Naples won't put up a fight with the clan on its knees. And with the family already in tatters, the lives of Magda's granddaughter and Rocco's lady become even more valuable. They'll agree to anything to save them. Then, we'll finish them off. For good."

"What's Zilli's reward?"

"He promised me part of LaTorres' territory when we are done. We cannot fail tonight."

Noises on the quayside interrupted them. There was a figure in the shadows. They heard a woman's voice.

"Hey, who's out there? It's Evie, are you t-taking me t-to Rocco?" the woman yelled from halfway down the dock. The men could hear the tremor in her voice.

"Over here," the man replied but cursed under his breath. "About fucking time."

"I'm expecting a baby. The flashlight has gone out. It is too dark. I might stumble."

"Where's the fucking maid?" he mumbled under his

breath to his mate. "It's okay. Stay where you are," he called out to her.

"We tie the girls in the boat when we get her. Then, we'll go through the people in the house. Remember, we throw in grenades first, smooth our way in. The explosions will help finish the job. I want no survivors. Then we'll leave in the boat, fast, taking the hostages. Got that?" he whispered to his mates.

"Yeah! Let's finish this," they acknowledged.

"And don't forget to kill that goddamn maid," he finished off.

"I'll fetch the bitch now. You come with me," the man issuing orders whispered to his comrade.

"Yes, boss."

"You stay in the boat and watch the kid," he said to the third man. "Let's get that slut." He climbed out of the speedboat. His partner-in-crime followed him.

∼

Evie

Evie remained still. Doubts seized her. She was risking Lola, her own life, and the baby's if this went wrong. Her breathing became shallow. Perspiration hit her forehead. She wiped it with her hand. "Hey, are you still there?" Evie blurted, not seeing anyone. She didn't know what was going on.

Two shadows emerged from the boat onto the jetty. They walked toward her. The moonlight slipped through from under the drifting clouds as the men approached, casting shadows on their faces.

Suddenly, bright, fluorescent lamps came on, illuminating the jetty and the entire area.

"Shit!" Evie mumbled. "Not now. Not yet!" They should have waited until she got Lola.

Too late.

"Freeze!" the leader of patrol guards yelled.

"Make sure you don't kill her. She's no use to us dead!" the man on the jetty said to his companion. He hesitated for an instant but nodded.

They put their hands up for a moment, but Evie saw his hand drop as the men went for their guns. They shot toward the big lamps and the patrol. The fellow in the speedboat also fired.

Evie screamed and threw herself down. She landed on her side, struggling to escape the fire line. A hand protected her head, the other her belly.

Sweet Jesus, help us! "Mommy will see you in heaven, sweetheart," she pledged to her baby, caressing her tummy.

New shots rang behind her, and the patrol guards responded to the assailants. She was caught in the crossfire.

They hit the guy in the boat first. He plunged into the water.

"Get her!" One of the abductors on the jetty tried to grab Evie, but she kicked and punched him. More bullets circled them and struck him in the chest. He slumped down on her, dead. She screamed in horror, trying to push him off her.

The corpse on her took two more stray bullets, thus saving her life amid the confusion as she lay under him. A surge of pain boomed through her body as a third shot hit her forearm as she battled to take the man's limp body away from hers.

The last assailant booted his lifeless mate off. He grabbed Evie with brutal force. He was too strong and pulled her up on her feet, turning her back to him. The shooting stopped. Her neck was in the crook of his elbow. He pointed a gun at her temple.

"I'll kill her!" he yelled at the guards. Evie's body was

shielding him. "Don't move!" The man pressed the gun harder at her head as the guards were advancing steadily on the jetty, pointing shotguns at him. "Lay down your weapons. I mean it. Or she's dead."

The guards froze. It was too risky, and they lay their weapons on the quay. Evie's eyes were closed in fear, praying.

"Go back. Do it!" he called out. The guards backed off. "Leave us, or she and the child will die!"

The patrol could not endanger them; they had to comply. The assailant retreated toward the boat. He dragged Evie with him. Her heart was thumping fast with an overwhelming sense of dread. Another wave of pain shot up her injured arm as he pulled her forward.

"Get in! Move," he said as they reached the speedboat. Evie climbed onboard, and he followed her in. Her trembling hands landed on her slacks as she steadied herself, and remembering, she fingered the items she had placed in her pockets. Her breathing was wheezing in her ears as the man stood facing her, gun in hand. From the corner of her eye, she saw movement. A shadow was slithering at the bottom of the cabin. To her dismay and horror, Evie realized Lola crouched under the bench, scared and whimpering.

The child recognized her.

"Evie!" Lola screamed and jumped up to her, standing between them, distracting the man for a second.

It was all she needed. Evie pulled out the knife from her pocket, flicked it, and stretching her arm, she stabbed his hand with all her might, sinking the blade deep. He wailed in pain, dropping his firearm. It bounced at the bottom of the cabin.

Dropping the blade in the water, she withdrew her own gun from her pocket in a bat of an eyelid while the man hesitated for an instant, still in shock and in pain, at the stabbing, not expecting it.

"Don't move!" Evie warned him, pointing her pistol at him, clutching it in both hands. Her palms were sweating and trembling, shaking. "Lola, stand behind me! Now. Quick," she blurted. The whimpering kid complied. The man recovered and made a slight movement.

"Stop right there, I said." Evie glared at him.

"You won't fire on me." The arrogant bastard smirked, watching this terrified, pregnant young woman with shaking hands pointing a weapon at him. He tilted to reach for his handgun. She read his intention and shot at a padded seat on the bench on his left, close to his leg.

"Your last warning! Kick the gun toward me with your foot." Evie's voice pitched, her breathing erratic with fear, gasping, her grip unsteady. *Oh, God!* She reckoned this could be the end of her and Lola. Adrenaline whooshed through her body.

"Brave, ha? You'll get yourself killed, you stupid girl." He jolted toward the weapon on the cabin's floor. Two shots rang out of Evie's gun. Lola screamed. One bullet hit the man's forearm, the other hitting him square on the shoulder, shattering his collarbone. The man went down, howling in agony.

"Next one will be to your head," she said. "Understand?" She paused to take her breath, then screamed for the patrol. "Help, guards. Quick, come over to the boat," Evie yelled at the top of her lungs to alert them, pointing the revolver at him as the man wailed in pain. "I've got him!"

She kept the weapon in one hand while touching Lola with the other, without turning, to ensure she was still behind her. The child was crying.

The man on the cabin's floor was not done yet, though. He slithered toward the handgun, and Evie stepped on his injured collarbone with all her weight. He cried out obscene curses in Italian. A bliss, she didn't understand them.

"Don't try me, or I'll finish you!" she hissed with vehemence. The man was in agony. He bled profusely from his shattered collarbone and forearm, the pain wrenching through him, as her foot pressed harder.

"Evie!" Zeno's voice reached her first as he approached the boat. It was the first time he had used her first name.

"I've shot him!"

"Jesus." Zeno paused as he flashed a torchlight at the man's face. "You captured Nico Columbano!" He went on with incredulous eyes, glancing between the wailing fellow at her feet and her face. His white teeth glinted in the moonlight with a grin.

"Nico? Bloody hell." She kicked Nico's injured arm. The man screamed. "This is for Oreo, you piece of garbage!"

"Enough!" Zeno pulled her off him. Two guards dragged Nico up to his feet. He squealed in misery at his throbbing collarbone as they took him away. Another guard probed the man lying on the pier. He was dead. So was the third attacker, wounded in the speedboat, who had fallen into the sea. Whether because of his injury or because he drowned, they didn't know, but Evie watched his body disappear under the water.

"Are you all right, Lola?" Evie turned toward the child.

"I think so."

"Are you sure? You are not hurt?"

"I'm fine." She nodded, still sniffing and trembling as Evie checked her from head to toe.

"You are safe now."

"I'm cold."

"Come, sweetheart, let's get out of here." Evie put her arms around Lola, squeezing her hard to her, still full of adrenaline.

"Yes." The child gave her a sad grin.

Zeno escorted the girls off the boat and onto the jetty. Lola's legs wobbled with delayed shock as they walked along, and Zeno carried her.

"You know how to use a gun, Miss Logan?" he asked, reverting to her last name.

"I'm a farmer's daughter, Zeno. I do."

"Well, Mrs. LaTorre will love you now." He chuckled.

But Evie shivered all over, fully aware of the risks she'd taken to herself, Lola, and her baby. *Rocco'd be appalled,* she thought. Even if her limbs were shaking, she managed a smile of triumph. But a guard had to scoop her up in his arms as her legs had finally turned to mush with suspended fear. She felt exhausted and went limp.

Zeno called out reinforcement off-duty from town and sent three of them to free Romina's mom. They stormed the modest house and immobilized the guy who held her hostage. They brought them both back to the villa.

Zeno had the unpleasant task of informing Magda about what had happened.

The news had the clan's matriarch realizing the attacks in Naples had been a decoy for the real target, her home and family on the island.

CHAPTER 31

Evie

After the night that struck at its core, the household was in turmoil. The mood was somber.

The women huddled up around the long wooden table in the kitchen, comforting each other.

Evie cuddled Lola in her arms, trying to be strong for her. The child peeked at her now and then with a blank expression and a faint smile. They were still shaken up despite their attempts to be brave.

Romina's mother still shuddered in shock beside them. Her clammy hands clasped on the counter, praying, shaking her head in disbelief at her terrible ordeal. Her face was black and blue with bruises.

Romina sat opposite her, relieved that her mother and everyone in the house were finally safe. But she wondered what would happen to her now. She joined her mom in prayers.

They were under Zeno's watchful eye. He had restored some normality as he waited for the rest of the family to return from Naples. New guards arrived from town. The men patrolled the perimeter walls while they restored the sensors and switched on the security cameras. The house was secured once more.

"I suggest we let everyone sleep off the drugs. Heart rates are stable, as is their breathing. The sedatives may last a few more hours. These were potent pills, powerful drugs. Romina did well not to give them what they instructed her to administer. The antidepressants alone, doctored as they were, would have killed them. As it is, they'll be fine, with no damage done. They'll feel a little groggy, tired perhaps, on waking up, but it will pass. I'll check on them in the morning," Doctor Murino, the family physician and clan's doctor when they were in Italy, said after examining those who'd been drugged with the barbiturates.

"Thank you, Doctor," Zeno said, still feeling a little dazed after the strong sleeping pills. Despite this, and his youth, he had everything under control in the villa within the hour.

"Let's see to Evie now," Murino said, turning to her.

"I'm okay, I have only a couple of scratches." She had insisted the doctor look after the people who had been drugged first, and reluctantly he had obliged.

"No more arguments, miss. Your turn."

He treated her wounds and administered four stitches where the bullet, luckily, had only scratched the skin on her upper arm. He also mended the slight cut Romina had caused with the switchblade, giving two more sutures to the wounded flesh. The doctor listened to the baby's heartbeat to ensure all was well. A calming tisane had gone a long way to settle her nerves and steadied her uncontrollable shivers. Evie wished Rocco's return home with all her might. She couldn't wait to see him again.

"Can I have ice cream?" Lola cried out when Evie returned to the kitchen.

"Sure!"

"I'll get it. Who else wants some?" Romina asked. Everybody put their hands up, even Zeno.

"What's going to happen to Romina?" Evie asked Zeno while the girl was out of earshot. "Sebastiano and Rocco won't do anything to her, will they? She's only a young girl. She was under duress. They threatened to kill her mother, look at the state of the poor woman. She had to listen as they tortured her."

"I don't know, miss. That's for Sebastiano and Mrs. LaTorre to decide. But in her defense, she didn't do what those renegades wanted. This will help her, and she cooperated with you and me in the end. She could have killed you. She could have poisoned everyone with those barbiturates, but she didn't. Thanks to her, everybody is still alive. Besides, Sebastiano has more pressing matters to deal with than Romina, right now. My guess, they'll give her a real scolding but will let it pass, this time, with a warning."

∽

Rocco

They were heading back to the villa in the choppers. They left Salvo in Naples to smooth things over.

Rocco was beside himself.

He realized the attacks in Naples were only a decoy for the real target—his girl, his family and clan on the island. Even if he had talked to Evie earlier, it still troubled him. The thought of someone attempting to kidnap her made him shudder. Worse, she could've been injured or killed. The thought sent his body into fibrillation. She could have lost the baby.

He tortured himself with these thoughts, blaming himself. His mind was agonizing with self-recriminations.

He had placed Evie in the line of fire by dragging her into his family, into the clan's harsh reality.

Is this what's in store for my unborn baby? To be part of a world of conflict, controversy, suspicion, violence and death? Rocco's existence was embedded in the mafia, deep into the Camorra, and he had never despised his destiny more than at that time.

Did he wish to condemn Evie to be his girl—the woman of a warlord? This a poorer choice for her than if she had married Jake with all his faults.

Evie could have died! What would he do then? The thought of living without her was too unbearable to contemplate. His heart sank. Then it dawned on him. Like a bolt from the skies, it hit him.

He loved the girl.

Rocco's heart belonged to her. And she cared for him. That much was clear. But he had repaid her by bringing her into his wretched world where she could be harmed.

I should let her go. I'll send her back to England, to her family, away from all this. Forfeit his child for his own good! He should give them a chance to have a peaceful life.

There was a sharp pain in his soul. He massaged his chest as if it physically hurt, a grimace on his face.

"I'm sorry, son, that hurt never goes away." Magda paused. "But you'll get used to it. They are fine now. They are safe." She squeezed Rocco's hand. He turned to her but didn't reply. Their eyes met, and he grasped that she had been there before, with those exact sentiments.

Could he do it? Like his mother did? Day in, day out?

He knew his mother had those same emotions many times over for her children and Salvo. She knew too well how irreverent her realm was to human life. As his mother, she would feel a deep pain in her soul for all her children, for him. Silence reigned as the helicopter returned to the island, each returning to their dark musings.

"Wait until I put my hands on that fucking traitor!" Rocco grunted at last. Anger flared out of his reverie and misery.

"Stay cool, Rocco. Zilli is behind this. It has his hallmark. You have to know the full truth from Nico. Make him talk. I need all the details. Vengeance is best served cold. And when we deliver it, we'll make it count. You have my word!"

∼

Rocco

He was frantic. Even knowing Evie was okay. Rocco took Evie into a powerful embrace.

"Rocco, I cannot breathe," she whispered. He clasped her as if the winds would take her from him. He mumbled little endearments in Italian, kissing her all over her face, feeling relieved. It was the first time he had thanked God since childhood. A miracle she was still in one piece.

He loved her! *So much.*

"Darling, you can't stay here after what happened. It's too dangerous for you and the baby. It would be best if you went home to England. Far away from all this. I'll hide you somewhere where they can't find you. I'll make sure you'll be safe, well hidden. I'll make a plan and—"

"Rocco LaTorre, stop right there! I didn't shoot a man so you could send me home. No, sir! If you think you are dismissing me—"

"Evie, sweetheart. Listen, I—"

"No. Stop. You listen for once! And listen well." She stomped her foot in vehemence. "I'm not going anywhere. Don't even think of it. I'm staying right here with you. I love you."

"You do?" He blinked, agape for a moment, astonished. But hearing her say it like this was music to his battered soul. Rocco was in too much turmoil to repeat the words back to her about how he felt the same. But his mouth crushed on hers in a passionate lip lock that took her breath away.

"You bossy-boots. Of course, I do," Evie whispered in his mouth, and he kissed her again. "I'm not leaving you. No matter what!" she added when the kiss ended.

It pleased his soul.

∽

Evie

She'd never seen him like this, vulnerable. When Evie was caught in the crossfire on the jetty, she thought her time was up and that she would never see Rocco again. So, she was bursting with joy at being in his arms. It was the sweetest of reunions. They were back in their suite as things had settled.

"*Dio Santo,* Evie! You and Lola could have died. You could've miscarried. Your arm is in shreds with stitches." He caressed her hair backward and kissed her forehead.

"Oh, don't fuss. It's two minor scratches on my arm. Lola and I are fine, and so is the baby," Evie assured him, caressing his face.

Despite Dr. Murino's assurances, Rocco checked his niece from head to toe, and Evie, too, to satisfy himself.

Since Melania and Fabio were still sleeping off the heavy drugs, Evie had Lola in her arms, rocking her after the stressful night. The child had dozed off.

"Please, Rocco, keep your voice down."

"A reckless plan, *micina!* How could you?" he uttered in disbelief as the enormity of what she had done slowly sank in. He realized if it weren't for her, half his family would have died, his niece abducted, and his clan decimated. She and Romina had averted a tragedy almost single-handedly.

"It worked. No one is hurt. We got Lola back," she whispered. "She needs to sleep now, poor lamb."

He shook his head and hissed, "Jesus, Evie. Promise never to do anything like that again!"

"Okay. I promise."

They tucked the sleeping child into bed. Evie settled beside her to watch over her while Rocco kissed her forehead and left the room. He had unfinished business.

~

Rocco

Rocco joined Sebastiano in the basement to interrogate Nico Columbano and his accomplice. He confirmed the involvement of the Calabrian 'Ndrangheta. He established Omero Zilli—in every respect and beyond doubt—the guiding force behind the assaults against them. Nico may have executed the strikes, but it was under the old man's orders. The Calabrian had funded the attacks on the villa that night and all the others.

"Zilli intends to get rid of the powerful clans like yours," Nico confessed as he bled. "Take over your territories. He promised me half of yours. He wants to be the *Capo di tutti*." He spat at Sebastiano's feet with the feeble strength left in him. Rocco punched him in the guts hard. It took him out of action for a while.

They knew the ultimate truth.

Omero Zilli wanted it all—be the new Boss of all bosses!

Rocco and Sebastiano extracted the confessions they needed from their prisoners.

Thus, Nico Columbano and his accomplice disappeared without a trace after the council deliberated the ultimate sentence for them.

The clan had finally vindicated the recent attacks in

Naples and the murders of Ulrico Di Marzio, Magda's nephew, and his men.

A long-awaited payback.

Even Oreo, the kitten Nico had poisoned in London with Mrs. Jones' cake, was avenged.

It was a sweet victory for Magda's clan. They had permanently solved one of their biggest problems in recent years. Though it wasn't quite over yet, the most significant task still lay ahead in the coming weeks.

They gathered evidence against Zilli and shared it with Carlo Santillo in Sicily, Federico's father and the head of *Cosa Nostra*.

The joint council considered the verdict. Zilli's fate was a foregone conclusion—they would wipe out the Calabrian clan. They needed to bide their time and plan carefully.

It was the next milestone. And when it came, they would have to strike with deadly precision.

CHAPTER 32

Evie

They were on the terrace overlooking the magnificent Punta Carena. Evie sat at the breakfast table.

She gazed at the dazzling blue waters of the Tyrrhenian Sea, a tad turbulent that day, glittering under the sunlight. The boundless swell of the sea, with its rolling, creamy peaks thumping on the rocks, reminded her of its power and beauty.

There was a gentle breeze wafting in. Its saltiness mingled with the scents of flowers and the citrus zest of mandarins and oranges on the counter. Evie's nostrils dilated, breathing the sweetness and freshness in.

Her sun-kissed skin felt glorious basking under the warming star.

They reached the table last that morning. Rocco sat opposite Evie and munched on a freshly baked croissant. Their eyes locked over the rich aroma as she sipped at her cappuccino.

After the incident, he had stayed with her for a week.

But he seemed restless. Everyone seemed nervous. The atmosphere was tense for a while. She could sense it. That was until Sebastiano and Rocco traveled to the mainland. They left in a flurry of activity with their men. They were gone for some time. She had no clue where or doing what.

She was sure he had gone to carry out some unfinished business after what had happened on the island. *What was that man's name Selina had mentioned? The one in Calabria?* Evie was young but not a fool. When Rocco wouldn't explain his absence to her, she wondered if some things were best left unsaid. She loved him unconditionally. So she opted for trust, despite his unorthodox business. He wouldn't tell her anything, anyway.

"You shouldn't be asking questions. You know I don't like it when you do," Rocco said. "Don't ask anymore. Evie, please," he went on over the phone one evening. In the end, she had learned to accept the mysteries in his life.

Besides, he had promised her that in a few months, he would take the role of CEO of Stream Net and forsake all clan business. She prayed it came sooner rather than later.

After returning late the previous night from his trip, Rocco had crept into bed with her and squeezed his powerful arms around her. She had slept like a log after missing him so much, at peace again after his absence.

Her pussy was still pink and swollen after their lovemaking at dawn.

He had awakened her to a delirium of ecstasy, her breathing choppy and erratic with his delicious suckling and licking off her nub. Raw pleasure had swept over her senses as two digits slipped inside her, thrusting hard, aiding his tongue on her clit. She soon climaxed, drenching his mouth with her juices. It was a great way to introduce a new day. She hoped it became a habit of his.

She entangled her hands in his soft hair, wanting to

keep him there forever. However, his lips sailed his way up over her body.

"Hello, *micina*," he mumbled in his silken, rich tone when he reached her lips. A thrill ran through Evie's spine just hearing his low rumble, still somewhat breathy. His cock entered her soft, wet folds sending her into a spiral of bliss as he stretched her hot pool, settling deep inside her.

"Ooh… hello, darling. Welcome home." She arched her body to him, wanting more as she bellowed out a loud moan. She thought she had awakened half of the household moaning and panting.

"The reason I opted for the more isolated second floor, *amore,* away from prying ears." He smiled indulgently at her loud pleasure. He didn't hold back his urgent thrusts, clasping her hips to steady her. She was aching with need again. His hands slid and palmed her buttocks hard.

"I love your ass! That's mine, do you hear?"

"Yes."

"Yes, what?" He slapped her ass.

"Yes, Sir!"

"Good. You are all mine."

"I'm all yours, Sir," she cried out as his fiery hardness, swelling, straining and throbbing, continued undeterred to bring her joy with smooth strokes.

"God! It feels great…" His control ebbed away as he plunged into her over and over until they climaxed in unison, his seed bursting in fiery waves.

She smiled at the memory and blushed as she watched him sip his coffee, his face serious and focused on the breakfast table. She wondered what he was thinking about.

He smiled when he peeked at her over the rim of his cup as if understanding what she was thinking. His moody, sultry green eyes were smoldering luscious lust, hungry, taking her in with wonder. She knew that look of his now. He wanted her.

They had made love for hours that morning, *does he want me again? A pregnant, plump lady like me? Wonders never cease!* Their sexual energy sparkled, still raw. Her urges did not surprise her, which, since her pregnancy, had mounted up. She was always up for it, and so was he, to her delight. Her pulse quickened.

He winked at her from the other side of the table, and her heart somersaulted. She felt her pussy throb. She would never get used to him looking at her with passion as if she were the most beautiful woman in the world. A wide grin spread across her lips. Her eyes gleamed at him. She would have given out a small fortune for him to return to that bed with her.

He tore at his croissant, and he gulped it down his gullet in two huge bites. He finished his coffee, got up from his chair, and came along to her.

"Finish your breakfast, poppet. Wait here. I'll be ten minutes." Rocco kissed the top of her head.

"Anything wrong?"

"No, all good." He caressed her cheek sultrily and brushed her hair behind her ear.

Then, he strolled over to Matteo. He talked in rapid Italian. She missed the meaning, and he moved toward the house with long strides.

"Where is Uncle Rocco going?" Lola asked her. The child had taken a shine to her since she had rescued her from the abductors weeks ago. Lola wouldn't leave her. Fabio had to work his magic trying to convince his daughter she could not always sleep in Evie's suite. They humored her, though. As it happened last night, the child had wanted to stay with Melania; thus, leaving Evie and Rocco free to delve into their unabashed lovemaking that morning.

"He'll come back soon, sweetheart."

Evie

"Are you all right, Evie?" Selina sat beside her.

"Fine," she replied with a sunny smile, caressing her tummy. "Why do you ask?"

"Nothing! I'm so fond of you; believe it or not, I already adore your child."

"I know, Selina."

"So glad you are my brother's girl." She winked at her with a big grin. While they were talking, Matteo opened a small case and smoothed out some papers. He got up from his seat and distributed a piece of paper to everyone. The staff received one, too.

"What's this?" Selina asked, but she winked at him. Evie picked up the sheet, but it was all in Italian. She shrugged her shoulders, thinking it must be some Italian quirkiness. Rocco would explain it to her later.

"Oh, sorry. This one is for you." Matteo gave her a second sheet of paper.

"Thank you." To Evie's delight, the new page also had the English translation and she read.

"Umm..." She glanced at her friend, who smiled, patting her arm. "What is this? It's wonderful." Her eyes were misty.

"These are the lyrics to a romantic aria from the opera, *The Elixir of Love*, by the Italian composer Gaetano Donizetti." Selina went on, "Nemorino, a main character, sings it in the opera. He's a young peasant in love with the wealthy farmer Adina, who shows him indifference. The woman is feisty, independent, strong-minded, the sort of girl you want to have as your best friend." Selina paused and smiled at her. "When Nemorino hears of the story of 'Tristan and Isolde,' and the love potion that causes them to fall madly in love, he wonders if such a thing exists. He loves Adina, though his love is unrequited. Or he thinks it's unrequited—so they bicker a lot. He finds a man who sells the love potion to him to make her fall in love with him. In reality, it's just wine. He believes the concoction made him more desirable to Adina, but she had feelings for him all along. So he sings the aria when he thinks the elixir to win Adina's heart is finally working. He sees a single tear in her eye, hence the name of the aria *A Furtive Tear*."

"Oh."

"Do you know it?"

"No." Before Evie could utter another word, the musical score of Donizetti's opera blasted out of nowhere and filled the terrace with its sweet, beautiful notes. A handsome, tall young man dressed impeccably in a tailored blue suit came out of the house. Everyone cheered. There was a chorus of applause.

Evie glanced around her. Everybody was excited. The staff had stopped working, applauded, and cheered wildly. Evie had no clue who he was, but she followed the lead and clapped her hands.

"A classical singer, a powerful tenor," Selina whispered in her ear, but Evie didn't catch his name. "He's very talented, from the San Carlo Theatre Academy in Naples. He seems destined to be the next Bocelli."

The fellow burst into song.

Evie glanced at her friend and blinked, astonished, but she fixed her eyes back on the young man as he belted out his tune. He had an extraordinary voice. He sang beautifully, with power and sentiment, as he approached her, stopping in front of her. Hair tingled at her nape.

Blast! And Rocco is missing it all! Where is he? Then, through the corner of her eyes, she saw him. She turned to him.

Rocco was leaning on a pillar, his arms crossed over his chest, seemingly carefree, feet crisscrossed at the ankles.

Though his ardent gaze was pinned on Evie, a wicked, captivating smile spread on his lips. She smiled back, and her blood pounded in her veins. She couldn't turn away from him as the melodic sound and lyrics floated in the air. The sight of Rocco had her hypnotized.

They gazed at each other. For an instant, everything disappeared around them. Only the two of them existed. The mellifluous voice of the singer carried them higher, to a place they'd never been. Her heart swelled in harmony with his. They forgot the rest of the world until the youth finished his aria in a crescendo of wild applause, bringing them down to earth.

Rocco walked toward the artist. He congratulated him on the stunning performance. Then, he marched over to Evie. His strides were long and purposeful. He reached for her hands and kissed her wrists. She thought she would melt in a heap of loveliness while liquid heat spread through her frame. *Was this meant for me?* She didn't dare ask, not wanting to make a fool of herself. He leaned over her and stole a quick kiss on her lips. A tear streamed down her cheek.

"A single tear sprung from her eye," Rocco repeated in his own words the apt phrase of the song, also recalling the single tear Evie shed long ago in the nightclub in London. "It's how it began, and Nemorino fell in love with the girl!" Holding her chin, he wiped Evie's teardrop with his thumb—this one of joy. Then he bent down on one knee and grasped her left hand.

It was then the realization hit her.

Evie yelped.

Her mouth hung open as she covered it with her right palm. Her heartbeat thundered in her ribcage. He chuckled a low rumble.

"Shush!" Selina hushed everyone. The family and staff

went silent. They stilled, staring at them. With not a sound, they waited with bated breath.

Evie blushed, sensing all eyes on her.

"When I think of you, I know no other woman will ever hold my heart as you do. I promise to cherish you forever," Rocco said, his words loud and clear. They had a note of emotion in them. He paused for a second and continued, "Evelyn Logan, will you do me the honor of becoming my wife?" He popped open a small velvet box carrying a sparkling, vintage ring with a square-shaped diamond over a gold band.

She struggled to muffle another shriek, and it boomed loud around them. She buried her face in her hands and trembled. She was speechless when she looked up at him. She squealed again.

"Are you going to scream all day, or will you deal with my question?" His eyes darkened. A sudden, real apprehension sneaked into his mind for someone so bold. Would she?

He had no reason to worry.

"Oh, yes, yes! I'll marry you, Rocco LaTorre!" she bellowed. And she rocketed into his arms as he rose, forcing him to stagger back a step, off balance, at her excitement. He held her down in a fierce embrace.

Cheers, shouts, and cries exploded around them. Milo and Matteo were thumping their fists on the table in buoyant delight. Salvo pressed Magda's hands, delighted and misty-eyed. The applause stormed up a notch.

Rocco placed the ring on her finger. Evie flashed at him in total adoration and kissed him. But they didn't smooch for long before the family mobbed them, showering them with hugs, kisses and congratulations.

∽

Evie

A few months later, baby Callum, named after her dad, was born to great delight. Three months down the line, Evie and Rocco tied the knot in a small family ceremony, and she became his wife.

Rocco took over as CEO of Stream Net shortly after as planned.

As the years passed, Callum's sisters, Flora—they wanted to honor Nonna Flora—and Ruby, like her own grandmother, were born. The children grew into beautiful young adults in a happy family.

Evie would never forget when Rocco first said, *'I love you,'* without actually saying the words to her. He declared his love for her many times after that, but in her heart, that morning on the terrace, when he asked her to marry him, was her most cherished memory.

ABOUT THE AUTHOR

Raffaella loves to write and read romance. She writes about strong, dominant heroes and clever, sassy heroines. Her characters range from handsome, possessive billionaires to powerful mobsters with a dash of kink; while the smart ladies in their lives give them a good run for their money. Above all, these are stories of passion, with all the complexities and struggles that sometimes falling in love entails.

When not writing, Raffaella's busy in her garden.

She lives in London, England, where she enjoys the city's many aspects, from the hustle and bustle of the West End to the leisure strolls around the beautiful parks.

Connect with Raffaella here:

Facebook: https://www.facebook.com/raffaella.rowell

Instagram: https://www.instagram.com/raffaellarowell/

Tiktok: https://www.tiktok.com/@raffaellarowell?lang=en

ALSO BY RAFFAELLA ROWELL

The Trouble With Mollie Series
The Trouble With Mollie
A Perfect Pairing
A Creature of Spirit

The Siblings Series
A Matter of Wife and Wealth
The Thrill of Seduction

The Lake Series
Book 1: Emotion
Book 2: Fortuitous

Standalones
Ice, Spice, and Red Lace

RED HOT ROMANCE

We at Red Hot Romance Publishing would like to thank you for your interest in our books.

If you liked this book (or even if you didn't), we appreciate your taking the time to leave a review on whichever site you purchased it. Reviews provide useful feedback in the form of positive comments and constructive criticism, which allows us to make sure we're providing the content our customers enjoy reading.

To check out more books from Red Hot Romance Publishing, to learn more about our publishing house, or to join our mailing list, please visit our website at:
http://www.redhotromancepublishing.com and receive a free book by Maren Smith when you sign up for our newsletter!

Printed in Great Britain
by Amazon